Righteous Reign Episode 4
The Ragged Remnant
by

T.J. MacDonald

To all the readers who stuck with me through bad proofreading and editing while I mastered this craft.

Forward

As I sit to write this part of the story, I recall that things were really tough. The OFSA had been routed by an unkown force we later discovered were called the Isesinis. With our forces scattered and a great deal of our territory captured things looked really hopeless by the end of September 2271.

Admiral George Bryant was still in command of the most powerful mobile tactical force in the Orion Federation and I still had IGB - now known as Zeta Command.

Little did I know how hard we'd struggle over the next while and that we'd use every capability at our disposal. And, though many had died and there'd been mass destruction, I didn't realize how terrible the losses could really get.

But we had no choice. We had to struggle on. We owed loyalty to the half trillion citizens of our Federation who were enduring a dictatorship.

Admiral Kurt Brubacher

Part One

Chapter 1 Chomping at the Bit

Wednesday, October 4, 2271

"It is better to be both right and consistent. But, if you must choose, it is better to be right." **Winston Churchill**

Well, we're again back to normal after experiencing another Isesinis test, yesterday. This has been occurring on a sporadic basis. We'll get a sudden warning from SOCC that a large formation has launched towards a section of the temporary border dividing us. Our response is to send all Tier One Local Regional Forces, all Epsilon Command Fleets and as many of Zeta's Fleets as are within three parsecs of the target. We have usually been able to muster around forty-eight fleets to the needy region before the enemy arrives with more appearing all the time. The Isesinis typically observe around eight hundred ships facing them. There are often as many as ten various level Headquarters' Ships, their security flotillas, and a few mobile hospitals farther off in the detectable distance. So, it can seem like a larger response than it really is.

After eyeballing each other across the boundary for a couple of hours, Kilkos' forces usually turn around and return to their normal deployments. But, when we withdraw, it is more careful. Frontline contingents will jump out, quickly. And, OFSA incoming Fleets continue to approach in case our adversary's departure is just a ploy. Another thirty to forty Federation Fleets will generally reach the hotspot during the next several hours as the first batch leaves.

I am not sure if the Isesinis are assessing our ability to respond or if, they're seeking to discover our sensing means. They have still not defeated our Covert Class Ships' cloaks. So, they don't know how we determine where they're going to land.

There is no real pattern to these maneuvers. A couple of times they've executed lunges just a few days apart. Other intervals have been as long as two months. We just have to ensure a Sub never falls into their hands. Even, the theory and concept of their shroud are unknown to most people, whether in the OFSA or not. Only a few Tier One Engineering Chiefs know everything. The rest is compartmentalized so no one person can "spill the beans."

For the most part, we've been on our best behavior since taking back the Kentaurus system at the end of March, last year. I've had more than a year and a half to think about it, and I believe we were incredibly lucky. The Isesinis laid a trap for us by giving ground to

1

lure us into a phalanx where they could finish us, and we had almost taken the bait. But, we finally saw through their duplicity and turned the tables on them.

But Isesinis' Governor Kil Kos had put a stop to our advance by destroying one of our inhabited Federation member worlds. It was a warning we couldn't ignore.

So, on the surface, we appear to have accepted our lot. We patrol an Orion Federation that is only fifteen percent its original volume as if our new borders are permanent. A stranger happening upon us would quickly conclude that this is all overkill. Nearly thirty-six hundred large warships, ninety thousand small fighters, and more than twelve-hundred covert subs, supported by all their mobile infrastructure, move throughout this region ensuring its safety. I am talking about a wedge of space that is forty-five degrees wide by sixty degrees high and extends out thirty-six parsecs from its central point at Sol. The Isesinis hold the areas above, below, and on both sides of this segment, leaving our only escape on the end at the Orion Federation Border. So, we are nearly completely surrounded. And though it is small relative to the size of the Federation or even the shard of space we manage now, that rear doorway is actually nearly eleven thousand square light-years, a pretty sizeable hatchway to attempt to close while maintaining pressure on all the other fronts.

But, we concentrate forces on that boundary, and those civilizations on its far side are Orion Federation allies and sworn enemies of the Isesinis. So, though they could impede our withdrawal, it's unlikely our opponents could prevent us from withdrawing if it ever becomes necessary.

What's been interesting over this eighteen months has been our technological developments and the growth of Fleet Admiral Savign's SOCC Headquarters' Command. The three Federation Worlds that possess our remaining nine orbital shipyards and all the manufacturing plants have devoted all their production capacity to the Covert Class Vessels and floating infrastructure like Carrier Flagships, Mobile Hospitals and Supply Ship Class Crafts she needed. As the enormity of her task became apparent, the OFSA R&R was rewritten again to increase SOCC strength. It is now a force of twelve hundred sixty subs divided into Fleets of seventy. Six Theatre Commands control three of these flotillas, each. And, two Tier Two Commands each run three of those subordinate operations. Standard Carrier Class Vessels serve as the Base Stations for each of the Tier One, Two, and Three Headquarters and are able to supply Raptor support, if needed. And, seventy-two Supply Ships have been added to their asset inventory. But, the real kicker was a technological advance developed by Vice Admiral Gojen Svjosloki. Half of their logistical vessels are now cloaked, too. It is probably the last special improvement he will generate for SOCC. Savign now has all her staff including her own Chief Engineer and the facilities needed for her to get the job done.

But, Gojen had sensed that the nature of SOCC's operations made covert resupply necessary. It was not an easy fix. The subs are smaller and possess relatively smooth bullet-shaped shells to facilitate cloaking them. But, Supply Ships are the length and breadth of a standard Carrier and have all kinds of jagged hull structures. This makes them very hard to surround with refractory shielding. So, he reasoned that a hybrid vessel was the answer. After six months development with the aid of a new ally who possesses this technology, the first ones were built and tested. In the last year, Savign received thirty-six of these ghost ships.

This all became necessary because SOCC has been tasked with mapping the locations of all Isesinis' deployments and finding the one that is the main Headquarters for their entire Orion Federation offensive.

For my part, I have Zeta Command's Tier Two Bases situated at Wolf 359 and Gamma Bootes. Wolf 359 is a relatively small red dwarf a little less than eight light-years from Sol, in the constellation Leo. Gamma Bootes is twenty-seven parsecs away near the other end of our sliver of territory. This deployment allows us to conduct our business over the entire region.

We have resumed our Investigative, Enforcement, Security, and Intelligence operations. They are necessary. But, this is mostly for show. We must all appear to be going about normal daily activities. I have divided my Tier One Headquarters. My Base Station and security flotilla reside in Barnard's Star system. El's is at Lambda Bootes. That way, part of the HQ is close to all the subordinates. To remain in sync, we communicate via the laser system daily, though we have to suffer through the one-day transmission delays.

The three regional Tier One setups have divided the space among them and sit at semi-permanent positions.

George Bryant's Epsilon Command is the only one that is actually floating throughout the territory, all the time.

Throughout this period, SOCC has amassed some incredible information on the Isesinis and has assisted General Sparks in placing personnel in key locations. One such mission yielded some valuable intelligence that led to an ongoing undercover mission that should permit us to determine the internal workings of the Isesinis' military operations.

Sparks has enlisted the help of a very special operative to act as his agent. And one new ally has been providing regular reports on observations they make throughout the Orion Federation. They are an ancient and advanced culture, and their entire Fleet employs cloaking technology.

Chris is now a full level ten General. Svesion is at grade eleven and is still the Zeta Marine Army Commandant. But, Sparks is no longer in direct control of I.S.I.E. He is Svesion's Deputy Commander. The I.S.I.E. is now a full Division with a Brigade-level headquarters in each Zeta Tier Two Headquarters' Operations and Divisional offices aboard the Examiner. And, I.S.I.E is among the two Corps that fall under his direct authority and is included along with four other Divisions. And, Sparks maintains extremely close ties with the new leader of his former operation. He takes a very personal interest in the well-being of the agents and officers under its umbrella. Chris especially loves the rush of the intelligence missions.

Whenever time permits, he makes the trip to Earth. He has become involved with Susan Sylvestry. She is the Speaker of the planet's Legislative Assembly and a candidate for President. She is also the person who turned us onto a great wine.

During the period since taking back Rigil, SOCC has used its ability to surreptitiously enter the Isesinis' Gigantic Polyhedron Headquarters Complex (GPHC). But, for now, they do not employ this tactic for assaults. Instead, it is tapped as a means of gaining information. And, these missions led to the significant discovery previously mentioned.

One of my most enjoyable tasks over the past short while was the promotion of Shane MacDonald. He'd been the master of the original Examiner back in 2257 and had taken over as Captain of its replacement. Since his promotion to the rank of Captain at the end of that year, he graduated from the War College and has steadily risen in level and assignment. Six months ago, I had the pleasure of elevating him to Admiral (10) and assigning him as head of a Tier 3 Headquarters. This was in preparation for his next move.

After three months in charge of his venture, he was offered Tom Steven's grade eleven position in Epsilon Command. After years of resistance, George Bryant had finally yielded to the idea of a Deputy and had reassigned Tom to the position. I will miss Shane. But, I know he has all the attributes to do a great job Commanding Epsilon T2-1.

Last January, all the Tier 1 Commanders headed back to Earth to attend King David's wedding. It was a week long event. First, his fiancée was granted the rank of Baroness and crowned Lady Elizabeth Montefiore Baroness of Wildwood. The rest of the week was spent in preparatory festivities like the bride's shower, the rehearsal, its dinner, and the groom's bachelor party. On the next-to-last day, we celebrated the wedding and joined in the fabulous dinner party. The next morning, Lady Elizabeth was crowned Queen. That was followed by another gathering. Then, we all returned to duty. It had all been marvelous but left everyone with staggering hangovers to nurse on the way back to our assignments.

Last March, we celebrated Bryant Edward's ninth birthday. He is already in grade seven. He has now skipped two grades, and I am sure he is smarter than his dad. Fredricka missed the party. She spent a year at the Academy on Earth and has been at the one on Rigil for the past three months. There's quite a story behind that.

The Commander in Chief, the Secretary of Defense and all the other member of the C&C Commission had intensely resisted us setting a wedding date. I knew it was because of her position as a journalist. It is in direct conflict with my high-security job. George Bryant finally sat down with me in August last year and discussed it.

"Do you want to resolve you wedding conflict of interest problem?"

"Of course, George," I responded.

"I have discussed an idea I had with the King, SOD and the other C&C. They've agreed to the plan if you guys can get on board. Are you interested in listening?"

"I'd be glad to hear anything that might help solve the problem without forcing Fred to abandon her career."

"Okay. But, you have to listen to me without interruption."

"I'll try."

"Fredricka resigns her position with the AP. She joins the OFSA. Her Masters' Degree in Journalism qualifies her to attend the Officers' Program on Earth. After graduation, she is commissioned an Ensign but assigned to the Rigil Academy. Then, she spends the time on Rigil needed to finish the Command Program. With her experience and these two accomplishments, we promote her to Captain and assign her the public relations department, on the Examiner. At that rank, she can marry a Fleet Admiral without question. And, she still uses her skills. Except from then on, she employs them for the OFSA and the Federation. She can come here for any leaves. It's a relatively short trip." George finishes as he brandishes some papers.

I look them over. It is an offer from the C&C Chief of Staff Fleet Admiral Tonaka. It essentially spells out the entire plan.

"I think she just might go for it," I respond.

"Can we get her in here and present the offer? Or, do you want to speak to her alone, first?"

I called Fred in. Both George and I stumbled a lot as we attempted to outline the plan. I kind of shoved the papers into her hand, as I finished. But, I could see tears falling from her eyes.

"I'm sorry, Fred. We didn't mean to upset you." I offered in a barely audible whisper as I took her hands in mine.

"You are such a dope! I'm not upset. I'm as happy as anyone could be. It is the answer to all our problems!' She blurted as she smoothed out the last page of the papers and signed them. Then, she handed them back to George. 'I agree. And, thank you all for searching for a solution for us." She finished through her sobs of joy.

George excused himself to head down to Lowry's, leaving us alone to discuss the situation. We journeyed down to join him after a ten-minute conference.

Fredricka immediately gave notice and was headed for Earth's OFSA Academy two weeks later. Since then, I've seen her during her leaves, every three weeks. Near the end of February, this year, she graduated and was commissioned an Ensign. We had two weeks together before she had to report to the school on Rigil. She has almost completed the Command Program, now. She will be here for a visit this weekend.

When she's home, we spend our days with Bryant visiting our old haunts in the mall on the promenade deck. We usually see a movie or two and enjoy the restaurants and ice-cream parlor. Evenings are spent in close embrace. When she graduates, she will be promoted to First-Lieutenant at Rigil. But, I will have the honor of elevating her to Captain and reassigning her, when she returns for the final time.

At this point in each year, I always begin organizing my thoughts for the year-end reports I must do. They are very extensive and include budgets, assets, projections, and summaries of the past year and the outlook for the coming one. The first items are all based on reports I receive via my COS, but the review and forecast are based on my logs and memories. It always takes me a couple of months for the events of the last twelve months to gel into a logical story line.

I begin with our decision to lay back and "play it cool" which was made last April 10.

Chapter 2 The New Typical

Friday, April 15, 2270

"In politics, stupidity is not a handicap." **Napolean Bonaparte**

Posed apprehensively in the walkway between the Command Station and its surrounding technical posts, Commander Nedrif Elantham Captain of the FSS Shenzhen glances between the numerical presentations in the strip at the bottom and the spatial images displayed across the surface of the main screen. He seeks the anti-neutrino signature that tells of an impending Isesinis incursion, something that occurs regularly in this region. The Shenzhen and its sister-ships have had to repel almost daily intrusions by small squads of enemy vessels testing OFSA awareness, readiness, and strength.

Ned, as friends and associates refer to him, is a squat, rugged Barian very typical of the humanoids on his planet. And, he's always impeccably dressed in superbly tailored, carefully pressed uniforms, because neither the daily grays nor the mess and dress uniforms flatter the Barian figure. They are actually designed for the taller, leaner humans. Bari orbits HD156668 an orange / red dwarf in Bootes, emitting only thirty percent of Sol's energy output. It circles the star in an outer habitable-zone path that results in a cool climate in its regions that do support life. A significant portion of Barian society revolves around both a martial-art-like culture and an Arctic Commando one. Its people make great cold-weather, close-quarter warriors. In fact, the R&R was changed to include special weapons Barian Marines like to carry like a Hunga-Munga style blade used for throwing, slashing, and spearing in close hand-to-hand combat.

As a leader, Commander Elantham employs an assertive-consensus style of command. It means he will try to gain agreement but will enforce his own decisions, when necessary. It is considered the best way to run a ship. He is dedicated to his personnel, and they are completely loyal to him. Though he indirectly works for Admiral Bryant in Epsilon, he enjoys the knowledge that he leads a craft once headed by me - Fleet Admiral Kurt Brubacher. The Shenzhen has a proud and storied history.

Right now, his ship is patrolling a small sector around Mu Bootis, a trinary system on the extreme western edge of the corridor the OFSA now controls. It is right on the border and one hundred twenty light-years from Sol and has been the site of constant Isesinis encroachments.

The Shenzhen's position is a result of orders that rippled down through the chain of command from Admiral Stevens to Admiral Laft and then on to Vice Admiral Boets who leads one of four Fleets of eighteen of Epsilon's autonomous Frigates. For Boets' part, he had directed twelve of his contingent to take up a line from Mu Bootis to Kappa Corona Borealis a distance of about twenty light-years. The other six are patrolling places located halfway between those front-liners and a quarter light-year farther from the temporary border. It means that a ship is no more distant than a light-year from another and can call on six that are within less than a parsec. Depending on the skill of their Captains, the modified Frigates are usually capable of holding-their-own or even defeating two or three enemy ships by themselves. The two-hour arrival time for help is believed to be more than adequate.

And each ship's duty area has been chosen to be rich in natural protection while still neighboring Isesinis attack points. It is entirely possible for a ship to use the local cover for protection while inflicting considerable damage on the enemy. The entire Autonomous Frigate Fleet is also aware there are hidden SOCC assets along this part of the border but are not certain of their whereabouts.

While the Shenzhen is positioned at Sol-vector RA 231.12495° x Dec 37.37717° at 120 Ly, the FSS Taipei is situated at RA 226.57605° by Dec. 37.64574° @ 120 Ly, and the FSS Lisbon is at RA 224.96265°, Dec 37.37717°, distance 119.75 Ly. All three can reach each other in two hours at forty percent of "C" velocity. The Taipei is directed by Commander Gu Megret a Latarian and the Lisbon is run by Captain Shannon McLaoch who also heads the local six-ship Autonomous Frigate Squadron. The next outlying vessels under her authority are in a similarly tight formation placing them just four hours away from Elantham.

....

Aboard the Taipei, Megret is as tense as Elantham as he too scans the data readouts on his main screen for clues to incoming Isesinis Vessels. Every minute or so, the proximity of both the Shenzhen and the Lisbon interrupt other conscious thoughts. When the situation is this strained, it is important to know who to call for help. Megret is from Lata, known to the Federation as Xi Scorpius. His people are similar to humans but display several facial bone rills and larger, disc-shaped, rounder, protruding earlobes.

....

On the Lisbon, McLaoch has her XO monitoring the screen numbers as the Second Officer supervises communications. Both are reporting changes to the Captain as they occur. Shannon is a red-haired, green-eyed beauty with an elegance derived from her height and regal bearing. She is a real rarity. The fact her shoulder-length tresses are not dyed is almost unheard of. This genetic trait has died out for the most part.

She is ready to defend her own space or to order her ship and the others in the squad to a common battle site at a moments notice, if necessary. And she will call for additional aid if, things are too hot to handle alone.

....

On the Flag Bridge of the FSS Valkyrie Admiral Laft is receiving continuous patrol accounts from his Fleets' Vice Admirals each responsible for one-third of the seventy-two Autonomous Frigates under his control. Valkyrie is a recent acquisition. Until six months ago he ran the operation from Admiral Bryant's ship the Valhalla.

Among the incoming statements are the ones from Vice Admiral Boets who commands the dozen and a half Frigates guarding the stretch of the boundary from Mu Bootis to Kappa Corona Borealis that divides the remaining Orion Federation from the Isesinis. Laft watches Boets' commentaries intensely because those eighteen ships are in the most tested section of the entire perimeter.

He worries because he knows these picket duties are not as simple as they sound. The home position is the center of a cube. But, each Frigate must land, hurl long range sensors to all regions in the box that are not within normal transducer reception, and then begin to tour the assigned space. They're actually required to search a nearly five cubic light-year box that is almost five times the height on its Z axis as the length of its X or Y axis. And all these ships' tours must be synchronized. The Shenzhen has to be working in the same region of its workspace and in the same travel pattern as the Taipei and the Lisbon, so spacing never varies. They must follow their assigned paths as if linked by an invisible Pantograph. Haphazard execution could place the crafts as far as two parsecs apart, significantly increasing the threat to each. So each Captain is ordered to relay their exact position to their Squad Commander every fifteen minutes. In turn, that Officer transmits those chronicles to Admiral Laft. They are nerve wrecking operations for all concerned.

Each of Laft's Fleets does two weeks supporting duty, followed by seven days on that front, then a week-long stand-down. The work is so intense that the three of four duty-cycle is mandatory. If the ships did more extended deployments, their personnel would be burnt out in a couple of months.

....

We began our Commission Meeting aboard the Examiner, at eight-hundred thirty hours on Saturday, April 16. It was a fairly regular one with few surprises. But, we were all on the edge of our seats as George recounted the details of Epsilon's Autonomous Frigate detail. He literally read the reports into the record verbatim. The current contingent hadn't met any intruders yet, but the tension experienced during the watch was palpable in the ships' Captains' accounts. It struck me that we were using this force as an early warning system, the first line of defense, and a lure to draw the enemy into a larger attack. The annunciator on George's data pad chimes. He stops and scans it.

"I'm sorry. Can we break this, for a while? I'm receiving updates from Laft. There's some action, right now.

....

At thirteen hundred hours, thirty minutes, on Saturday, April 16, 2270, Commander Mu Megret is preparing for the Bridge Shift changeover, when his Executive Officer Lieutenant Commander Kim Chi will take control of the FSS Taipei for the next six hours. Kim is already on the bridge as Megret updates her - all the while, keeping one eye and a portion of his consciousness on the main screen readouts.

"We're in this part of the patrol circuit, right now.' Gu Megret advises as he points to Taipei's icon on the star map presented on his datapad screen. 'We need to complete this." He adds as he traces the course indicated on the screen. 'Shenzhen is here... ...and Lisbon is here." He supplements again directing Commander Kim's attention to two screen images. 'There's been no unexplained activity. All systems are typical. Velocity is set at forty percent of maximum IPE output. We are still synchronous with both Shenzhen and Lisbon. We're just coming up on..." Megret tensed as he ceased the evaluation suddenly, then took a single step forward, standing rigidly still, and peering intently at the main screen.

"Activate tactical alert! Charge all weapons systems! All port side arms to salvo mode. All starboard armaments to independent. Synchronized bow and stern placements with port batteries. Heading twelve degrees starboard five degrees positive Z-axis! Increase IPE to maximum on fifteen-minute acceleration ramp! Change starboard two and port number five screens to long-range sensor images! Load all torpedo tubes and hold for solutions! Ready all launchers and cannons! Port side weapons to auto sensor control! Starboard ordinance to manual control! Communication - establish a constant link to the Shenzhen and the Lisbon. Tell them we've made contact." The Captain bellowed the commands as some numbers at the bottom of the main screen rose in value rapidly.

10

The Taipei veered to its right with an upward attitude accelerating at a barely tolerable rate. Though everyone could feel the G-forces, all personnel would have seated and belted or secured for conducting necessary operations, in response to the initial battle-stations' warning. Hums and soft vibrations were more felt than heard throughout the craft as its hundreds of weapons rotated to their readiness positions and loaders filled launch tubes with deadly anti-matter torpedoes.

The "Tactical Alert" order had triggered a ship-wide broadcast continuously repeating the announcement - "All personnel to combat positions! Secure all systems for conflict! Seal all atmospheric compartments! Shields to maximum!" - In a soft, calm, firm, feminine voice, while annunciator panels throughout the vessel flashed red indicators and continuously streamed the same message in bright red lettering. Lighting levels were automatically reduced by thirty percent at the same time, to facilitate graphics viewing and conserve energy.

Three silvery tear-drop shapes suddenly burst into normal space about a twenty thousand kilometers to the Taipei's upper port-side bow field of view.

"Port-side weaps - initiate release of anti-matter torpedoes and missiles in salvo mode. Starboard batteries target those ships specifically. Fire all particle cannons - launch spears in wave one. Follow that with a flurry of anti-matter missiles!" Megret snapped.

Chatter received from sensors, shield control, various engineering stations, and all the arsenal stations was continuous but sequential. The system only allows one audio report at a time. Each post understands how to be concise and brief, and the system is designed to indicate each department's turn. The Command Station's internal comm control can override everyone else, so the Captain can always issue an order.

The primary display image suddenly filled with energy flashes and streams of assorted projectiles each following its relentless path toward the metallic targets. Beams struck first, rocking the opponent ships. Then, AM torpedoes were followed by the dreaded "Spears of Fear" which were trailed by a volley of Anti-matter Missiles. The Isesinis hurled their response. Some ammo sought incoming ordinance. Others were directed at the Taipei. Most of Taipei's initial bombardment was absorbed by shielding, but a small percentage did limited damage. Sensor monitors reported their antagonists' energy barriers were diminished considerably by the initial barrage.

"All weapons stations execute a second attack!" The Captain hollered - seeking to launch a second assault before Isesinis charges struck his ship.

As another torrent streaks from the Taipei, it rocks violently in response to multiple concussions. The darkness of space becomes the brilliance of a dazzling sunny day as explosions strain all four vessels. Most arriving threats are absorbed by shielding, but violent shocks rupture cooling lines and conduits that required rerouting to sustain operating systems and weaponry. Departmental commentaries are continuous as are the Las-Com communications from both the Shenzhen and the Lisbon which are well on the way. Damage and casualty data are continually revised amongst the details in the bottom band on all the monitors.

An hour and a half into the scrap, a torpedo destroyed one enemy ship's starboard bow weapons' assemblies and another's hangar bay. But, shortly after, the Taipei pitched viciously and slid violently to its starboard bow, temporarily losing the lane of the course it was following.

"All systems' departments report!" Megret bellowed.

As he received the narratives it became apparent the starboard, aft AMPE engine was gone, and all local sensor transducers and shield emitters in that section of the ship were either missing or inactive.

"Shutdown anti-matter regulators to that AMPE unit! Emergency repair teams to Starboard Engine Room! Increase power to shielding to the hull of compartments four - eight, four - eleven, three - eight through three - eleven, and five eight through five - eleven. Adjust course to heading five degrees port, minus one degree Z axis. Weapons armories at starboard aft concentrate on defensive only fire! All other batteries target those ships and fire!" The Captain barked.

The pace of status commentaries elevates and now includes regular reports from Sick Bay. But, the Taipei battles on, continuously darting in and out of the naturally occurring rocky debris as it launches munitions volleys at its pernicious foe in response to Megret's directives. The third enemy ship vomits flotsam and bodies from somewhere near its engine room. He eyes a change in the video sensor readouts. Minutes later, the Shenzhen breaks into regular space.

"Can you use some help, Captain Megret?" The Barian counterpart calls out over the comm system.

"Wow. Am I glad to see you! I've given these guys a few black eyes and bloody noses, but they've hurt us badly." Megret responds.

"I'll protect your rear. Continue launching as much as you can. We'll join in."

The Taipei's Commander sees the Shenzhen take a position to its rear and commence firing at a ferocious rate employing mostly Spears targeted at the opponents damaged areas.

"Concentrate on protecting your damage. Just give me a little covering fire!" Commander Elantham calls out over the radio a few minutes later.

Suddenly, Elantham's ship accelerates, pulls ahead of its partner, then begins an arc that Gu realizes is the start of a giant loop. By the time the Shenzhen reaches the enemy vessels, it is traveling at high velocity, upside down relative to them, and launching continuous streams of AM missiles, torpedoes and spears down on its startled antagonists.

Almost simultaneously, the three ships all suffer a series of catastrophic explosions spraying spiraling parts, scrap, metal, plastics, and armored figures and body parts throughout the local region. Then, one at a time, they erupt into blinding fusion energy balls, damaging anti-matter storage systems and ending in still brighter annihilations.

"Thanks, Ned." Commander Megret breathed barely audibly through a sigh of relief as overwhelming exhaustion replaced the tension draining from his body.

"You're welcome. You'd have done the same thing." The Shenzhen's Captain responded cordially as his ship was moving to join the Taipei.

The Lisbon erupted from a conduit just as the Shenzhen pulled up alongside. A few minutes later the three were in formation.

"Engineering, can we use our lone AMPE to get back?" Megret queried over the intercom.

"Aye, Captain. But with that and all the other damage, we'll be limited to seventeen percent." The response came.

Megret advised HQ the Taipei was out of commission and would be limping home. Vice Admiral Boets would have to determine the handling of the situation. It was likely Admiral Laft would actually change the entire duty cycle moving the next eighteen ships into the region and assigning this one to a rest period. So Boets would probably order them to Rigil or Earth for leave - except for the Taipei which will need to land at Lambda or 44 Bootis for major repairs. And, Megret was advising them of one hundred ninety-seven casualties. Fifteen were dead and the rest suffered from a variety of injuries of varying gravity.

Chapter 3 Formulating Strategies

Monday April 25, 2270

"Age wrinkles the body. Quitting wrinkles the soul." **Douglas MacArthur**

It took us from April 10, 2270, to April 15 to get our Commands into reasonable formations and sit together for a C&C Commission meeting on Rigil. I chuckled to myself when I entered the large boardroom. Grace had her new gavel on the table. Though the old one was somewhere in the building, she now preferred the one scavenged from the wood of Lowry's bar rail.

After she called the meeting to order, we spent five days hashing out the handling of the current situation. Each of the three remaining Regional Tier One Commands was deployed to a sector representing a third of the Orion Federation Space we now occupied. We spent fifteen minutes discussing the hair raising scuffle near Mu Bootes. Epsilon would resume it's Mobile Fifth RAC responsibilities and tactics. Bryant would employ its autonomous Frigates to patrol our trade and travel corridors instead of using SOCC subs. And, Zeta would resume all of the objectives described in the R&R. We would again conduct HQ, Tier two and three, Fleet, and planetary audits and examinations. We would enforce the rule of law. And, IGB would resume its security responsibilities of protecting world and Federation dignitaries and infrastructure. And, we would conduct any military operations required of us.

SOCC would face the biggest change in goals, obligations, and range. It would conduct surveillance and reconnaissance throughout the entire region of the Orion Federation currently occupied by the Isesinis. First and foremost was the need to find this Governor Kilkos. Second was the need to map each and every installation throughout that region. Their third most important task was to observe and report on Federation member worlds and others inhabited by innocent pre-industrial species.

"You've got to be kidding?" Savign challenged.

"What do you mean?" Grace inquired.

"It's too much to handle, with a force the size of the SOCC. You are ordering eight hundred and forty ships to surveil nearly eight million cubic light-years. It's impossible!"

"How so?"

"The sheer volume. Over three thousand OFSA ships could barely handle it all before. And subs are small. They don't hold a lot of fuel, food, gases, supplies or ammunition. They need more frequent resupply. So, they're less efficient for long patrol or recon missions. We'd need more vessels and a much better logistics system than SOCC is currently endowed with."

"Can you give us an idea of your needs? I mean the SOCC requirements to be capable of executing your orders." George inquired softly.

"Yes, Admiral. But, it will take me a couple of days to crunch the numbers."

"Okay. Let's break until...' Grace looked at the calendar on her datapad. Then she continued. '...until Thursday, April 28, 2270, at eight hundred." She barked as she hammered down the mallet.

....

When we returned on April 28, Savign was loaded for bear. She passed out a document that justified her requirements. All the numbers were solid and indisputable.

It proved she would need at least one-hundred-eighty, seven-ship hunting packs to come close to covering the entire region's targeted systems over each ninety-day period. That amounts to twelve hundred sixty subs - one and a half times the number stipulated in the R&R. It would all require eighteen Fleet Commanders instead of twelve and an additional dozen Task Force Commanders on top of the original twenty-four. Sixty extra officers would need to be elevated to the Captain's rank to run the new hunting packs. Seventy-two supply ships would be able to keep the Subs stocked. But, there would still be one problem. Subs would have to leave their covert missions every week to reach positions where they could be replenished without risking either vessel.

It was a complicated issue that would necessitate a lot of thought and planning.

"Though SOCC cannot meet the objectives outlined on April 25, we can continue to run missions inside the occupied regions. We can locate and map enemy fortifications. But, we will be limited to a maximum of sixteen parsecs from Sol. That is the largest area we can currently cover in ninety days and allow the time for Subs to return to safety for resupply. If you all agree to the increases, we will be able to do much more. But, we will still be limited by the visible FSS vessels that must tag along. They will always be in danger and may reveal the position of our Subs, too." Savign finished and sat down.

"Okay then. It's quite obvious we hadn't thought this out well enough. We need time to look over this report from Savign. Then, we should come back to decide what we're willing to do about it." Grace injected.

"Yes, but maybe, we need to consider our method."

"What do you mean, George?" I asked.

"Do we need to surveil the entire occupied space in ninety-days? Or do we want to do it in stages?"

"What do you mean by stages?" Steven Nichols inquired.

"Would it serve our purpose to know the region out to say - ten parsecs? Then, we attack it and take it back. We follow up by reconnoitering the next thirty-five light-years and take that back. Can we leapfrog like that? If so, we would only need the eight hundred forty subs and the supply ships for them. But, I can see a big drawback in that plan. We would not know where the forces are outside our surveillance region. And, if we aren't sure where Kilkos is, we can never know how he'll counter. He could elect to destroy another inhabited planet. And catapulting could also eliminate the possibility of a preemptive strike where we destroy his Headquarters and all the Isesinis pull out. So, personally, I figure we need to expand SOCC to what meets our original objectives. Anyway, we all need to think it over and come back to discuss it and vote on a strategy." George finished.

"Okay. Let's break until Monday, May 16. We'll all study the SOCC document and consider our goals and objectives with respect to the occupied territories. In the meantime, Savign will continue SOCC operations as she has so far and Sub production will remain as planned. All in favor, please raise your hands.' Grace said. Each C&C indicated agreement. 'Meeting adjourned!" Grace yelled as she thwacked the gavel again.

....

Like a canine whose ears perk when he hears something, Gojen Svjosloki had stiffened in his seat when he caught and understood the issue of resupplying a Covert Vessel from a standard Supply Ship while in enemy territory. He'd been sitting with several other senior Flag Officers in the gallery section during the Commission meeting.

When the session adjourned, he began his study aboard the shuttle as he headed straight back to his office aboard the Examiner which was a day away at Wolf 359. He called up the 3-D CAD drawings of the Supply Class Vessels and began examining them. After an hour, he loaded the schematics for the Covert Class Ships and spent time investigating them.

Then, he went out into the general office area and began a staff meeting. When it was over, he was satisfied with the ten-person team he had assigned various tasks to. Together, they would determine if his idea for the supply vessels had credence and was attainable affordably.

Chapter 4 Another Expansion

Monday May 16, 2270

"You can not expect loyalty if you do not give it." **Gen. George Marshall**

It didn't take very long for us to realize we hadn't thought everything out all that well. Continuous reports from Savign to the C&C COS highlighted the need for a much larger covert force to meet all her objectives and conduct the diverse operations she planned. It also seemed apparent that resupply was a peskier issue than we'd thought - especially for remote "Subs" on deep covert missions.

But the previous Commission meeting had served to categorically drive the point home. And Savign's statement reinforced the entire issue. Now, her daily accounts seemed to support the need, if you read between the lines. I spent many hours in the days between April 28 and today crunching the numbers. No matter what angle I looked at the problem from, I could see she was absolutely correct. And, examining it from the perspective of George's little thought-experiment didn't resolve the issue. There is no way we could just run covert missions over a thirty to thirty-five light year radius and keep leapfrogging until we took back the whole Federation. It would not work. We would always be susceptible to attack from the regions that are unknown to us. And Kilkos is another issue. If we cannot surveil the entire expanse, we won't ever probably know where he's at. Unless we are extremely fortunate, we will likely never be able to "cut the head off of the snake" and end the entire encounter quickly. In the end, I concluded that Savign has to be able to run endeavors throughout the whole of the Federation. And, to do that, she requires what she specified - at a minimum. And, no matter what we decide, the issue of dangerous resupply appears to be something we're stuck with. It will influence her efficiency dramatically.

....

After the session was called to order, I interrupted Grace to head-off everyone else.

"I would like to make a statement regarding the SOCC objectives and requirements."

"Please feel free Admiral Brubacher," Grace said with palms upright and extended towards me.

"I have spent a great deal of time over the last two weeks examining this issue. I considered what George suggested at the end of the last meeting. My conclusion is that we cannot be limited to a ten-parsec window. It leaves us susceptible to strikes and counter-attacks. And, it is likely that course will eliminate the possibility of taking out this Kilkos creep early and ending the war.

So, accepting the idea that we need to surveil the entire occupied region, I crunched the numbers and analyzed the argument provided by Savign. And, I find she is right, if not conservative. It may take even more than she is requesting to get the job done as we were trying to outline it. And even if we do provide enough resources, SOCC efficiency is definitely reduced by the supply issue. They will need to interrupt covert missions and move Subs to safe locations for resupply. Then they'd have to return to the task. That is the concern that leads me to believe her request may be moderate. But, at this point, I see no other alternative but to grant the application and divert production to fill SOCC needs to reach the goals we would like to impose on them. Does anyone else have a comment?"

Admiral Nichols cut in. "Yes, I went through the same soul-searching process. We are asking ill-equipped operations to fulfill our pipe dreams. I agree with Kurt. We want SOCC to travel through the entire region. And to do that demands the equipment. And, I have the same concerns about efficiency. My calculations indicate it will actually take closer to fifteen hundred SUBs to scrutinize the entire region every ninety days and conduct the deep cover missions we require. But, I concur that we should at least agree to equip Savign's operations as she requested."

"That falls in line with my thoughts. I don't need to say anymore. Kurt and Steven have said it all." George piped in.

"I don't usually speak in these matters. But, I struggled through this one, too.' Ian Malcolm paused then continued. 'I had to seek out George and Savign to understand how the assets relate to the assignments and how this supply issue reflects on efficiency. Now that I understand, I agree with them. It is like me asking a mechanized division to engage a Corps equipped with superior armor. If you don't give someone the equipment to meet the objectives, you shouldn't send them, in the first place."

"Anyone else?" Grace asked and looked around.

"I motion we leave the SOCC objective as we had most recently set them. To achieve those ambitions, we alter the R&R to increase SOCC maximum wartime strength to fifteen hundred Subs. The appropriate infrastructure and staffs, and ninety supply vessels. But, I also propose we set current numbers at the requested twelve hundred sixty and seventy-two supply vessels with appropriate commands." I offered.

"We have a motion on the floor. Does anyone need it repeated?' Grace asked as she surveyed the negative head wags around the main table. 'All in favor of Kurt's motion...'

18

She trailed off and watched as all C&C hands were raised in the air. 'The proposal is carried - unanimously.' She whacked the gavel. 'We need King David and the SOD to approve this and the changes required in the R&R. The Chief of the C&C Commission will submit it for authorization. We're adjourned!" She hammered the gavel once more.

We all rose and left the room.

....

The constant chiming forced me to examine a message on my pad from Gojen Svjosloki. I went to see him, as he requested. He explained his idea and showed me the work conducted to date. I asked him if he could come up with a working plan in a week. He explained that it was almost complete, now. I advised my partners we needed to reassemble for a Commission meeting in a week because I had new information that would not alter the asset requirement but could alleviate the resupply issue. Everyone agreed to the meeting.

....

I decided enough was enough. I had been stressed by Savign's plight because I should have seen the need. I am the only other person who really understands all the ins and outs of employing Subs this way. SOCC used to be one of my Commands, and I participated in the development of all the special tactics. So, I should have known. So, I texted Bryant. We'd go downstairs for tomorrow and make nuisances of ourselves on the mall. I thought a couple of hours playing video games could be the highlight of the day. I advised Roh while in route to the Examiner. She would ensure all appropriate personnel was notified.

The next day we had a ball.

Chapter 5 *Admiral Svjosloki*

Monday May 23, 2270

"When placed in command - take charge." **Gen. Norman Schwarzkopf**

The man is definitely amazing! It only took Gojen Svjosloki a week to come up with an unsolicited idea that could be the answer to Fleet Admiral Savign's covert resupply dilemma. He is often included with level eleven and ten Admirals in the gallery during our Commission meetings. I choose to invite him because of his active mind. He envisions an idea and its development before we realize the need to reach our objectives. He had been present at both previous sessions and was able to predict the SOCC requirement for covert resupply of units executing deep cover missions. He came to me with a suggestion on Saturday. I accommodated him requesting a special meeting of the Commission only.

"I requested this session on behalf of Vice Admiral Gojen Svjosloki. Though I am unapprised of the nature of his proposal, too, I have sufficient confidence in him to know this must be significant and will likely result in improvements we can use. So I will turn the meeting over to him." I explained as I extended my right hand toward him.

"Thank you, Admiral. I will start by explaining that I attended the last two Commission meetings and was privy to the expansion, objectives, and deficiency of SOCC. I spent a little time mulling it over. I came up with an idea for a cloaked supply ship to fill Admiral Savign's unique requirements.

Of course, this seemed to be a major problem, at first. The nature of logistical vessel's responsibilities means they need to be very big. So, we have always employed the Carrier footprint without the island for them. On the other hand, a covert class craft needs to be smooth-hulled because of their cloaks. And this type of projection system would expend more energy than a standard supply vessel could generate. But, I am also aware that we cannot just design a brand new class within the timeframe required. So, after considering it in my head, an idea struck me like a bolt of lightning.'

The Vice Admiral stopped to engage the projector and select the appropriate presentation on his datapad.

'On the front screen, I am projecting a standard Supply Ship. Now, we'll peel away the skin.' He paused as the video graphically removed hull plates, one at a time. 'This is the basic unit without its cover. Now, let's add more power generation.' He paused again as the fission and fusion reactors, turbines, alternators and cooling towers were magically removed and replaced within the framework of the skeletal image. 'These are stock power units employed in the Supercarrier Class models. You will note that there is still adequate clearance between all the systems on the engineering deck. Now, we'll add the receivers, projectors and control system that create the cloak image.' He paused again as the animation put all the appropriate hardware in place. 'Finally, let's put the skin back on this big fish.' Again he waited for the projection to apply the paneling. But, it was different from what had been removed. In the end, the ship boasted an elongated cigar shape with a smooth homogenized surface, free of any irregularities. 'So, what you have now, is a nine deck vessel that devotes two entire levels to logistics and is crewed by five hundred thirty personnel. And, it employs the basic footprint and technology of existing hardware. The only new production requirement is hull paneling. Even its gun turrets are beneath its sheath. We could either build new ones - or skin and rebuild existing supply vessels. Are there any questions or thoughts." He leaned back on his heels in silence - ear-to-ear grin emblazoned across his face. He tapped an icon on his pad, and the animation replayed over and over. For over five minutes, silence dominated the atmosphere of the boardroom as the attendees sat mesmerized by the animations.

"What's the cost of one of these?" Grace finally broke the stillness.

"Building it from scratch costs eleven percent more than a standard logistics carrier. Rebuilding existing ones would amount to twenty-five percent more than a full reconditioning of an existing unit."

"What about defensive weapons?" George inquired.

"They're the same as a standard supply unit. But, the batteries are all internalized for the cloak."

"What about production time?" Savign queried.

"We use the latest three-dimensional Computer Aided Design systems, so we always go right from design to production. And production employs state of the art Computer Aided Manufacturing. There are a few dies to acquire. We could be ready to begin manufacturing in two weeks. Production could have the first hulls available a week later. Assembly time will be the same as regular units. So, the first ones could come out of shipyards in a little over a month. The nine yards would be capable of producing thirty-six of these in two months. But, to accomplish that, they'd have to cease all other production once they begin receiving hull panels."

A hush ensued again as the Commission members thought and looked for positive signs from each other.

"Vice Admiral could you wait outside the door while we discuss this?" Grace requested.

"Certainly," Svjosloki responded as he turned and stepped out the door.

"I didn't ask him to leave for a discussion and vote. I think we all agree this is the answer to a big problem. I wanted to discuss the Vice Admiral." Grace offered.

"What do you mean Grace?" I asked.

"Well, it seems to me your hogging all of this man's incredible abilities. We lost our OFSA Chief of Aeronautics and Engineering during the invasion. We don't know what happened to him. I believe he was taken by the Isesinis. So, the OFSA needs a new COAE. He can stay on the Examiner. We've proven you can run a central department from any Headquarters. But, I think we should promote him to level ten and assign him as OFSA COAE." Grace finished.

"Wait a minute! That means I'd have to find a new COE for Epsilon." I yelped.

"Yes, but if Gojen is still on the Examiner, he can assist in the search and help the new appointee acclimate," George said with a big smile. I think he was enjoying my discomfort.

"Okay, I agree. And, I wouldn't want to stand in the way of someone's advancement. Especially someone so deserving."

"Steven, would you be willing to take charge of production and assembly. It'd only be for a couple of months. I was thinking of how you got so much out of the plants and yards during previous expansions. If we could increase production, we could have all the new Supply Ships in service sooner. That way we can return to regular production earlier. Your DC can run your operation for that long." George inquired naively.

"Yes, I could do that. But, that's really an operations issue. Shouldn't Grace be asking?" Admiral Nichols responded somewhat anxiously. George gave a big smile and a nod. He was enjoying our agitation.

"And, I was thinking of something else that might speed up the whole process," George added.

"What's that?" I asked abruptly. I knew the other shoe was about to drop.

"Well, I was considering that maybe Kurt could oversee the proofing, so the ships move from the yards to assignments much faster."

"I'll do it! But, I think you're just trying to piss everyone off volunteering us for all this extra duty. I'll have to let Elasima know. He can run Zeta for a month." I could hear myself whining.

22

"So, let's formulate a motion. A suggestion has been placed before the Commission to adopt the new designs. When pre-production is complete, we will divert all manufacturing and assembly to these Covert Supply Class Vessels. Fleet Admiral Nichols will oversee their production. Fleet Admiral Brubacher will manage their space worthiness. And, we will elevate Vice Admiral Svjosloki to Admiral level ten and assign him as OFSA Chief of Aeronautics and Engineering. All in favor?" Grace called out.

All hands rose though some were less enthusiastic than others.

She slammed the gavel on its sound block. "The motion carries. And this does not require any additional funding or authorizations and falls within our authority. That was arranged when we had the R&R changed. We will advise the CIC and SOD, but we do not require their assent.' She slammed the mallet again. 'Let's get the Vice Admiral in here, again. Kurt, can you present the offer to him. He's your man, right now."

"Yes, of course," I responded.

Grace's DC marched to the door and opened it. He nodded to Svjosloki who returned to the room and took his seat.

"First, I'd like to explain that we have agreed to adopt your new design. And Fleet Admiral Nichols will oversee production while Fleet Admiral Brubacher manages the testing and trials. That will speed up the entire process. You will need to get designs to the manufacturing plants as quickly as possible and advise them and the assembly yards throughout the whole operation." Grace explained to Gojen. Then, she nodded to me.

"Gojen, we've asked you to leave so we could discuss you. You have been a major contributor to the OFSA over the past many years. So we would like you to take the position of OFSA Chief of Aeronautics and Engineering. You can run the operation from the Examiner. Other service-wide departmental commands are managed from mobile Headquarters. Or, you can move to Rigil after a few months to help pick your Zeta replacement and aid that person in becoming acclimated. The choice would be yours. You would be promoted to level ten Admiral. And, you'd get your own Admiral's Craft because the OFSA COAE needs to travel a lot. You'd have a large staff and expansive offices on either Rigil or the Examiner. And, a Grade 10 makes twenty percent more than a Vice Admiral. I have to be honest. I hate losing you. But, you are too valuable to keep you in Zeta when you could be so useful to the entire service.' I paused to let him digest what I had related. Then, I added. Do you need some time to think about it?"

There was a pause of a couple of minutes as he considered what I had offered.

"No, sir. I can decide now. I would like to take the promotion and reassignment. But, I'd like to stay aboard the Examiner. I'll have to figure out how to coordinate between there and the staff at Rigil." He responded.

"Okay. The ceremony and celebration will be tomorrow. Congratulations Admiral!" Grace offered a handshake as the rest of us gathered around to congratulate the man.

"I will need you to pick a replacement for Zeta. And, that Officer will want your help for a few months. But, after that, you'll have the near-impossible task of divorcing yourself from our operation - except when the two Commands need to coordinate." I mentioned when the others had finally backed away.

"I have a recommendation, in mind. And, I should be able to stay out of her hair once she's indoctrinated." Gojen responded.

....

On Tuesday, May 24, 2270, Gojen Svjosloki became an Admiral and OFSA COAE in the elaborate customary ceremony. It was followed by one hell of a bash in the Rigil Headquarters and aboard the Examiner.

....

Wednesday saw him in meetings with the full Rigil staff. After an hour of familiarization, he presented them with the animations and explanations. He opened the session to questions and discussion. When all difficulties had been resolved, he demanded the hull designs and die plans by the following Monday.

The schematic files went to the production plant and die-makers on Monday. They did the conversion to CAM and began preparing for production of the hull panels by Tuesday. After receiving the stamping dies, the first few samples arrived at the assembly yard on Friday for trials. After satisfactory fitting of representative parts, they were approved for release to all the shipyards.

....

While Gojen was in his meeting on May 25, Stephen Nichols was in flight to 44 Bootis. It was the yard best suited to increased production rates because it had a pool of available skilled workers on the planet. But, he ordered all the production plants and assembly yards into round-the-clock production. He required they stop all current construction and begin production of the Modified Supply Craft skeletons, immediately. They discussed and planned for the designed interior changes. He would advise me when the first unit was three days from assembly completion.

....

May 30, 2270, was a historic day for both Commander Mu Megret and Commander Nedrif Elantham. The Taipei was returned to Megret after almost two months in space-dock. The ship needed conduits and cooling lines throughout - not to mention the one AMPE engine and the surrounding superstructure. There had also been damage to many of her electronic systems. Outnumbered three to one for around two hours, the Taipei had taken a real pounding. The extensive damage had been assessed as so heavy, it was decided by Vice Admiral Boets that the vessel should have its full overhaul. Admiral Laft had approved. The entire crew was first granted a month's leave, then moved to the Rigil Academy for training on the new systems incorporated in the rebuild. During the construction, Megret was busy selecting midshipmen and graduate crewpersons for assignment to fill positions created by death or disability. He made many trips to Rigil's OFSA Medical Complex to visit those recuperating from battle injuries. When Megret finally stepped aboard the Taipei, he was shocked. It was like taking command of a new vessel. Their first assigned duty was to execute a shake-down. They would spend the next two weeks proofing the Taipei.

For Ned, it was a little different. He was being recognized for his rescue of the Taipei. Logs and control records indicated he had pushed the Shenzhen to its limits traveling at forty-five percent in FTL to get to Megret on time. And, it was also evident that though the Taipei had fought shrewdly and valiantly, the timely appearance of Nedrif Elantham and his crew saved nearly a thousand people and the warship from total destruction. The final detail was his spontaneous inventive maneuver that stressed his ship to its strictures but placed it in a position so unobstructed, he was able to destroy all three opponents.

For that, he and his command were awarded the Orion Federation Medal of Valour. And, Nedrif received the King David Award for Tactical Excellence, which includes a substantial monetary reward. He was also promoted to Captain and replaced Shannon McLaoch as Squad Leader. Meanwhile, she was promoted to Commodore in command of a Task Force.

For her part, Admiral Laft, along with Commodore McLaoch and Vice Admiral Boets put a little pressure on the newly minted Captain. They pressed until he agreed to take the War College Program because Laft saw him as potential Flag material.

Chapter 6 ISIE New Tactics

Wednesday, June 22, 2270

"A good military leader owes his success to his troops." **Admiral G.T. Bryant**

Now that it was possible to keep a Sub under cloak and in uninterrupted deep covert missions indefinitely, Sparks modified the ISIE agent's assignments in cooperation with Admiral Savign whose people would have to facilitate the operations. They would now enter any GPHC Base ships under cloak to enable agents to plant monitoring devices inside. It would not be an ideal source of intelligence since the Subs can only navigate in the orb hangar bays. But, they might pick up some information, and it's better than not having any. They would be able to plant listening devices while inside. And, with the addition of the covert supply vessel, Savign could keep an invisible team within close proximity of a Base Station for extended periods.

So, Admiral Savign set about developing the first assignment. First, she sought advice from Sparks on which Marine SF contingent would be the best for the first assignment. He chose the ten-man force headed by Lieutenant Colonel Velky Kaule. General Sparks has confidence in Kaule since his efficient completion of his planetary assignment on HAT-P-11E when he successfully destroyed the most important military equipment manufacturing facilities the "Inscrutable" possessed. It helped to end a very protracted war. Kaule was promoted from Major to Lieutenant Colonel after heading that operation. He now commanded a battalion of seven hundred Marines spread over a seventy ship fleet of SOCC subs and ran his own assignments from his home vessel the FSS Nautica.

So, Savigne chose the Nautica for the first penetration operation. A single GPHC protected by a flotilla of two hundred eighty-four warships was located in the 15 Sagitta system. This stellar organization's central star is a yellow-orange that has a large hot brown dwarf orbiting it on a seventy-eight-year long path. Both bodies have satellites, but 15 Sagitta B is the parent of a barren earth-type planet with a habitable moon. The Isesinis Orb is parked in a stationary orbit of this sphere.

Savign found the earlier reconnaissance reports of this formation's location and traffic particularly interesting. It was relatively distant from inhabited and occupied systems and enjoyed a lot of visiting traffic that included several ships resembling Federation civilian craft. The last point had really piqued her curiosity. Who in the hell from the Orion Federation would be associating with these heartless monsters?

So she dispatched the Nautica to the target. Its orders were to spend as much time inside the orb as feasible and the rest of the visit nearby, compiling all the intelligence they could gather. Meanwhile, Kaule and his team were to conduct as many EVA's as possible to place as many monitoring devices as possible.

Savigne was waiting to see the results. If Nautica and the FS Marines were effective, she would schedule many more of these capers.

....

Commander Ignot advised the Fleet Commander of Nautica's arrival at the GPHC target on Monday, June 27, 2270. Ignot is a ten year veteran of the OFSA and served the last seven aboard covert vessels. He was promoted and assigned to his current Command a year ago. At six foot five inches and two hundred forty-five pounds, Ignot is a big man for a human - especially within the confines of a Sub. In his travels throughout the ship, he's always ducking superstructure, piping, and conduits that others don't even consider. The CSS Provider, a covert class supply ship, was placed under his authority only a few days before departure. It could provide for the sub and itself for six months if necessary, and except for FTL mode or unless ordered otherwise, it is always six hundred meters off the starboard aft corner of the Nautica. It also provided the extra accommodation needed for Colonel Kaule's enhanced unit. Aside from the usual ten SF Marines carried on the Nautica, the Provider held the other fifteen that made up the full SF platoon.

Ignot advises the Provider they will observe just off the GPHC for a day before resupplying the Nautica. It will then slip inside the orb for reconnaissance and exit for another resupply a week later. He commands the Provider's master to withdraw his craft to a position five kilometers away from the Polyhedron for the period the Sub is inside the Orb.

Over the next twenty-four hours, they watch as Isesinis ships enter and exit on a regular basis. But, they are astonished at how soon they get to observe an Orion Federation registered civilian shuttle gain access. Not long after, a different one leaves. Over the day, this is repeated a half dozen times as the Nautica sensor station records the activity - including images of the crafts and their registry numbers.

Once inside the GPHC, the Nautica crew observes and records humans disembarking and boarding these transports. Ignot and Kaule conference to discuss their mutual feeling that two of the Orion citizens look familiar. But, the interior lighting within the Orb is extremely bright forcing humans to wear filtering eye protection. Between their beards and sunglasses, it is hard to be sure of identities. Near the end of the first day, a unique character disembarked a small transport. The Isesinis all wore silver, green, or red armor - except this person. His was dark graphite-gray with white markings, and he seemed to be very well protected, accompanied by a large staff, and he strode with an arrogant swagger. He slipped quickly into deeper regions of the Base Ship and didn't reemerge for five days. Whoever he is, he is obviously stationed on this vessel.

On Thursday, the Nautica moved to within ten feet of a hangar wall and held there for four hours as Kaule and his people conducted missions to place monitoring equipment. They repeated this process at each wall over the following days and on the ceiling on the sixth day. On Tuesday, July 5, 2270, they followed a big Isesinis Carrier Class warship out the massive bay doors, and then signaled the Provider.

The two ships withdrew to a point one hundred fifty kilometers from the giant Headquarters. One day was spent resting and the next restocking the Nautica. Then, another two were consumed just relaxing. On Saturday, July 9, they slid to within two kilometers for another two days of monitoring. Then, the Nautica re-entered the Orb and conducted four days of EVAs to determine all the surveillance equipment was still intact and untouched. On Saturday, July 16, 2070, the Nautica and Provider withdrew beyond the system's heliosphere to file reports and take two weeks for R&R. This type of operation is extremely draining.

....

When Admiral Savign received the Nautica's report on July 22, she was ecstatic. Though the Nautica and Colonel Kaule were not aware of it, she believed, they had located Kilkos on their very first mission. In fact, she was sure of it. He was the only person wearing the distinctive armor that passed through the Orb in a two-week period. She sent all the image files of the human visitors to her ISIE intelligence contingent aboard her flagship the Carrier FSS Sleuth for identification. Savign had found some of the people vaguely familiar as she viewed the videos. But, eyewear, bright background lighting, and beards made identification nearly impossible. Perhaps intelligence would have better luck.

But she copied the file for presentation to the C&C Commission. Then, she sent a memo requesting they convene a meeting.

....

"This meeting is called to order!' Grace yelled as she slammed her gavel on its base. 'So what's so important, Admiral Savign?" She asked.

"I believe the nature of the information I have is Ultra Secret." She responded.

"Clear the Room!" Grace yelled as she pounded the little wooden hammer into its base. There was a delay of a few minutes as the gallery emptied.

"This is now a US session!' Grace barked as she thwacked the mallet on its block, again. 'Please continue, Admiral Savigne." She added.

"I have a report of interest to the entire Commission. It's from the Nautica which is conducting our first long-stay intense surveillance mission. The target is a formation at 15 Sagitta. It is of unusual configuration with a single Base Ship and a two hundred eighty-four vessel protection flotilla. The unoccupied system and the amount of traffic to and from this contingent led me to believe I should target it first.' Savigne paused to activate the projector and tapped the appropriate icon on her datapad. The video began to play. She stopped it at the figure dressed in graphite armor with white markings. 'We need to confirm, but I believe that's Kilkos. Over a two-week period, he is the only person wearing that armor. And, he's protected by a six-person security force and accompanied by a large staff.' She restarted the presentation which focused on the human visitors. 'There seems to be a lot of human participation. I.S.I.E. intelligence is analyzing this and attempting to identify these individuals. So, I would say this all needed viewing by the Commission." Savign finished. There was a substantial silence.

"So, when do you think you'll have I.S.I.E.s conclusion?" I ask.

"It could take a week. They are also examining the audio tracks. There is dialogue. We are hoping to pick up something relating to our suspected Governor. And, we might get voice identification on the humans if we can't get visual." Savign explains.

"Good job, Admiral!" Steven Nichols admiration was palpable.

"It's a team effort."

"Yes, but your leadership is evident. You selected the target based on you logical examination of evidence. And - yes, your people deserve a pat on the back."

"Have you other targets in mind?" Grace directed at the SOCC chief.

"Yes. But, we're limited until we receive more CSS class ships and fill them up. The Isesinis formation at 82 Eridani has taken a strange turn. There are four of the GPHC base ships and fifteen hundred warships there. They may be massing to attack us. We need to get in there. I'm dispatching one of the covert hunting packs there, next week with their own cloaked supply vessel. We should begin to receive some information about five days after their departure. The group at Sagitta was ordered to report weekly, but I will have the Eridani deployment touch base with us every three days. And, we need to keep the pressure on 15 Sagitta in case it *is* the leadership, and they discuss the Eridani force."

"It does seem you have it all under control. Keep us informed Admiral." George inserts.

"Is that everything, Admiral Savign?" Grace queried.

"Yes, Grace. That's the gist of it."

"The US session is closed. You may re-admit the gallery.' Grace directed to the Sergeant at Arms. 'The Regular Commission Meeting will continue!" She yelped as she hammered the mallet down, again.

We headed to the Rigil HQ pub after the meeting and traded stories for an hour.

....

When the CCS Infiltrator, the rest of its group, and CSS Purveyor arrived at 82 Eridani, they found the situation in a state of flux. The massive Fleet was being redeployed to other locations. When the action ceased, only one Base and four hundred ninety-seven warships remained. It was an occupying force. This was probably a regional Command that had dispersed the others to diffused locations.

So, the Infiltrator transmitted an immediate report. Then it hugged the Orb for a day before entering its gaping Hangar doors behind an arriving shuttle. They too spent days in the *belly of the beast* planting monitoring equipment and watching the comings and goings. They exited and distanced themselves from the flotilla to facilitate a message. They resupplied and returned to reenter the GPHC and check on their equipment four days later. Then, they departed the system to send Savign their data and relax for a week's R&R.

....

In the FSS Sleuth's intelligence office, Captain McGrave was directing her analysis team as they combed the Nautica files for information. It was the audio file that first revealed additional valuable information.

Amplification and enhancement allowed isolation of an individual aide speaking to the Governor. In one instance, he called him Lord. In another, he referred to him as Kil - as if it were some kind of title. In the final one, he discussed him as Kil Kos when conversing with another staff member. So, it was confirmed. The Isesinis in the graphite armor is Governor Kil Kos. And, Kil is a rank or title.

The humans were another matter. That took a lot more effort. Manipulating imaging to remove beards and sunglasses resulted in five to ten possibilities per person. So, a week was spent on voice analysis and matching as the audio tracks were enhanced enough to decipher the speech. They identified former Rear Admiral Lee Chan as one of the humans. He had been tried convicted and sentenced to prison for embezzlement back in

March 2256. Though they could not yet identify the other human participants, McGrave's people assembled enough understandable audio to prove Chan was conspiring with the Isesinis and had given up a lot of information that helped win the day, when they attacked. And, just how much he hated the Federation was readily apparent from the audio tracks. The information was forwarded to General Sparks.

....

Chris came to see me on August 2. He presented all the information.

"Do you think we should authorize an assassination?" I asked.

"No, I have a better idea. I think we can use Chan to our advantage. But, I need to take a trip to Harrington in Saint Pete's, first. Then, I'll let you know."

"You mean the maximum security prison. Who the hell do you know there?"

"Trust me. You don't want to know who or why. And, you don't want to know my plan. Chalk it up to an intelligence operation. Don't worry, though. I would never do anything that's illegal or contravenes our charter in the OFSA R&R. It's just a harebrained idea, right now. If it works out, I'll make sure you're informed." Sparks explained with a smile.

"Okay. But, I will order you to tell me if it creates a lot of heat."

"Yes, sir. I understand. I better get going."

....

On August 8, Chris reported that he believed he could have an agent inside Chan's Isesinis operation in a few days. He'd keep me up to date on any intelligence resulting from his secret plan.

I examined IGB orders for a hint or clue. There were two issued to the prison warden at Harrington. The first was a warrant dated August 2. The second was some kind of official IGB request for a secret court order on August 4. Both were in a locked, encrypted, and secured file folder. I was unable to access them without the General's assistance. And, JAG was no help. Secret Court Orders were not even mentioned on their site. There are twenty-two hundred prisoners at that institution. I was unable to use deductive reasoning to determine who he'd visited and what he was doing. I'd have to wait for him to include me.

....

Fred arrived for a week's leave on Saturday, July 2, 2270. It was her second trip home from the Academy. The first had been just a three-day off-base pass. So, by the time she left on July 8, Spark's little scheme was the farthest thing from my consciousness.

Fred, Bryant, and I took my Admiral's Craft to Rigil and enjoyed the sandy beaches and refreshing lake waters. We scoured Rigil New York for attractions, distractions, restaurants, and ice cream parlors. After three days, we returned to Examiner for a couple of days on the mall. Each night was a new adventure in sexual experimentation.

And throughout her visit, she recounted tales of various incidents, classes, professors, and the workings at the Academy. It all brought back so many memories. Then, she was gone again.

Chapter 7 A Serious Challenge

Wednesday, July 6, 2270

"What one has to do usually can be done." **Eleanor Roosevelt**

By two o'clock in the afternoon, we've been in a pitched battle with the Isesinis for nearly four hours so far. I sent orders to Zeta 1 and had the Examiner and its Flotilla launch from Wolf 359 when we received SOCC reports nearly five days ago that a large enemy contingent would land just outside the border between Tau Bootes and HR 5273. These two systems are over eight light-years apart which is a substantial distance to cover. I sent a memo to Savign asking her to examine the trajectories and try to be a bit more specific. Then, I directed my people to make forty percent of maximum FTL velocity to vector RA 202.5° by Dec. 14.25° at fifty-one light-years from Sol, which is a position halfway between the two. That is a fourteen and a quarter parsec jump from where we were at Wolf. So, we arrived here in four days five hours. SOCC reports indicated that would be just after of the Isesinis Fleet. However, Gamma and part of Epsilon landed before our antagonists. We did make a single course correction when Savign forwarded a more precise position projection. So, this little squabble is occurring just outside the Tau Bootis system.

To Nichols and Bryant's surprise, Kilkos' forces continued rapidly forward after landing, on this occasion. By the time we arrived, space was flickering brightly from all the weapons' explosions reflecting off the smoky clouds, and there were collections of swirling debris strew over the entire battlefield. I contacted both Headquarters on the way to the site. Steven was fighting from above, and Epsilon had taken up the perimeter. I sent fourteen of my sixteen Fleets low so thcy could come in from below.

Now four hours into the confrontation, the battle site is littered with even more wreckage and body parts. The Captains of our battleships would be ordering their Bridge crews to map all these flying obstacles. From reports, I am now able to monitor regularly, it is apparent that Epsilon has lost three Carriers, five Cruisers, and seven Frigates. Seventeen Gamma warships have been destroyed or disabled. Zeta has lost a Frigate. And combined, we have suffered the destruction of one hundred fifty-seven fighters. But accounts and observation also indicate that two hundred seventy-one enemy ships are the biggest part of the drifting scraps. And, OFSA loss rate has decreased since Zeta's two hundred twenty-four warships began driving into the Isesinis soft underbelly. The escalating pressure appears to have caused a significant change in the struggle. We are now the offensive force while the intruders are on the defense. At this stage of the game, we are restocking each vessel regularly because our warships are expending ammunition at an incredible rate. Sheets of anti-matter charges are followed by sheaves of spears and salvos of cannon fire. But, this ferocity also means the Isesinis are unable to risk resupply and have begun to ration weapons' fire. More and more of their vessels are annihilating as less of ours are battered.

Four and a half hours into the confrontation, the entire deployment disappears. We analyze their trajectories. They are heading for 82 Eridani. It is over. We've lost a lot of good people and technology. But, we destroyed more than half the attacking Fleets, in the end. And, more Tier Three level Commands are still arriving.

Unlike the land wars of old, casualty rates are usually skewed towards those killed in action rather than people wounded. This is because we fight in the environment of open space. A hull rupture does not result in a lot of injuries, usually ending tragically in one hundred percent fatalities within the affected compartments. OFSA forces have suffered forty thousand eight hundred and seven lives and nearly thirteen thousand injuries. There will definitely be a day of mourning, and we will fly our pennants at half mast for five days. This level of losses hurts deeply. It is an insignificant consolation that an estimated two hundred ten thousand Isesinis died and a lot of their hardware was destroyed.

....

Examiner returned to Wolf 359 a day ago, and I am working away on the After Action Report for the Tau Bootis venture. Each headquarters involved will present one. Defensive operations are always discussed and debriefed at the next scheduled Commission meeting. But the account needs to be completed while the details are fresh in our minds. My data pad annunciator sounds off while I'm working on the summary.

It's a memo from Sparks. He has intelligence he'd like to discuss. I advise him we will speak at the next Intelligence meeting in two days. As the head of Zeta, ISIE falls under my overall command. Each of its four arms meets with me weekly, and Sparks has to attend each one of those sessions. I also meet with each of the two Tier Two Commanders four times a month and with the Tier Three heads and their bosses, every fourteen days. This is a system that we developed when IGB was first formed. It serves several purposes. It allows me to stay in the loop on every detail of the organizations under my authority. It permits us all to plan ahead and lets me mandate special missions or tasks. And, it is an opportunity for those requiring approvals at my level to seek those clearances. Of course, we discuss the mundane management issues like personnel, assets, and budgets.

35

Sparks responds that it's a US matter and he needs to see me outside that venue first, and if I decide, it can be discussed within the weekly conference that will be satisfactory. Chris presses hard, and Ultra Secret subjects are not usually dealt with in wider meetings. So I call Roh and ask her if there's anything special, this afternoon. She informs me that there's nothing she can't reschedule. I ask Sparks to appear at fourteen-thirty hours. That'll give me time to finish my report.

"General Sparks reporting, as agreed, sir!" He is in my doorway promptly at two-thirty.

"Come in and take a seat."

He steps up to the desk standing rigidly at attention as he holds a salute to his right brow.

"Relax, General.' I return the gesture. 'Grab something from the serving bar and slow down a little.' I offer as I round the desk corner and head for the counter. For me, it's a bottled water from the half-refrigerator. Sparks takes a coffee and sweet roll. I direct him towards the conversation area.

He had information on the Isesinis.

"You remember that secret little mission from a few weeks back?" He asks.

"I do. What's up?"

"I don't think you should know all the details, yet. Plausible deniability could be essential, in this case. But it's bearing fruit."

"What kind of information?"

"I can confirm Chan is at the Isesinis base off 15 Sagitta B. And, Kilkos is there. But, I am not yet sure if that's his permanent base of operations. He may be there for a visit. My source is unimpeachable, and I have documentation." He finishes.

"How? And, I don't mean you should give up all the details. How, do you come by this intelligence?"

"I now have a man at Chan's right hand. Chan made him his second because he knows and trusts him. And Chan believes he's averse to the Orion Federation. He has an ironclad cover."

"...any more information that's more specific? Little details convince my partners of the mission. They add a sense of reality to the narrative."

"Yes. As a matter of fact, I do. For instance - it's not Kilkos. It's Kil Kos. Kil is a rank equivalent to Supreme Tactical Field Commander. His name is just Kos. And, he is not as diminutive as his compatriots. He is one of a minority percentage on their homeworld considered to be giants. These titans are around six feet tall and a couple of hundred pounds. They are considered exceptional in their society and are always used to lead warfare. Kos is extraordinary, though. He is particularly clever and thought to be the equal of a revered legendary warlord from a century earlier. The other piece of gossip that's of importance is that Chan has sixteen Federation traitors with him. This group serves as an advisory council to the Kil. They have his ear. And, my agent sits in at planning meetings. If something happens to me, he will send information to you. It will be signed OFN. That's his identifying code."

"Okay. I will advise the C&C. I'll be very stingy. But, I need them to know the mission is running. And, you were right to see me independently. Place OFN in any memos requesting time with me about this. I am officially authorizing the undertaking on the basis it is not illegal or in breach of the R&R. Enter it in your secured journal under OFN. I will do likewise. After the Commission meets, I will forward you a mission number. You should tie OFN and the Mission Number together in the protected log. From that point, all communications on the matter should refer to the Mission Number.

Will we see regular reports?" I asked.

"Regular but sporadic, sir. The agent can only send out transmissions when it's opportune. And we will need to get SOCC to him with code updates, from time to time. He is running ten page OTC and could only take so many ciphers along."

"No problem. Savign will help without a lot of detail. She understands what we do. Is there anything else?"

"No, sir." Sparks rose.

"You realize that when you're ready to give up the details, we'll have to read your boss into this circle. We'll tell him I asked you to find a way and because it's Ultra level, and only the two of us were in the original chain. You have to work with General Svesion. I don't want him thinking you went over his head or were running rogue."

"Yes, sir. And, thank you, sir." Chris saluted, turned, and marched from the room.

I advised the C&C I needed a meeting. I also asked Savign to meet with me prior to the gathering. She's quite remote, now, so it took five days for her to arrive. In the meantime, the Commission session was set for July 22 by Grace.

....

"It's good to see you, Kurt." Savign voiced as she strolled into my office at ten hundred on Friday, July 22, 2270. The Examiner was now parked at Rigil for today's meeting.

"I'm always happy to see you, Savign. How are you?"

"I'm busier than a one-armed paper-hanger with the crabs."

"Well then, grab something and take a load off. You've got to stop and sniff the petunias once in a while."

"You mean roses. Petunias don't smell so good." She turned up her nose, and we both broke into uproarious laughter. We were both still chuckling as we helped ourselves at the bar. Then, we headed to the comfort area. 'So, what's up? You asked *me* here."

"Yes, I did. And, I'm glad you made it before the Commission meeting at thirteen hundred. I needed to speak to you before it."

"What do you want?"

"I need your help. Sparks has an Intelligence Mission going at 15 Sagitta B. His agent will need a sub to deliver code updates and retrieve reports, every so often."

"How often?"

"Oh... say once a month."

"That fits."

"What do you mean?"

"I suspect that Governor Kilkos guy is there. So, we run a week-long mission every month. Your agent's timing fits ours. Wait a minute!' She yelped with eyes wide. 'You have an agent inside?"

"I'm sorry. I can't talk about it. But, I can tell you the Governor's name isn't Kilkos. It's just Kos. Kil is his military rank."

"Oh my!' She yelped again.

"Will you do it? This is Sparks' doing - by the way."

"I will."

"Good. I have to inform the Commission, today. I need to add that we have the means arranged for communications and updates."

"Wow! I can't wait to hear the rest of this."

"You won't hear much more. I am obligated to advise the C&C. But, details are not required for Ultra Secret missions. But, thank you. I appreciate your help."

"How will I know your man?"

"You won't. And, I did not say it was a man. You'll drop and pick up at a prearranged location. You will only see the agent if extraction becomes necessary. We keep the NTK chain short for missions like this. I don't even know the agent's identity. Only Sparks does. I have the agent's code name, only."

"Wow. This must be seriously classified. That's real cloak and dagger shit." She says and drops in silence.

"Would you like to have brunch. It would save us rushing before we shuttle down to the meeting."

....

"Quiet please! Let's bring this meeting to order!" Grace yelled over the din as she slammed her gavel loudly on its sound block several times. The noise level died off until there was silence.

"This C&C Commission Meeting is now in session!' She slammed the mallet, again. 'Fleet Admiral Brubacher has the floor. He asked for special time.'

"Thank you, Admiral. This is an SU matter."

"Clear the room!' Grace bellowed as she hammered again. All monitors, gallery guests, and COS rose and left the room which was now only populated by the C&C. 'Go ahead." She said as she nodded to me.

"I need to inform the Committee of an SU mission. It was planned and is executed by General Chris Sparks. He now has eyes within 15 Sagitta. We have confirmed Chan heads sixteen humans in an advisory council. No one knows the officer's identity but Sparks. The NTK chain was very short, until now. It only included Sparks, me and Savign. We need SOCC for drops, pickups, and extractions."

"That's amazing. Does the agent know if we are seeing Governor Kilkos in our intelligence?"

"I cannot confirm many details, yet. But the agent says his name is not Kilkos. It's just Kos. Kil is his rank. He is Supreme Commander of all forces in this operation. And the General is not small like his confederates. He is a six-foot-tall Isesinis - a giant within their society. Chan's committee has his ear.

That is already more than I should say. This is a fluid situation, and it is very sensitive. But, I needed to fulfill my obligation to the Commission as outlined in the R&R. Any intelligence of tactical importance resulting from this mission will be forwarded to all of you by the fastest possible means as we receive it."

"Do you personally have confidence in the agent?" Steven Nichols asked.

"That's not the way it works. To protect the agent, only the handler knows who it is. I don't know who this person is. I do have the spy's code name, for communications purposes and I am his or her backup contact. And, SOCC will only see this Officer if extraction is needed. They will be doing blind drops and pickups, monthly."

"Thank you, Admiral Brubacher. A motion is now on the floor to authorize this mission, its needed assets, and any OFSA assistance required. All in favor, please raise your hands." Grace's volume was a little higher than conversation level as everyone jabbered about the amazing accomplishment. The motion passed unanimously.

"Admiral Brubacher, I am assigning Mission Number OFSA-CC-7128412 to this motion. We will all refer to the operation by that number from now on. All communications will be encrypted at the Ultra Level. I remind everyone that even discussion of the assignment's existence could jeopardize it and endanger the agent. Your mission is authorized, Admiral Brubacher.' Grace thwacked the gavel. Then, inquired more softly; 'Should we issue an arrest warrant, for Chan?"

"Not yet - we don't want to tip our hand. It's too soon after placing the agent. A new addition would be the obvious suspect." I explained

"Okay, let's get this show on the road. Bring everyone else back in.' Grace ordered.

"There is a motion to replace next Wednesday's meeting with this one. All in favor?' She observed as all hands went up.

'The motion carries. This meeting will replace the next regularly scheduled one. Is there any other unusual business before we hear the Headquarters' Reports?"

"I have one issue, Grace." George inserted.

"The chair recognizes Fleet Admiral George Bryant."

"It concerns the R&R and the section that describes the Headquarters' Commands and the C&C Commission.

I realized before our last major combined mission that there is a problem. I've had lots of time to consider it, and I still feel that way. We disagreed on the timing. The Commission had agreed to give me a veto in tactical matters but was still willing to override my decision to hold off. That in itself doesn't bother me. We can disagree, and mistakes could happen. But, what concerns me is that there is no determinative voice within our group. Everything is by majority vote. And, in that case, my argument finally won out because everyone at this table listens and considers all the details carefully. This entire topic is not a problem if it's a matter that requires the CIC and/or the SOD. It is problematic if it falls entirely within our purview. So, I would like us to propose to our superiors that the Chief of the General Staff should be able to employ some kind of overriding force. I know this could have worked against me before, but we need to reach finality on these matters. At some point, discussion has to cease, and a decision must be made. We are rather uncoordinated without that leadership."

Discussion on the matter went on for several hours. Towards the end of the day, King David appeared in the room. He had arrived for an appointment scheduled for early the next day, with Grace. He heard an impassioned argument from Fleet Admiral Tso Shah supporting Fleet Admiral Bryant's original proposal.

"We may need to execute a hastily arranged and urgently required tactical operation lacking a majority agreement of this Commission. It is imperative that final authority should rest in one person's hands. And, that Admiral should always be one who will consider all the other's arguments. In such a case, the Commission could become too unwieldy to be efficient. And, I agree with George. That power should rest with Grace. She handled it well when the C&C was a two-person job." Shah finished just as the King entered with the SOD and stood quietly at the door.

Everyone jumped to attention as David moved further into the room.

"Please sit. You are discussing an issue I've pondered for a long time. In fact, I've been surprised you have been able to function so smoothly, until now. There is no one to break a tie vote. I also think the OFSA C&C Commission needs a single face to represent it. It's very cumbersome when the Secretary and I wish to order an operation. Technically, we need to coordinate getting you all to Rigil, Earth, or some other central point to discuss it. Can you adjourn for half an hour so I can read the meeting transcript and discuss this privately with you?"

"We will take a one-half hour break!" Grace called as she whacked her gavel.

King David read silently for a few minutes. Then, he handed the minutes to the SOD pointing to something on the first page. After they were both up to date, the two men circulated through the room discussing the proposal with the C&C and even some gallery members.

"This meeting is called to order. I would like to note for the record that King David and the SOD are now in attendance and participating. King David, you have the floor." Grace directed.

"My feeling is that those arguing for a Supreme Commander are right. There are circumstances where an expeditious response is needed within a timeframe not possible if the entire Commission had to be included. And, there is the possibility of tie votes.

I am also satisfied that I can work with Grace. We've done that before. But, I still believe we are better off with a system employing some degree of consensus. So, here's what I'm thinking.

41

First of all, I don't like the term Supreme, so I will suggest we call this position Chief or First C&C. And, I think in matters of ultimate tactical urgency a First C&C should have the authority to order *all* others to conduct operations. And on large-scale multi-HQ Operational affairs, a Chief should have the mandate to dictate execution. But, that license should be subject to review by a majority vote of the rest of the Commission within a fixed period - say thirty days. That would temper whoever that leader is to consider what the other members would think of any order. But, those two channels of influence should be split. That was the intent of the original R&R that inaugurated the dual C&C concept. And, only in cases of tied votes on all Commission matters the First C&C would exercise two votes each.

In the minutes, I read Admiral Bryant's initial argument, and I understand that he was not referring to being on the losing end of an argument. He was just expressing the notion that someone has to be able to make a final decision in matters within the bailiwick of the Commission members. And I agree.

And, I would think Grace would be best for Operation First C&C. But, I think George would make the wisest choice for Tactical Chief. Anyway, you all need to decide on your preference and give me your proposal. This has to be something you can live with." David sat back in his chair as he finished.

There was an awkward moment as we all looked at each other to start the discussion.

"Do you mind if we take a five-minute break for a huddle, your Majesty." Fleet Admiral Addison Blythe requested.

"No, of course not."

We discussed the King's notion in whispered tones in a corner of the room. We were all surprised at the wisdom of his suggestion. But, it took as long as it did because both George and Grace needed to be convinced. We returned to our usual places at the table.

" I would like to offer a motion which proposes we recommend to the CIC and SOD the adoption of a modification to the C&C definitions within the R&R. We wish to have one member having preferential authority in service-wide Operations, and another in all-inclusive Tactical matters. The selected Fleet Admirals with the approval of the CIC and SOD would have the power to unilaterally order OFSA-wide operations subject to review by the entire C&C Commission within a one-month period. Further, these representatives' votes would weigh as two in matters falling within their particular

42

expertise the Commission is unable to resolve by majority vote. These Officers will be known as Chief of C&C. All other tactical or operational topics involving a single Headquarters' Command matter will remain under the control of that C&C within the bounds of the OFSA R&R and otherwise immune from outside interference. We recommend the selection of Fleet Admiral Grace Tonaka as Operations Chief of C&C and Fleet Admiral George T. Bryant as Tactical Chief of C&C." Stephen Nichols announced.

"A suggestion has been tendered regarding a change in the definition of the C&C within the R&R. Are there any objections' Grace paused. 'Okay then. We will vote on the application presented on the screen as described by Fleet Admiral Stephen Nichols. All in favor, please raise your hands.' Surprisingly, six assenting votes were recorded. 'Any opposed, please raise your hand.' No hands went up.

'Okay. I will record the vote as six for and one abstaining. Admiral Shah, may I ask why you're abstaining?

"Yes, you may Grace. I understand why everyone wants this and to a large extent, I agree. But, I resist because this does put absolute authority within individuals' hands - even if, it is only for thirty days and only regarding matters affecting the entire OFSA. I am not worried about Grace or George. But, the future concerns me. So, I elect to abstain."

"We understand, Admiral. The motion carries by a significant majority. My COS will prepare it and send it off to the CIC and the SOD. Do we have any other unusual business?" Grace inquired.

"I have an SU matter," David said.

"Clear the Room, please!" Grace called out. It took a couple of minutes to empty the space.

"Your Majesty...?" Grace let it hang.

"Yes, I noted a previous break on SU grounds and the issuance of the Mission Number OFSA-CC-7128412. I would like an update on the matter."

I took over and spent ten minutes filling in the King. He was satisfied, and we returned to regular business just long enough for Grace to gavel an adjournment, until the following morning.

Chapter 8 Pleasant Surprises

August 2, 2270

"If everyone is thinking alike then someone isn't thinking." Gen. George Patton

I am not yet sure if we can use their help or not, but, another species has offered assistance against the Isesinis. They are somewhat reclusive, almost to the point of xenophobia and anchor their group of worlds on a planet in the Beta Ursa Minor system just over forty parsecs from Sol. That's eleven light-years from the new border, so needless to say that between their location and quest for isolation, we were completely unaware of their existence.

George advised Captain Nedrif Elantham Captain of the FSS Shenzhen to forward the information to me, when people calling themselves the Suvayeek contacted Ned directly, on July 28. It was ship-to-ship communications initiated by a crew that had traveled a great deal out of their way to reach out to us. George felt I should handle the meeting and any negotiations because I'd conducted so much diplomacy since the Isesinis attack. Our new friends gave only a communications position and advised Elantham they would wait for a response for a couple of weeks.

I ordered the Examiner, her security group, and two Fleets from Zeta T1-1 to accompany us to Lambda Bootes just over three parsecs from the parked ship. We raced there at forty-percent so we could reach our destination in enough time to meet the rendezvous deadline. On August 11, we began transmitting continuous hails to the location via the laser communications system.

Communications' lags were nearly nine hours each way. We did not receive a response until midday August 13. We were invited to meetings on Beta Ursa Minor. However, it is a yellow/white star emitting incredible amounts of solar, ultraviolet, and infra-red radiation. So, we advised the Suvayeek of our inability to cope with their environment. A day later, they suggested we meet at Delta Bootis which falls somewhat between us in neutral space and is a very familiar system to us. We had used it to begin our lunge into the wedge of territory we have recovered. I agreed.

When we finally arrived in the stellar arrangement, we were treated to an extraordinary display by the Suvayeek, who uncloaked nearly one hundred fifty vessels of all types and sizes. Every single ship in their combined fleet enjoys the protection of this technology.

....

Shoy Cap almost reaches the ceilings and has to duck through the hatchways of my Admirals Craft. He commands the Suvayeek HQ ship. His species generated some shock when he and his compatriots came aboard on August 15. I will endeavor to describe them as best I can. But it is hard to put into words.

After getting over the initial amazement, I actually found these creatures somewhat cuddly in appearance - kind of like giant childrens' Teddy Bears. The five-member contingent ranged in height from almost two hundred to about two-hundred-twenty centimeters tall and weighed in between a very thin forty-five to a solid one-hundred-twenty-five kilograms. Their bodies are segmented into three sections and covered by tan and gray sections of folded hide and natural armor that make them seem dressed in oversized, overstuffed, hooded snowsuits. Eyes peak from beneath a fold near the top of the head. Mounted on either side of the skull below the same crease are two openings I assumed were comparable to human ears. There is no nose, and the mouth is perfectly circular with snow-white lips adorned with six black dots.

Six appendages protrude in pairs from either side of the middle segment and are employed as arms. Only the top twosome are jointed, and all six end in three sharp talons extending from paws. A fourth shorter set of legs are mounted at the posterior of the rear body portion and are double hinged at the equivalent of knees and ankles. The Suvayeek can walk upright on these or use them to sit in a crouch.

In the eight hours of our first meeting, it became apparent how valuable this species would be as allies. With a civilized record of over half a million years and a fossil and DNA history dating back seventy thousand millennia, they believe they are the oldest advanced life forms in the entire galaxy. It was also obvious they are incredibly intelligent. Later, we discovered their multi-lobed brains are exceptional at problem-solving and pattern recognition. Though they communicate amongst each other with telepathy, this analysis capacity gives them an amazing ability to acquire and use languages effortlessly.

We would class the Suvayeek as vegetarian, but they don't actually consume vegetation. Instead, they subsist on juices and saps from succulents and meaty fruits and vegetables they suck the fluids from. Six siphons extend from the dots in the lips to pierce and penetrate their meal offerings.

They can withstand near absolute zero and temperatures higher than the boiling point of water without damage. And, they can exist without food or water for up to ten years. This gift is facilitated by cellular-level control of fluid levels and pressures, protecting them from cell damage. Self-repairing DNA allows them to tolerate radiation levels a thousand times higher than humanoids can stomach.

Though they usually speak very modestly, they love to profess that a form of their species exists on every planetary system they have investigated, so far. And, though nearly microscopic in size there are trillions of a related genus on both Earth and Rigil, and we have found them on other planets in the Federation.

The Suvayeek are exceedingly technologically advanced and enjoy the protection and exploratory benefits derived from their Fleet of over six thousand spacecraft. Formations of these patrol their own territory and travel through the entire region extending over seventy parsecs from their borders. However, it is not normally their way to accumulate intelligence. It is more a matter of satisfying their curiosity. But, they do observe and note anything that may become a threat to them. And, it was this aspect of their operations that led to the breach in their profoundly guarded concealment.

Shoy Cap explained that they have watched the Isesinis closely for two centuries because of their very aggressive nature. The Suvayeek had long ago concluded they were a threat to a large part of the Orion Arm of the Milky Way Galaxy. But, they stressed it was not the Isesinis who triggered the invasion of the Orion Federation, in April 2267. Admiral Chan had already entered the picture by January of that year when the Suvayeek began to comprehend that some kind of offensive military operation was being initiated. By February, Chan had completed seven round trips between the Federation and the Isesinis Empire returning with additional associates, each time. By mid-March, the human advisors numbered twelve ex-OFSA officers. Cap declared the Suvayeeks' unconditional conviction that these traitors were responsible for the entire invasion plan.

The Suvayeek became concerned about their own sovereignty when the April attack began and spent the next couple of years debating whether to get involved or not. Now, they were certain the Isesinis needed to be repelled and contained.

Cap explained their surveillance of the region had also included the Orion Federation. And, he noted that they had observed our wars with the Grays, Spiel, and the Sec. I had to ask who the last ones were. When he was done explaining, I realized this is the species we referred to as the Inscrutables. Shoy clarified, explaining they'd monitored as we defeated each of those attackers, then settled back into peaceful life without taking revenge. And, they've concluded we are essentially a passive group that doesn't impose our way on others.

Shoy Cap took us on a tour of his Headquarters' ship - mostly to impress us with its advanced systems and power. He explained, their flotilla had never before been used for offensive purposes, but had been developed as a means to protect and defend the Suvayeek Dominion. At the same time, he managed to express how distasteful his people found combat. But, as second-in-command of the military and a senior member of their ruling council, he had the power to negotiate an alliance. He holds the rank of Hek Lider something akin to our Fleet Admirals or Marshals, yet more powerful still. He succinctly offered the Suvayeek help - in any way we could use them.

I explained that as one of the C&C of the OFSA, I did have authority to discuss and commit to terms of a coalition, but I wished to include our King in such an important diplomatic arbitration. We agreed to meet again within two weeks. The date would be confirmed after I communicated with King David.

....

I initially met with David for two days before revisiting Delta Bootis. We returned to the mediation with a goal in mind.

After all the proper introductions, I stressed to Shoy Cap that we did not expect to have the Suvayeek actually participate in battle because war is so revolting to them, but we would appreciate their support. Then, we spent several hours understanding just how deep the knowledge of *our* capabilities went among the Suvayeek. It was apparent there was no point in attempting to conceal any of our competencies, capacities, or resources from them. They knew all about us. Likewise, they had an in-depth awareness of all Isesinis' facilities, abilities, and potentials.

It quickly became equally apparent that the Suvayeek wished an open affiliation and would be unrestricted in sharing their technological know-how. There would be no surprises in the relationship.

King David handled the remaining discussion, which focused on Suvayeek services we would like to avail ourselves of. Particularly because of their stealth technology and covert proficiencies along with their distaste for violence, he asked they act as an intelligence source for the OFSA. In return, the Federation would occupy the previously unclaimed space between our border and theirs and ensure the security of that region in perpetuity, after our restoration.

The Hek Lider embraced the offer but asked for one other consideration. He explained it is their nature to fastidiously examine all the regions they patrol and approach governing bodies if there is a resource they might use. Shoy Cap added that they had found

47

such an uninhabited system in our territory that contained succulents they would like to transplant to their territory.

In answer to our inquiry, they gave its position in Galactic coordinates that we seldom use. After converting those to an Orion Federation location of RA 231.225°; Dec + 58.9666° at 98.119 Ly we realized they were referring to Iota Draco. It had been extremely strategic during our encounter with the Inscrutables in 2262. But, its importance was reduced when our borders expanded to the thirty-seven-parsec radius from Sol. Its principal star is an orange/red giant orbited by a brown dwarf. The secondary unit anchors several planets of its own. Two of those satellites possess abundant water and plant life.

King David not only agreed to the biological transfer but offered to allow the Suvayeek to harvest crops for consumption directly from these worlds provided they employed sound management practices so those forests would not be depleted. Shoy Cap agreed and was overjoyed. To show his gratitude for sharing this flora, Hek Lider Shoy Cap added technological collaboration to the discussion. This was a major concession since Suvayeek science is so much more advanced than ours. A contract was prepared and on August 30, and we were allied under the terms of a Mutual Assistance Treaty.

....

To our advantage, it was agreed Admiral Gojen Svjosloki would spend considerable time with Suvayeek engineering people, over the next several months. The first thing he came away with was a deeper, modified understanding of the construction of space. The Federation was correct in believing the primary substance of the universe is dark energy and matter, and all other types derived from those. But, dark matter is not as homogeneous throughout the void as we believed. Superior Suvayeek sensors can directly detect and map it. It forms a honeycomb. And matter accumulates just off these strands of dark matter. This spongy construction surrounds bubbles of genuine emptiness where all types of matter and energy projected into them can move unlimited by the constraints of standard space. These regions are literally ungoverned by some of the laws of astrophysics we take for granted. And a majority of these voids are not totally enclosed within the construct but meet one or more spaces within other compartments. Our inadequate understanding has curbed our creative process, limiting us to employing methods that fit within the physical principles we do grasp. As an example, Suvayeek scientists used their communications systems to demonstrate the possibilities achieved with this realization.

Photons traveling through space are confined to the regions that make up the honeycomb. The Suvayeek explained that they understood they would require a zero-mass particle to achieve FTL communications in the substrate of space. So, they searched for a way to isolate Grayons which they discovered did not need the physics we typically employ. Grayons are massless Bosons detected two centuries ago by the Suvayeek. They are similar in nature to gluons but may combine with dark or standard-matter quarks to form more complex units. But, unlike Gluons, Grayons may exist freely, can inhabit either the structure or substrate of space and possess a charge. They are found within Baryons of materials formed on the boundary between space and its substrata. They are more easily freed from these combinations to form a fluidic plasma (GFP). GFP is injected into the spatial cells in high-frequency digital streams. This energy is instantly reflected throughout all the other interconnecting compartments of the substrate ultimately propagating throughout all these bubbles like some giant "Hall of Mirrors." It is picked up by all the other converters and translated back to laser digital by the targeted receiver. By information in a Grayon based digital stream, the Suvayeek are able to communicate anywhere within the Milky Way's Orion Arm nearly instantly.

The energetic, fierce reactions required to generate these types of signals are too dangerous to create inside a moving vessel which is subject to all kinds of changing conditions. So signals are first transmitted via a laser system like ours and projected to the nearest SSSR (spatial sub-strata relay). It is essentially a collector and reactor continually breeding the GFP. When the signal is received the relay converts it to GDS (Grayon Digital Streaming) and transmits into the nearest pocket. Receiving units regenerate it as a laser signal by recombining the grayons with quarks to reform Baryons. This process generates energy fluctuations relative to the changing signal. These are detected, converted to laser, and redirected to the addressee by transmitting the beam through a vortex, like the Federation does, now. The greatest lag-times are in reaching the dispatching SSSR and in the receiver relaying the message to its recipient. But since the Suvayeek own nearly three-quarters of a million SSSR units deployed throughout all the territory they navigate, delays are limited to no more than four minutes. Each relay rests just inside a honeycomb cell with only its laser transceiver unit protruding into standard space, so they are incredibly hard to detect.

For our part, Admiral Svjosloki says our standard communications system will work in conjunction with the relays, so we should not need to change ship-borne hardware. But, we'll need to design, build, program, and deploy our own reactor/relays. He christened this our SSCS (Sub-Strata Communications System).

The Admiral and his team had spent considerable time examining the Suvayeek prints and understanding the sub-strata theoretical principals. They had no doubt they could create a working system that could interface with existing OFSA technology, within a condensed timeframe. The biggest problem was adding new transducers capable of detecting the construct of our spongy universe so the relays could be properly deployed. We also needed to acquire materials suitable for harvesting Grayons.

Svjosloki enlisted the team he needed, authored a calendar, advised production facilities, and set up a lab within a week of returning to the Examiner. After just three weeks, he had two prototypes that were deployed seven parsecs apart to assess their capabilities. Communications that would have taken nearly twenty hours to travel the distance were received in seven minutes. Meanwhile, Fleet Engineering Departments throughout the OFSA were installing the sensor modifications in all vessels.

After rigorous analysis and a lot of refinement of the exemplars, modified plans were transmitted to production facilities for manufacture. By late September, we were all in the process of deploying these units in the region we controlled and just outside Federation boundaries, while SOCC began to plant them throughout the occupied portions Federation. In the end, we would build and install thirty-five thousand of these throughout and around our territory. There would be one in every two hundred twenty-eight cubic light-years of space, meaning a vessel would never be more than two parsecs from one. This would provide a maximum communication's time of sixteen hours anywhere in our eight million cubic light-year sovereignty, instead of the previous five-day worst time. The ideal situation is two ships speaking to each other within a few hundred thousand kilometers of their respective relays. No matter how far apart they're positioned, the transmission would seem almost instantaneous. It's a considerable advantage over the Isesinis. In the future, once we have recovered all our territory, our goal would be to triple the number relays so we could reduce the distances and lag-times to one and a half parsecs and two hours between any two points in the Orion Federation. By positioning Headquarters Stations correctly, we could virtually enjoy instantaneous communications anywhere, allowing for video links between Commands. And, Gojen was sure we could adapt this technology to our long-range sensor systems!

Chapter 9 A Fly on a Wall

Tuesday, August 28, 2270

"Spying has gone on since ancient times." Vladimir Putin

It's almost two months since Sparks met with me about OFN. We've had one interim report arriving as a very brief transmission. But, I am now looking at a much more detailed account with pictures and videos. The entire assemblage is most impressive. Somehow, the agent was able to acquire photos of a Planning Group meeting around a boardroom table. Two images display about two-thirds of the group each, as viewed from different perspectives. But, the spy was careful to ensure he or she was not included. I still don't know who Sparks' infiltrator is. The package was retrieved by SOCC from a standard blind drop.

But, the mole is still uncertain of whether or not this is actually the Headquarters of Governor Kos. During the period the Kil has been present as often as he's been absent.

One major revelation regards the sudden lunges made towards the border. Some are designed strictly as tests. Even if we didn't respond to those, the Isesinis would not advance past the boundary. But, others are actually redeployments in advance of a discretionary attack. These forces may or may not proceed depending on our response. They are planned well in advance to allow for reorganization, resupply, and preventative maintenance. Our intruder has included the schedule for the next six weeks in the package.

On top of that, the data on district Headquarters is also documented within the bundle. This includes supporting assets, regional boundaries, and Chain of Command. On examination, this material overlays our regular intelligence acquired by SOCC. Though it is not new knowledge, it adds to our understanding of these formations.

Once satisfied I understood the significance of all the pieces, I asked my partners for a Commission meeting for US topics, only. This would mean no gallery or COS personnel would be in attendance. We all agreed to ten hundred hours on Thursday, September 1, 2270, aboard the Examiner.

....

"This meeting will come to order. Let's get this show on the road!' Admiral Tonaka slammed the gavel on its sound block. 'It's all yours Admiral Brubacher." She added.

"Thanks, Grace.

I wanted to discuss a recent intelligence report from our agent in the field at 15 Sagitta. He places a total of at least fifteen human collaborators there. They seem to sit as equals on a war council headed by the Governor. And, Kil Kos spends a lot of time at the site even if, it's not his base. We are analyzing photo and video information in an attempt to identify all the traitors. But, the human leader is definitely Chan. That in itself is important. But our spy sent us more valuable material than that.

The Isesinis plan these little lunges to our border well ahead of execution dates. Some are designated fakes, and others are designed to stop at the boundary and then continue an attack. But, we now have the schedule for the next six weeks." I finished as I tapped a screen icon on my datapad to forward the document to each of them. There was a pause as everyone eyed it in silence.

"This is incredible! We need to determine how we're going to use it." Fleet Admiral Tso Shah blurted out.

"What do you mean by that? We cream the bastards!" Fleet Admiral Addison Blythe barked.

"It's not that simple, Addison. We must maintain the appearance that we do not know their plans. We can arrive at each site a little earlier and with some additional force. But, we don't dare take pre-emptive moves or counter with an abnormally overwhelming force. It wouldn't take our enemies long to realize we have inside information if we act like that." Admiral Nichols explained.

"Yes. Of course... I just got a bit enthused."

"There are three actions on this list. One will infringe on Stephen Nichols region and the other two on Admiral Shah's. Can you align coverage so you can move a robust enough force to these positions without additional help?" George asked.

"Certainly," Stephen responded.

"I'm okay for the first one but, I may need help for the next. They're scheduled pretty close to each other." Tso answers.

"All right. You two build your plans. But Admiral Shah should include an additional two-Theatres force. I'll supply that for you, so send me those orders, and I'll pass them on to Shane MacDonald. He can assign a couple of Theatres to your fight. He'll probably want to come along." George returned.

"That'll be good. And, it's valuable to have the advance knowledge." Tso Shah gave me a nod.

"Yeah, thanks, Kurt," Nichols added.

"Thank Sparks, when you see him. He set up the whole enterprise." I responded.

"Anything else... ?' Grace queried as she eyed all of us. Then, she added.

'There is one more thing of minor importance. The Assembly, CIC and SOD approved the suggested changes to the R&R, as recommended." She tapped her screen. Each Admirals' pads chimed. They all quickly scanned the section involved. Each nodded their assent.

"We're adjourned!" She slammed the gavel, and we all headed for lunch in the pub.

....

Captain Nedrig Elantham, the Master of the FSS Shenzhen, had settled into the Bridge Command Station. Like every day so far this week, today was turning into a very routine shift.

On Thursday, September 1, 2270, he had received new orders from Vice Admiral Boets, his Fleet Commander, who was relaying them directly from Admiral Tom Stevens the Deputy Epsilon Headquarters' Commander. Their entire Autonomous Unit was being redeployed to a new region. An overview included in the orders explained there was reason to believe the area they had patrolled would settle down and the new area of focus would become a hot spot. So, they all jumped out for LTT 18350 to redeploy in a formation between 59 and 70 Virgo on the easternmost side of the wedge the OFSA fully controls.

....

Sparks and I sat in my office quietly discussing OFN, on Tuesday morning, September 6, 2270. He had the latest field report on 15 Sagitta.

"This is a list of all the various level Headquarters the Isesinis have positioned throughout the Orion Federation.' He forwarded the document to my datapad. 'You'll note that it includes their importance within the hierarchy. We know which are regional or local ones. And, we can see the strength each is responsible for."

"This is good work. The Commission will be surprised. We've always assumed there were ten of these orbs, but there are a lot more." I injected, after studying it for a minute.

"And this block diagram clarifies the relative positions of those who report to Kos." He directed the schematic to me.

"If you put the two together, you can see who's who."

"Yes. We can even see which Officer would supplant Kos if something were to happen to him. Dac Kil Mes, his deputy, would be the likely candidate. And, this is a directory of the sixteen humans in the advisory council." Chris forwarded the register.

"Shit! These are all ex-OFSA people. They were caught up in the rebellion or were charged with various crimes."

"Yes. And, that directory shows them by authority. Chan is the leader. The number two is my man. That's why his contact-handle is shown. And this final file is a very important timetable converted to our calendar." Chris sat back with a look like it was something extraordinary. I studied it carefully. It took a couple of minutes before I realized its magnitude.

"Dammit! This is Kos' schedule for the next month.' Thoughts were streaking through my brain. I stopped to consider them. 'Can the agent keep these coming?"

"I can ask in the next drop. But, I think it would be regular intelligence if these reports continue to be available."

"Two of these have created an issue, for me."

"What's that Admiral?"

"The appointment ledger creates opportunities to intercept and capture or eradicate the Governor and his immediate subordinates. But, acquiring approval and planning a mission like that will require much more certainty of the veracity of all the information.

The second concern is the number of OFSA personnel in this consulting group. It will lead to concerns there are more, and some are still active within the service."

"You mean, this material creates a need for a counter-intelligence operation?"

"Exactly. So, the time has come where I must ask you for the hidden details of the mission. I will have to share them will the Commission, and we will need to include General Svesion."

"I understand, sir.' Sparks paused to compose his thoughts. 'Well sir - when we believed we saw former Admiral Chan helping the Isesinis in that video, I got an idea. I thought we might be able to place a spy. Chan - if it was him - seemed to have quite a contingent of humans in tow. It kind of seemed like his personal staff. I got thinking that if he's helping our enemy, he is probably using a group of similarly disaffected Orion citizens to aid him.

I realized I might be able to place a spy. But, it had to be someone he'd accept without question. A person who *might* be equally pissed at us. And, I believed the agent needed to be someone he knew who was in a similar situation. So, I went to the prison to interview former Admiral Naabaahii. What I came away with is that he is a patriot. He did what he did because he believed it was the right thing to do, at the time. He says he could see over his years in prison that everything worked the way the King and Admiral Bryant thought - and that he knows now he was wrong. I spent four hours with him. When I left, I firmly believed him."

"All the people involved in the rebellion of 2257 were patriots. They were sure the proposed Constitutional changes were going to destroy the Empire and that it would not survive as a Federation. Anyway, continue with your report."

"Sir, I asked him if he'd like the chance to redeem himself. He convinced me he would use an opportunity like that effectively. So, I filled him in regarding our suspicions of Rear Admiral Chan and asked if he'd like to go undercover for ISIE and attempt to infiltrate Chan's operation. He approved. So, I had him sign an agreement, and I arranged for his parole on the grounds of Federation Security needs but instructed all parties the parole warrant and the prison files could not reflect that purpose. So, he was released three months ago."

"...the secret Court Order?"

"Yes, sir. Meanwhile, I arranged for him to *steal* an FTL capable shuttle from us. His cover is that he was finally paroled, after thirteen years and promptly pilfered a shuttle and went looking for the like-minded Admiral Chan. The appropriate reports have been filed on the theft, and Investigative Command is probing the crime without knowledge of the underlying mission. His Parole Officer reported him missing, six weeks ago. He would have been due to appear at his office on July 10, so he's well overdue, now. He is now wanted as a fugitive, and even ISIE Enforcement is searching.

So the cover is well established, and everyone is playing their part to the tee - unwittingly. He's in. It turned out to be Chan, and he was so happy to see Naabaahii, he threw a big bash in his honor, and he made him the number two."

I advised the Admiral he may have to actually participate with Chan to support his cover and that would be okay. I offered him immunity for any involvement. He has no secrets to share with them. He's been out of touch too long. So there's no conflict there. He's been in prison for thirteen years and out of the loop." There is a long pause. So, I assume Chris is finished.

"When did Svesion receive his last clearance?"

"We ran it two months ago. The General is as trustworthy as they come. We renewed our recommendation for his Ultra Clearance level."

"That's right. I remember it, now. I okayed his new Identification based on that. So, let's call him in here. I have a reason for wanting him included. But, you better let me take the lead. I will take the blame for initiating the mission without his knowledge."

"Okay. If that's the way, you believe we should play it."

"Yes. I do." I said as I tapped out a message for Svesion to appear, immediately.

When he arrived, he showed his surprise at being invited to a meeting already attended by a subordinate.

"Grab something and take a seat, General. I'll explain everything.' I said as he headed for the bar - then to a sofa with coffee in hand.

'This meeting is *Ultra Secret Need to Know* only. An agent's life depends on keeping this circle as small as possible.

A few months ago, when it became apparent former Rear Admiral Chan may be involved with the Isesinis, I asked Sparks in for a secret meeting because of the Intelligence nature of my request. I asked him to see if he could find a way to infiltrate the human participants helping this enemy. He did and has an agent in place as we speak. But, I have two reasons for widening the NTK circle. The first is that this is an extremely hazardous operation and Chris is your subordinate. I will discuss the second reason with you after we finish this update. For now, I'd like General Sparks to fill you in on all the details since taking on the mission.'

Chris began repeating the same dissertation he had already presented to me.

" Naabaahii - he's a fucking traitor! How can you consider using him?" Svesion snapped when Sparks got to that part.

"He's not a traitor. He's a misguided patriot who committed a treasonous crime. There is a big distinction between the two. He believed in what he was doing, even though he was wrong. He's served thirteen years and only wants to make amends. And, he's the right kind of agent for this particular job. It's easy to convince someone like Chan that Naabaahii would want to join. And, Chan knows him. There is already trust there." I injected, then extended a hand to Sparks to continue.

"I have to admit, it's a damn good plan. And, you're right, Admiral. I know what you're trying to convey. He is a man who believed what he was doing was best for the Federation. I'm sorry for the outburst."

"So, you're okay with this? You're on board?" I asked.

"Yes, sir. You can keep me within the chain. I will not expand it unless I clear it with both of you."

"Our communications must be verbal on this. You can both keep a detailed journal to support your recollection of the details, but make sure it's properly secured. Record this as Mission Number OFSA-CC-7128412. The only communication between us should be to request a meeting, and it should reference that ID. There should be no other written documents, except encrypted messages to the agent."

"That's understood, sir. I'm amazed you've already gotten results." Svesion observes.

"What results?" I query.

"You already know it is Chan. Confirming that was important. And, your man's been placed in a leadership position. Naabaahii is obviously the right choice."

"Is that it? Is everyone okay? Or, do we need to discuss anything else about this or any other subject?"

"No, sir." The two men chorused.

"Will you stay behind General. I need to discuss another matter with you." I directed at Svesion as Sparks rose to leave.

"With your permission sir?" Sparks said as he stood at attention bearing a salute.

"You're dismissed, General." I snapped as I returned the gesture.

"What do you need, sir?" Svesion inquired when we were alone.

"I was thinking of Sparks. Unless a spot opens as an Army Commander, he will be stuck at Level 10 General. He's a good man. I was thinking of all the different planetary resistance operations he keeps functional. And then there's this latest mission. Though I may have started the ball rolling, the entire scheme is his plan. It's absolutely ingenious. So maybe we could do something for him. I need an idea for something that would show our appreciation and maybe even give him a little reward for all his hard work."

"What if I nominate him for the Federation Award for Tactical Distinction. That's approved by the King and carries a cash award. If he grants it to Chris, we can present it at one of those big dinner/ dances for the entire Zeta Command."

"Great idea. Can you prepare the submission without any details on this mission? You may mention a special intelligence operation and the mission number without any specifics, and we can explain it to King David when he reviews your suggestion. He's one person we can add to the NTK circle. I need to expand it to include the other C&C and the King, anyway."

"Okay, sir. I'll get right on it." Svesion responded enthusiastically as he rose and saluted.

"You're dismissed, General." I snapped.

As soon as Svesion was gone, I requested "Ultra Secret" time at the next meeting and asked Grace to invite the King and SOD. She responded later, advising me that both had agreed to attend.

....

"Clear the room!" Grace yelled as she slammed her gavel on the sound block, after formally opening the meeting at nine hundred hours on Thursday, September 15, 2270. Everyone but the C&C, the SOD and the King rose and left. Not even the Fleet Admirals' COS are included in these sessions. I spoke when the room was clear.

"I need to advise the Commission and the King of details of US Mission Number OFSA-CC-7128412 being run under the direction of General Sparks for Zeta Command. For the record, I initiated it. General Svesion is informed. General Sparks is the operator, and one agent is conducting the covert mission. To this point, no others outside the C&C Commission have been included in the Need To Know circle except Sparks and Svesion. All communications are verbal, but we three Senior Officers are keeping encrypted and appropriately secured journals of the operation.

You all remember the video we had a few months ago that appeared to display former Rear Admiral Chan in collusion with the enemy. At that time, I asked General Sparks to see if he could come up with a plan to get an agent close to Chan - if it was him.

Sparks reasoned it would have to be someone Chan or anyone in cooperation with the Isesinis would easily trust. The person would need to have a background known to Chan and easy to verify. He felt we could not risk building a cover for an agent in this position. It had to be someone with the proper history already in place.

So, he approached Admiral Naabaahii in prison and interviewed him. He rightly determined that the Admiral was not treasonous but was a misguided patriot who committed a seditious act. He tested him on loyalty and found Naabaahii now views his past disloyalty as a mistake and would do anything to aid the Orion Federation. He knows he was wrong back in 2257 but says he believed the changes proposed to the Constitution would destroy the union, at that time. He went into that operation thinking he was saving us all. And, I must say that I concur with that perception. I supervised all the investigations, then. These people all felt they were patriots doing what was best for the Orion Federation.

So, Sparks explained the current situation and the belief Chan was involved, and his contribution may have actually precipitated the incursion. He expressed the thought that because of his record and their previous friendship, Chan or any other human it may be would likely readily accept Naabaahii as a compatriot. The Admiral agreed to the plan. So, General Sparks had him released. They faked the theft of a shuttle and Naabaahii made his way to the Isesinis formation. He has subsequently confirmed our suspicions. The leader of the human component of this attack is former Rear Admiral Chan. He accepted Naabaahii without question and installed him as the number two in the organization. It is now an ongoing mission. And, he has been the source from within."

There was absolute silence in the room. It went on for what seemed like an hour.

"So, you're saying we released Admiral Naabaahii from prison and helped him get to the enemy. And, with your approval." Grace inquired.

"Wait a minute.' The King interrupted. 'Think about it. It's a brilliant plan. And, yes - it could fail or backfire. But, we needed to get an agent in there. You're never going to place one unless it's someone like Naabaahii." David finished.

"I agree. It's brilliant! Who the hell thought this up?" Fleet Admiral Tso Shah inquired.

"I asked Sparks to look for a means. He came up with the entire plan and executed it to the point we're at now. He's been receiving regular reports. That's why I asked for this time. I have information that is probably going to force me to widen the operation."

"So, there was automatic trust there?" George queried referring to Chan.

"Yes. It sounds like it was immediate acceptance."

"That's because you two chose the right person for the job. You're right. Naabaahii never thought of himself as a traitor. He believed he was a patriot and probably still is.' George observed. 'It is inspired." He added with a chuckle.

"I must reinforce that I requested and approved it, so if it fails, it's my fault. But, Sparks developed the plan and executed it. He deserves any credit if it goes well." I injected.

"Do you need any tactical or equipment support from us?" Nichols asked.

"No, Admiral. All I need is your moral support and the approval of the Commission and the CIC. We have everything under control. If it's successful, I will ask the King for special considerations for Sparks. And, he may want to do something for Naabaahii if he serves the Crown well."

"Is everyone okay with this. This is a motion to approve the US mission outlined by Fleet Admiral Brubacher. All in favor?" Grace called out.

All hands went up quickly.

"The motion carried unanimously. I will enter it in the record under the reference number which will refer to the entry in my private journal - also secured and encrypted.' She yelled as she slammed her mallet. So, what is the new information Admiral Brubacher."

"We now have a list of all of Chan's human compatriots. And, it is extensive. All of them are former OFSA. This led... ."

"Do you think there are more still active in the service?"

"That's what I was about to say. So, I believe a CI operation is warranted to seek out any spies."

"I agree! But, don't we always run CI?" King David inquired.

"Zeta constantly looks for spies in our ordinary course of business. But, this is different. We would need to focus a group of agents on the specific task of searching for Chan's moles. It requires a different approach.

But there's more. We now know where each Headquarters is and its position in the authority structure. And, I have Governor Kos' calendar for the next six weeks. I don't think that's enough time to use it effectively. But, I believe we can use it to discuss how we can react to the next six-week schedule after this one. This data means we'll probably get an opportunity to grab or assassinate him."

There were several murmured expressions of amazement and a couple of low whistles from around the table. Then, there was complete silence.

"Do we need a short break?" Grace called out finally breaking the hush. There were nods all around.

"We're adjourned! We'll reconvene in half an hour!" Grace slammed the mallet.

We all went about the business of washroom breaks and retrieving refreshments silently. As we returned, the swelling congregation stood in groups speaking in soft whispers. We slowly worked our way back to our table positions.

"The meeting will come to order!' Grace thwacked the gavel on its sound block. 'Does anyone have any questions or comments about what we heard before the break?"

"As far as CI activity goes, I believe we should agree it's necessary and leave it all in Kurt's hands. It's his area, anyway. But, I think we need to form a sub-committee to look into possible actions around the calendar. We may or may not be able to plan and execute around the current one. But, it's more likely Kurt is correct, and we'll do better with a future version. I know he's a busy guy but, I feel Kurt should be part of that unit with Admiral Nichols, Savigne, and me." George offered.

"I agree with both views. Counter Intelligence is definitely Kurt's area. I think we should just authorize it. And, I concur with his view of the Calendar operation, except that, I'd like to be included in the sub-committee." Fleet Admiral Tsoh Shah injected.

"I agree with Admiral Shah, entirely!" King David added to our surprise. He did not usually insert himself into our OFSA operational discussions.

"Okay. A motion is on the table to authorize a CI operation under US Mission Number OFSA-CC-7128412. All in favor?' Grace paused and looked around. 'The proposal is unanimously passed.

A second tender recommends we form a sub-committee to insinuate a military operation into the Calendar schedule previously discussed. Before we vote, I would like to add a comment to this topic for consideration.' Grace paused and looked around for assent. Then, she continued. 'I believe this should also fall under the direction of Fleet Admiral Kurt Brubacher since it has the smell of Covert Special Operations to me. I envision a small secret force engaging the target. Should we reopen discussion or should we vote on the original proposal?" Grace concluded.

"I think we should vote on the original proposal because the subcommittee will also look at the method and may determine it should be a Zeta operation. But, they may also end up viewing it as best handled as an offensive military one. Either way, they'll have to come back here for endorsement." Fleet Admiral Bryant offered as the others around the table nodded agreement.

"All in favor of the initial plan?' Everyone raised their hands including Grace. 'The request is approved unanimously! Let's go on to regular business!" She banged the hammer again, and several of us rose to invite the gallery in. The meeting continued.

....

Two days later, I sat in my office with Svesion and Sparks.

"The Commission has authorized another mission - or rather, an expansion of US Mission Number OFSA-CC-7128412.

We are to branch-off a Counter Intelligence covert operation. We will be combing through the regions of the Federation and the OFSA Commands we can reach looking for any who may be Admiral Chan's confederates. The two of you have to determine how wide you want the scope to be. Then, you'll build a plan, enlist your candidates and execute the assignment. And, it goes without saying that this motivation must also be articulated to our regulars in enforcement and investigation who may be able to pick up clues in regular audits and examinations. But that must be done without a hint of the Intelligence or Covert Counter Intelligence actions.

I know you have a lot on your plate right now, Chris. But, my feeling is that this should be directed by you under General Svesion's supervision, because you are the head of ISIE. And, the General has several other commands to manage. However, you would be wise to create a temporary control under a Senior Officer to actually administer the day-to-day. It could become a relatively large venture. So, I would suggest at least a Major or maybe even Lieutenant Colonel. But that person must understand the nature of this beast and that it is an SU mission running under an identity number, only. The team should only know what they're required to do to complete their task but should never be aware of the other side of this setup. They should never be aware of OFN. The two operations should remain completely disconnected from each other up to your involvement.

Do you have any comments or questions?' I eye them both carefully. There are negative head wags. 'Okay then. I need a plan on my desk by nine hundred on September 20. You're dismissed!"

Both men rose, saluted, and exited my office.

....

I spent September 18 and 19 with Bryant and Fred. It was a great weekend. Fred arrived at my station on Friday, September 17 and had to depart the following Monday. She was doing exceptionally well in the Command Program. It won't be long until she comes home for good.

Chapter 10 Analysis

Friday, September 30, 2270

"There can be no prestige without mystery. Familiarity breeds contempt." Charles DeGaulle

It's the most incredible problem we've ever experienced - kind of like having so much money you don't know what to do with it all. But, in this case, I am referring to intelligence and information, in general. It's great to know a lot, but you need to be able to compartmentalize and analyze that data and convert it to some form that is usable.

This torrent has been especially overwhelming to Zeta Command since we are the organization tasked with acquiring the protected materials of others. The Intelligence division of ISIE retains a total of just over fifteen thousand people. Thirty-five hundred of those are covert agents. Their missions included undercover work within OFSA and Federation operations and secret assignments in unfriendly regions. Besides that, another group of over a thousand "Paid Informants" continuously report on a variety of matters throughout our own and enemy territory.

Nearly twelve thousand support those actions. All are considered ISIE "Staff." But, only half of those actually manage personnel, payroll, accounting, and all the other accommodating areas that aid operations. The rest is a combination of general and specialized analysts who sift through the data to discover its meaning, put it in practical forms, and determine how it affects us. In some cases, the senior specialists even suggest how we may use it to our advantage.

Right now, we are receiving an abundance of accounts from a lot of different sources. There are the typical agents', and PI feeds - at about a thousand items a day. SOCC observations are being collected by the hundreds, each day. There is also the new feed from the Suvayeek. We are taking in as many accounts from them as the SOCC. And finally, there are the sporadic scoops from our undercover spy at the 15 Sagitta location. So, our evaluators are now overworked. I am receiving completed assessments about a week after reception of the data instead of within two days - and that lag time is growing. And, "Urgent Matters" are dealt with within twenty-four hours - not the usual hour-and-a-half. I call in Generals Svesion and Sparks.

"Gentlemen, we have a serious issue developing within the Intelligence Division," I announce once they're both seated comfortably.

"Do you mean the crushing workload created by the prodigious amount of information they're handling?" Sparks inquires.

"Correct. I am assessing evaluations on a very delayed basis. Even burning issues are taking a day or more to get to me."

"I may have a temporary solution. But, in the long-run, we will need to hire more analysts when we recruit from the Academies." Svesion offers.

"We're in the middle of a war. We need something, right now! What's the temporary solution?"

"Well, Sparks here has a large Investigative Division which isn't being fully utilized because of the current conflict. All of those are Academy grads who have the required military background. All have been suitably trained in criminology which has similarities to intelligence. And, all of them have a lot of experience in ISIE and have dealt with matters that overlap with Intelligence. Many have great minds. Some may even have transferred out of Intelligence for some reason or another. I suggest we take a couple of hundred of the most qualified people with methodical, reasoned, logical aptitudes and move them." Svesion suggested.

"I can do that! You're right when you say, the Investigative Division is currently under-employed. So, it makes a lot of sense. But, this won't be instantaneous, in most cases. Anyone with a previous background in Intelligence will be able to get up to speed in a day or two. But, the rest will need two to three weeks." Sparks injected.

"That's a lot better than the six months it takes to develop a good Analyst right out of the Academy. Let's make it happen!" I said as I rose from my chair.

Both Officers excused themselves, paid the mandatory respects, and departed my office.

....

I'd been receiving delayed reports for over a month but, the pace picked up about a week later as the lag times began to decrease. Suddenly, I'm becoming the bottleneck. Another ten days later, it became daunting, and I called in Elisma. I knew that once Intelligence was ordered to echo him, he would be exposed to even the US items. So, I read him into all the operations during our six-hour meeting. Several times we interrupted it to travel to mess-halls or the pub, to relieve the intensity. We were always careful to discuss only generalities during these interludes, returning to secure details when in the confines of my office. He was stunned at the Suvayeek and Naabaahii activities. Once he was familiar with the basics of all the strands of the web, I reviewed protocols for handling the material. He could employ aids in anything classified to the level of "Confidential," but all information at security levels above that had to be dealt with by only the two of us or the contributing parties.

When handling this data, the first course is to separate out those items that concern only Zeta. These would be reports that require direction for additional or different covert actions. The other pile is sub-divided into categories involving particular Headquarters. And, a final stack will need tactical decisions on a service-wide basis. None of these are released directly to the recipient. Instead, a more generalized report is prepared that includes recommendations and is forwarded to the appropriate Command. I gave El examples of these communications and provided him with one additional proviso. Anything requiring OFSA tactical responses should be filtered through my office before transmission. Once I was certain he had grasped all the procedures and rules, I issued a directive to Svesion and Sparks.

....

MEMO
CLASSIFIED - SECRET (NTK)
ENCRYPTED - *Authentication Root I.D. ZETA-8571A&740}+*

From: F. Admiral K. Brubacher C&C Zeta HQ Commander

To: General Svesion Zeta Marine Army Commander, General C. Sparks ISIE Commander

C.C.   C&C Commission Members, CIC, SOD, Admiral (11) Elasima DC Zeta Command

Date: October 19, 2070

Re: Intelligence Handling Protocol

Generals,

Please be advised that effective immediately, due to overwhelming volume, Admiral Elasima, Zeta Commands' Deputy Commander, will be included in all Intelligence normally forwarded to my office. Please divide these reports evenly between us. He has been fully briefed and instructed in handling regulations. It will not be necessary to separate materials by source, topic, or expected direction of communication.

Regards,

....

I advised my COS Rohkea Sielu of the change and the resulting meetings I would need with El. She revised my calendar increasing my daily session with El by another hour. All other appointments were rearranged accordingly and notified of the change.

Almost immediately I could begin to see a reduction in the workload. And, Elasima called me via Vid-Com and asked how the hell I ever handled it all, since he was grading only half of it and that part is enormous. I reminded him there had been a significant recent uptick in the job.

....

Like all good plans, there appeared to be a hiccup we identified at our meeting of October 26, a week after the adjustment. Because of the division, each of us was seeing some of the data from the Suvayeek. But after discussion, we realized we could turn that apparent problem into an advantage. Instead of just dividing reports from this source arbitrarily, we'd have Sparks' people separate it by regions. That way, each of us would be able to develop images of our distinct zones that we would totally understand.

The sessions also quickly morphed into longer discussions. Going it alone meant follow-up actions were always based on my point of view. By discussing each and every matter together, they were now tempered by both our outlooks, though I always retain the right of making a final decision. Some events I would have just forwarded to a Zeta operation were now directed to other Headquarters. It's hard to understand the effect of the Intelligence Division on the various Commands. But, since the rise in information, we were now dividing nearly four hundred analyzed reports among the Field Headquarters, with another fifty directed at Rigil, each and every day. And throughout each twenty-four hour period, we'd monitor several hundred orders issued as a result of those accounts.

....

I was in the middle of a wonderful weekend with my son Bryant and Fredricka my fiancee, when I received notifications` of a serious US intelligence matter. I had to excuse myself, dress in proper attire, and head to my office. I needed a secure location to study the issue.

There was a significant Ultra Secret memo from Sparks, regarding our agent at 15 Sagitta. Naabaahii had activated a signal requesting an extraordinary pickup from the drop location. SOCC had retrieved the package and immediately forwarded it to Sparks. He'd received it yesterday, Saturday, October 29, 2270. It was an updated calendar and contained information on four impending actions. Two would be feints. But, the other two would be optional attacks.

The file was extensive containing the complete battle plans. It appeared the Kil was a micro-manager because all but the reactive components were included. And, even general guidelines for responses were there. Every single field maneuver was preplanned. This record held so much data, it made me happy we operate by "guided design." We transmit a general strategy with basic configurations, objectives, goals, and rules of engagements. Individual Commands determine their own force deployments, reserves, and battle tactics.

I scanned available information from SOCC and the Suvayeek. It confirmed movement to staging points that would facilitate the actions. They involved areas patrolled by the three remaining Local Headquarters and may also require both Epsilon and Zeta assistance, so I notified the entire C&C that an urgent meeting of the C&C Commission was essential to discuss tactical matters.

Our emergency session on Monday, October 31 resulted in new orders to most of the Headquarters' dependent Commands.

Chapter 11 New Fronts

Monday, December 5, 2270

"You cannot escape the responsibility of tomorrow by evading it today." **Abraham Lincoln**

There are lot's of changes, today. As of now, the Examiner is Fredricka's base of operations. I prepared for her arrival by contacting the Examiner's Captain for office space and quarters. The Examiner has a Amenities' Officer to allocate discretionary areas so, the Captain placed the task in her hands. Because her job is a Command-wide responsibility, Fred's office is down the Staff Offices corridor, on the Flag Bridge, not that far from mine. And, her need for quarters is just temporary. For all our advanced attitudes, outlooks, and technologies, parts of the Orion Federation are still rather prudish. It would scandalize some if the Headquarter's Commander were living with someone while in an unattached state. So, we will continue to live as we have, until the marriage.

I first held an official meeting with her, as I would with anyone joining the team at a Senior Level, directly within my Staff. Roh, El, Fred, and I sat quietly discussing the matter in the conversation pit within my office.

"I'd first like to welcome you to Zeta Command, Captain.' I rose from my chair to present the official handshake. 'I thought we'd better hold this little gathering to sketch out your responsibilities and protocols.

First, you'll be provided with a staff of five. They're to be used for research, to compose, and in some cases to makes less sensitive statements to the Press Corps when you're not available. As your department grows or demonstrates the need this can expand. You'll have generous annual expense and capital budgets. And, you may need to travel to Rigil, from time to time, for meetings with your peers from other Commands.

You will be the public face of Zeta Command. As you know, it's sometimes necessary for the Commander to address the public through the press, but it's usually quite disruptive to our schedule. So, a Press Secretary is a major benefit.

Your pipelines will be very sweeping. We cannot include you in all our discussions and meetings because Regulations limit what we can share. But, we'll involve you as much as possible. That means you will often be privy to information that's Classified at various levels. Usually, this is for your benefit, only - so you have the background picture. It permits you an in-depth understanding of a situation. But you may not share secured data unless authorized by Roh, El, or me.

Contrary to the common feelings of the Press Corps, we consider them a valuable asset. Sometimes, they may point out the egg on our faces. But, usually, they do us much more good than harm. They spotlight the many benefits of the OFSA and the sacrifices most of its members endure to support the Federation.

So, your job is to give them as much as you possibly can without compromising our operations. If you're conducting operations appropriately, they should be informed without the need to be underfoot. Your job helps keep everyone happy."

MEMO

From: **Fleet Admiral K Brubacher C&C Zeta HQ Commander**

To: **All Zeta Command Operations**

All Zeta Command Personnel

Dist: **All Zeta Commands**

Re: **OFSA HQ Field Public Relations Office**

Date: **December 7, 2270**

All,

Please be advised that the Office of Field Public Relations will now be housed aboard the FSS Examiner. I am also pleased to inform you that Captain Fredricka Whitehead will Command this operation for the OFSA. Fredricka holds a Masters' Degree in journalism and is working toward her Doctoral post-graduate certification. She brings several years experience to the position. Her most recent pre-service assignments were with the AP news services. Though Captain Whitehead will have no direct tie to our tactical operations, please join me in welcoming her to the Examiner and Zeta Command.

F. Adm. K. Brubacher

As soon as she was comfortably aboard, Fred and I announced our wedding date. We scheduled it for Saturday, January 14, 2271. That permitted time for all the attendees to receive and reply to invitations, and to make their way to the Examiner at Wolf 359. I ordered the Investigator here for four days starting January 12. The expected attendance at the wedding dinner would require both ships. For the ceremony, we included the entire Royal Family, Secretary of Defense, Defense Committee, C&C

Commission, all Tier Two and Three Commanders, and many Admirals at all levels we considered friends or close acquaintances among the four-hundred summoned, with their spouses or significant others. Previous experience suggested the Flag Bridge of the Examiner could manage eight hundred for the military ceremony. All other Zeta personnel were added to the wedding list for the dinner party. The new Suvayeek inspired communications' system really helped. It allowed for delivery to most recipients in less than a day.

MEMO

From: Admiral Rohkea Sielu Zeta Commander Chief of Staff

To: All Zeta Command Operations

All Zeta Command Personnel

Dist: All Zeta Commands

Re: Personal Announcement

Date: December 9, 2270

All,

We wish to invite the entire Zeta Command team to participate in a day of festivity to help us celebrate the joining of Captain Fredricka Whitehead to Fleet Admiral K. Brubacher as man & wife, on Saturday, January 14, 2071.

The ceremony will take place in the Hangar of the FSS Examiner at eleven hundred hours. This venue has been selected to allow attendance by a much larger group than would be possible on the Flag Bridge. This Bay is capable of comfortably seating nearly nine thousand people. Since Zeta Command employs many hundreds of thousands, seven thousand guests will be chosen by lottery, and one thousand have been specially invited by the bride and groom. Details of the sweepstakes will follow in a couple of days.

To celebrate this special day, two dinner/dance parties will be held aboard the Examiner, Inquisitor, Investigator, and Interrogator. The festivities will start at seventeen hundred hours thirty minutes on Saturday, January 14, 2071, and at zero hours one minute on January 15, permitting any who want to put in an appearance and enjoy the festivities the ability to do so.

Those attending the marriage should be dressed in full mess uniforms. OFSA dress attire should be worn to the celebrations.

On behalf of all within Zeta Command, I wish to offer Captain Whitehead and Admiral Brubacher our congratulations and best wishes.
Admiral Rohkea Sielu Zeta HQ COS

....

Until now, we knew very little regarding our assailants except a general direction and probable distance supplied by the Spiel. But, our friendship with the Suvayeek changed all of that. They sent a message asking to meet with me at a place of my choosing. I inquired as to who specifically wished to see me and was advised it was Shoy Cap, Hek Lider of all Suvayeek forces. I suggested 44 Bootis because it was almost exactly halfway between our current positions.

....

"I am honored you wished to consult with me, Hek Lider." I bowed as I paid my respects.

"Please dispense with the formalities. I believe we are friends - and equals."

"Thank you, Shoy Cap. How may I be of service to you?"

"You may not. I hope I can be of aid to you!"

"How's that?"

There was a considerable pause which I finally realized he needed to interpret my abrupt response. The Suvayeek do not use the informalities we humanoids employ in our execution of the English language.

"We have information you may find extremely enlightening."

"You already do us a significant service providing the intelligence you send us daily," I responded.

"Yes. I know you appreciate that. But, this is much more distinctive. I have a definitive location for the Isesinis Homeworld to give you. And, we have sensor readings and images of its defenses for you." Shoy Cap used the uppermost talon on his right forepaw to tap at his console. My pad annunciated reception of mail. The Lider had been provided all C&C communications addresses.

I whistled. Shoy Cap looked about.

"That was me. I'm sorry about that. It's a human reaction to startling information."

"That's very interesting. It kind of sounds like your melodies." He observed.

71

"Actually, we use that ability to make music, sometimes." I offered as I broke into a couple of bars of "If I Only Had a Brain" from the Wizard of Oz.

"This is most fascinating. You can entertain yourselves in a most pleasant manner. But, I digress. What were you going to say?" The bearlike Officer inquired.

"I was going to thank you. This is incredibly valuable information to us. How can I show my appreciation?"

"That is not necessary. Partners do not expect payment for a favor. My payment is in seeing the pleasure it gave you. Especially your... ?" He pointed to his own white lips.

"You mean whistling. We whistle to make music and show satisfaction."

"Seeing and hearing that is payment enough," Shoy explained.

I paused as a thought began to gel in my mind.

"Hek Lider, may I formally ask for another favor?"

"What do you need Admiral?"

"I was wondering if you would make your communications relays in the region available and provide us their locations?"

"I assumed you would need to use them." He acceded to the request as he tapped a key on his system. My annunciator chimed again. It was a list of area relays and frequency bands available for use.

"Thank you.' I responded earnestly. 'I don't know how we'll ever repay you."

"Maybe someday in the future." I thought I saw him shrug but realized I must have imagined it.

We spent another hour just passing the time. Shoy Cap asked about David. I devoted ten minutes updating him on the Royal Family. Then, we went our separate ways.

I was back in my office by eight hundred on Tuesday, December 12, 2270. I enlisted ISIE analysts and spent my time during the return analyzing the data and formulating a plan. On the Monday before my arrival, I asked for a meeting of the Commission on a US matter. It was scheduled for Wednesday on Rigil.

The session on the day after my return was short and sweet. I presented my compatriots with the Suvayeek intelligence and a proposal. It took half an hour for everyone to study Shoy Cap's report. The initial responses were much like my own.

Then, another half-hour was expended studying my proposal before the discussion began. After hashing it over for a few more hours, the pitch was approved, intact and US Mission Number OFSA-CC-7128415 was applied to it. George, Savign and I stayed in place when the meeting dissolved to refine the authorized plan. The timing of the operation was dependant on Admiral Svjosloki who was executing a program that would affect ours.

....

For the next month, I conducted very moderated business, depending on Roh and El to keep things running on an even keel. Though Fred was establishing her new offices, she authored a schedule to full functionality over a two-month period to allow for a vastly constrained workload. We were busy finalizing all the minutia of our impending wedding.

George Bryant agreed to serve as best man. King David accepted the role of Ring Bearer, the other male C&C will be ushers, and Marie Bryant would be Maid of Honor. The remaining bridesmaids included Grace Tonaka, two of Fred's former AP associates and Admiral Savign. All the servicewomen in the wedding party are to wear the formal military dresses, and Fredricka will don the official OFSA wedding gown. My first wife Helena designed both in mid-2257 for that union. And, they were approved as official OFSA formal Dress Uniforms, at the time. A muted sadness still overcomes me when I think of these things. Though I love Fredricka dearly, Helena will always occupy special places in my heart and mind.

This event is to be the biggest one yet. Over the years we've been part of George and Marie Bryant's, Steven and Oliva Nichol's, and my first ceremony and dinner. They were ostentatious but limited by the numbers the Flag Bridge could accommodate for the nuptials. In this case, it was Fred who requested we hold the wedding rite in the Hangar Bay so more Senior Officers and Regulars could attend. She felt we owed them that.

Fredricka questioned the wisdom of the decision when she viewed the cavernous space the day before the affair. Nine thousand seats atop inclined bases were arranged in four long blocks, creating three elongated aisles nearly three hundred meters in length. The entire configuration faced a raised dais in front of the massive viewing windows on the port side of the Examiner. Fred wore her formal service gown to the evening rehearsal to test her ability to make such a long march in the outfit. The sleek train, trailing less than a meter behind could pose a hazard. The two dresses are identical except for color, so this one served as an excellent model without appearing in her wedding garb in front of me. She had no difficulty making the extended trek to the platform.

Following the trial run, we all retired to the Examiner's Flag Mess for the rehearsal dinner. It was a most enjoyable evening with delicious foods, fine wines, a dozen toasts and great conversation with a lot of laughs. I was "roasted" by George and Fred by Marie.

Then, we split up. The men all marched off to Lowry's for the "stag party." Fredricka and nearly a thousand women attended her bridal shower in the Examiners large amphitheater.

No one tried to get me drunk, this time. They remembered how reserved I was before. And, we're all a little older and wiser, now. But, we did have an amusing time filled with boisterous jokes and a lot of toasts, in our honor.

Fred was stunned by what happened at her gathering. She received nearly nine hundred gifts and wasn't sure how she'd be able to make use of them all. Among the offerings was a cheque from King David and his family for one hundred thousand sovereigns. Fred asked me about it feeling it was much too generous. I explained it was fruitless to attempt to argue the matter.

....

I stood on our wedding altar facing the massive view-windows scrutinizing the dazzling scenery arrayed outside. We moved and turned the Examiner this morning to achieve the effect. We now circle Wolf 359 in a trajectory similar to Mercury's as it travels around Sol.

Wolf 359 is a small red dwarf about one-tenth the mass of our home star. Very dim and emitting in the infra-red range, it is a variable flare star that produces delightful stellar displays, if you're close enough to observe it clearly, without being singed. It is an uncommon system because of its lack of planetary companions but boasts a considerable ring of asteroids and moon-sized member satellites ringing it. And though impressive, it's subdued enough to allow unobstructed viewing of the incredibly scenic space surrounding the system. Our slow but constant change in perspective continually offers the sights of all the different wonders around us, including Sol - and always with the vibrant ruby jewel anchored in the center of the presentation.

The Hangar's center aisle is lined by two hundred Special Forces Marines in full Mess Uniforms with all lanyards, medals, ribbons - and their ceremonial swords. On cue from the orchestra, their Master Sergeant barks the "present arms." Each draws his sword and crosses it with the soldier on the opposite side of the walkway as the Zeta Choir accompanied by our Zeta Orchestral Ensemble break into a soft rendition of Train's Marry Me.

When she appears, Fred draws gasps. She is a gorgeously, elegant porcelain collectible. The sleek white silk, satin, and taffeta white and off-white jacketed gown seems as if it was designed for her slim statuesque frame. The jewelry-like rank and assignment insignias offer just enough glint to tastefully garnish the dress and complement her diamond earrings and necklace. Her cafe-au-lait skin tone and striking features do as much justice to the outfit as it does to her. Though accompanied by her father, hardly none even notice him. Two tiny, similarly attired neophytes scatter flower petals ahead. She is trailed by her Maid of Honor and four Handmaids. They are all dressed in the same chic gown in colors reminiscent of our standard Dress and Mess Uniforms. I couldn't help but wonder what Fairy Tale this scene had been wrested from.

The slow-march over the three hundred meter span took nearly three and a half minutes - a delay no one seemed to mind as they drank in the dazzling exhibition and the surrounding panorama. At the platform, Fred's dad hands her off to me with a smile. But, as he turns under the diverse lighting, I see reflections tracing shiny lines of tears that are rolling down his cheeks. My angelic figurine steps forward taking her place at my side.

The highlight of the wedding rite occurs when a rising magnetic arch bursts into a breathtaking stellar flare behind us as we engage in the kiss that seals our matrimonial contract. Its tongue stretched so far and fast that appeared it would lick the side of our ship. There were audible gasps from all nine thousand attendees - even those more familiar with such phenomena.

....

By the end of January, it was our turn to travel for a wedding. King David was marrying a beautiful young woman by the name of Elizabeth Montefiore. Elizabeth comes by her blue blood honestly. Though few noble pedigrees survived through the centuries, she is one of a rare group of people originating from an ancient royal family. George, Marie, Fred, and I were all selected to join the couple as members of their wedding party. First, we attended Elizabeth's elevation. Already the Countess of Birmingham, she was crowned Baroness of Wildwood.

The rest of the week was busy with an assortment of functions. The bridal shower was the day after Lady Elizabeth's elevation. The rehearsal was the following day. That evening we joined the wedding party and family members in the most magnificent dinner. Though the bride and groom hosted it, I was the Master of Ceremonies. And though I didn't get to roast David, I lobbed many jestful gibes throughout the evening.

The next night found all the male guests appearing at the castle for an "impromptu" stag party. Of course, you don't really conduct any event in secured locations spontaneously. King David's people were acutely aware of our intentions and fully informed on the guest list. Though we had a delightful experience, no one got out of hand, and King David maintained his sobriety in anticipation of the next day's events.

On Monday, January 30, 2271, King David and Lady Elizabeth Montefiore were wed in a public ceremony reminiscent of royal weddings throughout history. There were horse-drawn carriages, red carpets, and thrones for every venue. And all wore tuxedoes, gowns, or full military mess-style uniforms complete with lanyards and sabers or cutlass. And, though it took only seventy-five minutes, another two hours were consumed in an elaborate coronation rite raising her to Queen Elizabeth Delnikov. Those ceremonies were followed by a light luncheon. Many hours were spent in the royal residence throne room receiving the several hundred of us bearing wedding gifts and bestowing blessings upon them.

Following a two-hour break, three thousand sat for the wedding dinner. There's no point in describing the function. Though smaller, it was much more extravagant than those we'd attended before.

We unintentionally stole the show when the two were opening their gifts. They unwrapped and opened two boxes which each contained a gilded bridal and ornamented Western Saddle.

"You know a saddle should be fitted to the horse?" David explained quietly.

"They both were," I responded.

There was a pause then a glint of realization.

"They're out back in your stable." I offered

"Let's go look!" David said as he quickly grabbed Elizabeth's hand, rose, turned, and exited to the stone patio with thousands of guests in tow.

"Oh my goodness!" He gasped as he spotted the two new black Arabians. Tears streamed down the couples cheeks.

"You shouldn't have." He said.

"It's far too generous," Elizabeth added.

"Nonsense, just enjoy them," I responded as Fred nodded her agreement.

Fred, Bryant and I left Wildwood on February 1, to return to the Examiner at Wolf 359, having witnessed a fairytale scene.

Chapter 12 Shifting Scenes

Monday, February 6, 2271

"Intelligence is the ability to adapt to change." Stephen Hawkings

"I was surprised at how much extra would be involved in moving the central office for Public Relations into my Command," I mumbled to George as we left the Rigil HQ boardroom after our Commission Meeting.

"What do you mean? It's just another Headquarters. Marie's is aboard the Valhalla."

"Yeah. I know. But, this is different. It turned out to be much more involved than I ever imagined. Fred needs a dedicated briefing room. And, over a hundred reporters from various services required quarters and office space within the Command. And, that's all added to the agency space for her and staff that's needed."

"I wouldn't have thought of all that either."

"And, that creates a new set of security issues. Besides the typical AP HQ contingent of journalists, I've got this extra large group roaming through the Examiner and Interrogator always trying to unearth some big newsworthy secret. I know they're just exercising their investigative instincts, but it's a real handful!"

"I really enjoyed your wedding ceremony, Kurt. Especially the processional and recessional music. It made the whole ceremony quite unique. I especially liked the old, "Signed, Sealed, Delivered, I'm Yours" by Stevie Wonder. It's been a classic for two and a half centuries, but I've never seen it used at a wedding."

"Thanks, George. I'll tell Fred. Both pieces were her choices. Did Bryant behave for you and Marie during the first week after our marriage? He always loves to go to *Uncle George's* and *Aunt Marie's*."

"He was a perfect young man. And, he and Atina got on well. We were happy to do it. He made a stimulating addition to our family. We went to an amusement park on Earth for three days. He really loved the Jurassic section. He relished all the rides and knew so much about dinosaurs, Marie and I were awe-stricken by him. Where did you go on that week of your honeymoon?"

"We spent two days drifting a slow trip between Wolf 359 and Earth. That was just for us - quiet times alone - if you know what I mean? Then, we landed in France and reveled in the culture and culinary advantages of Paris. We shuttled to Cadarache for a day. We both adored the ancient fusion plant there. Everything is so massive. I'd never been

77

there before, but you spoke so highly of it. Now, I see why. It's a genuine relic that reveals a lot about history and our past. We will go back."

"I'm glad you both enjoyed it. What'd you do the week after?"

"After retrieving Bryant, we cruised to Rigil and spent five days on the beaches. It was very relaxing, and my son always loves the water."

"It sounds like you had a great honeymoon."

"We did - both alone and with Bryant. Thanks again."

"We both thought your gifts to the King and Queen were unique. The really love to ride. The horses were absolutely magnificent." George said.

"We both feel that David and the Federation have done so much for us. We wanted to express our feelings."

"So, how do you feel about the discussion and plans from this session?" George asked referring to the Commission meeting.

"I'm just glad we got the intelligence we were looking for. It's past time for a response."

"I agree. But, things weren't right before. It was important to exercise patience."

"I know. But, I can't help thinking about all those billions of suffering Orion Federation Citizens. I don't report on local information I receive through ISIE unless it's of tactical significance. But, I can tell you there's been a lot of atrocities. There've been mass executions and hundreds of accounts of interrogations involving torture. There are daily search and seizures. People are held without due process. The sooner we do something, the better."

"I didn't realize there are that many incidents. If it's not NTK, you should talk about it. It's got to be hard keeping it all inside. You can always bend my ear." George sounded concerned.

"No, it's not Need-to-Know. And, sometimes I would like to share it. It does bother me. But, El and I discuss it among ourselves. That helps too."

"...want to head to town for lunch and a drink?" George inquired.

"Sure, let's do it!"

We walked out the main gate of the Rigil HQ campus onto Center Street in Rigil New York. It was only a few blocks to the City Centre walking mall. George and I passed Banerjee's Custom Clothiers on our way to the Winchester Authentic English Pub frequented by just about everyone in the OFSA. We'd been coming here for years.

I ordered the Gluten Free Chicken Pot Pie while George selected the English Style Fish and Chips. Though its "pub-style" cuisine is famous, everything on the extensive menu is always freshly prepared at the Winchester which is owned by Geoffrey Blaise, a Cordon Bleu Chef. And though it specialized in tapped beers, the Winchester was also renowned for its wide-ranging bar fare, broad array of select coffees, and invigorating teas from worlds all over the Orion Federation.

The Winchester's mealtime entrees are always accompanied by a side dish, appetizers, soup or salad, dessert, and coffee, tea, or soft drink, so we ate rather sumptuously for a lunchtime. The Winchester boasts an excellent Gluten Free Beer made from malted rice instead of barley. It's superior to those brewed from sorghum. So, we each ordered a mug of their world famous micro-brewery beer to glug down while waiting for table service and the meal but stuck to a robust cup of coffee to accompany the desert. We exchanged family information and general conversation on our respective commands. But, the Winchester, or any other outside venue, is not the place for topics broaching policies or secure operations.

We took the long way back to the HQ station, stopping at Banerjee's first, to scan the latest offerings. And, fancying what we observed, both of us scheduled appointments for fittings. Lunch was well-settled when we arrived at the base in time for the fourteen hundred hour afternoon conference.

....

Back in my office on the Examiner parked outside the Wolf 359 system on Monday, February 13, I prepare orders referencing US Mission Number OFSA-CC-7128415 to fulfill my obligations created a week earlier. I direct Svesion and Sparks to attach another thirteen hundred SF Marines to Savign's SOCC operations. She will distribute two to each of six hundred-fifty subs in preparations for coming actions. Then, I order Zeta1-2 Command to send a full Theatre to specific coordinates on Sol vector 340.70° x 30.20° @ 168 Ly where they will meet a large SOCC contingent. This is sixteen parsecs outside Orion Federation borders and about one and a half light-years from the Eta Pegasus system. They will ferry the Marines to Savign at that location and must arrive by March 10. I monitor communications from Admiral Bryant to his Theatre Three Commander ordering a full Tier Three Command to the same position, on the same date.

At the same time, Savign quoted US OFSA-CC-7128415 to order one Wolf Pack and Supply ship to Eta Pegasus system, under cloak. They were to continuously surveil the system and report every four hours - twenty-four hours a day and join other forces at

340.70° x 30.20° @ 168 Ly, on March 10. They were to provide their final report to Laft, at that time.

Savign again refers to US OFSA-CC-7128415 to separate the rest of her contingent into three groups - one for Epsilon, one for Zeta and the rest to run additional covert intelligence missions.

The next day, Admiral Svjosloki citing US OFSA-CC-7128415 cryptically notifies George that his order will be complete by the end of the month. That triggers another flurry of memos directing Admiral Laft to have half his forces at the same position, on March 10, too. Each and every note alluding to OFSA-CC-7128415 had an attachment providing all the Suvayeek communication stations' regional locations and available frequencies. Laft completes more imperatives, commanding a quarter of his unique ships to join Epsilon and the rest to unite with Zeta, immediately, in preparation for a future action.

As the regional HQ Commands forwarded orders repositioning their forces, George and I did, too. Flotillas dedicated to the OFSA-CC-7128415 operation required us to redeploy defensively to fill in for their absences. Meanwhile, we all spent the next two weeks planning our own individual inside moves corresponding to the March 10 actions outside our borders.

....

Vice Admiral Boets scans the list of delivery dates for the Frigates under his Command. He spots the Shenzhen in the group and selects it because Captain Nedrif Elantham and his people are the most experienced Crew in his Fleet. He orders Ned to report at his earliest convenience.

Elantham shows at his office on February 16. Boets advises the Shenzhen's Captain to report to Rigil for a refit which will be complete by the nineteenth. Then, he provides special orders for a daring mission Ned must complete immediately upon receipt of the vessel. They spend an hour deliberating over all the details of the assignment.

....

Sunday, February 19, 2271, finds Ned at the Shenzhen's Bridge Command Station with his heart palpitating in anticipation of the orders he's about to dispense. They're currently orbiting Rigil.

"People, on my signal I want the following. Helm, continue for one more complete orbit. Then, accelerate toward breakaway speed slowly. Begin to spiral outward when you're directly over Rigil HQ. Widen the orbit to a three-light-year radius over the next two orbits while increasing to maximum normal space speed. At one hundred-two by minus sixteen and three-quarters degrees at three light-years adjust all settings for FTL on a heading for 82 Eridani."

"Sir, that's inside occupied space!" The helmsman interrupts.

"Lieutenant, follow your orders to the tee. Propulsion, I want standard orbiting speed until the end of the next orbit. Then, I want a steady, gradual increase up to maximum velocity over the subsequent two orbits. At the Helm's signal, I want AMPE from current to thirty percent of light-speed over half a billion kilometers. Hold thirty percent to 82 Eridani.

Kasimir Control - I want a threshold three hundred thousand kilometers from when the helm turns us toward 82 Eridani.

Shields, I want maximum shields at all times.

Sensors, I want all long-range sensors and station reports from 82 Eridani.

Weapons, all ordinance systems to ready.

Tactical, stand ready for instructions.

Now, I want everyone to listen carefully to what I'm saying. We are on our way to test a new system installed in this vessel during that last refit. It is risky business. But, if it works we will have the upper hand in coming skirmishes. Let's do it!" Ned bellowed.

Each department station reads back settings as they alter control panels to meet his commands.

It's just over three and a half hours when they reach the final ninety degrees of the last extended orbit. Ned watches both the chronometers and the position readouts on the main screen oblivious to everything else in the command center.

"Tactical, activate Vanguard." Ned snaps suddenly.

"Aye, Captain. Vanguard engaged."

"System status?" The Captain calls.

"All readings are acceptable and show Vanguard operating properly."

"We'll see at 82 Eridani.' Ned mumbles. 'All stations return to normal operations. This is a sixty-three-hour flight. I want this crew on the stations in sixty-hours. Everyone call for relief, now! I need to see this team in the boardroom when you're relieved." The Captain barks.

Over the next fifteen minutes, the Bridge is destabilized by the irregular change of shifts, and the Exec runs off to calculate a new schedule. She wants to rotate the full bridge crew in equal periods permitting the current lineup to be in place in sixty hours. She ends up with five-hour duty cycles for the four groups. Then, recalculates for standard six-hour intervals, after that. When everything finally settles down, everyone relaxes into their revised roles for the next two-and-a-half days.

Captain Elantham spends a half hour in the boardroom with his shift's personnel explaining the upcoming mission. Then another ten minutes are expending answering nervous Bridge Officers' questions.

....

On Monday the twentieth, I meet with El and my Tier 2 Commanders at eight hundred in my office. There are no Chiefs present except my own.

"This meeting is Ultra Secret. Admiral Sielu will record the proceedings. All orders emanating from this gathering will refer to US mission number OFSA-CC-7128415. This mission is to be conducted in conjunction with a parallel one. There is no chance of crossover so you will not be made aware of the other one's details and they will not know ours. I can only tell you that it is a diversionary operation.

A third skirmish will be conducted by Epsilon Command. They will be supported by Fleet Admiral Tso Shah and some of his ships. We will not discuss any of their details either.

We will attack this system at eleven-hundred hours on March 11, 2271.' I point to 82 Eridani on the star chart. 'A preliminary test of specialized equipment is in progress there, right now. If it is successful, we will have the use of our new communications system in the space around the system under attack. Zeta -T2--1 has ordered one of its Tier 3 operations to support the other simultaneous assault. So, it is not available for the raid.

But, its other Tier 3 unit and our T2-2 outfit are entirely available. We will send all Three theatres against the target with two from Gamma Command. The enemy formation will already be primed by SOCC. The base units and about half the supporting enemy vessels are mined. There is a headquarters supported by three hundred fifty Cruisers and five Carriers. Please use previous attacks as your guidelines in your planning.

Our objective is to destroy the HQ and as many crafts as possible. In fact, the entire OFSA operation is designed to cut the head off the snake. Your plan must include a reserve of at least twenty-percent and a good exit strategy should something go wrong. You will have control of the mine detonators, so how you employ them is up to you.

As far as rules of engagement go, the goal is their total demolition. But, if a unit is helpless, you are expected to take it.

....

The Shenzhen breaks out of an exit threshold just six hundred fifty million kilometers from 82 Eridani at nineteen hundred hours on Wednesday, February 21, 2271, at thirty percent of light-speed. That's far enough away to avoid standard systems and too near for customarily deployed long-range sensors.

Ned barks out a series of orders. "Hold velocity at thirty. Balance shielding for one hundred ten percent in the forward half of the ship. We don't want to sustain a puncture at this speed. Maintain this heading but be ready to make evasive moves. We should travel right through the main body of the Isesinis support ships, at high speed. Sensor Station, keep an eye out. I'm looking for *any* response to our presence!"

Captain Elantham only subconsciously hears the team echoing his commands as they set all stations to meet his edicts. At thirty percent, six hundred million kilometers passes in just over half an hour.

"Sensors?!" He barks.

"No sign of change, Captain!"

There is silence for another fifteen minutes.

"Sensor station report!" He bellows again.

"Still nothing, Captain!"

"...reports every half minute for five minutes. Then, I want to hear from you every ten seconds."

"Aye Captain."

"Tactical, give me the status on the VG!"

"Vanguard readouts are all within expectations, Captain."

"Okay people! Stand ready! We're going right through hells furnace!" Ned yells as the images on the screen are quickly growing larger. Then, they streak right through the heart of the formation.

"Sensor Station?" Ned's insistent voice is just above a whisper.

"No reaction to us, sir." The lieutenant sounds relieved.

"Reduce engines from thirty of C to maximum space normal speed over the next five million kilometers. Helm take us out to five-million and plot a turn to bring us back on a return trajectory through the middle of the formation, again. ...Sensors to maximum. Shields to maximum. Maintain weapons at the ready - all cannons charged, all missiles launchers active - all torpedo bays loaded."

Again the response is only barely discerned as Captain Elantham leans against the inertia of the slowing vessel without seeking support. It takes nearly ten minutes to make the distance and begin the turn. Then, another ten is consumed making their way back - finally, cruising through the formation of hundreds of warships.

"Sensors?" Ned yelps.

"Still no response, Captain." Now there is amazement in the voice.

"Helm take us out the other side to two million. Turn and return to the enemy flotilla."

"Engines slow us from maximum space-standard to five percent over the next trip. All other stations hold steady."

There is a chorus of acknowledgments.

This time the forward strain on his body is less as Elantham refuses to sit through the test. It's kind of like his feet are glued to the decking.

Twenty minutes pass making the excursion at the ever slowing speeds. They enter the mass of vessels.

"Reduce from five to zero velocity over the next five minutes.' There is a pause as the ship slows further. 'All stop! Engines to station keeping."

They sit in the middle of the enemy configuration for fifteen minutes. Ned listens to the sensor report every ten seconds. He steps forward to get a better look at the screen.

"Helm take us to that ship.' He points to the screen. 'Then, I want you to circle it.

Propulsion, give us fifty KPH forward velocity!

The Shenzhen begins a turn as it crawls to the designated vessel and begins a close circuit around it.

"Take us out the way we originally came in. Propulsion to ten percent maximum space-normal speed. Sensor maintain maximum. Take us to one and a half million and turn back. Then, go to all stop and station keeping!"

They sat quietly in the distance eyeing the enemy Fleet.

"There's one more task for us to perform. We need to plant four of the new substrate relays in this region and record their positions." Ned explained.

The bridge crew went about the business of moving to four different sites and stopping long enough for each deployment. In the meantime, engineering was in the hangar bay preparing the units and assisting the launch personnel in their send-offs.

"Okay people. I'd love to take out a couple of these bastards. But we can't unzip, yet. It's time to go home. Plot a course to Rigil. The show's over.

You all did great people. You will get a generous leave for this."

....

At just about the same time, two covert supply vessels were dropping relays at 15 Sagitta, I met with Svesion and Sparks for an intelligence update before the Commission meeting on Saturday, February 25, 2271. I received current information funneled through them from the Suvayeek, the resistance networks, and our agents in the field. Most of it was excellent. But, one report was disappointing. Despite that, I was able to prepare proposals that would allow the C&C to conduct operations that would advance our agenda.

The session was a busy one. We were all excited by the Shenzhen's test results which were forwarded by Admiral Laft. We now had powerful covert warships that are capable of inflicting a lot of pain and suffering.

When the meeting adjourned, we all returned to our vessels to transmit another flurry of directives. Most of us were putting the March 10 / 11 operations on temporary hold. OFN had advised us that our primary objective would be returning to his homeworld for a short visit, at that time. He was expected back in two weeks. So, we reset the execution dates to March 25 / 26, tentatively. But we also approved an SU Intelligence Operation for immediate implementation so, I quickly sketched out the mission on my pad and called in Sparks and Svesion.

"Generals, the mission we had planned for early March is delayed. But, I have an important one I need you to start, now. It is US mission number OFSA-CC-7128422. I will pass my pad to you. Please read the mission parameters. You may not copy it or print it. You will need to commit it to memory." I turn the data pad to Sparks. Svesion leans over and reads along, too.

"Colonel Kaule is the best man for this task," Sparks observes.

"I agree," Svesion chimes in as the two smile and nod to each other.

"Why Kaule?" I ask.

"He's one of about a dozen men trained for precisely this type of mission," Svesion explains.

"And, he's already there. He's on the Nautica and its UC at 15 Sagitta, now." Sparks adds.

"It has to be around the twelfth. Kos leaves two days before that. And Mes will just be getting comfortable as his temporary replacement."

"No problem, sir. We can have a message to the Nautica, today. We have permission to use the Suvayeek transceiver, there. That gives Kaule time to prepare." Svesion clarifies.

"Good. Let's get it done!" I snapped as I rose and recovered my pad.

The two men stood, saluted, turned, and left the room without a sound.

....

Colonel Kaule sat at the small desk in his tight quarters decrypting the message, himself. It had been received by Communications an hour ago. But, they did not have the appropriate cipher to interpret it. He raised an eyebrow as he finished and read it in its entirety. Then, he rose and removed a long case from his personal locker. Kaule laid it on the bed and lifted the lid. Inside was an array of both conventional and directed-energy hand weapons. He chose one pistol version of each and a single long-barrelled laser-emitting gun ideally suited for distance shots. Then, he returned the luggage to its home and removed a specialized set of EVA gloves and mitts. The latter worn over the others would keep him warm in the cold harshness of space should that equipment be required. He'd remove the protective mitts for a few minutes and use only the gloves while actually targeting and shooting. But, he really hoped to find a place to conduct business free of the constraints imposed by EVA equipment. He consulted with the Commander Ignot Nautica's Captain who had been in charge of monitoring the Kil's movements for the last several months. Then, he set about developing a plan. He wanted to live through the experience.

....

On March 10, I received reports from both OFN and the Nautica indicating Dac Kil Mes arrived at 15 Sagitta on the ninth and Kil Kos left for his home on the tenth. I knew I'd be full of apprehension over the next few days. In fact, everyone down the line that was involved in this scheme was probably feeling that way.

....

The Nautica had surreptitiously landed Kaule on 15 Sagitta B on March 8. Reports he read indicated the Kil visited the Isesinis installations there, every second day and there was no reason to believe the Dac Kil would handle things any differently. Kaule's first requirement was a perch within close proximity of the official structures. After that, the need for a nearby temporary housing structure had to be filled. He needed to stay put for a couple of days.

Hiking and climbing the surrounding low mountains provided an ideal location. An outcropping forming a flat ledge surrounded by a low rocky border molded a perfect perch. And, just to its rear was an opening in the mountain leading into a cave Kaule could make a home of. He cleared it of vermin and insects so he'd be comfortable. Then, he set up a bed, communications/computer station, a cookstove, and a small folding table and chair set. It wasn't home, but he'd be comfortable enough. After a quick meal, he moved to the brink of the niche and began watching with high-powered field glasses. The task would take up most of his next couple of days. He needed to understand the timing of normal operations. Especially those that would continue on regardless of the Dac Kil's presence. Several times, he engaged the laser functions in the glasses to determine target range and alignment. The shot is almost two kilometers. But, Kaule has been accurate to three before, with the chosen weapon.

From time to time during breaks, the Colonel spends some time perusing the area about the ridge. A variety of escape routes may be required after completing his mission. The entire cavern and shelf are part of a trail that originates below and rises to his east as it circles around the peak. This particular route would take him completely out of sight. So, he spends time walking the path until coming upon a more substantial but similar protrusion that is big and sturdy enough to land a shuttle on. He contacts Commander Ignot who advises he can have a supply-ship shuttle there if he is given an appropriate schedule.

"If you let me know when the target is coming down, I'll let you know when to do the retrieval," Kaule advised Ignot.

Chapter 13 Second Acts

Wednesday, March 1, 2271

"If you're going through hell - keep going." **Winston Churchill**

Bryant will turn nine on Friday, March 24, so we sat and talked today. I was concerned that activities now provisionally booked for March 25 may heat up earlier or may require a great deal of my time on the twenty-fourth.

"How old are you now, son?" I tried to sound as if I sincerely didn't remember.

"I'm eight daddy. But, I'll be nine soon."

"Yes, I remember. And, I want to talk to you about that."

"Is something wrong, daddy?"

"Nothing serious. But, your birthday is on Friday, March 24 and we have actions that may take my time on that day. So, I wanted to know if it's okay to have your party a week earlier on Saturday, March 18?" I held his eyes so he would see my genuine need.

"Yes, that will be fine. You scared me though. I thought you were going to say I couldn't have a party, daddy."

"The day might come when that could happen. But, I will try everything within my power to make sure you always have a birthday celebration, Bryant."

"I know, daddy. I know you would never miss unless you couldn't help it."

"Okay. I'll tell your mother." I referred to Fredricka as Bryant does. He has taken to calling her either that or mommy.

On March 10, ISIE received a report via Admiral Savign that Colonel Kaule has developed a plan and been in place since March 8. We will get updates when there are changes.

Earlier in the day, the SF Colonel had walked his escape route one more time. But, on this occasion, he'd hauled all his gear to the pickup point. The call from Ignot had precipitated the move. Dac Kil Mes was on the way to the compound below.

Now, Colonel Kaule spies on the assemblage over a mile away through his binoculars. Several armored soldiers are walking about the complex. One's in graphite with white markings. He is pointing to various things as he explains something. The two men closest him keep calling up others who run off quickly with new orders. All three seem significant. The Colonel checks a photo. The Kils wear the dark armor. This must be Dac Kil Mes.

Kaule picks up the rifle, shoulders it, and puts his right eye to the scope. He activates the laser range-finder. Electronic icons show him distance and wind direction. He touches a button as he rights his aim and takes a deep breath. The viewer indicates a trajectory, but the trio's continuous movement is shifting Mes in and out of the cover of the others.

The Colonel squeezes the trigger as he exhales ever so gently. The invisible beam is quite discernible in the eyepiece as he sees it instantly burn a hole through the center of one subordinate's suit. The target drops to his knees and then keels over on his face. Kaule sticks with Mes and clinches his finger one more time. A smoking perforation appears as the beam drills straight through from back left to front right of his head. Mes tips over, falling across the other body. Kaule fires another quick shot at each prone figure. Others run toward the fallen victims. The third officer looks up and pans towards Colonel Kaule's position. At this distance, he cannot be seen, but it's time to move.

The SF Officer now works quickly, quietly and efficiently. He packs up the weapon, closes the case and begins to move toward the pathway in a crouch without even looking back. He knows the enemy will be scrutinizing the hill with field glasses to find the position of the shooter. So, popping up to look only gives them the clues they want. He reaches the extraction point in a few minutes and presses a button on his communicator. He's out of sight from the location of the remaining enemy officers and troops, now. A shuttle descends a short while later. They pile his belongings in. Kaule boards and they're gone before anyone can make it up to his nest.

....

Kil Kos returned quickly after the assassination of his deputy, arriving at the Sagitta Headquarters on March 16. Absolute confusion set into the operation following the murder. And the Kil was angry there were no suspects and no clues. The only thing his people knew for certain was the approximate trajectory of the shot. They had searched the mountainside for days but found nothing.

On his return, his subordinates accompanied him up the pathway - first driving as far as possible, then walking the rest of the trail. After several passes, the Kil decided correctly where the nest must have been. He noted the cave and ledge were both a perfect hiding place and an excellent perch. But the couldn't be positive because the perpetrator had left no evidence. There was not even a footprint. The small party ambled up to the landing point out of sight of the lowland. Once again, he decided this was the place the perpetrator must have escaped from, but there were no clues here either. It was a five minute trip from the cave - maybe ten if someone was laden with equipment. And the sill was stable enough and extended far enough to accommodate a sizable shuttlecraft. He ordered his people to have forensics investigators concentrate on the two areas and the footpath between them.

Kil Kos was in a foul mood. Terrified minions scurried about when confronted by him and tried to stay out of sight when not needed. Inside, he was experiencing a mixture of anger, disappointment, and guilt. Dac Kil Mes had not only been his deputy. Mes was Kos' best friend. They had known each other since primary school days and graduated the military college together.

In the early years of his career, Kos had chosen assignments off the beaten path. Usually covert and risky, they paid big dividends when productive. When he reached the rank of Sul, he was forced to command brigade-sized operations and proved to have a penchant for broader tactical planning. So, he continued to rise through grander assignments until becoming one of two full Kils. The other commanded Isesinis territorial, defensive forces.

His friend Mes had climbed the ladder a little slower choosing more traditional military jobs. They were rejoined when Kil first became Sul, and Mes was assigned as one of his Batallion Commanders at the rank of Dac Sul. From that point on, they had risen in lockstep. Every promotion for Kos meant one for Mes. Mes had been unusually gifted, purposeful, honest, and a great friend he could confer with and confide in. Someone will pay!

....

By eight hundred on March 19, I am in my office reading the report Sparks presented from OFN. The Isesinis' HQ is presently suffering from widespread confusion. Kos had been trying to decide on a worthy replacement for Mes but didn't really trust his other immediate subordinates enough. So, he announced the transfer of Sec Kil Res to the Sagitta Command from one of the territorial outfits. He would be elevated to Dac Kil and assigned as Deputy Commander. He was not expected to arrive until April 6, so Kil Kos was now overburdened with the work of both positions.

And, their investigation had gone nowhere. There were no clues except a single footprint they'd found at the extraction site after an exhaustive examination. They were not even sure if the imprint was made by OFSA military boots or shoes with similar soles. I decided to ask for a US session to share Naabaahii's latest account. As I awaited responses from my peers, I recalled yesterday's events.

....

I had taken the day off for Bryant's birthday celebration and organized my personal staff to prepare the large meeting room for the event. Then, I went down to the childrens' store in the mall on deck four. It is quite large and is sectioned by age, offering wonders for kids from infancy through their youth. I had ordered a new bicycle for my son. He'd grown out of the last one. And this was a ten-speed with colorful streamers flowing from the handlebar grips and racing stripes on the wheel yokes. The youngsters ride them along a marked section of the walking mall and often take them on planetary excursions.

From the toy store, I sauntered down to the entertainment one. It is full of audio offerings along with videos presented in two and three-dimensional formats and holographic display mode. I picked up three rings containing old science fiction shows Bryant had grown to love. They had now replaced his earlier obsessions. This interest had developed by sitting with me while I enjoyed different ones. Soon, he began to watch them on his own and developed preferences. So, I was acquiring episodes of his three favorite programs originating two and a half to three centuries ago. He says none of our present day entertainment compares and often adds that those generations were the luckiest of all.

It is all the rage for juveniles to wear the rings containing all their favorite shows. Some children have two on each finger and one on both thumbs. The more valuable games and videos you have on your hands, the more prestigious you are. Every generation seems to have their own unique customs that vary by age group.

We invited Bryant's entire class, Atina, and several other youngsters he's close to. So, there were about forty kids at the party. There were also a dozen adults, though we stayed out of the children's line of fire for the most part. They had a ball playing video games and eating pizza and cake. Edgidio did his usual stellar presentation baking and decorating and incredible cake and preparing all the food. That included the gluten-free fare for me. I've still been putting off the suggested treatment because of our busy circumstances.

I grabbed all the other parents to peek in on the youthful revelers when I entered the entertainment room and found them playing math games. It completely astonished and pleased all the adults. Fred had purchased a selection of small gifts for the attendees. So, I spontaneously turned some of them into prizes, taking care to ensure each child won a suitable reward. Later, the children switched to a game they called "Constellations." They were very good at identifying a star system by its position on a chart. In the end, all the gifts were spent as prizes.

....

As I turn my attention back to Admiral Naabaahii's account, the import of a small notation I'd read earlier strikes me. I summon Sparks and Svesion to report, immediately. They arrive at my door ten minutes later, and we all sit after attending to the usual courtesies and acquiring a beverage and our favorite treat.

"We have a problem, gentlemen," I mumble.

"What's that, Admiral?" Svesion inquires.

"We have one or more moles among the upper echelon of our HQ Commands."

"Why do you think that, sir?" Sparks queries.

"It was something in the OFN report I just read. It was just a casual point, so I missed it the first time. When I reviewed the report an hour later, it hit like a sledgehammer."

"I didn't see anything in the summary that would lead me to believe we've been badly compromised, sir." Sparks offers.

"OFN says that the Isesinis Sagitta Command issued an order to stand down from their preparations for March 10 and resume them later for expected execution around March 25," I explain.

"I don't see the gravity of that statement. It sounds like a change in routine deployments." Svesion injects.

"No, you wouldn't. And neither would OFN. But, thank goodness he is so meticulous, and included it."

"Why? I don't see the significance." Sparks questions.

"As you know, we are planning some major actions. This is top secret information. But, they were originally scheduled to begin on March 10 and eleventh. Circumstances required us to tentatively move those operations to the twenty-fourth and twenty-fifth. I don't think this is a coincidence. And, only the C&C Commission and their upper subordinate Commands realize those dates. Everyone else only knows they are preparing for some action. They aren't supposed to have a grasp on the overall plans or proposed timetable. So, either someone in that inner circle is a mole, or one or more of us has been bugged. I've already requested an Ultra Secret Commission Meeting. We can suspend our operations, temporarily. But, we need to find the leak!" I raised my voice to impress the weight of the order.

"It falls under my Command, Admiral. ISIE will find the infiltrator." Sparks promises.

"It may just be a device. There may not be a spy." Svesion argues.

"With all due respect, General - someone has to place a tap. So, there is obviously one or more agents involved, too.' Sparks explains as Svesion nods. 'I'll have all the areas frequented by the involved Officers swept for listening devices, and all data systems scanned for that type of malware. It will be easier to follow a trail if we find a mechanism. But, one way or the other, we will uncover the snoop." Sparks mumbles.

"Could you please start with my offices and equipment. Then, spread out to Roh, Elasima, Grace Tonaka, and George Bryant's areas. I need to be able to talk to them. After that, widen to the rest of the C&C and the boardroom we meet in at Rigil. If and when we're all clear, we'll be able to discuss the action plan that's compromised. Once all that's complete, you need to include everyone and everywhere involved in these campaigns. This is very urgent, General!"

"Yes, sir. I know. I can send out ten teams, today. There'll be a group of techs in your office within the hour. We'll look after Admirals Sielu and Elasima, at the same time. We can have other teams at the other HQs later in the day."

....

George Bryant was stunned when an ISIE Marine Major and his team of eight ISIE agents appeared in the office doorway that afternoon. He was handed an Inspector General Branch Warrant and asked to leave as the Officer indicated the need for silence. It had to be profound because the document was signed by Brubacher, himself. There was no further explanation, so he departed for the Flag Mess knowing this kind of action meant there was a security breach somewhere. He understood that elimination was as crucial as discovery, in these cases. And, he knew that IGB authority was absolute in criminal or security matters.

Two hours later, the Major summoned him back.

"I'm sorry for the inconvenience, sir. We have swept this room completely and scanned your systems thoroughly. It is safe to talk here, so I'll tell you there's been a serious penetration. I am not privy to all the details. But, our teams have been ordered to clear Admiral Brubacher, you, and Admiral Tonaka, first. And, we have to sweep all the areas you meet in and examine all data systems connected to each of you, your COS, and Deputy, today. I am authorized to say that Admiral Brubacher has asked for a Commission Meeting and will discuss this with all of you, once our teams have completed our immediate investigations. He just needs to be sure your discussion won't be compromised, first. It'll take us another twenty-four hours. Tomorrow, we will repeat the same process with all your subordinate HQ Commanders and their operations.

I am also to advise you that Admiral Brubacher is undergoing the same process, now. We will notify you when he is unrestrained so you can discuss this with him. However, please don't share this with anyone who hasn't been certified."

"I understand. And, thank you, Major." Bryant responded.

....

At the Rigil complex, Grace went through a similar process. So, it was not until twenty-two hundred hours that we spoke. We used the new relay system so we could conference in real-time on a secure channel.

"What the hell is going on, Kurt?" George yelped.

"We've had a perturbing breach of security. OFN included something in the last report that set off all the alarms. I don't think the agent even realized how critical the information was.

But, it involved large-scale enemy troop movements. The execution dates were being altered from March 10 to the twenty-fifth, if..."

"Son of a bitch!" I was cut off by Grace.

"So, it looks like we're being monitored, somehow?" George interrupted.

"Yes. I think our missions are doubtful. That's why I wanted you, and Grace cleared, first. The leak has to be among the Commission members and our Tier 2 and Three Commands. We're the only ones with the information in question. We can deal with that. We'll find the source. But, this creates another problem, too." I add.

"What's that?" George asked in a barely audible inquisitive tone.

"OFN may be compromised. If we have someone releasing this high-level information they might know of our spy. I would guess that Kos realizes who the agent is or at least that there is one. But, we won't know until we plug the hole."

"Can you get your infiltrator out of there?" Grace queried in a concerned manner.

"We probably can. But, I'm not sure that's necessary, yet. The best thing is to drop it in the eavesdropper's lap to determine how to handle it."

....

Lt. Commander Chak, Captain of the FSS Provider, is aware his crew is in need of a break. And, it has to be even worse for Commander Ignot and his people aboard the Nautica. The two-ship Covert Unit has been in close proximity to the Isesinis Headquarters

94

for several months without a break, now. The only intervals resembling rests are the times they back away to resupply the sub. It's just as tense when the Provider leaves to replenish itself because the covert supply ship must make most of the trip behind enemy lines. And, it's moments like the current activity that make it worse.

The Nautica has been ordered to make an unscheduled entry into the giant Polyhedron under the protection of its cloak. They need to drop an extraordinary communications packet for the agent who's clandestinely operating within. The two Captains are not privy to the information. Only the spy has the means to decode the cipher.

....

On Wednesday, March 22, Sparks' technical investigation teams discovered two listening devices. Both were in the Rigil complex, so this makes the rest of the task a lot easier. One was in the Rigil Deputy Commander's office. The other was in the small amphitheater where we conduct expanded Commission meetings.

General Sparks sat with his Brigade Commander constructing a directory of all who would have had access to both locations. Though it included everyone, they'd concentrate on engineering staff. The placement of the second unit made it seem as if the mole had to be a specialist because it was in an air vent over the stage. Non-maintenance personnel using a lift or ladder to work in an air duct would have drawn suspicion. Both taps were sent to labs for forensic testing, and the grate and ductwork were carefully examined. Then, Sparks had them reinstall the one in the amphitheater.

The ISIE crime scene people struck paydirt. The agent had likely caught a hand on a screw protruding from the ductwork. There were tiny specks of blood near the device that were traced to Specialist Covess, a Gian HVAC technician holding a Leading Crewman First Class rank. Covess has been with the service for fifteen years.

But, the one hundred ninety-eight centimeter tall Covess was able to answer for his own actions. He had an ISIE order for the installation that appeared to be signed by General Sparks, himself. The Gian was held while it was determined this was not just a ruse.

In the meantime, the search took a turn toward the ISIE, itself. First, the document was examined thoroughly. It indicated all the correct approval and registration numbers. This meant it was definitely created by someone with access to the Command. But the diversionary manner of data routing made it seem obvious that the spy wanted it to appear Sparks had generated the order.

It took nearly two days for programmers, network specialists, and systems people to find the beginning of the chain. The directive had been created in General Svesion's Command Offices. The particular terminal was the hub for nearly eighty personal data pads. It took another day to find the offending unit.

When he was sure the culprit wasn't Svesion, Sparks summoned him. They examined the device owners OFSA history, finally determining that as a Lieutenant Colonel, he had been the Task Force One Marine Battalion Commander when Admiral Chan had been in charge of that operation in Phoenix Fleet. Svesion and Sparks petitioned the Secret Court located in the Examiner for an arrest warrant and detained Major General Stephen Hickock on March 25.

Interrogation is an art. Civilized societies do not allow for enhanced means to acquire information. But, gaining the accused person's trust is the first goal. Then, questioning over any period needed to develop inconsistencies is the next step. This stage is critical because the interrogator must continuously ensure respect between the two. So, questioning occurs with adequate breaks for eight hours a day. The prisoner is not denied any needs. But, the detainee generally realizes that this will be a never-ending cycle, after the first day or two and begins to feel a type of uncertainty leading to submission. And, known information is compared to testimony in a search for inconsistencies. Finally, turning those discrepancies against the suspect usually results in the offender just giving in. And, it was this classic confrontational assault that forced the dam to break a week later.

Hickock was not working alone. There were additional arrests within the ISIE investigation and intelligence divisions, another in engineering and one more in Svesion's offices. But, it was evident that Hickock was the ringleader.

First, Sparks determined that only the audio tracks were being forwarded to Chan. There was no clandestine communication of documents or observations from Hickock or his compatriots. The only written transmissions were in the form of requests from Chan and responses by the Major General to the ex-Admiral. Once installation dates were compared with logs and other information, Chris was confident that OFN was not compromised.

The five parties arrested were charged with one count of Treason and one of Espionage, each. Though it was unlikely, they could be executed under current Orion Federation law - not to mention the stronger measures allowed under the existing state of Marshal Law.

We were finally able to meet for a Commission Meeting aboard the Examiner on Monday, March 27, 2271. The meeting was long and drawn out. Most of it led to decisions to hold off actions and planning for a few weeks. But, there was a fascinating discussion about the recent arrests and the repercussions of the espionage.

"So, why are we meeting here?" Grace asked after opening the session.

"Because your amphitheater and General Svesion's offices are still bugged," I explained.

"When are the devices going to be removed?" Marine Marshal Ian Malcolm enquired.

"I thought we shouldn't remove them. We can use them to our advantage."

"How's that? It's pretty inconvenient not to be able to hold our sessions in the main HQ." Grace injected.

"We can still hold Commission meetings there. We just can't use the small amphitheater for the *real* ones."

"What are you getting at?" Nichols queried.

"I am suggesting we hold *fake* gatherings there, at the usual times and dates. Then, we hold the real conference elsewhere, immediately after. We feed Kil Kos all kinds of bullshit during the first one."

"Yes, yes - that's a great idea." Tso Shah observes.

"I thought so. We can do our cause some good with a little disinformation program of our own. It's sort of our way of having a direct contribution to the counterintelligence operation."

"I love it! It's so devious!" Fleet Admiral Addison Blythe howled drawing a chuckle and simulated smile from Savign.

"We'll need to script those bogus meetings, so we feed Kos what we want," I explained.

"Do you have something in mind, now?" Grace asked.

"Not specifically. But, I can focus on a lot of topics that deflect information OFN gives us. In the most recent communiqué, the agent has directed suspicions of espionage toward one of Chan's people and one of Kos' senior officers. I think we can confirm those mistrusts - if you know what I mean."

"So, let's schedule a meeting in the Rigil facility for April 1 to play a good April Fools' joke on the Kil." Grace barked with a laugh.

"There's one more item!' I shouted to regain attention. 'There is one compromised computer system in General Svesion's Command. Any orders we would like Kil Kos to see should be modified to be relevant to the Marines and should be sent through that unit - if you catch my meaning." I suggested.

Everyone agreed.

....

After we disbanded, I spent the rest of my day preparing a script. Large portions dealing with day-to-day operational crap were very generalized. But the dialogue around OFN's actions was very specific. Each C&C would have to read their part, carefully. I even added a section where we call in Svesion and Sparks to discuss the matter, for realism.

Chapter 14 Slights of Hand

Saturday, April 1, 2271

"All war is based on deception." **Unknown Origin**

"Come on people. Let's get this show on the road.' Grace thwacked the gavel. 'I call this session of the C&C Commission to order!' She whacked the mallet again silencing the particularly rowdy group. 'That's better. What the hell got into you all, today?" She added with a smile.

We spent the next hour and a half discussing the mundane business of the entire organization with a goal of putting any listener to sleep with the boredom. Then, we dropped our bomb.

"Are there any other issues that need to be discussed here?" Grace inquired.

"Yes, I have an intelligence matter." I volunteered.

"What's the issue, Admiral Brubacher?" Grace queried.

"It's about our agent at 15 Sagitta. I think some of the pressure is off the Brigadier, now."

"How's that?" Fleet Admiral Addison Blythe questions.

"He has help, now. Someone to divert attention from him. An unhappy Isesinis Brigade Commander is covering."

"Who's this guy? I don't trust any Isesinis."

"May I bring in Generals Svesion and Sparks?' I requested. 'They can put this in perspective for you."

"Certainly," Grace said as she nodded to her COS who went to the door and invited the two men into the room. Both were holding their copies of the script, as were everyone else around the table.

"Gentlemen, don't look so nervous." I directed at them.

"It's just that we don't get brought before this Commission usually, Admiral," Svesion explained.

"Well, you can relax. We're not going to bite your heads off. That's our enemy's way." We all chuckled on cue.

"What may we do for you, Admirals?" General Sparks asked.

"General Svesion, did you authorize General Sparks to plan and execute an operation at 15 Sagitta?" I inquired.

"Yes, sir. I asked him to see if he could get an agent in there." He answered officiously.

"And, was he successful."

"Yes, sir. He found a satisfactory candidate. The spy has been in place for several months."

"General Sparks, can you please summarize your plan and the subsequent actions?"

"Yes, sir. When the General came to me, I thought hard and long until I came up with a scheme to get a spy into that enemy Headquarters. It occurred to me that I should employ someone Admiral Chan trusted. And, that person should seem to have a beef with the Orion Federation. So I chose a Brigadier who'd been jailed for five years for disreputable conduct and who had worked directly for Admiral Chan for several years. He has been able to get information to us on a regular basis. And things are even better, now. He has help from within. Dac Sul Jek is ensuring he has some cover. He is extremely disheartened because of two reprimands he's received. And, Isesinis corrective measures are not verbal, I should explain." Sparks finished.

"Do you consider the information accurate?" I queried.

"Yes, sir. It's limited, so we have to be careful. Our agent does not have access to the entire picture. So, he will know of force redistribution and advise us. But, we have to be careful in case other things are happening we don't know about. So far though, his data's been spot on. Without it, we wouldn't have been able to conduct the recent assassination." Sparks responds.

"Any other questions?" I asked my peers.

"You're dismissed, Generals - with the thanks of this Commission.' I snapped.

'Well? What do all of you think?" I asked the other C&C.

"I think your people have a good operation going, there. But, you should caution your agent. I still don't trust this Dac Sul Jek guy. He could be a plant." Tso Shah argued.

"I know it's a risk. But, lack of information caused us to cancel our operations planned for the end of last month. We have to take this chance if we're ever going to take back the Federation." I recommended.

There was a chorus of verbal endorsements and agreements all around.

"Is there anything else?" Grace called out and received negative head wags.

"We're adjourned!" She hollered as she whacked the hammer on its sound block.

....

We met in the large Boardroom in the Rigil Headquarters, the next day for our real meeting. Orders were issued to return to regular patrols, for the time being. Everything appeared to have returned to normal - without thoughts of our principal assault.

....

Sparks requested a meeting on April 8. Svesion was with him when they appeared at my door. They tantalizingly held a datapad in the air and taunted me about its contents.

"Wait'll you see what we have on here!" Sparks howled mischievously.

"Stop fucking around and show me!" My frustration was apparent.

The General placed the pad on my desk and tapped an icon. It played a half-hour video of a very slowly conducted and grisly dual execution. I muted the sound to silence the terrible screams. The whole thing reminded me of a middle ages slaying. Both parties were nearly drawn and quartered as great pains were taken to keep them conscious until the very end. It was very revolting. I did not know Jek. But, I did recognize Brigadier General Yskeni Vrosnikov.

Now, I was fairly confident that OFN was secure and safe, for the time being. And, I could be just as sure his information would be uncompromised.

....

A week later, we held another Commission meeting in Rigil's small amphitheater. During that, we discussed the tactical plan for a multi-faceted assault on the regional Headquarters Polyhedrons at 37 Gemini, 83 Leo, and Delta Pavonis. The scheme called for forces of four-hundred-fifty warships to be deployed to each location. I sent the following memo to Svesion's DC.

MEMO

From: *Fleet Admiral K Brubacher Commander Zeta HQ*

To: *General David Rottinger Deputy Commander Zeta Marine Army Command*

Re: *Pending Actions*

Date: *April 15, 2271*

General,

I am writing to you since General Svesion will not be available for the next couple of days. You are required to comply with the following and ensure the General is fully informed when he returns.

On May 25, the OFSA will commence actions against Isesinis Regional Headquarters units at 37 Gemini, 83 Leo, and Delta Pavonis. Zeta Command will be specifically targeting the 83 Leo operations while Gamma will engage at 37 Gemini and Epsilon will confront the contingents at Delta Pavonis.

Please ensure all OFSA Zeta Marine Army personnel are primed and ready for their support roles in the upcoming scuffle.

Fleet Admiral K. Brubacher

....

April 17 found the entire Commission back in the large Boardroom at Rigil for another meeting. This time, it was for planning our actual assault.

First, I reported on current intelligence and displayed the execution video, after warning everyone in the room of its offensive nature.

By the time the session was over, we had fundamentally adopted the original plan. The preliminary portion would begin on May 25. The three dominant thrusts would commence on May 26.

Finally, we agreed to have Fredricka release a public statement on those murders expressing our disgust with the practice, on April 24. And, we scheduled another meeting in the large amphitheater for April 25. This timing would allow us to discuss the executions as if we came by the information through the grapevine.

....

The scene on April 24 opened with Fred standing at a podium on a stage in front of the official seal of the OFSA and the Orion Federation Flag in the Briefing Room.

"This is an official press report regarding the uncivilized nature of the Isesinis occupation of our Orion Federation. I will share portions of a video. This is an edited version of two executions - reduced in length to facilitate this venue. But, the entire presentation is available from my office, in its original unedited format. We feel this is an authentic report. It was received from a concerned Orion citizen near the site of these horrendous acts. We have verified as much as possible to determine its accuracy. We believed it was filmed with a personal device.

I must warn you all that, though this is truncated, it is still very graphic and quite violent and disgusting. So, anyone who cannot deal with explicit, brutal, and bloody aggression should turn away. It is especially important to protect children from this exposure.

With all that being said, If you watch the flat screen, we'll begin the video."

As they watched, most reporters and attendees cringed or turned away. Several had tears streaming down their cheeks while a few vomited on the floor of the room. A couple yelled out to mute the volume. There was a communal sigh of relief when the ten-minute movie ended. Everyone looked exhausted and shaken when it was complete.

"So, I've asked my superiors, and they're unfamiliar with the men who were killed. As far as our people know they were not spying for the OFSA. The human victim did work for the OFSA over a decade ago. But, he has since served a prison term and has had no contact with our organization over the period since his employment. He was recognized but is unknown to any current OFSA executive. The C&C Commission has a copy of the complete presentation, now. They'll be discussing appropriate responses, soon. Are there any questions?" She asked the group.

Hands went up all over the room. Reporters made their inquiries and Fred answered throughout the next fifteen minutes.

"I'm sorry. I have other business to attend to. I'll have to end this conference, now." Fred called out, turned, and abruptly left the room.

....

The next day found us in the bugged room conducting another charade.

"Admiral Brubacher, do you have anything to report to us before we discuss planning matters?" Grace queried after she brought the meeting to order.

"Yes, I do. I'm sure you've all seen the video that was presented, yesterday. We have pretty much verified its voracity. The Isesinis did indeed conduct these disgusting execu..."

"Do we, or did we know those two people?" George interrupted.

"As far as I can tell, Brigadier General Yskeni Vrosnikov served in Admiral Chan's Command up to ten years ago. He was arrested and convicted of fraud, misappropriation of funds, and conduct unbecoming and served a lengthy prison term. Since his days commanding a Brigade, no one at the OFSA has had any contact with him. My information says none of the current administration has much knowledge of him.

As for this Mek guy, no one's ever met him. In fact, I don't think any OFSA people have ever met an Isesinis and lived to tell about it except those that are prisoners on occupied worlds." I explained. There was a thoughtful silence.

103

"Do you suppose we're being bugged or monitored, somehow?" Tso Shah mumbled.

"Why do you ask, Admiral?" I responded.

"Because at a previous meeting - not so long ago - we spoke of a Brigadier we are using as a spy. Do you think we could have been overheard? Maybe this Kil Kos guy mistook Vrosnikov for our agent." Shah conjectured.

"It's possible. But, I doubt it. We sweep all our facilities regularly for listening devices." I don't see how they could be eavesdropping." I explained.

"So, what about the planned assault?" Nichols questions.

"We go ahead - as scheduled. On May 25, we attack the three locations in our blueprint." George responded.

"Should we start ordering flotillas into position?" Savign asked.

"Yes, we need them at their assembly points by the fifteenth. Some will require up to ten days to reach their targets, at reasonable velocities." George responded.

So Grace loudly placed a motion to execute the assaults at 37 Gemini, 83 Leo, and Delta Pavonis on the date scheduled. Considerable disagreement and discussion erupted. But, in the end, the vote to persist was unanimous. It was all done with a great deal of embellishment.

....

At the meeting in the large boardroom a day later, we decided to position Theatre Commands in locations that were suitable for launch to dual landing sites. It would look like they were going to one of the three fake targets. But, it would be no farther to travel to the real objectives from these starting points. A burst of encrypted orders originating from reliable stations on secure channels initiated the redeployments.

For my part, I redirected the bulk of my forces to 61 Virgo, just inside the temporary border. It is marginally under forty light-years from 82 Eridani and slightly over eleven and three-quarters parsecs from 83 Leo. By leaning just a little toward Leo like we have, it makes it all the more acceptable that it is where we're headed. Zeta reserves would jump late from Wolf 359. They would appear to be staying behind for regular patrols.

The trip to 82 Eridani from 61 Virgo would take nearly a week at a rate of twenty percent of superluminal speed within a vortex. So, my three and a half theatres would depart the Virgo system on May 18 for their May 26 attack. The four reserve Fleets would use up precisely four days to reach the target. So, they will leave Wolf 359 on May 21 and land a light-year from the goal with all my Command Headquarters, the Mobile Hospital Commands and the security squads for all of them.

The majority of Epsilon will jump from Rigil. It is fifty-eight light years to both the fake and real objectives from there. The two exceptions are a half Theater level reserve and Epsilon's autonomous Frigates. They need ten days to reach their destination. So, they will leave on May 15 for their assault on the twenty-fifth. A portion of the Autonomous Frigates will fly with them while a small group travels with Zeta. The rest will depart for a position at vector 340.70° x 30.20° @ 168 Ly, immediately. They will take a circuitous route that won't attract attention and will meet some of their mates and a considerable number of subs already on-site. Action there will begin on May 18.

Nichols will stage his forces for a jump that will never happen. Gamma, Beta, and Alpha operation will protect the recovered territory.

The entire scheme is a giant slight of hand with the distraction of a suggestive diversion and the benefit of total surprise. Many have suffered for a long time while waiting for us to manipulate the situation to create the advantages we need. Over the next few weeks, we have to watch the Isesinis even closer than usual. We need to know if they've taken the bait or suspect a deception.

MEMO

In the Clear

From: Fleet Admiral K Brubacher C&C / Commander Zeta HQ

To: Gen. C. Sparks Commander ISIE, F. Adm. Savign Commander SOCC

Re: Pending Actions

Date: April 26, 2271

   Sirs,

   Please intensify you surveillance efforts. Contact me should you wish additional details.

Fleet Admiral K. Brubacher

Short and sweet, it should get the results I want.

Chapter 15 Naabaahii

Thursday, April 27, 2271

"Military Intelligence is a contradiction in terms." **Groucho Marx**

Admiral Naabaahii was thankful the Isesinis monitor OFSA Communications. He was also grateful he was in the inner circle of advisors. As a matter of course, he was included in a meeting that watched the female Captain do the Press Conference denying knowledge of the executed men. He was also privy to the Kil's personal thoughts. There had been a time not long ago when Kos was distrustful of all human partners. Now, the leader did not believe their opponents and showed nothing but disdain for the two he had murdered. He was entirely convinced they were the source of the deceitful stream of leaked data. They were the cause of his best friend's death.

The Admiral could not help but admire the strategy used by ISIE. He was sure it was Brubacher, Sparks, and their people that had devised the twists and turns that absolved him of any suspicion. Putting out information on false spies, and then denying it, was a strategy of pure genius.

But most importantly, Naabaahi was included in meetings that listened to recordings of captured OFSA C&C Commission meetings. Spies had placed devices in germane locations and had compromised a primary computer system. But the Admiral was convinced by the exchange of words that the members of the Commission were performing for an audience. It seemed especially so when Tso Shah suggested they were bugged and Brubacher so promptly dismissed the notion. But, just to be sure, he'd mention the surveillance in his next message.

Though Naabaahii hated Kos for what he'd done to the Federation, he could not help but admire some of his attributes. He was an incredible organizer, strategist, and tactician. He was otherwise quite intelligent too and had even mastered the English language in short order after meeting Chan. And, the Kil didn't just remember his immediate subordinates. Despite his brutality, most personnel like him because of his genuine interest in them. If you didn't fail and were loyal to him, there was no limit to the advantages he would bestow on you. Except for his new Deputy, promotions were usually from within.

Admiral Naabaahii thought about the new second. He is the proof that not all Isesinis are brutal killers. Dac Kil Res is a genuinely civilized person who is concerned for everyone in the organization. But, he is unconditionally loyal to Kil Kos. There is no daylight between them. Though he showed discomfort, he unequivocally supported the Kil's decision for such a vicious termination of the two traitors.

But, Res is much like Kos in most other ways. They are from the same Isesinis tribe which is much bigger and more intelligent than the others. They are always the chosen military leaders in their society. The Dac Kil was the only person that shared unrestrained light-hearted discussion and even laughs with Kos.

Even the Isesinis who speak English experience difficulty pronouncing Admiral Naabaahii's name. So they have nicknamed him Nabby and often refer to him as Admiral Nabby, in a friendly way. He watched as everyone in the meeting swallowed the bait regarding the attacks. He would include the fact they were ready for the impending assaults on 37 Gemini, 83 Leo, and Delta Pavonis. If they were real, the OFSA would alter them when his message was received. If they trying to goad the Isesinis, it would give the Service the assurance it needed to proceed.

Admiral Nabby never prepared messages in his sumptuous quarters. He was never sure if they were tapped by audio and video surveillance equipment. So, he always went to the Headquarter's administration center where there were desks and apparatus people could use. The observation equipment was evident there, and he could sit in plain sight, where he gained an advantage.

The most perilous problem was always the drop point. Nautica could enter and exit the big sphere at will, but Nabby went for long "walks" throughout the vessel to conceal his ultimate purpose. And, they included a stroll on the hangar deck. He would always ask permission. They would refuse him if they were opening the doors but quickly granted approval, otherwise. He'd ask how long he could stay and then saunter around appearing interested in this or that, often stopping passing Officers to ask questions. Around forty-five minutes into the venture, he'd make his way to the cross-member that served his purpose and plant the data chip in the head of the designated rivet. When the Nautica retrieves these units they insert them in an interface unit, plug them into a datapad, and transmit the information to the ISIE. And, he always destroyed his copy of the OTP cipher immediately upon completing the message. So even if the communication is discovered, it will never be interpreted.

But, all the tension in these surreptitious operations made him feel he was aging rapidly. He felt very old now and hoped he'd decide on asking the Nautica to extract him, soon. It was all a matter of sensing that he'd accomplished as much as possible.

To relieve the pressure, Nabby often attends the Kowaka games. The sport is like a cross between ball-hockey and lacrosse with full-body contact. It is quite violent, and the bulkier men like Kos and Res are not permitted to play because of their unfair advantage. It is something to see these diminutive people rolling along the floor or bouncing off it after a solid hit. They are genuinely fearless and resilient. Though it's brutal, it is almost hilarious to watch a penalty being awarded. Penalties are based on the "eye for an eye" principle. If a player slashes with a stick, the victim is granted a whack at the offender. But, somehow, there never seems to be any life-threatening or debilitating injuries. There are twenty-four teams throughout the Regional Commands, and they are often transported to 15 Sagitta for matches the executive can watch.

So today, he ambled to the Admin Center for an hour stay. He prepared his message then hung around and just "shot the shit" with several Isesinis and humans who passed through the facility. When he was satisfied, he strolled about the unrestricted areas of the big HQ until arriving at the appropriate Hangar Deck. They delayed him for half an hour as they were closing doors and repressurizing then let him amble about "getting his thoughts together." He took a little longer than usual to ensure he wasn't being watched. The executions had convinced him not to take unnecessary risks that could result in getting caught. An hour and a half later, Nabby went over to the Senior Officer, leaned against his desk, and started up a conversation. They chatted about Kowaka for quite awhile before he excused himself to get ready for tonight's game - which he did not want to miss.

....

Colonel Velky Kaule almost bumped into the Admiral when he came to place the computer chip in the rivet head. The cloaked Nautica had entered the Hangar Bay just before the spy. It had taken him long enough to get around to the drop that Kaule was already in the midst of his EVA. But, he was still inside the covering energy veil so Nabby couldn't see him. And, the agent got so close to the Nautica, he didn't even notice when one arm disappeared behind the cloak. But, he had to shift his weight to plant the message, and that little move extricated the limb from its dilemma before any nearby attendants noticed. The Nautica had to wait until a ship was coming or going. So, the undercover guy was gone before them.

....

The next morning, Nabby was sitting with Res talking when he observed he could use a vacation.

"What's a vacation?" The Dac Kil asked.

"It's when you take a week or two rest to get your head together and sort things out."

"Oh, I know this. We do the same. But, the translator did not get it." The Isesinis General laughed.

"Before I came here, I was in prison for a long time. After, leaving the jail, I stole a shuttle to make my getaway. From the day I arrived the Kil has always expected a lot of me. He demands a lot of everyone. But, I started without a break. I don't expect to go home. I'd be arrested - and probably executed. But, I'd really like a couple of weeks on the shore of a cool, clean, clear lake."

"To sun yourself."

"Yes. And to swim."

"Humans swim? Only fish swim on my world! My people are terrified of water that is over our heads." Res was truly amazed. And, Naabaahii filed the information away for the next report.

"Most of us love the water. We enjoy the exercise and the refreshment."

"We never think of humans like that."

"Like what?"

"We never think of you as getting tired and needing a rest. Of course, it is natural. All the universe needs a break. I will speak to the Kil for all of you."

"Thank you, Res. You are very kind."

"Don't ever say that in front of any of my people!" He said. Then, we broke into laughter.

"Are you going to the game, tonight?"

"Yes. Kos and I will attend together. What do you think of Kowaka?" The Dac Kil asked.

"I love it. It's exciting and similar to a lot of games on my homeworld. We have many competitive ones like Kowaka. They are rough and tough, too. Maybe not quite as violent as Kowaka. But, they're pretty stormy."

"I must leave. I have work to do. I will speak to Kos about humans getting vacation. He rewards those who succeed. So, I don't think he'll refuse." Res explained as he was walking away.

Naabaahii considered how Kos has used the humans. They originally came to him with information that helped formulate a plan of attack at a time when the Isesinis were jealously eyeing the Orion Federation. He incorporated the data into the original assault plan but realized their assistance could be valuable if he used them correctly later. Their knowledge of strategy, facilities, and technology is dated and becomes less relative with each passing day. But, their general comprehension of the Federation, the OFSA, and how it thinks and operates could be invaluable. So, he had Chan form them into a team of intelligence analysts. Throughout the war and the subsequent occupation, they had been instrumental in providing him with counsel based on surveillance and observation. But, the small team had been required to work nearly day and night with few breaks to keep up with the countless occurrences funneled to them daily from throughout the expansive territory.

The Admiral's thoughts drifted to the other human's motivations. He considered those in relation to his own past. When he and his compatriots challenged the OFSA and the Federation, it was because a significant alteration to the Constitution was to be imposed on everyone. And, that modification would fundamentally change it from a Monarchy to a Constitutional Monarchy. He opposed it because the Federation was comprised of a hundred members spread throughout four million cubic light-years, at that time. He and his associates believed the government would lose control and the whole thing would collapse under the new system.

To some degree, they were proven right, later. After a couple of years, the document required further editing reapportioning control a little more towards the King. But, from his prison cell, he'd seen them work that out peacefully. So, he knew the rebellion was a mistake, and his entire group had lacked faith in the people involved who will do whatever it takes to maintain a robust and healthy union. But their reasons for the revolution had unquestionably been patriotic, nonetheless.

But the human rebels involved in the Isesinis attack were not motivated by nationalism. They were a group of misfits who had committed dishonorable unlawful acts. Most were imprisoned for those actions. And, they were seeking revenge against a Federation they hated for jailing them. They also wanted a shortcut to positions where they could wipe the slate clean and begin new lives as influential leaders instead of criminals.

The Admiral employed a very circuitous route to return to his quarters. It was necessary for him to always appear to enjoy these long hikes to reinforce his need for those jaunts in the Hangar Bay. He washed up and changed for the coming sports event. Then, he left the room for a long walk with a datapad in hand and earpiece in place. He chose a music playlist he enjoyed listening to and turned up the volume until it leaked from his earlobe a little. As he moved along the corridor, Naabaahii removed an interface unit and placed the tiny chip inside. He plugged it into the datapad and brought up the opening document. After reading the heading, he selected the decryption app and directed it to the correct OTP cipher. Then, he minimized the entire operation and continued his march while the computer did its work.

"What'ya got there?" A voice from behind him asked. It was Chan.

"...just listening to a little music.' Chan refused the offered ear hoop. 'It relaxes me. I've assembled these long playlists for my walks." Naabaahii explained as he turned the screen towards the other man.

"You on your way to the games?" Chan queried.

"Yes, but I'm taking the long way. You know how much I enjoy my walks. They give me time to think and center myself."

"Sort of like meditation?"

"Yes, I guess it is. I never thought of it that way, before."

"Well, I'm taking the regular route. See you later." Chan said as he veered off into a corridor on his left.

....

In the Admin Center the next morning, Nabby sat in a safe position with his datapad in hand. This particular desk places him with the monitoring camera behind his pad. And, he can see those coming in and out, just in case someone enters who may wish to speak with him.

He raised a video game to keep on the screen, then opened the message. Sparks wanted to remove him for his own safety. He expressed his concern over the recent near-miss and explained they have all the intelligence needed from him. They would remove him during his regular Hangar Bay walk the next day. It would leave a big mystery for Kos and his people. They may even think he got blown out into space by being in that section when the doors were opened. He ran the special digital cleaner. It essentially does a standard wipe. Then it zeros all unregistered memory so no information can be reconstituted. After that, he always starts the Defragment application to further muddle everything by moving data around, which overwrites previously used memory. And the record of the Defrag explains the state of the unit. The sudden inspections of all Isesinis data pads had never revealed anything that shouldn't be in his system.

....

Later that morning, Kos put out a memo to all humans allowing them to take leave, with approval. But, they were not permitted to return to unoccupied regions of the Federation. They all understood that proviso.

After a full day's work analyzing incoming surveillance and observations and preparing reports for Kos, Nabby showered and changed. Then, he left his quarters for the usual stroll. In the Hangar Bay, he sauntered about showing interest in this or that and standing on the main floor looking up at one of the big warships for nearly half an hour. As if waking up, he began to move along the side walls studying piping, conduits, and hardware as usual. As he passed the back side of the cross-member used for the drop, he suddenly disappeared.

Both he and Kaule peered out from inside the cloak. No one even noticed the Admiral evaporate. Everyone was just going about their business. After a few more minutes, Kaule ushered the agent inside the Nautica's hatchway. Half an hour later, it backed out of the Polyhedron behind the departing warship Naabaahii had been examining a while back. The Admiral was prompted to maintain complete silence while inside the big base ship with a visual cue.

"Welcome aboard, sir." Captain Ignot offered a hand when they were clear of the giant Polyhedron.

"Thank you. I was glad General Sparks wanted me out. I was beginning to suffer from exhaustion."

"We'll have you home in less than a week. We're going to meet a Frigate that will take you the rest of the way. Unfortunately, we are still needed, here."

"You have a Frigate in occupied space? I'm not sure that's a safe way to travel."

"Not to worry. We have cloaks on a fleet of seventy-two Frigates, now. Let's get you some quarters and show you the way to the mess hall. You must be tired."

"Very!" The ex-Admiral replied.

They walked in silence along the hallway, stopping at a doorway. "This will be your room for the next day. But, you're welcome to wander the ship, if you're so inclined. I'll show you the dining area." Ignot extended a hand in the same direction they'd been traveling.

They moved a hundred feet along the walkway which opened into a concourse. To the right were the tables and serving counters. To the left, there was a communal entertainment room.

"Make yourself at home. I have work to do. But, if you need me just go forward to the Con." The Captain offered warmly as he hustled away.

....

"Sir, we're here!" A young Ensign had poked his head through the small room's doorway.

"Where? How long have I been asleep?"

"We're nearly to your transport. You've slept almost a full day."

"Dammit! I had a report to finish. I need to transmit it, so it gets to Rigil quickly. I should have asked someone to wake me. Did you know the Isesinis are afraid of water?" He asked, then realized he was still half asleep.

"Sorry, sir. I didn't know!"

"It's not your fault Ensign. I never thought I'd sleep that long or I'd have set the alarm. Man, I feel like I've been on a big drunk. I slept too long." Naabaahi said with the coarseness that comes from a dry mouth and throat. "And, I must have been snoring. I could drink lake Okeechobee dry." Nabby observed as he moved toward the sink.

"Are you going to be okay, sir."

"Yeah, I'll be fine. How long do I have?"

"We'll meet the Frigate in about an hour and a quarter. But, that's not important. You're the guest of honor. They'll wait."

"That gives me time to shower and eat. I should be okay by the time they're here."

An hour later, the Admiral found Commander Ignot in the Con. Outwardly, he was wide awake and fresh. Inwardly he felt like he had a rolled up wool blanket inside. He was sluggish and lackluster.

"You finally came out of your hibernation, eh?" Ignot smirked.

"Yes. I guess I was more exhausted than I realized."

"Half a year undercover will do that. I've never done that kind of work. But, we transport agents all the time. Some are intelligence and others are Special Forces, but all are clandestine. They come back in various states depending on the length and stress of their assignments. But, none have ever slept a full day before." The Captain observed.

"It was a long, nerve-wracking assignment. There was the constant fear of discovery. Did you see the report of the executions?"

"Yes, I did. They were particularly uncivilized."

"Yes. And, those people were innocent. It was me the Isesinis were really looking for. General Sparks misdirected them to look elsewhere."

113

"Holy shit. The Isesinis did that to two innocent people?"

"Not entirely guiltless. The human is a traitor. And the other guy is the enemy. So, from a strictly OFSA point of view, they deserved it. But, they were not spying. I was the agent."

"We're here. All stop! Engines to station keeping!' Ignot barked. 'We won't decloak. The transfer will take place behind full screens. Enjoy your trip home. And good luck." He directed softly at the Admiral as he offered a hand.

....

"I think your incompetent people killed him!' Admiral Chan yelled at the Dac Sul commanding the Hangar Bay. 'You opened the fucking doors with him inside. How could that happen?" He added.

"I don't know. There are safety systems. People are automatically monitored on entry. We receive a warning if people are inside when we're trying to land or launch."

"And, what happens when you get this alarm?"

"We check all internal sensors and do a quick physical sweep. If no one is found we assume, the detectors missed someone exiting, and we depressurize and open. This is a busy station, Admiral."

"So, if an individual gets sick and passes out on a floor in some hard to see area, you could blow them out the door?"

"Yes, sir. I suppose it's conceivable. If instruments don't detect anyone and we can't see them, then I guess it is possible."

Chan abruptly exited and marched to Kil Kos' Command Center. They spent half an hour discussing the matter - first heatedly then more calmly. In the end, Kos locked down the station and the rest of the day was spent searching for Nabby and trying to recover any evidence that might enlighten them. A fleet of shuttles searched the surrounding space for nearly fifty kilometers around the station.

"I think we should hold a memorial for him. Naabaahi was loyal to both of us. And, he provided valuable insight into all the information we received. He had the ability to analyze it from the point of view of those in charge of the OFSA. And, he worked tirelessly. I know for a fact, he was feeling exhausted."

"I agree. We will do something for him. I will have Res handle it. I am not good at these things. He seems to understand sadness and remorse much better than me.' Kos assessed candidly. 'And, we will initiate steps to improve safety on the hangar decks." He added as he stood up indicating it was time for Chan to exit.

Res arranged the observance quickly. The next day there was an assemblage in the Hangar Bay. Kind words were spoken. Fifty fighters did a fly-past, and fifty guns fired reduced charges. Even Kos rose to make a brief statement thanking Naaby for his service.

Chapter 16 From Intelligence to Action

Wednesday, November 2, 2270

"Thinking will not overcome fear but action will." **W. Clement Stone**

The following Wednesday, Beta and Delta both deployed three of their four Theatre-level Commands to sites that would see the feints. They would all arrive just after their opponents at three hundred hours fifteen minutes on Monday, November 7, 2270. Each would hold the fourth operation in reserve. But, neither expected to see real action.

But, Admiral Nichols issued orders splitting Gamma along its two Tier 2 operations sending them to border "no-mans'-land" positions at RA 237.325° x Dec 47.6° at ninety-five light-years and RA 211.755 x 47.6 at ninety-five light-years, respectively. These regions are directly across from each other on opposite sides of the wedge we have recovered. He had provided them with the detailed enemy preparations.

Each OFSA Tier 2 Command had elected to hold only three Fleets in reserve throwing the other thirteen into the boundary area scuffle. But, an Epsilon twelve Fleet Theatre was added to Gamma-T2-1, and an eight fleet Zeta one was included with Gamma T2-2 forces. There would be twenty-five Fleets on one border and twenty-one on the other. The distribution was based on information received regarding the strength of enemy formations scheduled to attack at each position.

At both, the OFSA ships would land and wait a light-year inside the border, since the enemy battle plan was to land beyond it, then immediately make another lunge for the interior and begin a slow, steady push toward the middle. The objective was to cut our wedge in half. If they succeeded, thousands of warships accompanied by Base Stations would enter through the rift and begin to push us towards either end of our archipelago. So, a significant and efficient response is required.

....

It took nearly four days in the vortices at forty-percent of light-speed for the two Gamma contingents to reach their staging places then, relaunch to their assigned positions. The group on the eastern boundary arrived to find the Zeta flotilla already engaged in fierce fighting. The western deployment also found the Epsilon task force deeply involved in combat. The two Gamma T1-2 level Headquarters were positioned a parsec inside each border, away from the fighting at either place. The T1-3-level Headquarters were stationed a light-year from each site with their Mobile Hospital Units with security flotillas and reserve forces.

Fleet Admiral Nichols' Gamma T1 HQ the FSS Supernova, along with my Examiner, and George's Valhalla are situated beside one of the new SSR transmitters at Gamma Bootes, on vector RA 224.4° x Dec 38.31° at just over twenty-six and a half parsecs from Sol. That places the Central Command about twenty-two light-years from either conflict. All seven subordinate Base Stations have each been carefully situated beside one of the new SSR relay units so we can employ the new Substrata Communications System. Cloaked SOCC Subs also sit at each battlefield transmitting sensor images via SSR units near them. And, because the new technology is so heavily deployed within the corridor, no Carrier in the battle zones will ever be more than fifty thousand kilometers from one. So, all Senior Commanders are receiving reports, logs, and visual representations in near real-time and can return new orders as quickly. This is the first field testing of the Suvayeek inspired technology during an actual campaign.

In the west, Epsilon's Pacific, Atlantic, and Arctic Fleets are clearly visible with the other ten a little too distant to see clearly. Likewise, to the east, most are hard to perceive, but Kalahari's FSS Prosecutor, Sahara's FSS Defender, Gobi Fleet's FSS Witness, and Negev's FSS Accuser are distinguishable. Epsilon and Zeta had both employed new naming protocols during the last R&R change, freeing standard nomenclature for the Regional Tier 1 Commands.

And, as expected, our opponents arranged in disc formations, static and heavily protected around their perimeters but sadly weak below and above. All the while, both Epsilon and Zeta forces kept moving, reforming, and re-attacking from the same side atop and beneath. From the left frame of the Western and right rim of the Eastern battle screens, large contingents streaked towards the Isesinis launching Raptors and firing all weapons at a ferocious pace. Gamma T1-1 divided into two arrows to fortify the Epsilon assault. T1-2 Headquarters had separated its Fleets into three to aid the Zeta operation. Within a minute of their appearance, over six-hundred fighters had also joined the fray at each location.

But though the initial ferocity hurt the Isesinis, it cost us, too. Before Gamma arrived at each battlefield, both Epsilon and Zeta had incurred severe losses. Epsilon's T2 Theatre One Command had seen the destruction of several vessels among two Fleets that had formed the point of one spear. Atlantic Fleet lost the Cruisers FSS Kadesh and FSS Tanagra while Pacific Fleet lost the Carrier FSS Vinland, the Cruiser FSS Carchemish, and the Frigate FSS Pittsburgh. Pacific's Vice Admiral Gargata quickly rolled Vinland Group into Kaupanger Group so the remaining ships would have guidance. Two more Fleets suffered critically damaged vessels that were still space-worthy. Arctic Fleet's Carriers FSS

Odense and FSS Tynwald and Antartic Fleets FSS Runeston were badly mauled. Epsilon casualties totaled nearly twelve thousand dead and eight thousand injured by the time Gamma arrived. Zeta's price was not quite as high. But Admiral Anne Arce's Negev Fleet lost the Carrier FSS Integrity, and all of Admiral Tom Hurst's Chihuahua Fleet Frigates were annihilated. We suffered almost eleven thousand deaths and five thousand injuries during that period.

Combined, Anna's and Tom's Theatre Commands still had two-hundred fifty units up against the remaining three hundred twenty-four Isesinis ships and had already destroyed thirty-one of their Frigates and Carriers, when the two hundred fifty-six Gamma T2-2 formations landed. And at the other location, the original four hundred twenty-six assaulting enemy vessels had been reduced to three hundred seventy-seven, to face Epsilon's balance of three hundred seventy-nine warships, when Gamma T2-1 arrived. That was the point where our communications came online, and we saw the Gamma deployments heading in with all guns blazing and hundreds of Raptors launched.

At each locale, they broke into four columns. Two traveled above existing armadas and two below. Two were to the Sol side of the fray the other on the galactic facing edge. All fired a torrent into the centers of the Isesinis formations. Within a minute of the influx, thirty to forty Isesinis craft were destroyed at each location turning the field into a brilliant flare flickering off the smoke and debris from all the sudden destruction. The massive attacks triggered the first flexibility in our antagonists' tactics we have seen to now.

On the western line, they broke into six separate Fleets. To the east, they divided into four groups, which reflected the loss of one of their Carriers. On both fronts, the detachments opened up like starbursts placing considerable distance between the various flotillas. And each individual body of ships widened their footprint. It all served to create an atmosphere that reduced the chances of vessels falling victim to chain reaction annihilations. And, they were able to fortify their outer perimeter by defending it in layers. But, they still could not adapt to our three-dimensional style of assaults, failing to adequately reinforce the territory above and below their new configurations.

In response, Gamma reformed into a single mass as it completed its first pass across the enemy, then re-split into two far-flung convoys as they made their turns for a second sprint. All the while the Epsilon or Zeta force stood its ground. And, off in the distance at each location, thirty-six exit threshold formed spewing an additional force of OFSA frigates into each battle. Admiral Laft had managed to get his typically diffused forces together and into the confrontation in time to be a vital benefit at both positions.

These independent units displayed an entirely unique tactic. Each Captain must have gauged friendly and enemy fire on their trip from jump exit to confrontation. The Frigates all zig-zagged throughout the maelstrom avoiding both sides' streams of ammunitions while lashing enemy vessels encountered on their erratic paths. Several times, at both sites, I saw Frigates make runs then complete a loop for an inverted pass above the frenzy. One at a time, they would withdraw to the outer edge of the tumult to meet a supply ship for restocking. Then, they'd return to the mission, at hand.

At both locations, OFSA forces respond to the widening enemy formation by altering their tactics. Instead of streaming in from either side, they now ring the top and bottom of the enemy assemblage, continuing the crippling onslaught. All our Fleets concentrate on those enemy units forming the outer perimeter of the widened disc, while offensively-tasked Raptors launch wave after wave against those toward the center. All the while, thousands of defensive fighters protect their parent Commands and provide cover to supply vessels moving in and out to replenish ammunition being expended at a merciless rate. And through it all, communications channels are ripe with flying orders intended to direct a response to an action or take advantage of a newly perceived weakness. Some are transmitted down from Theatre Commands, but most are at Fleet, Task, and Group levels.

These counter-moves result in multiple benefits. First, it defeats the Isesinis attempt to break the conflict into regional skirmishes. Next, it forces them back to a defensive mode and prevents them from restocking diminishing ammo. And, most readily apparent is the steadily rising increase in their rate of destruction and the decrease in damage to our ships.

Space is thick with dusty smoke drifting between the spiraling fragments of destroyed warships - some OFSA - but most are Isesinis. Lightning-like flashes and flares from warhead detonations and exploding enemy hardware reflect eerily on all this litter creating ghostly flickering shadows and images on the remaining members of battlefield formations.

As I watch, I realize it's not our technology as much as our tactics that provide this turn towards our favor. And it's our capacity to react logically and quickly to changing events and our ability to think and execute in a three-dimensional fashion. Though we all have our rehearsed part in this play, it must seem confusing and utterly arbitrary to our opponents. This time, we don't even have the surprise we enjoyed in previous encounters with the Isesinis. But, it appears we will prevail because of our flexibility.

119

Our antagonist's reaction to our reorganization is almost instantaneous. They flee both regions. We track them back over the provisional boundary on trajectories that terminate at Epsilon Eridani. We had been expecting a sustained fight to divide our territory in two. It left us all scratching our heads in wonder. There'd been no hint included in the intelligence that they'd break so easily, and to fail and live is not an option with Governor Kos. So there must have been follow-up orders to avoid a massive loss. And, Kos must view the attack as a means to keep us in check. Cutting us in half would have been a bonus.

....

On Tuesday, November 15, 2270, we begin a very remarkable Commission Meeting. It starts with the Tier Two and Three Commanders present so we can review the battle that ended a few days ago. The debriefing goes well, and we devote considerable time, effort, and discussion to analyzing our response. In the end, we agree we countered the attack fittingly. We were just late enough to remove the feeling we might have had advanced knowledge. This is important if we are to maintain the intelligence advantage and protect all our undercover forces from suspicion. Though our success is unambiguous, our losses were substantial, in the end. Epsilon and Zeta had been the first responders, this time. So, our forfeitures were higher than the others. Our combined operations suffered nearly sixty-five thousand deaths, and almost fourteen-thousand were injured or wounded. We need to replace twenty-five warships in various classes and nearly two-hundred fighters. Acceptable at a rate of four-and-a-quarter-percent of our engaged forces, the lists of casualties is still tough to bear.

Gojen Svjosloki attended on the second and third days of the session to make a very fascinating report and an attractive proposal. His work with the Suvayeek has borne added fruit. He and his team spent some time and effort studying and analyzing our ally's cloaking technology. We have never been able to incorporate cloaking together with the shield system we now use. And, we could never use cloaking on other than covert class ships because their structures, exterior hardware, and external weapons placements create such an irregular shape. We were only able to accomplish the change to supply vessels because of their reduced weaponry. But, Gojen feels, we can enjoy invisibility and stronger protection at the same time by employing a modified version of the Suvayeek equipment. They are able both hide and protect very irregularly-contoured warships.

It would be impossible to modify all the nearly four-thousand OFSA ships, but the Admiral is proposing we do change all SOCC subs and all Epsilon Autonomous Frigates.

This would give SOCC an offensive capability they do not now enjoy and would endow the Frigates with the ability to get a complex weapons' platform into a battle-site, undetected.

Admiral Svjosloki provided drawings, costing, and scheduling for the entire proposition and it was quickly approved as suggested.

....

I booked the period from November 25 to October 13 off. Fredricka arrives Friday and will leave to return to the Rigil Campus on the following Saturday allowing us seven full days together. The three of us spent the first day traveling to Rigil. Bryant always enjoys these trips. The Lounge's expansive view-windows provide him with hours of entertainment staring into space to examine its infinite marvels.

We spent several hours playing board games, disembarking to a shuttle on the twenty-fourth to head down to the Rigilian beaches. Fred and I spent a lot of intimate time together when Bryant was sleeping. We had a wonderful week together before shuttling her back to the campus. I stopped in to visit. Then we traveled over to Headquarters for a short stop before heading back up for the return trip to Wolf 359.

This would be Frericka's last visit. She will finish her program with a formal graduation next weekend. Though I was to handle her final elevation on the Examiner, she will now be commissioned a Captain, at that ceremony by Fleet Admiral Tonaka and assigned as Field Public Relations Commander. Then, she returns to the Examiner - for good.

Chapter 17 Kil Kos

Wednesday, May 3, 2271

"Only the winners decide what were war crimes." **Gary Willis**

"Are you okay, old friend?" Res asks Kos in response to his pointless tirade.

"I'm sorry, Res. I know I'm nasty, right now. It's that idiotic Federation Military outfit."

"What do you mean, Kos?"

"I know they're up to something. They're a sneaky bunch - pretty good tacticians and worthy opponents."

"Do you think they're plotting again?

"I'm not sure, Res. We are pretty confident they're heading for what they call 37 Gemini, 83 Leo, and Delta Pavonis. But, something doesn't seem quite right. They formed up for the first two. And there was a formation already in position to land at the third system on the same date as the others. But, we lost them when they jumped out. We're not sure where they actually went. Then, there are the seventy-two Frigates that disappeared. We don't know where they are. And, Chan's made us aware of those invisible ships they call Subs. We never identify where any of those ones are. I'm just uneasy about the whole thing." Kos explains to Res who is the only person he can bare his soul to.

"Maybe you're just tired and need a break."

"I can't!' The Kil snapped, then added in a softer tone. "Sorry. But, the last time I took a breather my deputy died. The two of you are my only real friends. I could not lose you, too." Kos' concern was genuine.

"You can't concern yourself about that. We're all soldiers and prepared to die, anytime. You need a break. Don't worry. I'll be okay."

"What if I went home for six weeks. If I travel at maximum, it'll give me ten days on the planet. I could spend some time relaxing and a day or two with the Emperor. I need to see him personally, anyway. I have to twist his arm - threaten action from the opposing houses. We aren't getting enough support."

"I'll be fine, Kos. You need a rest, and you have to attend to your political responsibilities." Mes counseled.

"Okay, I'll leave in the morning."

"Give the Emperor my regards, please. And, try to enjoy some of the time."

"I will."

The two men parted company. Res went to the central office to check duty rosters, departmental summaries, and deployment tactical reports. He wanted to hit the ground running the next morning.

Meanwhile, Kos returned to his quarters to prepare orders and pack for the trip.

....

On the morning of the nineteenth, Kos was aboard a cruiser orbiting 15 Sagitta. He is always comfortable aboard these sleek tear-drop-shaped vessels. They are the height of efficiency requiring only five hundred thirty crew to pack a punch equal or better than any opponent they'd met so far. Despite that, they have very generous and relaxing quarters for General Officers and some enjoyable diversions. And, he'd spent a great deal of his career on these and the Carriers before he was promoted to Dac Kil ten years ago. From then on, he was always aboard the giant Base Stations unless traveling.

The Kil was looking forward to reaching home. Aside from official functions, it is always a time to walk around freely without the cumbersome armor that all Isesinis military wear like a uniform. That shell provides both protection and the illusion of imposing ferocity to his ordinarily diminutive minions. But in his case, it only serves as a security shell. And reaching the planetary capital always means he'll be able to attend a Zaltka tournament. This is a series of gladiatorial competitions where captured enemies and criminals engage in gory, violent death matches employing ancient throwing, hacking and stabbing weapons.

Kos is from the Yalobaga, a once-isolated-tribe of fierce warriors that inhabit a string of equatorial islands off the southern coast of Isesin's expansive, single continent. With the exception of their pug-faced appearance and cranial ridge, they are similar to their Orion Federation humanoid opponents, though some are more robust than an average hominid. And, as a sub-class, they have been gifted with more powerful intellects than their cousins from other genus on their world.

The Kil draws attention when he walks the streets of most major cities on Isesin. Tall and powerful he is fair and nearly blonde appearing much less swarthy than most of his compatriots. And, his regal - almost arrogant bearing and erect militaristic posture only add to the sense of leadership he emanates. He commands respect wherever he goes whether in or out of the rigid martial attire and draws the crowds of a celebrity.

Since it is not the custom of his people to attach appellations to inanimate objects, the Cruiser has a registry number but no name. It is one of the seventy-five hundred throughout the fifteen regional commands under his authority. And for this trip, it will use the older "Jump Technology" to ferry the Kil to Isesin. The faster more-contemporary FTL technology poses too great a risk to transport one of the two most significant leaders of the Isesinis military. From 15 Sagitta, the journey to Eta Pegasus is just over one hundred eighty-three light-years. At forty percent of superluminal in its vortex, the ship will complete each leg of the trip in a little over sixteen days permitting Kos ten days on the surface. He will need a recovery day or two to compensate for dilation, so he sends a request to the Emperor for a visit on May 24.

Then, the Kil strips off his exoskeleton, showers, and changes. He will relax in a textile uniform for the majority of this excursion.

Chapter 18 A Big Wet Kiss

Saturday, May 6, 2271

"Success is where preparation and opportunity meet." **Bobby Unser**

"Admiral Naabaahii, you have done a magnificent service for your people, and we are grateful. We wish to show our gratitude to you.' King David spoke to the man in front of an extended Commission meeting that included all the Tier One and Two Commanders, General Svesion and General Sparks.

'A long time ago you led a revolt that caused my father pronounced consternation. Out of loyalty, you once made a blunder that you paid a high price for. And, we all see it as that - a mistake! So, I am going to make a proposal to you.

First, by order of the CIC, I will grant you full exoneration and purge the record of your crime and your incarceration. I am not speaking of a pardon but the elimination of the account of your conviction and imprisonment. It will appear as if the incident and its consequences never happened. Next, we will restore you to service. But, if you accept, you will be transferred to the Marines and granted the level-eight rank of Major General. You will have your choice of working within either the Analysis unit or in charge of a Brigade of Field Agents for General Sparks. He has expressed his belief in your loyalty and his faith in your ability and value. And, we will grant you back pay at the Level Eight field rate for all the years you were imprisoned. Finally, your OFSA personnel file will be wiped clean and amended to show a transfer to the Marines on the date of your arrest and service for the years since, at the new rank. In short, you will be able to make this new career reach whatever heights you aim for.

I assume you've had time to consider the actions that led to your fall. And, that you would never act rashly again. I believe you would now have the wisdom to allow our internal events to work themselves out, as they always have. I know you only acted as a patriot.

Do you need some time to consider the offer?"

"No, Your Majesty. I accept, with thanks. And, I'd like to add that I will not disappoint you, again. I will try to make you all proud you made this decision."

"General Sparks!" David barked.

Sparks came forward. He and Naabaahii spoke quietly for a few moments. Chris tapped on his datapad. Then, he forwarded documents to all the C&C and King David.

They examined them and keyed the appropriate icons on their devices before returning the orders. After that, Chris conducted the ceremonies inducting Naabaahii into the Marines, elevating the new soldier to Major General, and assigning him duty in charge of active Field Agents.

"You're out of uniform, Major General. I am granting you week's leave on Rigil. I'd like to make it longer, after what you've been through, but we need you. So, I expect you in my doorway, rested, and in full uniform, in a week."

"Aye, sir!" The Major General responded as he snapped to attention. He did not salute because he was in civilian clothes.

"May I be excused?" He directed at the King.

"You're dismissed!" David snapped.

General Naabaahii was quickly followed by Svesion, Sparks, and several Admirals as he quickly exited the room.

"Congratulations, General!' A familiar voice bellowed from behind him. It was Tso Shah who appeared to be genuinely pleased. 'It's great to see you again." He held out his hand as the others congregated around the new General. They spent half an hour together. Then he, Sparks and Svesion went to the pub. They each ordered a beverage and talked for a few minutes. Chris forwarded a pass and his transport authorization when it was time to break up the gathering. Finally, Svesion handed him his Zeta - ISIE credit card.

"You'll need this. We'll cover your vacation, and you'll want your new uniforms. You're authorized for the full complement of daily, mess, and dress ones fully tailored, along with all the necessary accessories and underclothes. So, enjoy your trip to Banerjee's. He has the requisition. And, I'd like to welcome you aboard, General Naabaahii." He said with a wide smile as he extended his right hand.

"Thank you for your faith, sir. And thanks for this." Nabby responded as he raised his pad and the credit card. "And, please call me Nabby. It was a nickname given to me while I was undercover. Though I don't much like any of those people I dealt with, I kind of appreciated the handle. Everyone has so much trouble with my real name."

They chatted a while longer, then they all rose and left the pub.

....

When the Commission session resumed after lunch, only the C&C, their COS, and some Deputies were in attendance. None of the extras present in Naabaahii's restoration were needed.

I shanghaied the meeting for intelligence purposes.

126

"What is it, Admiral?" Grace sounded a bit annoyed at my tactic.

"I have an intelligence report that needs to be presented before we discuss impending actions. Depending on how it's received, it may force us to change some decisions."

"Go ahead. The floor is yours."

"I have a report from the Suvayeek at 15 Sagitta. It is verified by the FSS Nautica. It's the sub watching the GPHC that's parked there.

They are both recounting the departure of a Cruiser headed for Eta Pegasus. This is unusual in its own right. In two years, most travel between those two locations has been by supply ships. The only exception was the last time we monitored Kil Kos leaving when we dispatched his deputy. That wouldn't be enough by itself, but the sub was in the Base Station's Hangar and saw the Kil board the Cruiser." I explained

"George, the balls in your court." Grace barked.

"I don't think that account changes anything. We'll still be able to deal with Kos whichever location he's at. This is the plan for the upcoming events.' George explained as he raised a very thick bound brief from the table. 'It is eight hundred pages. But it's laid out by responsibilities in order of Command. It is sectioned into Beta, Gamma, Delta, SOCC, Epsilon and Zeta parts. So, you only need to examine the elements reflecting your operations. But, I do recommend you read the rest. I'm sending it to your pads, right now.

It was prepared from a basic concept and modified with input from all of us. So, I presume it will be satisfactory to everyone. But, if you do find an issue, please direct your concerns to me immediately, bearing in mind there are some changes I made for tactical reasons.

Once you're satisfied, send your acceptance to me and issue all your orders to any subordinate Commands you want to control directly. You will receive one update before launch date. Very late on the twenty-fifth, I will send you each a report on the diversionary bombings. Just in case we don't get a chance to meet again - Good Luck Everyone." All our annunciators chimed as Admiral Bryant finished his presentation.

....

As a student of tactics, I did study the entire battle plan, carefully. It was a complicated but ingenious combination of moves and assaults designed to confuse, disrupt, and eliminate our opponents. Epsilon's part was especially grueling. Though Gamma would aid in some confrontations and SOCC in all of them, Epsilon would bear the brunt of two separate arms of the strike and even assist Zeta in our endeavor. And George had

127

enlisted Admiral Savign to do her usual thorough work preparing the enemy for the assault - or priming their ships, as he referred to the mining action.

Intelligence reports showed that SOCC subs, Suvayeek warships, and Federation observation platforms had tracked Dac Kil Res back to his base command at Epsilon Eridani. But, no one was actually sure of Kil Kos location. But whether he was home or on his station, everyone was where they should be.

....

TACTICAL ACTION MESSAGE #ZETA HQ-0016531
CLASSIFIED - TOP SECRET (NTK)
ENCRYPTED - Authentication Root I.D. ZETA-2292XS431*&

From: *F. Admiral K. Brubacher Commander Zeta Headquarters*

To: *Admiral G. Astinov Commander Zeta-1, Admiral Urquhart Commander Zeta-2*

C.C. *All C&C Commission Members*

Re: *Coming Action Plan # CC-1345987*

Date: *May 7, 2271*

Admirals,

You are ordered and required to execute the following.

1. *Refer to the plan listed above for the Zeta Operations included.*

2. *Check SOCC reports for the current disposition of enemy forces at the Zeta target location.*

3. *Together, divide your Commands into the required assault arms as previously agreed.*

4. *Issue orders concerning each sub-division of Theater Units under your individual controls to achieve the tactics, goals, and results indicated in the above-listed Action Plan.*

5. *Have all deployments launch from Wolf 359 at a velocity to arrive at their assigned destinations in time for a single rest day before the attack date specified in the scheme.*

6. *Reserves specified in the blueprint will be held at your stop-over point with all HQ Commands, Mobile Hospital Commands, and their accompanying security flotillas.*

7. *Maintain a constant link with the Examiner and Interrogator throughout the strike.*

8. *Report status of all divisions and departments along with battle assessments once every fifteen minutes via the direct network.*

9. *Report casualties, deaths, and hardware losses continually using your communications connection.*

F. Adm. Kurt Brubacher.

Though most of our orders were transmitted only along their respective lines, George had the courtesy of sending me a copy of his directives to Admiral Laft and his subsequent orders to his subordinates. Half of Vice Admiral Boet's covert Autonomous Frigate Fleet would be accompanying us to our destination and would aid in the destruction of the Polyhedron. The other half of that Fleet would join SOCC forces at Sol Vector 340.70° x 30.20° at 51.509 parsecs, for an exceptional project the day before the other strikes.

Over the rest of the day, I was copied on a flood of orders issued by all the Commands down the line. Tier 2 directed their Tier Three operations who commanded their Fleets who dictated to their Task Forces who passed the most detailed instruction to their Group Commanders. Even the mandates they gave their ships were echoed to my system. And all ships were ordered to join a common communications link for the duration of all actions. So, even individual ships' tactics will be accessible to me. Though I wouldn't interfere and would always use the chain of command, I would be able to monitor everything.

Those of us from Zeta Command still at Wolf 359 left to join the rest of our Command at 61 Virgo, immediately. It's a distance of almost twenty-three light-years. We'd arrive late May 11, traveling at twenty percent of C in our vortices. The jump to 82 Eridani would be made from there. That journey of almost twelve and a third parsecs would consume another week at point two of superluminal. So, we'd leave the 61 Virgo staging area early May 18 to arrive a light-year and a half from our target in time for a day's rest there. But, that all shouldn't be too apparent. The diversion should be impressive enough to draw Isesinis attention.

....

While we're in transit before a battle, there's little I can do. Most of my duties involve directing forces to new assignments and monitoring results. But, all my Commands are currently engaged in executing my previously issued orders. And, I won't have anything to monitor for a while. Aside from a little administration and housekeeping, there's very little to occupy me. So, rather than sitting around worrying about the coming confrontation, I decided to spend the trip with my family. It's no problem for Fred. Her daily briefings are canceled. There is always a press blackout around significant actions.

....

Vice Admiral Boets and his fleet of eighteen covert Frigates joined Admiral Korgos Basi and his SOCC contingent at the position at Sol vector 340.70° x 30.20° distance 51.509 parsecs on May 15. Basi is Savigne's Deputy Commander. She'd dispatched him with the Fleet of subs run by Vice Admiral Kononga to oversee the entire positional objective. Boets reported to Basi aboard the FSS Challenger fifteen minutes after arriving. The two ships docked under cloak to avoid being spotted. Basi decided to temporarily move his pennant to the FSS Chicago also being used by Boets as his flagship. The two would run the joint operation from there.

Basi asked Boets to have the Chicago moved to a position inside the Eta Pegasus system so they could view the activity around the inhabited planet there.

"You won't believe what we're facing here.' He said as the ship crept up to the globe around a hundred million miles from its central star. 'There's so much traffic that can't see us, that avoiding crafts dropping into an orbital path is a major consideration. Since they're blind to us, many have tried to settle right on top of some of our subs.

Boets could see a vast assortment of ships.

"There are two circling multi-bay space assembly yards, a pair of the GPHC units and a couple of dozen warships in orbit here. The Frigates' paths are synchronized with each other. They essentially form an impenetrable web around this world. My subs have been moving in and out of here, covertly priming this nest for the coming action. Fifteen minutes before our assault, they will detonate the whole shebang. We should only have to do some cleanup before executing our orders. And, there's a lot of traffic. Tons of civilian shuttles and what seems like a merchant fleet drop into stationary orbits every day. And there are dozens of Fleets of military vessels within ten parsecs of here. I have individual subs monitoring each for unusual movement. I estimate we'll have under three-hours to conduct our duties, here." He finished as Boets watched all the space traffic through the view-window and on the main screen.

"So, you've mined the big Bases and all the Cruisers?"

"Yes, and the shipyards, too. We don't want them replacing losses too quickly." Basi explained to Boets.

"So, there'll be a lot of debris flying around, when we land."

"Uh-huh. But, that's why the fifteen minutes. It's not really long enough, but it's all the time we can risk. Hopefully, everything will be disbursed or have settled into a trajectory we can track by then."

"Our shields should withstand hits from the shrapnel. And, the subs should too, with their recent upgrades. All I'm worried about is that stuff deflecting off of us makes us targetable." Boets offered.

"I agree. But we have to chance it. So, the plan is that I'll press the button detonating all the mines at five hundred forty-five hours. We'll jump to exit here at five hundred hours fifty-five minutes. We'll have five minutes to secure positions safe from debris. At six hundred, we'll all decloak so they can see the thirty battleships surrounding their planet. We'll each fire two volleys, recloak and move to positions fifteen hundred miles east of the first ones. Then, we'll decloak again and fire two more salvos. We'll all re-establish our veils and move to new locations five hundred miles west of the second ones. We will remain cloaked as we bombard the planet until we expend seventy-five percent of stocked ammo. Four covert supply ships will restock us for the trip home. They're at the staging point, now."

"Can you send me all the Frigates' positions?"

"It's not necessary. The biggest and most important installations and population centers are in the northern hemisphere. SOCC will stay south of the Equator and Epsilon will remain north. You can assign your people their original firing points. You're a big boy, Boets. And, I hear your damn good. I'm sure you don't need or want me holding your hand." Basi joked with a smile.

"Thank you, sir. Shall we head back?"

"Sure. I'd like to make it in time for supper."

"You're welcome here, sir. We have much more elaborate galleys and a Flag Mess. We can have a nice dinner and a little wine with the entire senior Command if you'd like."

"That's a terrific idea, Admiral. Let's invite the rest and get back so we can throw this little shindig." Basi joked lightly.

Admiral Boets sent out memos to his two Task Force Commanders and his squad Commanders. He also transmitted invitations to Basi's Fleet Commander, Task Force Commanders, and Pack Leaders. They were all to meet their two bosses aboard the Chicago when it returned. He did not typically use the small Flag Mess. He usually preferred the noise of the Officers' dining area. So, he forwarded a memo to the galley and the service staff that there'd be a dinner in that FSS Chicago Flag Dining Hall starting at eighteen hundred. They were to expect up to twenty attendees.

Boets enjoyed Basi's company so much he failed to monitor the amount of food he was eating. When the evening was over, he felt bloated and distended. But, it had gone well, and his new association was good enough to call a blossoming friendship. He was impressed with the SOCC operation. Vice Admiral Kononga commanded seventy units, though only fifty-two are at the staging area. The other eighteen are scattered about the region monitoring enemy formations. And, SOCC has dropped a lot of the new relays within this region. So, he can communicate with and supervise the remote ships' signals nearly instantaneously. "You really have your shit together, gentlemen.' He'd observed admiringly as their party was breaking up. 'I am impressed with your operation and all you've accomplished here." He added.

"Thank you, Admiral." The two responded in harmony. Then, all but Basi made their way to the docking ports and departed. Basi occupied his new temporary quarters.

....

"Did you sleep well?" The Vice Admiral asked Admiral Basi when he arrived in the Officers' Mess at six-hundred.

"Very. The quarters seem sumptuous compared to that sub. I'll need an office, too. Have you been here long?" He signaled he was referring to the Mess Hall.

"No problem, Admiral. The Frigates and Cruisers are all equipped with three Flag offices. That was established in case a Carrier is disabled, but the Command is intact. On most, they are inactive. But, we use a couple in particular ships within Epsilon's Autonomous Group. There's still one available here. So, I took the liberty of having your gear sent over and moved into it. Your name is even on the door." Boets explained.

"When the hell did you get the time for that?" Basi sounded surprised.

"I was up at four hundred hours thirty minutes, so I organized the orders for your stay, first. Then, I cleaned up and dressed and arrived here ten minutes before you. I recommend the omelets. This chef is great with them." Boets suggested.

"Thanks. I'll try one. And, thanks for the early service. You're a real go-getter."
The two men enjoyed a great breakfast and conversation together.

....

When we arrived at 61 Virgo on the eleventh and with nearly a week to rest, I decided we should place the Examiner in a synchronous orbit of Alpia. That's the name the humanoids who inhabit the planet have given it. We decided to call them Alphans when we met. And, the name stuck even with them. Before that, they just referred to their species as what we interpreted to be "The People." They are rather diminutive in stature. The tallest male stands almost one hundred sixty-eight centimeters. But, they are gristly, fierce, and proud, with a culture heavily immersed in martial arts and military service. Though they're usually good-natured, you don't want to rub one the wrong way.

The system is very atypical. Its yellow star is a little dimmer and smaller than Sol. A very dusty, dirty and rocky ring revolves around it with three planets orbiting in close, hot trajectories. But Alpia circles in a nearly round orbit at a distance of one hundred thirty million kilometers making it a warm, green, water-rich world. It boasts many of the most exceptional recreational playgrounds in the entire Orion Federation.

So, I grant rotating leaves to all Zeta personnel over the next six days. Then, I head down with Fred and Bryant in tow. El schedules everyone's departures, so all get their fair share of time.

I've never visited this world so, I am shocked when we reach the recommended beach. Long sandy shorelines border a cool, clear lake. And, water rides, glides, and slides are available all along an extended section of the coast. Clumps of cozy, comfortable, furnished, and fully stocked cottages form small communities along the shore. By the time the dust settles, we end up with OFSA personnel as neighbors on either side of our bungalow.

Over the next four days, we get too much sun and fun and host four barbecues and parties open to all Zeta members. At each, I pull out all the stops. The Examiner, Inquisitor, and all the Tier Two and Three personal Chefs take turns working in groups at each one. The final one includes roasting a pig and three large prime ribs to go along with barbecued shrimp and lobster tail. At each, endless bars with alcoholic and soft refreshments from all over the Federation are open to all. In the end, it is one of the most memorable times we've ever experienced and requires a full day aboard the Examiner for recovery. I am glad it's still twenty-four hours until we leave. And, I'm happy it'll take a week to get to the skirmish. By then, everyone will be concentrating on their responsibilities and not distracted by the good times their remembering.

I wonder about Epsilon HQ. I'm sure George would have held the same kind of events on Rigil during their break. He and his COS Tahu Moahu are the masters of good times. They really know how to throw a party.

....

George, Marie, and Atina have taken a suite at the New Okeechobee Heavenly Haven, a sprawling three hundred fifty unit resort complex on the southwest shore of the expansive lake just north of where the New Mississipi River empties into it. Epsilon Command has contracted all the available space in it and six smaller hotels and cottage campuses within three kilometers on either side of Heavenly Haven. And, Moe has engaged the services of the Haven's restaurant to host eight barbecues over the next four days for all the Epsilon personnel.

The Bryant's apartment is situated almost in the middle of the edifice on the bottom floor with quick access to both the beaches and the expansive hotel patio. The six-room unit offers comfort and privacy. Tom Stevens and his wife of ten years, Anita are right next door. And, Moe and the Tier Two Commanders are on either side of Tom's and George's rooms. So, there'll be a lot of poker playing in the "quiet times" between scheduled events.

After checking on all the supper and dinner arrangements with Moe, Admiral Bryant and his family headed out for a day of hot sun and revitalizing water recreation. Between the outdoors' activities and the eight parties he'll host, George expects to be exhausted when he returns to the Valhalla in five days. But, there'll be time to rest before departure and during the trip to 15 Sagitta.

By the early morning of May 18, all of Epsilon Command had returned to their respective ships. Most people displayed at least a modest tan and seemed rested and happy. Orders were confirmed and reissued down the line. At nine hundred hours, the entire force jumped out.

Chapter 19 A Slight Hitch

Sunday, May 21, 2271

"Whether your having setbacks or not, the role of a leader is to display a winning attitude." **Colin Powell**

From their position on the bridge of the FSS Chicago, Vice Admiral Boets and Admiral Basi observe the Isesinis Cruiser as it re-enters standard space just outside the Eta Pegasus system and cruises at relatively high speed to an orbital position at the enemy homeworld. When the sensor station first reported the detection of a vortex termination and the formation of its threshold, Basi requested that the Navigation Station determine its origin. The Nav-Com informed him the flight launch point was most likely 15 Sagitta since it is the only inhabited stellar system on that trajectory. Both Flag Officers were convinced it was the ship they'd been advised was on the way carrying Kil Kos.

They tracked it carefully from their invisible perch, as it slowed and dropped into a synchronous path. By the transponder identification icons on the main screen, it looked like the Cruiser almost landed on top of the Resolute. An hour later, a shuttle departed for the planet. Both men believed it carried the Kil, though they couldn't be absolutely confident of that assumption.

"Let's get Sen-Com, Nav-Com, Weaps, Tac-Com, Communications' Com, and Intelligence into a meeting, right away," Basi ordered Boets.

The Vice Admiral moved from station to station ordering the various Commanders to the boardroom in twenty minutes. As they were being relieved by their substitutes, he directed his stewards to have sweet rolls and beverages in the room in a quarter-hour.

"Group!" An officer barked as the two Admirals entered the room. Everyone snapped to attention.

"Relax. Everyone make sure you have what you want. Then, please take a seat.' Basi said as he waved his right hand toward the buffet. Ten minutes were consumed as people rattled about acquiring their favorite snacks as the traded barbs and laughs.

'This is an informal meeting to discuss targeting. First, I want to know if we've identified all the government facilities?" Basi inquired.

"We've had sensors focused on three locations that appear to be planetary administration, sir." The young Lieutenant who is the First Shift Sen-Com answered.

135

"Intel, have we confirmed those locations?" Boets asked the young Marine Lieutenant.

"Yes, sir. We have designated them T-one, two, and three. Our operatives on the ground say the first is the ruling counsel's chambers. The second is the military headquarters. And the final one is the Emperor's complex including personal residence and offices."

"Tactical, I assume you have translated those into target coordinates. What about military bases and weapons and ship manufacturing facilities?"

"Yes, sir. All potential objectives have been mapped for weapons action. And, there are another two hundred fifty supporting bases, defensive platforms and production facilities on the list that have been confirmed by ISIE agents and plotted by Weaps. Those marks have been forwarded to the appropriate Frigate or Sub for bombardment."

"Intel, I'd like your ground personnel nearest the capital to locate and monitor Kil Kos. I have reason to believe he just landed on the surface, and I need to confirm his presence and know where he is when we execute our operation. I also need to be aware of any unusual troop movements on the ground." Basi ordered.

"Yes, sir." The Officer responded.

"Tactical, I need to be apprised of any changes out here in space over the next three day."

"Aye, sir. The Lieutenant Commander replied.

"All of you please make sure all departmental operations throughout our Fleet are aware of these critical points. And we still have three days, so let's make sure we have all the strategic objectives but don't accidentally hit a school or hospital. We're not trying to annihilate this enemy - just limit their ability to make war and draw their attention back to their homeworld.

Does anyone have any questions?' There were negative head wags all around. 'Finish your snack, but you're all dismissed!" Basi snapped, turned and headed out into the corridor followed by Boets.

....

This is the first time since adopting the new communications systems that George has needed to employ it to monitor sensor data while in FTL flight. The Comm station appears capable of continually shifting communications' clustered lasers from one relay to the next, smoothly. So, throughout the trip to the staging point near 15 Sagitta, there has been a constant stream of up-to-the-minute information. Connections between all other

136

Commands and the Valhalla are similarly steady and reliable. There have been some delays as distances from the Sub Strata Relays change, but they have been minimal. For the first time in his career, Admiral Bryant is able to conduct near-real-time operations, while traveling through outlying regions in FTL mode.

When they exit into open space a half parsec from their goal on May 25, George will spend the next half-day confirming all the intelligence they have on their opponents before completing a review and last-minute modifications of the plan.

....

Likewise, I am enjoying the ability to talk to my distant counterparts and receive outlying transducer information nearly instantly during my flight. It removes the doubts created by time lags. But, my thoughts drift from my tactical goals to one particular defensive worry. Five hundred and sixty-five vortices develop quite a disturbance. Space is very spongy, and a Minkowski spacetime essentially bends it by compressing a region while expanding another. And, the wormhole traveling through this bent expanse pushes against the void further squeezing space-time that is in contact with it. All this is perceived as changes in the ambient field strength within a section. Multiply that by a factor of nearly six hundred, and it is understandable that I'm concerned about detection by our antagonists.

....

My fears came to fruition when one of our covert vessels was captured near Mu Arae. This is a most multifaceted Sol-like system with six planets orbiting a star similar to ours. A century and a half ago, the fourth satellite was thought to be a Jupiter class one with a mass around half that of our most prominent gas giant. But, close visitation revealed it to be a super-Earth with five large moons. The planet and two of its companions support life.

There is an Isesinis Regional Command Center there. It is comprised of a GPHC accompanied by three hundred fifty Cruisers and five Carriers. That Base Station runs operations within a radius of nearly eight parsecs in all directions from Mu Arae.

The supply ship FSS Purveyor made a mistake when dropping one of the new communications relays there. The transceiver became visible during the operation making it apparent a ship was present. Though the Isesinis attempted to capture that vessel, they accidentally discovered and seized the Sub FSS Mysterious. The Purveyor escaped and used the newly planted and undiscovered transmitter to provide an instantaneous account of the incident.

We called an emergency Commission meeting and quickly developed a plan to either recover or destroy the apprehended Covert vessel. A flurry of orders were issued. All other offensive tactical operations were temporarily suspended.

....

By May 24, a majority of Zeta Command is relocated exactly a parsec from Epsilon Eridani between it and Luyten 726-8. A twelve-member squad of Epsilon's covert Frigates and two of Savign's packs are already at the target to provide cover during landing. We will launch at forty percent of luminal from here at seven hundred this morning and attack the Isesinis Epsilon Eridani contingent at fourteen hundred. The two covert operations will begin their assault ten minutes ahead of our reentry into normal space.

This strike is diversionary. It's designed to make a lot of noise and cover the main charge. George is scheduled to confront the forces at Mu Arae at sixteen hundred. The Zeta objective is the destruction of ten percent of our antagonists - then get the hell out.

Because of that, we will not activate any mines currently planted in or on the vessels in our focus. But, our lunge will be furious. We will form a hollow sphere surrounding all the enemy ships and fire in on them. We do not want to enlighten the Isesinis to our booby traps, and we need to take enough time to draw more forces towards this location. We are looking to accomplish our goal over about a two-hour period.

....

George looks out at his vast Armada currently placed at Gliese 676A. It is a small red dwarf that mothers four planets and is barely massive enough to facilitate fusion. It's uninhabited, and intelligence indicates that it is unused by the Isesinis. And, it is just three and a half light-years from Mu Arae. Though he can't see them all from this vantage point, Admiral Bryant can distinguish nearly half of the almost twelve hundred ships in his arsenal. Leaving a six hundred meter safety region around each craft means it takes up practically a cubic kilometer. This indicates his entire command uses over one thousand cubic kilometers for parking, plus the space required for Headquarters, Security, Hospital, and Supply ships. That places the most distant ones around six and a half kilometers from the Valhalla if it is in the center of either a cubical or spherical arrangement. Those are the standard parking patterns for flotillas parked in open space. Whichever formation is used, all vessels face out in a staggered configuration to endow the group with maximum protection against unwanted arrivals from any direction. This setup also allows all Carriers to launch Raptors without interfering with each other.

Since Epsilon is the primary assault body, it will employ mines. SOCC has prepared over half the enemy warships and the GPHC at this location. Booby trapping the Orbs involves three charges located in the central Hangar. A fusion cooling line and a magnetic conduit passing through the compartment each receive one. The third is planted on the hangar bay doors. Savign has provided Tom Stevens with detonation codes for this particular Polyhedron. He will trigger both the second and third units. The other would eventually lead to catastrophic failure. So, they will save that device until they've rescued the Mysterious or determined its recovery is impossible. Epsilon's objectives are to recover or destroy the Mysterious and annihilate all enemy vessels in this system so none can report on cloaking technology.

....

As we cross into the system, we are forcefully buffeted by the heliosphere which is exceptionally intense along this avenue of entry to Epsilon Eridani. It is unique because though it is a young star, one planet is inhabited. When we first entered this star's area a century ago, we found a peaceful space-faring society who called themselves the Teal. Tealians do not know how they got here. That information has been lost to history. But, their recorded chronicle indicates they've lived on this world for around six centuries and were technologically advanced when they arrived. Studies by paleontologists, geologists, anthropologists, and archeologist all point to a limited history. And, though their planet is green and blue and plentiful, they have been plagued by its very active mantle and tectonics, and a barrage of asteroids and comets during their tenancy. This is likely a result of Epsilon Eridani's youth. Our scientists believe it is just half a billion years since the sun ignited. It is a fast rotating and very active star. Despite that, Teal orbits its parent at a distance of almost exactly one hundred million kilometers giving it a warm but comfortable climate ideal for vegetation. And its relatively dense ozone layer protects it from the radiation created by all the solar activity and this world's proximity to it.

As we close the distance to the planet, I see the extensive enemy formation is trying to defend itself against a constant onslaught from an unseen and moving opponent. The twenty-six covert units are wreaking havoc without out aid. But, we swoop in from above ferociously firing all batteries and launching Raptors at a breakneck pace. The space around the Isesinis is filled with buzzing hornets within minutes of our appearance.

All subordinate commands are conducting their missions as anticipated but I ask the Tier 2-1 leadership to order a Fleet to concentrate on a group of vessels on the perimeter of the Isesinis flotilla to its western flank, on the side facing our galaxy. Then, I ask SOCC to detonate those mines under cover of our withering fire. There is a brief lag as the subs determine which mines are in that region. Then, there is a series of fusion eruptions that appear to be the result of our blitz. I repeat the same process but on the rim opposite the previous deluge. Twenty enemy Cruisers and a Carrier are destroyed in less than ten minutes with no casualties on our side. There is panic amongst our opponents. They are staggered by the realization we seem much more formidable - and considerably sturdier than in our initial encounters.

Following the original plan, and without additional new orders, our Fleets heap more and more havoc. An hour after entering Epsilon Eridani, we have destroyed fifty-two and disabled or severely damaged another nineteen without loss to our contingent. But, I am now getting reports from remote SOCC units and Suvayeek surveillance that enemy fleets within six parsecs are launching towards us. I advise George who is in route and almost at his target. He suggests we've done enough and should get the hell out of here. I agree and send out the appropriate orders.

While our unseen forces maintain their merciless attack, our overt units set course and leap back to our staging point. After meeting up with the rest of our outfit, we all jump back to Wolf 359. One Frigate and fifteen Zeta Raptors had been destroyed. I estimated our loss at around eleven hundred people.

....

Epsilon's approach to Mu Arae is handled in the same manner. Concealed forces fire ceaselessly on the already crippled opponent. Mines have been detonated throughout their formation including the one that blew the doors off the giant Base Station's large lower hangar deck and another that interrupted ion flow to its reactors and engines. The GPHC is running on auxiliary power without weapons or engines.

Because of the Isesinis' continuing mayhem, George's ample convoy is almost unnoticed as a portion bears down on the array's western edge and another contingent attacks upwards from the same side. All the way in, they lay down a barrage of mixed ammo as they launch Raptors by the hundreds every minute. But, the orders require all his vessels to avoid firing on the disabled Orb.

OFSA Frigates are much larger than Isesinis Cruisers, so the FSS Tokyo barely fits through the Polyhedron Hangar doorway on its way to rescue the FSS Mysterious. Admiral Bryant had decided to use this class because the Sub may need to be towed and another sub would labor under such a load. All the way in, the Tokyo hails the Mysterious offering identification codes. And it finally locates the captured ship by using positron beams. They

140

are bounced off it like radar despite its cloak which was still active. The Tokyo responds on the tenth summons. They had been a week in the bay without penetration by their antagonists who never did gain entry.

A few minutes discussion determines she is space worthy and able to leave under power. The Tokyo advised it would escort the Mysterious to the Epsilon staging area. Both would travel in covert mode. Mysterious would follow Tokyo's transponder signal.

Meanwhile, the battle outside persisted. The remaining functional enemy vessels waged a fierce defense. But, they had suffered overwhelming losses at the beginning of the encounter and were outnumbered nearly four to one, now.

As the Mysterious cleared the hatchway, the Tokyo advised the Fleet of their departure and the previously ignored GPHC became a target. As all Epsilon ships backed away from it, the last mine was detonated while anti-matter torpedoes were fired into its expansive opened doorway. It pulsed and flashed angrily. Then, it erupted in a fusion flare that sent more than fifty of its escorts to hell with it.

After that, things went a lot easier. Every passing minute saw the destruction of another Isesinis ship. But, the effort was not without sacrifice. Six hours into the battle, Epsilon Commands were reporting the loss of four Carriers, six Cruisers, fifteen Frigates and one hundred ninety-six fighters and their pilots. George estimated quickly in his head that they'd lost nearly forty-six thousand personnel. It was quite a price to pay to recover a single ship. But, the intelligence reversal caused by its loss would have been profound.

....

We were debriefed in a Commission Meeting on Monday, June 5, 2271. The losses we sustained were severe enough to hold off on any offensive actions for a while. Eleven of George's Fleets are affected in one way or another, as is one of mine. We need to replace the demolished vessels and slain people. And, we'd want to train with all the new elements in place before attempting anything major confrontation. We set the end of October as a potential launch period for our plan.

In the meantime, we also directed the Theatre Commander to reprimand the Captain of the Purveyor. His ship managed to turn a simple task into a near disaster. And, they put the nearly five hundred aboard the Mysterious at significant risk.

But, the Captain of the Mysterious was to be awarded a commendation and promotion. She'd made it impossible for the enemy to gain entry to the sub for over a week and managed to save her crew. She displayed a stubborn defiance that could be a great asset in the future.

Things went back to the routine we knew before the abduction. We ran our particular patrol missions while we restored lost hardware and people. We trained together to integrate our affected Fleet. But, Epsilon required much more extensive replenishment and exercises to bring it up to a full fighting complement.

In the meantime, we dealt with the sporadic Isesinis lunges at our boundaries.

....

I closed the application I was using to prepare my annual report. There'd still be another couple of months to edit it. But, I now have the basis for the year's chronicles. It's much too long. I'll have to revise it. But, it's always best to include everything in the first draft - though the sixty thousand words will have to be taken down to around ten - including the balance of the period.

The exercise also serves two purposes that are much more personal. It allows me to refresh my memory. We've been so busy that some incidents become blurry - as if they'd happened several decades ago. And, it helps me in the construction of my journal which I may put in print someday.

Part Two

Chapter 20 Shock, Evaluation, Judgement

Wednesday, October 4, 2271

"A lot of my work is a matter of reacting to surprises." **Alexander Wang**

Sparks and Svesion appeared at my office door this morning - unannounced. They'd arrived at a conclusion that required my attention, immediately.

"This must be remarkable. You two have never landed here without notifying me or requesting an appointment. Grab something from the bar and let's sit and talk about whatever this world-shattering news is." I said with a chuckle as I waved a hand to the buffet with its assortment of beverages and treats. Five minutes elapsed as we all selected our preferences and took a seat in the conversation pit.

"Sir, may I use your projector?" Sparks queries.

"Of course. Help yourself."

Chris powered everything and adjusted settings. Then, he lowered the lights and clicked an icon on his datapad screen. The area of space above this end of my office was filled with three-dimensional holographic images of stars and planets.

"The first reports we received were from the Suvayeek. Their accounts had the enemy completely abandoning their regional command at Chi Draconis. According to our friends, they sent the Station and all its support to join the array at 15 Sagitta.

I was concerned so I contacted SOCC who verified the observation. Then, I transmitted a request to our agents on the surface of our member planet there. They confirmed that all enemy ground forces had suddenly vanished.

The next report came from 70 Opiuchi and turned out to be primarily the same. All the hardware detached from there joined the Regional Command at 51 Pegasus. Again, I verified everything including the removal of landed soldiers.

That was yesterday. And by the end of the day, twenty systems had been cleared, and all their equipment and people moved elsewhere.

So far today, another ten reports of emptied systems have come in. And, in each case, the forces are redeployed elsewhere.

It appears they are fortifying a section from RA twenty hours up to seven hours and abandoning the other one hundred ninety-five degrees of our space. And they are only controlling as far in as three parsecs from Rigil. That's nearly sixty percent of Orion Federation Space!"

"I'm not sure we should be elated. There may be a method to their madness. Please remain here while I arrange a Commission Meeting. We will probably want your attendance." I said as I tapped out a message to my peers.

MEMO

From: F. Admiral K Brubacher C&C Zeta HQ Commander

To: All C&C Commission Members

Re: Changes in enemy deployments

Date: October 4, 2271

All,

I have received confirmed reports of enemy redeployments. These involve the abandonment of a vast region of Orion Federation territory and reinforcement of those areas still occupied by the reorganized forces. I would like to suggest an immediate meeting of the Commission. I will be accompanied by my Marine Army Commander and Deputy since their people received and verified the information.

Admiral Kurt Brubacher

Thank goodness for the new system. I had responses from all within half an hour. It would take us eighteen hours to complete the eight and a half light-year journey at forty percent of superluminal in FTL mode.

"Pack your bags, gentlemen. Plan for four days. It'll be eighteen hours each way, and we'll probably need a couple of days to determine a course of action!' I snapped off the order. 'I'll meet you at docking port four. My Admiral's Craft is parked there." I added.

"Aye, sir." The two Generals harmonized as they snapped to attention, saluted, turned, and exited the room.

....

"Please relax while you're aboard. There'll be no protocol unless there's crew present. You can come and go as you please. Sleep if you want. You can eat or drink in the recreation area. You can also work here. The lounge and seating area have full access to the complete Zeta information system. But, try to enjoy yourselves on both trips." I explained.

"Thank you, sir. We'll follow your rules." Svesion responded with a smile and a mock-salute.

We all decided to have a drink and order some lunch.

145

"Admiral, you seemed reticent about the information we presented to you. May I ask why?" Sparks queried.

"I have no doubts about the data. Your accounts are always accurate and the sources unreproachable. I won't elaborate, yet. But it's the Kil's motives I'm questioning."

"You think he might be luring us into a trap?" Svesion questioned.

"Not really. It's such a big area it would be easy to escape it anyway. I'd rather discuss it with the Commission, first. Sometimes, I'm a little paranoid. Let it rest, for now."

"Yes, sir. But, regardless of intentions, it's a positive turn. What I mean is that if Kil Kos is changing anything, it's because we're having an effect on him." Svesion observes.

"Yes, that's true, I guess." I responded as the steward served Gamay to Sparks and me and a "Neat" Scotch to Svesion.

"What's on today's menu for lunch?" I asked Dave Angstrom.

"The chef's offering a six-ounce New York cut, a grilled pork chop or a pastrami on rye with your choice of sides. Beef vegetable soup or a salad are available. He also has fresh Chiabata rolls - both regular and gluten-free."

Svesion selected the pastrami sandwich with the vegetable soup. Chris Sparks chose the pork chop with a side of roast potatoes and another of mixed vegetables. I ordered the New York - medium rare with roast potatoes and the garden salad. Both Sparks and I requested a bun.

We chatted about baseball until the food arrived. Once they dug in, neither General seemed interested in talking until their plates were empty.

"Boy, can this guy ever cook!" Svesion mumbled appreciatively.

"Wait until you have dinner.' I smirked. 'You should let him know how much you liked your lunch."

"I will."

"Me too.' Sparks added. 'Mine was incredible, too."

We reopened the baseball discussion. The sport had become more prevalent with all the Commands so close together over the past couple of years. Someone was always near enough to suggest or accept a challenge.

"We should also initiate hockey teams and tournaments," Sparks commented after we'd indulged ourselves in a half-hour discussion of hardball.

"I've thought about it. I love the game. I played a lot in Minnesota when I was younger.' I responded. 'I just don't see how we'd be able to do temporary ice as easily as we do a ballpark."

146

"No problem. It used to be done all the time."

"What do you mean?" I inquired.

"Back in the day, the old NHL would hold exhibition games in unusual venues and at outdoor parks. They developed portable rinks for the purpose. You set it up. Turn on the refer-unit. Then, you add two and a half inches of water. You top that with lines and your emblem. Then, you enhance it all with a half-inch of additional ice and viola - instant hockey rink. Sections of the floor including cooling tubing snap together. The Compressors go off to the side in a different room to reduce noise levels. Hoses link the two. The coolant is a brine solution that comes in barrels. Five hundred liters does the job. You could set the whole thing up for a few days skating and shinny. Then select teams. As far as equipment goes, it's sold on Earth. It's a popular game there, again. But, most groups went back to the rules of the very early twenty-first century. There's a collective feeling today that the pros tried to make it too much like basketball from 2005 on. It pretty much died during the apocalypse. But, if things had continued, there'd probably have been jump-pucks instead of faceoffs." Sparks sniggered.

"We have a sizeable chunk left over in our entertainment budget, every year. Maybe I'll invest in the rink and personal equipment. We can have intra-Zeta teams, for now. Maybe later, we'll be able to do inter-OFSA tournaments.' I speculate. 'By the way, there's a gym down the hall on your right if you need to work off your lunch." I directed, though no one seemed interested.

We yakked for another half-hour before I excused myself to begin some work. The others got their pads out and did the same. At seventeen hours thirty minutes, I suggested we grab another drink and some dinner. They were just as impressed with that menu and the food. Afterward, we enjoyed several hands of poker. No Sovereigns actually changed hands. We played for chips that had virtual values, only. But, it was a lot of fun.

....

"Come on, let's get this show on the road!' Grace called out over the din as she whacked her gavel on the sound block. 'This meeting is called to order!' She barked and hammered again. 'This is a special meeting to discuss recent changes in our occupied territories.' She added in a quieter tone reflecting the lower noise level in the room. 'Admiral Brubacher has a presentation for us.

It took an hour for Sparks and Svesion to outline the presentation and discuss its implications.

"My feelings are mixed about this," I concluded.

147

"You think it's a trap?" Marshal Malcolm queried.

"Not really a trap." Before I actually finished, George cut me off.

"An offering. Peace at the cost of nearly half the Federation. And, if we accept it, we'll spread out to manage our widened territory and be unable to recover the rest without a massive expansion. But, whatever we do, it means Kil Kos realized he can't hold it all. He's hoping we'll accept it."

"Maybe we should. Everyone's pretty tired of continuous war." Fleet Admiral Addison Blythe observes.

"No Fucking way!' Tso Shah blurted. 'Excuse me. I apologize for my outburst and my profanity within this venue. But, that'd be like rewarding a thief by letting him keep half the booty if he doesn't do it again."

"One of these days I'm going to propose we start a swear jar. We'd be able to throw a big annual binge with the proceeds." Grace's tone was tongue-in-cheek.

"What the hell is a swear jar?" Savign queried.

"You put a Sovereign in each time you cuss,' Shah answered. 'But, I could just swear in Navajo." He added with a laugh.

"We'd have to ding you every time you spoke your native tongue, then.' I observed. 'But, I agree with Admiral Shah. Declaring peace is not the answer - yet. I think we execute our original plan. But we need to change it to adapt to the strength at 82 Eridani. And, I presume the same is true at 15 Sagitta. But, we don't have reports on it, yet. Those two locations and our diversionary target are still relevant. We just have to change our proposal to deal with enemy potency at those places."

"I concur. If we hit the Isesinis as soon as we can, they'll realize we'll never give up. They may pick up and leave, after another encounter - if it hurts them enough." George expounded.

In the end, we decided we'd employ the same force at Eta Pegasi since nothing really changed there. But, we'd redouble our mining operations at the other two positions and ask both the Spiel and the Polemista to join us again. Steven Nichols agreed to split his Command for use at the two regional sites. That leaves Beta and Delta Commands to patrol our little corridor. And, we won't try to maintain the regions that were recently abandoned by the Isesinis. We'll concentrate on pushing them right out of the Federation and limiting their future ability to wage war on us.

So, by the end of the meeting, the ball was in George's court once again. It was up to him to modify the plan to fit current needs. And, it fell to me to discuss it with our two allies.

....

We all stopped outside the room when the session ended to just pass the time.

"So what's Zeta Command up to these days?" George inquired when we finally got together for a moment.

"Well, we enjoy baseball, still. But, we've been bouncing around the idea of starting up a hockey league - first intra-Command - then, inter-OFSA. Are you interested?" I asked.

"I love the game. I played a lot of it when I was younger. But, I haven't been on skates in years. And, I rolled the idea around and couldn't figure out how you'd put a rink in a Carrier."George observed inquiringly.

"No problem. You buy a portable rink. A company up north in what was Canada called Cold Fusion sells them. They specialize in all sorts of temporary sports venue set-ups for special events. I contacted them. They'd supply everything. But, we already have seating and bleachers. A single regulation-sized ice sheet - complete with boards, compressors, and cooling lines - is just under a hundred thousand Sovereigns. They only ask for a visit to teach us the setup. And, I found a wholesaler that can supply three makes of all the different sports equipment including skates. So, I figure we buy the unit and sell the gear to the players. That'll help keep it sanitary. I'm going to set-up skating sessions, first. Then, we'll add shinny to the menu. After that, we'll do organized hockey. It'll take about the same space as baseball does when it's in storage. And, I can have the Quartermaster issue the equipment on a payroll deduction basis - no profit - just recover the funds spent." I explained.

"Well, it's been so long, and I am getting older. I think I'd take up the skating again. But, I'd probably be smarter to coach or referee. But, I'm in. You get the first one done and work out the kinks. I'll come and visit. We'll go for a skate, and you can teach me how it's done."

"I think we could all have a lot of fun with this. And, it's another outlet for everyone. Our troops need and deserve it.

Should we go down for a drink?"

"Yeah. Let's head to the pub."

We proceeded down to the bar accompanied by each entourage.

....

"That was some experience." Svesion observed when we were back aboard my personal craft.

"Yes. And, I could see where all the orders come from. They are always small parts of a much larger plan." Sparks added appreciatively.

"Yes, that's true. But, now that you're privy to the general strategy, you must remember that you can't discuss it outside this group. I will end up describing our limited role with my Tier Commands. They will explain it in more constrained terms to their subordinates and so on down the line. Each Command only receives information on the part of the strategy directly related to their objectives. They are asked to produce a plan of how they'd meet those goals. They submit it to their superiors who edit and modify them, then assemble the pieces into a Theatre-wide plan. Those Admirals will send it to their Tier 2 leaders who may also adapt it. They construct a plan for their entire operation. The two Tier Two Commanders then tender to me. I also make amendments. Then, I present it to George as do all the other Headquarters. He examines all those pieces and constructs a tactical field plan and proposes that to the Commission for approval. Once it's ratified, we're all sent copies. Then, I generate orders to one level below, and they do the same to their subordinates and so on down the line until orders reach each individual Command, installation, and ship.

Our plans are very detailed. Besides including what tactics we'll use to meet our requirements, they spell out how we'll execute resupply, what our rules of engagement are, and how we intend to withdraw from the battlefield safely. They even set the numbers for what ratio of our force will be active or reserve and how and when these standby Fleets will be used. And, they determine our limitations, like whether or not we are to take prisoners. The next session will be much longer. We'll go through that entire scenario, discuss it, and vote on it." I finished

"Wow. It sounds complicated. I did not realize these major battles are so choreographed." Svesion declares.

"It's complicated. But, only because no one knows or considers everything, and no battle ever goes exactly as imagined. Requests go all the way down the line. Suggestions and plans come all the way back up the ladder. Then, orders go all the way back down. And, we have a lot of useful simulation tools. They help us determine if a plan genuinely makes sense. And, though it's very detailed, no one can predict all the little nuances like an individual enemy ship Captain's response to an action. So, there is a certain amount of flexibility that allows independent responses. Our scenarios mostly determine the gross movements all the way down to and including the Fleet level. From there all the way to single ship Commands, there is more flexibility at each stage. They are still required to meet the objectives - and they know their limitations - but are allowed to respond to changing circumstances. Let's order some lunch."

....

"I noticed how new the Rigil HQ looks. Do they always keep it that way?" Sparks asked after swallowing a mouthful of the seabass he'd ordered.

"Not always. It ages and deteriorates like anything else. Everything is refinished, resurfaced or replaced about every five years. But, it needed major repairs after the Isesinis occupation. They did a lot of damage. The refurbishment took about four months. But, it was like giving it a complete facelift. Even the OFSA badges and Orion Federation Flags and Emblems are new." I explained.

"Well, it sure looks good, now!" Svesion's comment was followed by complete silence as we all dove back into our meals.

Chapter 21 Preparations and Practice

October 25, 2271

"To be prepared for war is one of the most effective means of preserving peace."

George Washington

I'm working diligently on my battle plan. Two weeks ago, I had my Tier-Two Admirals in, gave them each an outline including objectives, and they prepared their Command-specific ones and sent them down the line. Mine was based on an overall plan from George that included employing two Gamma Theatres, Spiel, and Polemista Commands. A week ago their updates informed me the plans were on the way back up the Chain of Command. My two subordinates were working at combining the proposals of their secondary operations to present their homogenized versions to me.

Now, I have both those tenders, and I am working on editing and combining them into the Zeta combat doctrine while attempting to maintain its suitability in Admiral Bryant's original creation. Every level's proposal is included in its parent authority's composition. This provides additional depth and understanding but has made it a nine hundred page document before my revisions and amendments. I have my first rough draft which incorporates six alternate possibilities based on Isesinis responses. I need to run the simulations before finalizing it. I click an icon on my datapad.

"Hello!" Fred's pleasant voice says as her stunning face appears on my screen.

"Hi, Baby. Will you and Bryant be okay if I don't make it home for dinner? I think I'll be in the office until near midnight."

"We'll be okay. But, we'll really miss you. And, what about saying goodnight to Bryant?" She asked.

"Would you like to bring him up here? I could break for a quick dinner. Then, I'd go on when you two leave. He loves to see the ship and my work."

"Sure. What time?"

"How about five-thirty?"

"Sounds great. We'll be there."

"Can you let Ed know. I'll advise Dave Angstrom. What would you like?"

"Let's have a picnic?"

"Okay. I'll tell Dave fried chicken, potato salad, and cole slaw. I'll see you at seventeen-thirty."

"We'll be there." She said with a big smile as she disconnected.

I informed Dave and told him I wanted it served picnic-style - on a big beach blanket - on the floor. He actually seemed excited at the thought.

....

By the time they arrived, my simulations of the rough draft were programmed into the system and were moving holographs playing out in the air over the picnic lunch. Bryant was exuberant and mesmerized. He must have asked a hundred questions about the battle and how the simulations and plans are assembled. It turned into the dominant topic as we enjoyed our dinner. Even Fredricka enjoyed the entire presentation. She'd never seen how this part of my job is done.

"But, you know war is not a good thing, don't you son? People get hurt, killed, and displaced by it. And the money we spend on it and on protecting our space could probably feed an entire world."

"Yes, I understand. But the simolations are neat - kinda like a video game.' He struggled with the one word. 'Boy, you sure have a lot of work to do, Dad." Bryant reflected aloud as he admired the moving images.

"This is not all my work. Nearly six hundred people have contributed to this. But, it is my job to tell them what I need to get done and how I'd like to do it. When they come back with all their ideas, I build a final plan like this. But, it's not finished, yet. That's why I have to work late.

These projections are called *simulations*.' I emphasized the pronunciation. 'They *are* like giant video games that allow me to see how the whole idea works. I can see some problems in parts of it. So, I have to find ways to improve it and run the entire recreation again. I keep doing that until our plan becomes the best one I can create. I have to get it to your Uncle George, tonight. He needs a couple of days to include it with his plans."

"Gee dad. You guys are really smart. I think I'd like to do what you do when I grow up."

"If that's what you still want then, that's great. But, you may want to do something else by the time you're bigger. And, that's okay too - just as long as you try your best at whatever you do."

"Don't worry, dad. I'll be the best Admiral ever."

....

I spent until one o'clock in the morning modifying the entire proposition to a satisfactory state. By that, I mean it's my job to develop a scenario that's going to give us the biggest pop for our Sovereign with the least probable losses.

In the end, it didn't look much like what we'd developed when we were looking at executing in May. Our opponents withdrawal and redeployment changed everything. 82 Eridani now had three times the enemy strength we saw there back then. It required making the best use of all assets under my direction. Pre-assault mining, seven hundred sixty-eight of our warships, two hundred fifty-six Polemista Frigates, twelve Epsilon covert Frigates, and fourteen SOCC subs had to be coordinated in the most efficient possible manner to deal with the nearly thirteen hundred enemy vessels and three giant orbs. The latest edition included surprise, deception, and exploiting Isesinis tactical deficiencies.

An hour later, I was satisfied with the final version after running it through our editing application. The Zeta plan was nearly two hundred fifty pages including charts with an additional six hundred of lower echelon details and supporting documents. I e-mailed it all to George with the final sims and a suggestion to the timing of the overall operation. Then, I sent a memo to Roh and Elasima explaining my late hour, advising I wouldn't be at my desk until thirteen hundred, today, and copying the proposal to them. I will need their assistance. Both know their jobs well. And they'll ensure the daily orders and duty rosters are managed correctly.

....

I feel a lot better today as I take my place in my office. Despite my late start, yesterday, I felt hungover the entire day. The previous night's marathon had sapped me. I guess I'm unable to do the all-nighters' anymore without paying a price. As I power up the datapad, it indicates dozens of incoming mail items, but I am especially interested in the one from George. It requires decryption, so I'm sure it's a response to the submission I sent him thirty hours ago.

MEMO
CLASSIFIED - SECRET (NTK)
ENCRYPTED - *Authentication Root I.D. Eps-11571#W739/?*

From: F. Admiral G. Bryant C&C / Epsilon HQ Commander

To: F. Admiral K. Brubacher C&C Zeta HQ / Commander

C.C. C&C Commission Members, CIC, SOD

Re: Pending Operations

Date: October 28, 2271

Admiral,

You will find specific orders attached pertaining to our upcoming operations. I have also included the approved version of your general battle plan. There has only been one change to your proposal, and it is based on your suggestion regarding the timing of the overall assault. In this version, you will confront the enemy one hour earlier than previously discussed. Likewise, Epsilon will begin one hour later. The diversionary team will start two hours before you.

Regards,

Flt. Adm. G. Bryant

Over the next hour and a half, I see that copies of all the other endorsements are landing in my mailbox. These include defensive redeployments within our recaptured area and two feints that are planned to confuse our opponents.

Based on the approval, we have limited time to practice, so I quickly set about releasing orders to my subsidiaries. They were prepared in anticipation of the authorization and include directives relating to practice and war games. There is a set of instructions for each of my Tier 2 Commanders, and the Tier Two operation borrowed from Gamma Command. However, I'm careful to inspect all my documents because they were done on the day I was feeling so dull.

All the way down the chain, Commanding Officers would complete the same procedure. So, when my Tier Two Admirals receive their mandates, they will pass their directives to the Theatres, and so-on down the line. Since it is standard for everyone in the chain to copy me on any instructions regarding an operation originating at my level, I begin receiving copious amounts of mail. In the end, I monitor over a thousand communiqués associated with the campaign or its preparations.

Starting the next morning, I travel to a different Command's Headquarter's every day tracking their training measures. At first, they are conducted by each individual Theatre Command. Then, they are run in combination at the Tier Two level. After two weeks, El and I alternate supervision of "all-Zeta" rehearsals. Finally, we run all versions of the plan with a significant portion of Delta Command standing in as our opponents. But, Fleet Admiral Addison Blythe throws a little kink in our exercises. She comes up with responses we hadn't considered. I ponder them and amend my documents and orders. Then, I copy George explaining the reasoning, and he quickly forwards a modified master document and all the necessary approvals with his thanks to Addison for " a good catch."

So now, there are eight forms the Zeta assault may end up taking, depending on what we find at the moment of contact and the Isesinis response to our blitz. We continue practicing all of them. The intent is to see the enemy reaction and identify which alternative is required, immediately. Our attack must be flexible and reflexive, at all times. As a final test, Addison first counters with one method, then quickly changes to a different one. We do this several times to improve our effectiveness and hone our skills. By November 10, I'm satisfied. We're ready.

But, on that day, I receive a memo sent to George and me by Savign asking us to review the most current surveillance of our targets, carefully. I ask Svesion and Sparks to attend me with the appropriate files. What I view reinforces my belief in both Kil Kos' wily tactical skills and the security of our covert operations. He has altered the configuration of standing Regional Headquarters' Fleets. They are now within three-disc formations. The orbs are located at the hub of a central one. The other two contingents are positioned above and below the one holding the Polyhedrons.

It's evident from this that he has identified his troops' inability to think three-dimensionally and has adopted this scheme to compensate. It's also apparent, he's still not aware of SOCC mining operations. Kos has not realized that a great deal of our success has come from neutralizing a substantial portion of his flotillas before a shot is even fired. But, this does require a change in our initial approach. We've always entered the fields from above and below at one end with limited support around their perimeter provided by SOCC. We will need to emphasize the use of both our covert support units on the middle disc. And, we will need to ensure a majority of Isesinis' vessels are boobytrapped. I alter our plans and forward them to George suggesting a two-week delay in launch date for training. He approves.

I reencode my sims with the new parameters. I still end up with eight possible avenues that are very similar but vary with different responses from the protective enemy layers. I reschedule practice and war games. Delta employs the new enemy layout in their opposing role. By November 24, we're ready. George, Savign and I agree the big day will fall between December 10 and December 15. We will all grant leaves. Then, we'll conduct two more days of rehearsal and decide the precise date.

....

For their part, Boets' and Basi's roles haven't changed. And, they haven't had time to get bored. The constant delays have provided an interval to mine each and every warship, orbiting shipyard, and communications platform circling this world. And, they've been able to identify more ground targets which have either been penetrated by covert ground forces or entered into their ships' weapons targeting computers. They have also had time to receive Admiral Savign's approval of changes to their assault operation. They will now conduct four waves of bombardment, targeting three hundred and twenty surface installations.

Their combined operation is actually quite simple. On whatever date E-day happens, they will detonate all space-borne enemy assets at three hundred hours fifty minutes. By four hundred, they will be aware of all the speeding shrapnels' trajectories and will adjust accordingly. The order to fire the first wave of Spears and particle cannons will come at one minute after the hour. Bombardment will continue for one hour. It will be stopped for a two-hour period of resupply and damage assessment. Then it will resume for another hour. This will be repeated until all three hundred twenty sites have been hit. The final volley should be complete by fourteen hundred hours. They will take thorough sensor and imaging scans of the planet over the subsequent hour. After mission completion, the combined Command will reorganize and jump out as Isesinis support begins arriving.

....

On Saturday, December 2, 2271, we are so close to our staging launch that it is time to take all the exceptional internal actions we've secretly discussed. Though unsure of the innocence or guilt of all the parties mentioned, it's time to act on information that arose as a matter of course in reports from General Naabaahi's mission. In most cases, he was unaware these contact lists and journals involved names of people within the OFSA. He did not know if they were actually communicating with the Admiral. But, he included them because they originated with Chan.

Sparks had ordered ISIE to locate and initiate surveillance of all those people over six months ago. Some were clearly working for the traitor. Others were questionable. And, there was a group Sparks was sure had no knowledge of Chan's interest in them. But, in an abundance of caution, Sparks sought and received warrants for the arrest of all two hundred twenty-one on suspicion of espionage. One hundred ninety-three were Officers and Enlisted personnel within the OFSA. All were arrested today.

Each person would be thoroughly investigated and undergo grueling interrogations. Sparks knew he would drop charges in about a third of the cases. But, they would all be held until all Epsilon and Zeta Fleets had returned from the mission. There'd be no pipeline to Kos regarding this operation.

....

Admiral Nichols looks out over his reduced Armada contemplating the approaching maneuvers. It's a smaller formation because he's loaned one complete Tier Two Command

157

to Fleet Admiral Brubacher of Zeta HQ. His Headquarters is currently parked at Lalande 21185, a faint red dwarf just over eight light-years from Earth. And, his remaining two hundred fifty-six massive warships are still an impressive enough force to draw attention if they make a move. Which is what George Bryant is counting on.

Stephen had recalled them all from patrol duty to reconfigure in an assault arrangement by six hundred hours December 1, 2271. They'd been conducting drills to attack an Isesinis force of two hundred and thirteen Cruisers and Carriers. Addison Blyth had loaned Steven a part of Beta operations to play their foils in the rehearsals.

Several times Steven instructed his outfits to conduct a short jump as if practicing unified execution of an attack launch. And, every time the heading was as if leaving for Chi Orionis.

....

Similarly, Fleet Admiral Shah is conducting training at Barnards, where he has three full Theatre Commands staged in a strike configuration. Another portion of Blythe's flotilla is assisting Delta in their preparations. And, like Nichols, Tso has his people opening conduits and leaping in the direction of 107 Pisces repeatedly. There is a formation of two hundred eighty-four Isesinis ships at that system.

....

Zeta Command has all returned to 61 Virgo, now. It's twelve hundred hours on Tuesday, December 5, and I am in my office just closing off things so I can head out for lunch when my system annunciator sounds off. I receive up to a thousand e-mails a day, but with the pending actions, I feel I should check before my departure. It's from George.

TACTICAL ACTION MESSAGE #CC-CTO-0013435

CLASSIFIED - TOP SECRET (NTK)

ENCRYPTED - Authentication Root I.D. EPS-8467A+649*^

From: F. Admiral G. T. Bryant C&C Chief of Tactical Operations

To: All Field Deployed Headquarters Commands

C.C.   F. Admiral G. Tonaka C&C Rigil HQ Chief of Operations

Re: Mission # CC - 34612-C

Date: December 5, 2271

Admirals,

You are ordered and required to commence all operations included in the above action with the intent of launching the first phase for contact on December 14, 2271, at four hundred hours. All other subsequent engagements should be scheduled for launch and execution based on timing indicated in the above-listed Mission Plan number and bearing the above date and time in mind.

F. Adm. G.T. Bryant

As I released my own TAMs to my subordinates, I could hear my system as it repeatedly announced incoming copies of orders being sent throughout the entire OFSA. The alarms continued over the next several hours as the chain reaction spread all the way down to Supply Ships and Mobile Hospital units.

Since this had the potential to be one of the most intense fights we'd ever experienced, I left everything running and locked-up my office as I headed home to speak with Fred and Bryant at sixteen hundred hours, thirty minutes. I am sure other HQ Commanders would be doing the same.

"How's my beautiful wife and wonderful son doing, today?" I beamed my widest smile to them as I entered our apartment.

"What's up?' She asked inquisitively. 'You never come in like this."

"We're executing that big operation. I need you both to leave on my Admiral's Craft. I'm ordering all Commands to do the same. You'll all form a Fleet here at Wolf. You'll have five Frigates for protection and a supply ship to keep everyone fed until we return."

"Is that really necessary. You've never done that before." Fred whined.

"Yeah, I don't want to leave you, dad." Bryant whimpered.

"It's just a precaution. This will be a big one. And, it could get very intensive. Even the Examiner could end up involved, somehow. So, I don't want to risk you two. In fact, I don't want to endanger any of the innocents aboard our operations. The eight Admirals' ships can take over six hundred and their five Frigate security flotillas will handle the rest. And each Fleet Commander's yacht will be there, too. I don't want to have to worry about anyone but the troops." I explained.

"What time do we disembark?"

"Our launch time is very early. So, I think you should pack and be off the Examiner by twenty-one hundred, tonight. That's what I've asked everyone to do."

"Can we at least all have dinner together?"

"Yes, of course. But, let's go out to the pub. We can have some fun, too. But, I have to be back at my desk by seven-thirty. I'll break away again to see you guys off."

Chapter 22 Kick-Off

Wednesday, December 6, 2271

"The secret of getting ahead is getting started." **Mark Twain**

George's plan was full of devious deceptions. Epsilon and Zeta would launch, first, because each had to travel for seven days. Then, Nichols and Blythe would head out the following morning, since their trajectories were four days flight-time.

Admiral Bryant is satisfied as he turns from the view window to return to his Command Centre and strap himself in for the jump. He's just watched his nearly one thousand vessels execute the FTL leap from Sol in perfect orientation. At one hundred in the morning, he's a little dumpy feeling, but very satisfied they're headed toward Gliese 777 in Cygnus. An hour into the trip George feels the ship begin to speed up. It will do this portion of the journey at forty percent of "C." He heads off to his empty quarters to get some sleep though he's always restless when Marie and Atina are gone.

....

I was much more relaxed than on previous missions by the time Zeta launched into their conduits at nine hundred on December 6 at twenty percent velocity. Our trajectory was BD-05 1123 a binary system with a medium sized enemy contingent in Eridani. The Examiner and its security squad were the last to leave so I could observe the others. Their synchronization was near-perfect.

After an hour, I could feel the effects of inertia as the vessel accelerated from twenty to forty percent of superliminal inside its vortex.

....

Kil Kos receives his first intelligence report on Thursday afternoon that includes the two large Federation lunges. Based on the trajectory and the departure times velocities of the two Fleets he decides to wait a day to see what's happening. He has forces close enough to both projected destinations to land on time even if he makes the decision tomorrow. These may only be feints or diversions.

....

Admiral Steven Nichols verbally orders the execution of his forces' leaps at six hundred hours on Friday, December 8, 2271. The nearly three hundred vessels ramp-up to forty-percent of light-speed as they're approaching and entering their vortices at Lalande 21185 with courses set to Chi Orionis.

....

At almost exactly the same time, Tso Shah is also directing his four hundred units to jump for 107 Pisces at forty percent. Once in the conduit, he decides to go home for some rest. He's been working in preparation for this since noon, without a break.

....

Kil Kos is with Admiral Chan and Dac Kil Res when he receives the accounts of the Gamma and Alpha Departures, in the late afternoon on December 9. Based on trajectory, departure time and velocity he makes a silent snap decision these are the main thrusts. He's convinced his forces at Chi Orionis, and 107 Pisces will be attacked sometime on December 11.

"Gentlemen, I think these are the real main thrusts."

"Why do you believe that, Kil? The first two were bigger." Chan queries.

"Yes, and that's part of the illusion of a convincing diversion or feint. It has to look like a full-scale assault. But, the initial ones left first at relatively slow velocities. The second group of departures launched at much higher rates. No, I believe the first ones were to draw our response. Besides, it makes sense from a tactical point of view. Their targets are more valuable than what you call Gliese 777 or BD-05 1123. That's why I waited. There almost worthless strategically. Not to mention the forces assigned are much larger than needed."

"When you put it that way, I have to agree." Chan smiled.

"Res, order eight Fleets to assist at Chi Orionis and seven for 107 Pisces. Make sure they know the directions the conduits will approach from."

"What about the other locations, sir?"

"Calculate the estimated arrival time of the enemy. Have our forces leave those systems and return for half an hour after the OFSA should arrive. Tell them to attack, but don't stay to be destroyed. They should retreat when the fighting gets heavy. Don't worry about sending any help. They won't need it." Kos said confidently.

"Yes, sir. I will issue all the orders, at once." The Dac-Kil said as he snapped to attention, bowed his head, then turned and exited the command area.

....

George receives a steward's visit in his quarters late on December 9, to advise him the tactical department needs to see him. Dressed in off-time civilian garb, he heads up to the Flag Bridge and over to the Tactical station.

"You requested my presence." He smiles at the back of a Lieutenant who's examining the station's screen intently. The officer jumps to attention.

162

"Sir, I didn't realize you were there."

"Relax Lieutenant. I didn't mean to startle you. And, we don't typically follow those protocols during the day."

"Yes sir, I know that. I was just surprised."

"Do you have something to report?"

"Aye, sir. Intelligence sent up Suvayeek and SOCC accounts you may want to see. The Isesinis have started some redeployments. Two Groups are headed to these locations. Five hundred sixty-eight ships are going here...' He points to Chi Orionis. '...and, four hundred ninety-seven are traveling to this system." He moves his finger over to indicate 107 Pisces."

"Hook, line and sinker..." Admiral Bryant mumbles.

"Pardon me, sir?"

"Nothing. It's what we wanted Kil Kos to do. I'm going to get some rest."

"I'm sorry I had you disturbed, sir."

"Don't be apologetic. And, continue in that manner if there are *any* changes in enemy field forces. I needed to know what you had. I was just so calm because the enemy did what we wanted them to do. But, that's valuable information, too. It means our plan is working. So, thank you very much. And, good job." Bryant said softly with a warm smile.

"Your welcome, sir." The young officer responded as George turned and walked off the bridge.

....

At five hundred on December 9, my entire cluster exits their conduits and stops dead in open space. We are nearly halfway to BD-05 1123. As we wait for four hours, we resupply our Sub contingent with provisions and fuel. Then, I issue orders to move to Step 2 of tactical mission #CC - 34612-C. The entire formation activates Casimirs and projects new conduits directed at 82 Eridani. Then, we all accelerate and cross the thresholds at twenty percent of superluminal. Our staging location one light-year from our target is still five days away.

....

Automatic helm and FTL settings in all the ships bring the entire Epsilon contingent out of their vortices and to "station keeping" in the middle of nowhere. George waits only two hours before issuing the order to progress to stage two of Epsilon Mission Plan #CC-34612-C. He wisely uses the time to resupply his Subs, too. He can feel his body resisting inertia as the engines slowly increase velocity to twenty-five percent as they enter their

163

conduits to 15 Sagitta. It's five days until they'll land at their rest point a third of a parsec from the system.

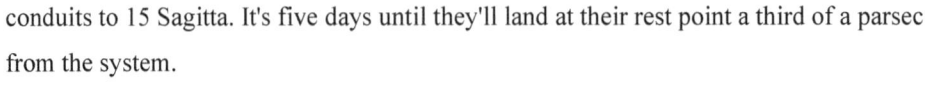

"See, I told you both." Kos sounds kind of arrogant as he makes the pronouncement.

"What do you mean?" Mes asks.

"Those two other conduits are gone. They're nowhere to be found. It looks like those groups turned around and left.

We're still reading the ones on the way to the sites you reinforced." He adds as he waves a datapad in front of their faces.

"That's why you're the boss, Kil." Chan offers with a smile.

"Yes. And, never forget that." He says to the other two men.

At thirteen hundred hours, on December 9, Nichols smiles as his entire HQ assembly crosses exit thresholds into no-mans'-land. He does not wait. Instead, he immediately orders his troops to head back to Rigil, in friendly space.

At the same time, Admiral Shah is conducting precisely the same sequence of operations as Steven Nichols. He smiles to himself too, understanding that if all went as planned, the Isesinis don't know the whereabouts of the two bigger flotillas. "You're a genius, George." He thinks to himself.

"The whole thing was a ruse," Koss says to the others as they stand on his bridge at eight hundred on the tenth.

"Why do you say that?" Chan asks.

"Because now, the other two formations turned around and headed home."

"This worries me."

"Why?"

"Because I know George Bryant and he doesn't make meaningless advances. We've missed something. I feel it in my gut. He's up to no good."

"Don't be such a worrier. There are no more OFSA conduits in our territory." Kos said.

Chan excused himself and left. But the nagging feeling that George had just put one over on them was causing raised goosebumps on the back of his neck. The fact executions were still ordered in the Federation for treason flashed through his mind. The image of George Bryant arresting him merged with the notion. He shuddered involuntarily once he was alone in the corridor.

Chapter 23 Preserving the Future

Wednesday, December 8, 2271

"...those who look only to the past and present are certain to miss the future."

John F. Kennedy

"Well, I think we've been here long enough. I know I'd like to get back home, for a while." Basi says to Boets.

"Me too. It's three hundred forty-nine and thirty seconds." Boets responds.

"I guess I'd better give the final order. This part of the operation does require my personal authorization because millions not in warships are about to die."

"Yes. It's a tough one. These are the hardest directives to give."

"You just have to remember what they've done and what this will do for us.' Basi explains then turns to the outer stations.

'Communications. Open inter-ship communications, please. Notify all Captains this statement will be broadcast throughout their ships. " He pauses.

"Sir, the channel is now active."

"Officers and enlisted of our Special Tactical Group, I just wanted to take a moment to address you all. We are about to conduct a bombardment of this planet. It is the most offensive operation we could perform. You must remember we execute this plan because it's necessary. Our objective is to destroy the Isesinis ability to organize an aggressive war. We are not attempting to annihilate them. We have tried to program our targeting to avoid the majority of innocents. Carry out your duties professionally and remember the responsibility for this is not yours. This is a decision made at the highest levels of the OFSA and the Federation.' He clicked off.

'Tactical!"

"Aye, sir!" A young lieutenant snaps.

"Tie into Tactical Field Weapons Control on the FSS Pacifica authorization number SOCC CBZ345167."

"The link is established, sir. My screen mirrors their command center."

"Activate detonation of all mines except the one designated 12521."

"Aye, sir!" The Tactical Officer says as he highlights all mines, marks them all active, then, deactivates the one specified."

"The system is asking for a senior Flag Officer's authorization."

"Punch in CB$798325 and hit enter."

"The system has confirmed. Detonation will be in ten seconds."

Basi is followed by Boets as they walk to the view window. The mines detonate in a programmed sequence. Defensive installations and warships are first. Communications platforms and orbital shipyards go next. Finally, all sensor and observation platforms are obliterated.

The three elevations all these devices had circled the planet in are filled with debris, smoke, and dust. The screen indicates the movements of several OFSA vessels as they reposition to avoid collisions.

"Time?" Admiral Basi calls out.

"Three fifty-one thirty-three." The FSS Chicago's navigator calls out.

"Let's send out our authorizations for step 2," Basi says to Boets.

The two sit and punch the commands with the appropriate authorization codes. All their ships in orbit will begin bombardment at four hundred hours and one minute.

They sit in silence. Both Admirals are watching for the first volleys, feeling for the vibrations of the Chicago's weapons' systems, and listening for the internal reverberations created by all the shots and launches.

"Holy shit!' Basi yelps as the first volley leaves the Frigate. 'It's nothing like a sub. We have one dual mount cannon we can fire with up to four torpedoes at a time. How many..."

"The Chicago would have fired forty missiles, eighty spears, and eighty particle charges simultaneously. We actually could deliver double that. But, we never leave ourselves defenseless. We're holding the rest in reserve in case someone counter-attacks." Boets cut in and explained.

They watched as several minutes passed for the salvo to make its way to all its various destinations. Mushroom clouds began rising from the surface.

"You weren't supposed to use any fission weapons!" Basi barked.

"They're not. They're what are called Spears of Fear. They use a massive kinetic charge delivered at high velocity. One of those expends between fifteen and twenty kilotons TNT equivalent. So, they raise mushroom clouds. But, there's no radiation. And, we're only launching missiles with chemically charged explosive warheads. Big bang but no fallout." Boets says.

"Good. We want to finish off this war. But, we don't want to annihilate the Isesinis civilization." Basi says.

"Sir, may I ask a question?" The Tactical Officers asks.

"Of course Lieutenant. It's the only way to learn anything." Admiral Basi answers with a chuckle.

"Why didn't we blow that one unit we christened 12521?"

"I think you'd agree that this is a major offensive operation in its own right. But, we're also using it as a diversion. Admirals Bryant and Brubacher are leading attacks on the two most important enemy Regional Field Commands in Federation Space. Those operations are timed to begin after the Isesinis receive a call for help from their homeworld. The device we spared is a transceiver. We will detonate that mine when we start the second wave of bombings. That should give them lots of time to get out their distress calls. And, after we destroy it, Kil Kos the leader of the enemy force that took our territory should find the lack of a response to his communication compelling. We hope that he will command half his Fleets to come here. But, the Isesinis still communicate the way we did. It'll take six and a half days for Kos to receive the hail and send help. But, we'll be gone before any Isesinis arrive. We're going home, as soon as this is done."

"Thank you, sir. It's a good lesson in battle tactics." The Lieutenant said appreciatively.

Boets and Basi watch in silence. They really can't make out much detail. Between the mess in orbit and the dust and smoke on the surface, it's hard to see anything. They keep monitoring infra-red, and radar sensors since those systems peer through the dirty clouds.

"All OFSA vessels, please move to step three of the battle orders," Basi calls out verbally at precisely five hundred hours. All weapons fire ceases as covert supply ships move in and begin docking with Frigates and Subs for replenishment. The resupply is on a tight schedule. Every craft must be restocked by seven hundred. Timing is critical because there are Isesinis forces within ten light-years that can arrive in a day. So, they must complete the final step and be gone today.

"Let's head to the Officers' Mess.' Boets suggests. 'There isn't much for us to do for awhile." He adds.

"Good idea. I can use some breakfast." The Admiral responds with a broad smile.

They return to the Chicago's bridge at exactly five minutes before seven.

"Tactical!" Basi calls out, immediately.

"Aye, Sir." The young female lieutenant responds. That's when Basi and Boets realize there's been a shift change.

"Tie into Tactical Field Weapons Control on the FSS Pacifica authorization number SOCC CBZ345167."

"I'm online, sir. My screen is showing their command center."

"Activated detonation of the mines designated 12521."

"Aye, sir!" The Tactical Officer says as she highlights the specified bombs.

"The system is asking for a senior Flag Officer's authorization."

"Punch in CB$798325 and hit enter."

"The system has confirmed. Detonation will be in ten seconds."

"Where is that charge?" Basi asks.

"Out of our line of site. We won't be able to see it. But, our sensor net will pick it up. We'll be able to confirm that way." Boets responds.

"Sensor Station, I want confirmation of that detonation when you see it," Basi calls out.

"I have the coordinates on my screen, sir. There's the flash!"

"Tactical, what's the feedback from the device."

"There is none, sir. The signal is gone."

"Good."

"Please cycle through the surface imaging your receiving, right now." The Admiral orders and the views from space quickly change to planetary ones and flash from one location to another. They see that the palace, the government complexes, and the military headquarters are demolished. Over a hundred bases and nearly two hundred factories have been replaced by craters.

Both men sit and type the authorizations to move to the next step.

At seven hundred, the second wave of shelling begins. Tier Two supply operations are hit. Over three hundred factories and distribution centers are demolished in this round.

Except for a meal, the two men repeat the same pattern as the first bombing. It ends at eight hundred, and again they can't make out much without using infra-red.

They order step five to begin. It's another resupply break. At ten o'clock they authorize the third and final round of bombings. Another three hundred fifty factories, businesses, military, and government operations will disappear.

At eleven hundred another resupply is ordered then everyone waits until the Admiral is satisfied with what he sees at fifteen hundred. By then, a lot of dust has settled, and clouds have risen high enough that imaging can see below them. The devastation is widespread and complete.

"Tactical, please have all strategic units report on the accuracy of their attacks and the resulting level of destruction. Copy Admiral Boets, please."

"Aye, sir."

"Sensors, tie into all other ships and the sensor net. I want every picture you can get of the surface and all the orbital tracks. Copy Admiral Boets, please."

"Aye, sir."

Half an hour later both their system annunciators sound several times. The two Admirals stand in the middle of the bridge examining the reports on our pads.

They order the final step, which is withdrawal, reformation, and launching to Rigil.

"It'll take us each a couple of days to write our reports to our bosses. But, for now, let's go down to the pub and get some lunch and a beer." Boets suggests.

"Good idea.' Basi says. Then he turns back and snaps one more order. "Captain, the Chicago is yours, again."

"Thank you, sir." A voice calls back as the two Admirals leave the bridge - probably for good. There won't be any need for them up here, anymore.

The two men were in the bar for about an hour and a half when Basi's received a message notification. He activated his datapad, opened the mail and began swiping at the screen.

"Take a look at these." He said to Boets as he angled the pad for the subordinate to see.

He very slowly and methodically moved from one image to another. Both men were analyzing the pictures for destruction and lack of damage to facilities and buildings surrounding the targets.

"Very impressive!" Boets observed.

"Yes, it is. There's no need for more. We've exceeded our objectives." Basi responded as he tapped on the screen to send the orders to all Commands to move to the next phase of their tactical plans.

They returned to their chat and drinks. An hour after Basi transmitted his instructions, they heard the ship-wide annunciators and felt the inertia of the Frigate breaking out of orbit. These were thruster and long-ramp IPE moves, so the force was minimal.

As they were signing their checks and rising to leave, there were additional announcements and the reaction to an increase in acceleration rate. They were headed for a jump threshold.

Both men returned to their quarters as they felt the G-forces of the AMPE engines kicking in. Then, there was the shudder and vibrations of them crossing a vortex event horizon.

They were on the way home.

....

Because of the new communications' system, both George Bryant and I saw the results of the Eta Pegasus bombardment on December 9 in near real time. We got on the horn to discuss it and agreed to wait until Kil Kos had time to receive any message from his home world and react to it. The Isesinis employ a laser transceiver system similar to ours but without the sub-strata relays that make it instantaneous. So, they experience the lags we once suffered. It will be another five and a half days before any distress calls arrived from the planet. But, waiting could mean attacking a much small force.

Chapter 24 82 Eridani

Wednesday, December 15, 2271

"...put your feet in the right place. Then stand firm." **Abraham Lincoln**

Today, started out very interesting. The Suvayeek, SOCC, and our own sensor nets are reporting intriguing enemy movements. Their accounts from throughout occupied Federation space are reflecting substantial redeployments towards Eta Pegasus.

ISIE ground agents in those systems are reporting the recall of around half the ground forces. At most of those worlds, half of all the Cruisers and Carriers have departed. Federation wide, seven of the big GPHC units have gone. Overall, the operation at Eta Pegasus has served to drain Isesinis strength in occupied Federation space.

In further discussions, George and I agree to execute Zeta's battle plan, tomorrow. Step One of my scheme is the detonation of half the mines including those in the two Orbs that are still here. But, since those explosives are now controlled via our sub-strata relay communications, we will also trigger the bombs planted in units that are returning to Eta Pegasus. More than half of the ships leaving my target won't make it home and therefore will not be available to assist here. The Zeta first phase will commence at four hundred hours.

....

I am watching both the primary Flag Bridge screen and the broad port-side window as I begin to record today's events.

"It's now seven hundred hours thirty minutes on Thursday, December 16, 2271, and we've been involved in an intense scuffle for over three hours. The site is full of smoke, dusty gas clouds, flying shrapnel, tumbling bodies and severed limbs. I haven't had time to do a precise count but, Zeta Command has lost somewhere around half a dozen Carriers, ten Cruisers, fifteen Frigates, four Supply Ships and about two hundred Raptors, to this point. But Dac Kil Res has lost his subordinate GPHC, and his station is severely battered and mostly disabled. We are trying to capture him. Mining reduced his force of nearly nine-hundred Cruisers and Carriers to half that before we even entered the battlefield.

The Isesinis were distributed in three disc-shaped formations. A central one was protected by one below and another above it. Before the assault, twenty cloaked SOCC subs and a dozen covert Frigates ringed the outer perimeter of the central disc. They have done their jobs quite well, keeping that layer's ships extremely busy while a portion of our Fleet concentrated on the Dac Kil's big base ship.

A second assemblage of Zeta ships lunged at the top Isesinis group from above, and a third pursued the lower one from below it. All moving flotillas approached from the same side of the Isesinis. Our three subdivisions reentered regular space at thirty-percent with a combined eleven hundred twenty fighters already deployed and another thirty-five hundred becoming space-borne within a minute of crossing our exit thresholds. And by that time, space was filled with anti-matter missiles, torpedoes, and spears all speeding toward the remaining enemy. All ships ran manually-helmed, evasive trajectories to avoid all the debris encountered in their pathways.

Our initial contact found the enemy seriously confused by the all the sudden destruction around them. So, we were able to assail them virtually untouched for the first few minutes, destroying another one hundred vessels and completing the disabling of the Headquarters Orb, during that period. But, our opponents' recovery was relatively quick, and they resorted to relatively standard defensive tactics until our first resupply round began at six hundred thirty hours. They began to concentrate on the Supply Ships and their protective cover, at that time.

In response to that tactic, I was forced to bring my Headquarters ship into the fray to take on the task of shielding the resupply. Each of those provides the broadest possible screen and is endowed with the greatest number of weapons of all ships in our group. So, for the last hour, the Examiner has remained synchronized with a supply vessel as it gingerly moves from one depleted craft to another. Likewise, the other seven SuperCarriers have taken on the same responsibilities.

So far, all our Headquarters have sustained some minor damage but are each capable of continuing their task. We have also been directly responsible for the demolition of an estimated forty enemy platforms. And, each Super Carrier is operating its protective screens at one hundred ten percent of maximum in an attempt to diminish further injury.

As I speak, large bodies of Isesinis craft have begun struggling to flee. But, for the time being, we are destroying their apertures to force them to continue the fight. There is also a steady stream of enemy shuttles from the planet below. I believe the Isesinis are removing ground troops."

I encrypted and packaged up the audio report transmitting it to all C&C. I knew it was punctuated by the sounds of weapons fire and concussions, in the background. George will undoubtedly recognize I'm not exaggerating and may start his initiative with the new enemy strategy in mind. But, I will contact him directly, in a short time.

Out the window, I see nearly fifty fighters defending the Examiner's perimeter. They are zig-zagging around objects and vessels to gain the best advantage. And our automated defensive weapons systems are intercepting hundreds of incoming shots every minute. The same is true as I locate the other Base Ships in the distance. The Examiner's scenario is repeated over and over again by the entire Headquarters group of SuperCarriers. Our outbound salvos are still intense and continuous while our unreplenished opponents are already beginning to measure their responses. Every minute, I can see the tide turning more in our favor. I keep reflexively trying to protect my eyes from the flashes of particle weapons, anti-matter detonations, and warship fusion eruptions. My watery eyes are hot and scratchy from the continuous flickering. I am sure they are bloodshot. It is much like looking into a lightning bolt or welding arc.

Though we had expected it to take much longer, I give the order to move to the next stage at sixteen hundred thirty hours. Our antagonists are now down to a Fleet of less than a hundred. Isesinis platforms are allowed to leave if they wish.

Two standard Frigates are attached to each Group Command. And, there are four Groups within a Fleet. So, eight Frigates make up a battalion of Marines. Fifty-two Marines make up the small Companies on each ship. They are each led by a Captain who is counseled by another Officer who is ISIE intelligence. The rest are split into two platoons led by Lieutenants. One Frigate in every Fleet carries a fifty-third Marine at the rank of Major and assigned as Field Battalion Commander in control of all eight Companies when they're combined for specific operations.

There is no need to employ shuttlecrafts because of the size of the GPHC and its docking ports. Sixteen Omicron and Graeca Fleet Frigates move for the Orb. Omicron's Marine Major Sinat has been placed in the leadership role. The eight hundred thirty-three soldiers will prowl throughout the complex disabling and securing remaining troops while hunting for the Dac Kil. Both Battalion chiefs have been provided a plan and the drawings of the Headquarters. And they have briefed all their people on its layout.

....

Major Sinat aboard the Baltimore takes control via the Marine communication's link.

"I need to know which units I have here. Everyone report now." He instructs into the video screen. He's eyeing twenty faces with nomenclatures in bands at the bottom of each of their panes on the split screen.

One by one they recount their identities to him.

174

"I need the docking position of each of your Frigates, now." He directs.

Each, gives the location of the GPHC docking port their particular Frigate is attached to. He adds that info to the information banner of each square under the appropriate face.

"Have you all got your Orb Maps?" He queries and receives unanimous nods.

Sinat spends the next fifteen minutes reviewing each Group's assigned objectives. Then, he has everyone synchronize watches. He signs off.

Though each one is small, sixteen charges exploding at the same time cause a powerful compression wave throughout a significant portion of the Orb. Groups of fifty-two soldiers dressed in black assault armor and helmets carry a variety of weapons as they lurch from one blindspot to another. Each warrior wears a radio headset with microphone beneath the head protection. The Major can hear the continuous chatter of reporting Captains punctuating their troop's individual assessments, as the units advance. Doors are rammed or vaporized and their interior spaces cleared. Isesinis are secured in groups of two to ten at a time.

"All platoons report!" Sinat's whispered words convey an insistent tone ten minutes in.

Each Captain gives a brief account without interrupting his Company's momentum.

This scenario is repeated many times over the following hour. Companies begin running into each other and forming up into combined Groups.

Three hours after entry, two bands of over four hundred are now searching the deck holding the Upper Bridge. Besides that Control Center, it contains mostly elegant quarters and a Flag-level Mess Hall. Prisoners are secured individually and in pairs on this floor.

At eighteen hundred hours-thirty minutes the entire eight hundred thirty-two Marine formation smashes in the Bridge doors but hold back in the corridor.

"Omaha Platoon - intrusion protocol!" Sinat calls referring to their platoon handle which is a derivative of their ship's name. He quickly points in the direction of eight locations within the space.

An eight-Marine "pitching team" moves into the doorway with a similar "ball boy" group behind them.

The lead group turns, and each receives an object from the man opposite in the rear.

They all press an activation button and simultaneously toss to various depths in the directions Sinat ordered. There is a series of sudden brilliant flashes and deafeningly loud bangs in the space.

"Let's go!" Sinat orders."

Crouched Marines enter twenty-five at a time with those behind covering. Sinat stops the advance when half the combined force is within the room.

"Hold here unless things get hairy!" He says to his counterpart than crosses the threshold.

"Check every crack and crevice. Look under and around every console. Check every closet and office!" The Major snaps.

"Over here. I think its PE One." The young Sergeant calls out referencing the identity they've given Mes.

The Major notices a graphite armored figure crouched below a desk with six Marine weapons trained on him.

"Stand up!" Sinat barks with an accompanying hand gesture. The soldier rises.

Sinat can now distinguish the graphite armor with white markings. He knows if this is Mes, he's almost as tall as Kos. So, his suit has a headpiece. It'll be one of the internally controlled robots, if not.

"Remove your helmet!" The Marine Officer yelps with associated hand signals.

Two latches are released on the neck. The Isesinis removes the headpiece.

"It's Res. Get pictures. I want confirmation." An ISIE intelligence officer takes two pictures and fingers his datapad. He waits. There's an annunciator chime. He examines his email.

"It's him. We have PE-1!' The Captain shouts to the Major.

"Let's get him and all the others to the ships. I'll be aboard the Examiner reporting." Sinat explains to the other Major.

....

"Despite all the damage, there were still over six hundred alive over there, including Res. It'll take until around twenty-two hundred to get them all in the brigs of our ships." Major Sinat reports at seven thirty in the evening in my office with Svesion present.

"And, you didn't lose a soldier?" I ask.

"No, sir. We have a couple of minor wounds. But, no one's dead. Everything went by the book."

"Good job, Major. Please have Res moved here, as soon as possible?" Svesion ordered.

"Yes, sir. Sir, may I be present during his interrogation?" Svesion looked to me as the Major made his inquiry. I returned an almost imperceptible nod.

176

"Yes, Major. You may attend the questioning. Just stay out of the way. You're dismissed!" Svesion snapped.

....

When we enter the interrogation room, Svesion and I note that though he no longer wears his headgear, Res is an imposing person. My guess is he is attempting to use that stature to intimidate. He will not sit down. I have brought a file with me, I will want the Dac Kil to see - when the time is right.

" Sit down, Dac Sul Res! You're not impressing any of us, and you're tiring yourself out!" I growled at the man.

"That's Dac Kil. A Dac Sul is like your Commanders or Lieutenant Colonels. A Kil is a full General or Admiral. A Dac Kil is like your Lieutenant Generals or Vice Admirals." He spits out the words arrogantly in perfect English, as he glared defiantly into my eyes and remained rigidly upright.

"Guards!" I hollered. Four large armored Marines quickly transitioned into the interrogation room.

"Strip this armor off and give this man something to wear!" I said to the squad's Sergeant who nodded to the others. They immediately sprang into action. Res stood naked moments later as the NCO quickly exited, then returned with a bundle.

"Put these on!" He growled as he slammed the bundle into Res' midsection.

Res quickly dressed. But resumed his erect vertical posture.

"Now, sit down!" I barked.

Res hesitated.

"I will have you forcibly chained to the chair if you don't comply."

Res sat down.

"What do you want from me, anyway. Kos is in charge. And all security protocols and strategy will change the minute they know I'm dead or captured. Nothing I can give you would help. It's all yesterday's news, by now."

"I understand that. But, you've already given me a lot."

The Dac Kil was momentarily startled.

"I've given you nothing. And, you'll get even less, from now on." The man said softly after recovering his demeanor.

"You and Kos are from the same tribe. You're big, strong, and confident. And, you're both obviously intelligent and good tacticians. Because of that, you're treated very

177

specially by your Isesinis brethren - including your Emperor. And that's made you both arrogant and careless.

By the way, your leader is probably dead. We laid waste to your world a week ago."

I dropped the contents of the folder I held on the table letting the photos and sensor images spill out. Res peered down at them. His shoulders drooped, and he expelled a long slow breath.

"So, it's over." He said, quietly.

"Not yet. But, it will be in a few days. Without any support your forces are finished."

"Am I a prisoner of war."

"I haven't decided, yet. I am holding you as a material witness. I believe Kos is a war criminal. I am not so sure about you. Give me your boss, and we'll keep the charges reasonable."

"How can I be sure of that?"

"I am Fleet Admiral Kurt Brubacher. I am one of a Commission of nine Admirals and Generals that run our forces. My particular Command employs slightly more than two and a half million people. Its designation is Zeta Command. But, it's functional objectives, and responsibilities are as the Inspector General Branch. We enforce Federation laws and the Constitution. We audit the member planets for compliance. We examine all the other Operations within the OFSA for conformity. We have full powers of arrest and seizure. We supply security forces for critical installations and Federation dignitaries. And, we are the intelligence arm of the OFSA. So, when it's time to decide what to charge you with, it will be me who makes the decision." I left the statement hanging in the air in silence.

"Is my world destroyed?" The man choked back sobs as he softly posed the inquiry.

"Not destroyed - that is not our way. We had cloaked vessels in orbit for the last many months and..."

"Oh yes, we know of your subs. But, we could never breach the technology."

"Not just subs - we now have warships and supply vessels that are cloaked. So we were able to sustain the operation for an extended period of time. We orbited beside each of your satellite sensors. And, we landed Special Forces to pinpoint leadership, and military bases and supply manufacturers and distributors. We have destroyed your entire detection grid and all your communications relays. Then, we demolished the Emperor's home and facilities and all the government complexes. We also devastated anything to do with defense production or operations. No schools, hospitals, regional governments, or residential areas were targeted. Provincial and municipal authorities are still in operation. Possibly up to a million are dead. But, billions are still alive, and your culture is intact. You will be able to rebuild."

"Under your yoke!"

"I know that's what the Isesinis do. But, that's not our way. We will build a buffer to prevent you from repeating if you recover. But, your destiny will be in your own hands. We have never forcibly taken territory. Some species we defeated have joined our Federation, and others are allies. But, they made their own choices. You may speak to some of those members if you wish. A good example is the Spiel who helped us defeat you. They are our ally. But, we defeated them in a war they started some years back."

"And, all you want is Kos?"

"No. I want the Emperor too - if we find he's still alive. And, I want Admiral Chan and his human associates." I watched Res stiffen as I finished.

"You said you run Intelligence?"

"Yes. It is within a division called ISIE under my command."

"You are very skillful. You even knew about Chan."

"Yes. I had an agent in that group of human advisors. And I ordered the assassination of Dac Kil Mes to show Kos we were a threat to be reckoned with. It could have been him. But, I decided it should be his second. For now, I consider your Emperor and Kos war criminals. Evidence may convince me it was just the Kil. But, Chan is a traitor. He was already a criminal in the Federation. It was me who uncovered his crimes, years ago.

Did you manage to send out a distress call when we attacked?"

"Yes, we sent out hails. But, it will take seventy-three hours for a message to reach our Headquarters.

And, Kos will try to stay and fight to the last possible moment. But, when all seems hopeless, he will finally go. I am not sure if he'll kill Chan. He never liked the Admiral. He tolerated the man so he could use him. But, if he decides to be compassionate, he'll probably take him along."

"Where does he plan to escape to?"

"Kos does not leave anything to chance. Sooner or later he will move to what you call Markab or Alpha Pegasus. Admiral Chan explained your curious constellations and their history. But, Kos will probably head to Gamma Capricorn first because it appears

179

very inhospitable from a distance. It is a hot very chemically peculiar variable giant star. So, most species stay away from it. But there is a gas giant in a reasonable orbit with a life-supporting moon circling it. There's no intelligent life there. The Kil always said even he needed others to maintain his sanity. He figured he could last a couple of years there - until the heat died down. Then, he'll move on to Markab.

Are you planning to attack his group?"

"I can't answer that directly. But, I think it goes without saying that we'll attack every contingent that's illegitimately in our territory."

"He won't leave. So, you'll have to evict him, in the end. If you want to catch and prosecute him, then he should be approached like I was."

"What do you mean?"

"Severely damage and disable his Base. Blow the hangar bay doors off like you did to my Station. With all the fighting there was no way for me to dock a vessel at a port. And without the Hangar, I couldn't escape."

"You will not be held in our brig..."

"What's a brig?" The prisoner asked.

"A jail aboard this ship," I responded as I waved my arms to indicate the brig was all around us.

"Where are you sending me?"

"I'm not. You'll be given quarters befitting your rank aboard my ship and treated with respect. But, you will be under heavy guard. Four Marines will go everywhere with you. You will not have access to any secure areas of the ship without my approval. But, you will be able to move freely, otherwise."

....

I returned to my office and prepared a quick report of the day's actions. I added the video of my meeting with Dac Kil Res to George's copy of the account. And, I suggested he modify his plan to launch his assault at 15 Sagitta on Saturday in the late afternoon or early evening after Kos gets the report of our encounter with Res.

Thursday, December 16, 2271

"The Isesinis have made me into a warrior and Epsilon Command is the tip of my spear." **King David**

Admiral Bryant was already considering the delay of his operation. His tap on the sensor net and SOCC scans had convinced him that execution was a matter of choice. But, when he received my report, the video, and my recommendation, that cinched it. He wanted Kil Kos to grasp the details of the battle at 82 Eridani for multiple reasons.

First, because the Kil had quickly ordered deployments to Eta Pegasus when it was attacked, George believed he might react the same way this time. Sending help to his friend Res would weaken his own position even more.

Second, George wanted Kos to realize that the second most essential field unit had been destroyed. It would increase his apprehension because he was bound to assume more was coming. But, with the first two thrusts so far-afield and widespread, he was likely to presume that the OFSA would need to regroup before making a stab at him.

And finally, George wanted the Isesinis General to appreciate that his friend Res was gone. He wouldn't be able to distinguish if the Dac Kil had been killed or captured but, he'd recognize his associate was missing. Bryant's awareness of their friendship caused him to imagine that even Kil Kos might experience remorse which would add to his stress.

So, now the Isesinis leader sat in his Base Station at 15 Sagitta knowing his homeworld had been attacked, his most essential remote Headquarters was gone, and he's unable to raise either.

Admiral Bryant advised all his forces to delay execution of their orders, until Saturday, December 18, at eighteen hundred hours thirty minutes. He followed-up by transmitting a memo to Savign who would place her forces at the site on hold, too. But, in that communiqué, he also advised her of the likelihood of Kil Kos escape attempt. She would deploy accordingly.

....

"You're useless! All you've been able to give me has been the obvious. You have no insight into those two Admirals' thinking. You've led me down a pathway to nowhere with all my people following closely behind." Kos was ranting at Chan. He'd received the plea for help from his home on December 15 and immediately ordered nearly half his force there. The problem was each detachment would hear those orders at different times spanning three days, and it would take all of them several more days to reach the planet.

"You're supposed to be able to anticipate OFSA moves. And though you know its workings, you haven't been able to predict one of their actions." Kos nearly spat the words.

Chan wasn't sure if he heard underlying disgust or contempt for him in the Kil's voice. He thought it better not to answer in case the remarks were rhetorical. Why make a dangerous situation worse. He'd personally witnessed a gruesome execution by the Supreme Commander.

"Nothing to say, Chan? Maybe it's better because I'd probably kill you where you stand if I didn't like your explanation."

....

"Listen to this! We just received it!' Kil Kos almost screamed the order at Chan as he touched a screen icon. He'd summoned the Admiral to his Bridge at fourteen hundred hours on Saturday, December 18.

Chan listened intently to a message being relayed to them. Concussions, explosions, and other battle noise were apparent in the background. He finally identified the voice as Dac Kil Res. As the audio played on, he sounded increasingly stressed and continued a running description of the destruction he was witnessing. Kos stopped the recording and tapped in a time index.

'This is the end. The whole thing is four hours long." Kos said as Admiral Chan listened, intently.

"We've been boarded...' A whispered voice Chan recognized as Res' was speaking. 'A regimental-sized force entered through a dozen ports and are coming from all different avenues. I am sure they are looking for the Station Commander. We've lost almost the entire Command. I may have to take drastic action. Goodbye, my friend. Don't mourn me. Just take care of..." Res was cut-off abruptly as other background pronouncements were detected by the system.

"Stand up! Come out from behind there! Drop that weapon.' The sound of nearby weapon's fire could be heard followed by the clang of something hitting the metal decking. "The son of a bitch was going to kill himself. I had to shoot him. Get a medic in here, ASAP!" The voice ordered as Kos shut down the recording.

"Here!" Kos barked as he offered an Isesinis ceremonial knife to Chan. It's slightly curved blade was about nine inches long, and the handle glistened ornately. The Admiral looked inquisitively to the Kil.

182

"If you don't I will. And, you know what that will be like." The General said calmly. Chan accepted the dagger.

What seemed like several minutes passed as he considered his options. Then, he resigned himself to the inevitable.

"First, I want you to know I was always loyal and I still am."

"It doesn't matter. You've failed me miserably." The Kil was almost soothing, now.

Chan put the blade to his own throat, pressed hard, and drew it from ear to ear without flinching. He stood looking at Kos as blood gushed down onto his chest and spurted in the air to either side of him. He smiled. Then the light behind his eyes dimmed as he dropped to the floor with a thud.

"Get this garbage out of here!' Kos barked as he stooped to retrieve his prized possession wiping it clean on the Admirals pant leg. He turned back to his console as two soldiers removed the corpse. 'And, get rid of all the other humans.' He growled loudly. 'I think the only one of any account was Admiral Naabaahi who died in the accident." He mumbled to himself as he recalled the man. He was impressive, to say the least. First, there was his rigidly military bearing. Chan had become slovenly. But, there was also a level of intelligence and tactical skills well beyond Chan's. He considered the man an equal and contemplated reversing their roles. And, he knew Naabaahi had been at the highest levels of the OFSA. He didn't get there by being obtuse. But then, Nabby had been sucked into space in the Hangar Bay accident. It was disheartening that events had taken their course.

....

Kil Kos was in his quarters at seventeen thirty contemplating the loss of his friend Res when he was rudely interrupted. The mammoth station shuddered violently as the compression wave of a massive explosion traveled through it and the lights winked off then on in quick succession. Claxons trumpeted their alarms and soldiers were rushing everywhere in the corridors as he opened his stateroom door to peak out. A hallway wall annunciator indicated a hull breach and depressurization of several sections. Turning back he took ten minutes to redon his official armor. Then, he made his best time through the chaos to the Bridge.

Once at his station, he eyed the giant screen, then peered out the massive view window. He could see no visible attacking vessels. But, his own ships were exploding in bunches. The two base stations that had recently joined his formation had vanished. Examining the screen's information band showed severe damage to the lower Hangar Deck. The enclosure was a total vacuum and sensors indicated its enormous doors were

183

gone. On top of that, both coolant flow and ion conduit interruptions prevented FTL flight and the use of weapons. The base was running on auxiliary power.

Kil Kos did not believe in coincidence. So, the fact the other two stations were gone and his had survived was not lost on him. The attackers wanted to capture him. He wondered more than usual about their intelligence operation. They seemed to know everything about the all the Isesinis in their territory before he comprehended it, himself. He checked communications. The system was still functional.

Kos ordered all his local Commanders to position their forces into a sphere protecting the Base Ship. They were to distribute the ships no closer than a kilometer to each other in case of further detonations.

But, as his vessels began to move, missiles appeared from out of the emptiness of the space all around them. Anti-matter salvos destroyed any ships trying to reposition. He understood. These were the cloaked vessels they'd never explained.

"Target those launch points and fire at will!" He directed the entire group. But, he knew, it may be of no avail. If the enemy fires and moves, Isesinis forces would need a lot of luck to actually strike one. But, he went to the portal to observe anyway and wasn't surprised when no enemy ships were hit by Isesinis torpedoes and missiles.

Console alarms sounded as dozens of large warships broke out of vortices on a highspeed vector aimed at their contingent's heart. Ten times as many of their lethal little hornets accompanied them, and more were launching at an incredible rate. Returning to his station, he noted on the screen that what he saw through the glass was being repeated on several different vectors. It was a massive formation, and his own Fleets had already been reduced by more than half.

"Belay my last orders. Target those visible ships, right away!" But, it was already too late.

Each Isesinis warship was being assailed by multiple sources. It was all they could do to attempt intercepting the incoming deluge."

"What do we have in the upper Hangar Bay?" Kos called as he activated the line to that station.

"The only thing here is a mid-sized supply ship, sir." The metallic response was barely audible over the din of hull concussions.

"Is it fully fueled?"

"Yes, sir. We were about to launch when everything went crazy."

"I'll be up there in a minute. Tell the Captain to prepare to go!"

"Aye, sir." The voice was almost drowned out by background noise and interference.

"Security!" The Kil snapped, and six soldiers took up positions around him.

Personnel ducked out of the way as the seven armored people marched quickly through the corridors, into the hangar bay, and onto the supply vessel.

"Captain set a course to take me to what the humans call Gamma Capricorn at maximum velocity.' He barked. 'And, you're trying to avoid a sizeable enemy Fleet. So, take us out the door fast and plot an evasive course until you're beyond this mess."

"Aye, sir."

Kos felt the force of aft thrusters until the doors were wide enough to exit. Once beyond the opening, he was compressed into his seat as the Captain "hit the gas" setting thruster and Ion Engines to the maximum. The Kil smiled to himself as five times standard gravity pressured him. They banked sharply left for a few kilometers then turned upward in the middle of the arc. Kos eyed the disappearing battle through the rear starboard portal. Then, he settled back for a long ride.

....

"Did we get sensor readings on that vessel that just departed the Polyhedron?" Bryant yelled into the comm system over the rumble of the Valhalla's weapons systems.

"Aye, sir."

"How many Isesinis?"

"Two hundred forty-seven."

"Tactical, how many crew members on the mid-sized Isesinis supply ship?"

"Usually, two hundred forty, sir."

"Helm plot that ship's trajectory and determine possible landing sites."

"Aye, Admiral. I need a couple of minutes."

While he waited, George watched the raging battle. It was mostly one-sided, and enemy ships kept trying to jump out. Occasionally one would succeed.

Thresholds suddenly appeared in his line of sight. I had ordered a significant portion of my team to 15 Sagitta. The remainder stayed behind to mop up at 82 Eridani.

....

"Captain, I need to use your communication system." Kil Kos quietly said to the ship Commander.

"It's all yours, sir. In fact, the vessel's yours. Whatever you need, please help yourself."

185

"Thank you, Captain."

"Comm - I want laser channels to all our Headquarters Stations in occupied space and to our Carriers at 15 Sagitta. Please record my message and send it out using the latest encryption. Your Captain will give you their positions.' The officer nodded as the Kil began dictating.

"This is Kil Kos to all forces under my command within occupied space.

Our opponents have successfully destroyed our formations at what the humans refer to as 82 Eridani and 15 Sagitta. And, it seems they have curbed our world's ability to support our operations. In response, I ordered a substantial portion of our Fleets home. With our forces dangerously reduced and no ability to resupply, I have no recourse but to recall all groups under my authority. Please make Best Speed to exit Orion Federation Space at the nearest boundary location and find your way to an isolated system near there. I will meet you in sixty-days at the system our enemy calls Markab. Then, we will make our way home."

....

Now that Zeta is on-site, it is our job to support Epsilon in any way we can. So, I attach my Theatres to their Tier One Commanders until the confrontation reaches its now inevitable conclusion. But, this time, I have the Examiner parked much closer to the battlefield, quite near the Valhalla. And, I intently eye both my large view screen and the port-side view window to ensure I know of alterations to enemy tactics, immediately.

By twenty-one hundred hours forty-five minutes our flotilla of over a thousand is now fighting just over a hundred enemy ships. But, seven suddenly break out and head for the Examiner at high speed. They are bearing down on us, projecting sheaves of missiles, torpedoes, and particle charges at Examiner and my security flotilla. Our starboard bow torpedo tubes, launchers and the shielding protecting them are damaged and knocked out of service making a response to incoming vessels harder unless we turn that side of the big craft towards the incoming enemy. But, they are closing the distance so quickly, we may not be able to complete the maneuver in time.

We detect a firing solution lock while our vulnerable area still faces the formation which is just one hundred kilometers off our hull. The pulsing alarm speeds up as the weapons' detection system is determining the Isesinis squad is reaching a point guaranteed destruction.

Then, just as the signal becomes constant, a massive hulk separates us from our opponents. It's the Valhalla and George has ordered it to protect us in our moment of need.

186

But, it is rocked by one blow after another delivered at point blank range. I discern gasses, scrap, and bodies exhausted from near its upper front region as momentum carries it past us.

We are now in position, with our damaged sections protected and all weapons locked on targets to our starboard side. The Captain orders the Examiner to fire. Hundreds of rounds close the distance in a couple of seconds. All seven intruders are destroyed instantly.

"Get me Admiral Bryant on the Valhalla," I order.

"Sir, it's the Captain. Admiral Bryant is unavailable."

I see the face on my screen. I do not recognize it. He requests a private conversation. I almost run to my nearby office.

"Report!" I bark. The fear is apparent in my voice.

"Sir, that part of the Valhalla was hit and is severely damaged. Admiral Bryant is missing. But, we haven't been able to get in there, yet. However, based on sensor readings, we believe everyone on the Flag Bridge is probably dead." He nearly whispers the account.

I fall back in my chair.

"Oh. I hope not. I hope I haven't lost my best friend!" I know there are tears on my face and my voice is cracking.

"I'm sorry, sir. I wish I had better news."

"It's not your fault, Captain. Look after your ship. And, get into that bridge as quickly as possible." I ordered.

After closing the line, I invoked my C&C rank and gave Tom Stevens temporary command of Epsilon. His people would probably have followed that protocol, anyway. But, an order from a member of the Commission makes it a certainty.

I turn my attention back to the battle. The field is a kaleidoscope of spiraling garbage orbiting more massive pieces of junk. There's lots of flotsam and scrap and a slew of floating bodies, limbs, heads and torsos. We are still in the middle of a confrontation, so despite my concern for George, I have work to do. It takes us another two and a half hours to completely overcome our antagonists. My eyes are burning by then. It's much like the problem welders have from accidentally flashing themselves. Only the Kil and six Cruisers got away. All other warships and two of the GPHC units were destroyed. The third base ship will be towed to where we can intensely examine and analyze it. Some of the metals employed in the hull are unfamiliar to us and superior to what we use.

I discuss the situation with Tom Stevens. I offer our help in the mop up. He agrees. So, I assign the appropriate contingent. Then, I contact him again and ask if I can board the Valhalla to help with the search for Flag Bridge personnel. He agrees. I shuttle over.

My journey from the docking port is uneventful and unimpressive until the elevator doors open on the Fifteenth Level. Everything is disheveled. The corridor to the Flag Bridge is a mess. All sorts of things have been sucked from spaces around on their way to the bridge. When I reach the doors, rescue teams are just gaining access. It's taken three hours to secure the area with temporary bulkheads so it can be pressurized. Everyone else makes their way slowly inward from the entrance. But, I march headlong to George's Office. I put my hand against the panel. It's cool but not as cold as if the other side was exposed to space. I call for pressure readings. I'm told they're low but rising. I stop for a minute to think that one out. It should mean George's office is intact and pressure atmosphere was drawn out through the gaps around the access way. Now, the pressurized bridge is forcing air back in.

I push on the door which releases but resists. I put my shoulder to it. There's a lot of crap up against its bottom half preventing it from sliding open. I am struggling to create enough gap and finally get my body through. I hear a groan from behind the bar which has shifted halfway across the floor.

I race to my friend. He's alive - barely. He has frost burns and broken blood vessels in and around his eyes.

"What happ..." He passes out.

"Get a medical team in here! It's Admiral Bryant, and he's alive!"

There is no observance of protocol in these cases. People don't acknowledge the order. They just act. They are using portable communications units to call for aid. Within two minutes, a team of three medical people arrives. They huddle around taking vital signs and attempting to restore his consciousness, unsuccessfully. One man inserts an Intravenous line and injects medication into it.

"He's stable - for the moment. Get him to sickbay - STAT!" The man says while he's placing sensors on Bryant's chest. He keys on his datapad and the remote traces and readouts appear as they negotiate their way through all the disorder. The ship's Captain arrives firing orders left and right. The Exec takes over for him.

The Captain and I are on our way to the medical unit when Moe and Tom Stevens appear in the hallway and join in for the walk.

"How is he?" Stevens asks.

"Alive!" I answer as I choke back a thankful sob.

"That guy's still tougher than nails."

"He's frostbitten and oxygen deprived. And that's not to mention he may look like a hungover raccoon in a day or two. He's got broken blood vessels all over, but it's the worst in and around his eyes. I bet that's going to hurt. But, the Doc says he's stable for now."

"Anything broken?" Moe asks.

"You know, I don't know. I was so concerned he might be dead, I never thought of broken bones. It's quite possible. The bar's halfway across the room, and he was behind it. I don't know about cuts and abrasions either. There's broken glass all over the place." I finished just as we were exiting the elevator doors facing Sick Bay. We enter in silence and just stand in place. Everyone knows who we are and why we're there. The area is full and interrupting would only interfere with the ministrations.

There's a limited waiting room but its big enough for all of us. We sit and wait.

....

"You're lucky to be alive," I observe quietly during my visit the next day.

"I don't feel very *lucky*. I have a partially crushed foot, a broken wrist...' He holds up his right arm. '...and the Doctor says there are over a hundred stitches in me in batches of two or three. My eyes feel like they're falling out and my face is killing me. And, to top it off, an artery ruptured in a lung, and it hurts like hell to take a breath. Aside from that, I feel great.' He started to chuckle. 'Ow, that hurts!" He finished and laughed again with a wince.

"It's okay George. Your Two-I-C is great. He'll keep the seat warm until you get back."

"What about losses?"

"I'll let Tom give you the exact Epsilon ones, but you lost around a dozen ships and forty thousand people including those from the Valhalla. You're the only survivor from the Flag Bridge. Thank goodness you were in your office. And, it's a bonus you had Tom off the ship.

Zeta lost fifteen ships and two hundred thirty-seven Raptors over the last two battles. Nearly fifty thousand dead. But, we're mostly intact, and the Isesinis have withdrawn from the Federation."

"So, now you can lay back and rest, eh?"

"You can. But, not me!"

"What do you mean?"

"I have work to do. Kil Kos got away. I'm going after him."

"You mean you're sending ISIE?"

"They're coming along with me. I'm hunting that bastard down myself. Chris Sparks is coming along, and we're taking fifty SF Marines."

"You shouldn't. You're C&C. We can't lose you."

"You won't. Sparks gave me an earful. If I want to go, I have to follow his rules. He says he'll arrest me for not following OFSA Regulation if I don't. But, I want to be in on it. And, it'll give EL a chance to run the unit for a month without me."

"What about Chan?"

"We found him dead. The Hospital Unit Pathologist says he slit his own throat. We found the other fourteen in a heap in the upper Hangar Bay of that Headquarters. Each had a knife driven through the temple."

"Gruesome bastards, eh?" George observes.

"You bet.

After we get Kos, you and I are going to Eta Pegasi. If you're not ready, Tom can take Epsilon."

"You going after their Emperor."

"You bet! He and Kos are the real criminals, here."

"Good Hunting - With Kos, I mean."

"We'll get him. You just get well old friend."

I turned and left the room. I took a few minutes to speak with Marie and Atina who'd been waiting for me to exit. I explained I had a mission to finish, but I'd be there whenever possible. And, in the meantime, they could call on Fred and Bryant.

....

We all traveled together at thirty-five percent to make Rigil for December 24. Being home for the holidays and New Years was essential. Tracking and traffic control was startled when fourteen hundred ships exited simultaneously and began to taxi towards the planet. They had just two hours to find parking spots for all of us. SOCC and the covert Epsilon force joined us a short time later.

The two Commands were greeted as heroes. But, none of us felt like that. We'd lost too many during this war. And, the strain had been continuous for more than two years. And then there was the concern over the injured. Not the least of those was George who was still bed-ridden. Between the foot and the lung, his doctors didn't want him running around, yet.

Tom Stevens sat at my side as I represented both of us at the Commission debriefing. Then, I dropped the plan to go after Kos. They all just about shit their pants. A C&C taking an active part in arresting a dangerous criminal, with six SF soldiers of his own - and on an unknown planet. They didn't like it. So, I called in Sparks who'd been waiting outside the door. He explained the rules and the care they'd take. Everyone relented, and the mission was approved unanimously.

Finally, I shocked them again with the proposed operation at Eta Pegasus. After explaining Epsilon and Zeta would conduct it together and we were up against a very depleted enemy with no means of support or resupply they again gave their consent.

So, the games afoot.

Chapter 26 When Pigs Fly

Saturday, Jan 20, 2272

"Evil is powerless if the good are unafraid." **Ronald Reagan**

Dammit, it's hot here. And, it's so humid perspiration can't even evaporate. The faint breeze is mostly blocked by the thick tropical forest. So there's no relief. And, I've been bitten by bugs that look like black flies. But, these suckers are about the size of a baby pig. I'm exaggerating in my thoughts, but the image makes me laugh aloud.

"Are you starting to lose it? What's so funny, boss?" General Sparks looks genuinely concerned.

I pointed at one of the insects.

"I was thinking about how big these buggers are and the expression "When pigs fly" came to mind," I said as I laughed all the harder. He caught the humor in the mental picture and broke out in a guffaw, too. Then, several of the fifty-man SF Platoon within earshot followed suit.

"Let's take a rest stop.' Sparks ordered. Then, he added, 'It's nice to laugh. There's not been anything funny in this place, until now."

"I agree wholeheartedly.' I chugged a few swallows from my canteen. 'What do things look like, now?" I asked.

Sparks pulled his datapad from the backpack he'd dropped.

"Orbital sensors continue to show their squad in the same place. There are still seven targets there. Two are moving around on guard duty. The rest are in the lake, there. Their shuttle's still on the other side of them.' He stopped in thought. 'It'd be nice to take a swim right now." He mumbled quietly.

"After we finish what we came for. We can dive in as soon as they're all secured. Any active sensors from their vessel?"

"Not so far. But, they may be weak or passive. We'll have to be careful on approach. Radio or Radar Sensors can be detected simply enough. But, we'll have to scan for infrared and laser. And, we need to think less technologically. Simple tripwires could be in place. We'll have to watch for mines, too.

"How much farther?" I asked.

"About two more clicks. We'll have to slow down and go stealth in about twenty minutes."

We sat around chatting for another short while, then picked up our gear and moved on.

Trudging through the forest wasn't all that hard. There were breaks in the trees and ground cover that permitted us to trek without hacking our way through. Though it allowed us to journey quietly, it did extend the length of our march. Periodically, Sparks would examine the screen on his pad as we walked silently through the woods.

Fifteen minutes later, he held up his right hand. We all stopped. He put a finger to his lips to indicate absolute caution and quiet for the remainder of the walk. Then he pumped the air twice to specify slow going and signaled we should all keep low.

We advanced slowly through the jungle from there. All fifty-two of us were crouched down to take advantage of the stumpy ferns and brush.

Sparks flashed a stop, suddenly. He held out a scanner as he eyed his screen examining the area for infra-red and laser signals. He removed two pairs of eyeglasses from a pocket, donning one pair, then the other, as he carefully peered through the maze ahead. He presented the "okay" sign, then thrust both palms in the air, again. He was telling us the way forward appeared clear but to move cautiously. Finally, the General indicated both his eyes with his pointer and middle finger and drew a line to the region ahead. I rose slightly to observe.

Two fully armored and armed guards ambled slowly about a semi-circular track surrounding the beachfront the seven men occupied. Five of the rigid uniforms lay about the area, and an equal number of near-naked men wandered about in the lake. Five pintsized ones in a group laughed, splashed, joked and soaked. A tall, blond, muscular hulk was off by himself just enjoying the refreshing break. I remembered what Res told me. The Isesinis don't swim and are afraid of water over their head.

"Kil Kos." I mouthed to Sparks as I pointed to the giant. He nodded.

He and I moved to the rear of the company and spoke quietly.

"Did you notice the pattern the guards use?" Sparks whispered. I raised both hands palms up.

"They cross paths once in every cycle. That's the time to take them. They're much easier to target together." He murmured. I nodded agreement.

Then, he gathered the others around us and directed Marines to specific tasks employing sign language. Four would target the guards each leveling a single shot to the body cavity of their suits. Four more would advance to secure them. Twelve would move to block those in the water from reaching their weapons and armor. The rest would be held

193

in reserve in case of a problem or hidden forces we had not detected. The group silently reformed to their appropriate positions. He held up a hand with all five fingers widespread, then folded them down, one at a time. When his hand formed a fist, four nearly silent "sputs" sounded as the two dressed men fell suddenly. Four of our party headed to them while twelve more stepped out and quickly secured the beach. Kos looked up - amazed.

"Kil Kos, I have a warrant for your arrest authorized by a criminal court of the Orion Federation. You are charged with war crimes. Specifically, you are accused of murdering or causing the execution of seventeen without due process of law. Generally, you are indicted in the deaths of over a million. Your guards will be charged as accessories after the fact." Sparks shouted.

A single particle round was followed by two conventional shots. I looked around. One of the armored guards had managed to fire a weapon. A Marine had promptly killed him. I scanned my compatriots. Blood was seeping from just below Sparks right shoulder. His breathing was labored.

Buoyed by the distraction, Kos made a sudden move. Two shots rang out as water splashed on either side of him. "Stay where you are! I don't care if we bring you in alive!" A Marine Captain called out.

The Kil froze.

"Medic!" I called out. One of the reserve group came forward as Sparks slid the knapsack from his shoulders. We helped Sparks to lay down on the sand. The attendant examined him.

"It didn't hit an artery. But, it did penetrate the upper lobe of his lung. The lung is collapsed. That's got to hurt like hell. How long until departure?" He directed the question at the Captain.

"Half an hour. I'll have the shuttle brought over here." The Captain responded. Then, he raised an open hand, closed and reopened it. Ten more men moved forward.

"Communications, call the shuttle. We need it here in ten minutes. Tell them to home in on us from the orbital images. Get those men out of the water!" He shouted the orders.

Twelve soldiers wade into the lake with hand weapons drawn, primed, and pointed. Each pair takes a different party. Kos tries to resist but stops when he hears the mechanics of a dozen or so weapons cocked or enabled from the shoreline. Once the Isesinis in the water are handcuffed, they are brought to landfall. Then, they are chained with shackles that permit a stride while securing feet and hands together.

194

Five minutes later, the large short range vessel appeared overhead.

"Do the Isesinis follow any customs with bodies after death?" I ask.

"If they died honorably we bury them. If not, we just discard the carcass. These men failed in their duty." Kos waves at the dead guards.

"They'll be buried. Your soldiers didn't fail. They were overwhelmed by a surprise superior force." I advised.

The Marine Captain picked eight to dig the two graves. The sand is soft and the contingent large so the job was quickly completed.

"Do you have any words to say over their bodies?" The Captain inquires.

"I don't consider their deaths honorable." Kos spits at the Captain.

"If these men believe in an afterlife, we hope they reach their Nirvana. They were soldiers asked to do an impossible task who died honorably. We salute you." The Marine Captain conveyed the prayer in solemn tones. We hold a moment of silence. Then, we all snap to attention and salute the graves.

"Let's get out of here!" I yelp. Everyone turns towards our craft.

"What do we do with that?" The Captain asks directing our attention at the Isesinis transport.

"Destroy it!" General Sparks moans.

Four "Specialist" Marines move quickly to place explosive bundles.

"We'll detonate when we're two hundred meters in the air, and out of the way." A Sergeant says.

A dozen soldiers enter our shuttle. Then, the prisoners are prodded in. Finally, the rest of us board. Sparks is provided a little extra room in the crowded space.

"Let's go!" He attempted to shout the command to show he's is still in charge.

"Watch for a blast wave from the surface, when we blow that ship!" The Sergeant calls to the pilot.

We rise and move south of the lake looking down on the scene.

"...you ready to detonate?" The Sergeant asks a Corporal.

"Aye, Sarge." She nods assent. Her boss watches through the portal.

"Call out our altitude, please." He yells to the pilot over the internal background noise.

"One hundred meters... ...one hundred fifty meters... ...one seventy-five... ...one eighty... ... one ninety... ...*two hundred meters*!" The pilot emphasized the last read out.

The sergeant raises a hand with three fingers up. He folds down to a fist and signals the Corporal. Those near the portals saw the devastation as the enemy craft was demolished. My only regret was that we didn't move it. A few larger pieces of shrapnel spiraled out and fell into the lake. A second later there is a shudder as the wavefront buffets us.

....

I was surprised when one of the Kil's personal guard asked to see me a few days later aboard the FSS Interrogator. I had moved my flag while the Examiner was being repaired.

I ordered the translator activated when I landed in the corridor in front of the appropriate cell.

"You asked to see me?"

"Yes, Ad... ..Admiral. I wanted to take a moment to speak with you." The swarthy man said, uncertain of my title.

"What may I do for you?"

"First, I will introduce myself. I am Sec Was. A Sec is an Officer commanding a group of up to fifty."

"That would most probably be similar to a Captain in the OFSA Marines."

"Regardless, I have been asked to thank you, by my men. And, I feel the same way." I was surprised by the Sec's command of English. The interpreter was confusing me.

"Turn off that thing, please. This man's English is excellent.' I said to the Marine Lieutenant in the hallway.

"Why do you feel it necessary to thank me." I inquired as I turned back to the prisoner.

"You have treated us fairly and with respect. And, you honored our burial customs. The Kil would not have done that. Our system is very rigid and unforgiving."

"You are very welcome. This is our way. We do not disrespect our opponents."

"What will happen to us?"

"Probably nothing. We'll likely send you home. It's Kil Kos and your Emperor we wanted. We also have Dac Kil Res in custody aboard another ship." The man was startled and appeared concerned.

"Sir, none of this was his doing. And, he only followed tactical orders. He never killed or harmed any prisoners. In fact, he is considered unusually compassionate within our society."

196

"I will bear that in mind. And, I'll tell you that, I already consider him an honorable man."

"The only consideration we would ask for is to meet with the people who prepare our food. We are having difficulties digesting our meals."

"Of course. I'll make sure the Galley Chief sees you right away.' I reply. 'Is there anything else?" I ask.

"Just that...' there was a long pause. '...I hope you execute the Kil. He is unusually brutal - even in our system."

"I have no say over that. Our courts are independent and follow strict rules. In this case, a jury of nine will determine if Kos is guilty of the charges or not, from the evidence presented. A prosecutor is required to prove guilt beyond a reasonable doubt before the court will convict. And, a defense attorney will be presenting his version of the data. He will make a real effort to disprove the Kil's guilt. We believe it is a just system."

"Too fair," The man replies. I turn and leave with a shrug.

....

"Kil Kos, Supreme Commander of the Isesinis field forces that invaded the Orion Federation, you are accused of numerous war crimes. The clerk will please read the charges." Judge Onasta ordered from behind the mahogany counter designated her "bench" - well raised above the rest of the courtroom seating. She is a tall but slight, gray-haired, elderly, jurist with a soft voice and very regal bearing and manner. The Interrogator's sizeable courtroom was filled to capacity, muffling the echo usually conspicuous at this stage of most trials.

It took the court officer nearly a quarter hour to complete the task.

"Kil Kos, you have heard the charges. How do you plead?" Onasta calls.

"I do not recognize your authority. I refuse to participate in this farce!" Kos snaps belligerently.

"I order a plea of not guilty entered into the record. And Mr. Kos, I will advise you that you are being tried by a legally chartered court of the Orion Federation. Many of the allegations in our documents have also been leveled by four other sovereign Federal authorities in our spatial neighborhood. So, I'd say you better take this seriously because this proceeding has broad universal recognition. Whether or not you recognize it is irrelevant. It will determine your future and may, in fact, establish if you live or die. And, that will happen even without your participation.

But, under our laws, you are innocent until proven guilty beyond a reasonable doubt. And, you are allowed to present a vigorous defense. A panel of nine individuals will weigh all evidence and arguments presented and will decide your fate. So, if you care about your life or prospects you should consider joining in."

"My defense does not matter. I failed at my task. I shouldn't be allowed to exist!"

"Since I sense a high degree of ambivalence, I will appoint a solicitor to act on your behalf. Our laws are very precise regarding trials. The bar to prove your guilt is incredibly high. And, the most significant allegations even require the Federation's attorneys to present convincing evidence that your intent was malicious. So, I recommend to you that you cooperate with your counsel.' The Magistrate turned away from Kos to view the general courtroom.

'Is Commander Simmons from Cag present?"

"I'm here, your Honor." A young uniformed Officer stood and stepped forward.

"Have you got someone in your group to represent this defendant. And, I warn you to be careful. I understand the emotions involved here. But, this man deserves a fair trial, under our system!"

"That is an issue. So, I've decided to represent the General myself. I am sure I can control my own feelings. But, I would never be absolutely convinced of someone else's mindset."

"So entered! Commander William Simmons will defend the accused! This case is adjourned until February 15. I will hear pretrial arguments, then. I am hoping to reach the jury selection phase by the end of that month. So, let's not make a mockery of this. Put your noses to the grindstone and get to work!" She slammed the gavel down and rose. The courtroom stood in deference to her as she exited.

Sitting among the gallery spectators, Admiral Gojen Svjosloki takes note of the beautifully crafted wooden mallet and sound block. He ponders why he never thought to steal one from a courtroom instead of cutting up the Examiner Pub's handrail all those years ago. He'd been lucky when he took that chance.

....

El is communicating with me daily as the Interrogator travels to meet him. He'd moved to the Examiner for the duration of the completed mission so its Engineering and Maintenance crews could complete repairs on its damaged bow hull, shields, and weapons' units, while I'm away.

Of course, I am receiving all the usual mail. But, El is ensuring I got the flavor of how our operations are proceeding. He says things are returning to normal very quickly. The Isesinis did little damage to infrastructure. We may find out from the Kil, but I believe they intended to use what they could when they felt secure. But, we never allowed them to get to that stage.

The Federation Council and King David have decided the four worlds most severely affected shouldn't pay Federation taxes for six months. That frees a substantial amount for each to recover. They will still enjoy the benefits of the Federation, in the meantime.

Susan Sylvestry has won election as Earth's President. She will do well. She's very impressive, understands government and politics and is very popular. Most of us from Earth see her as the one who led our people in tough times.

Here aboard Interrogator, Sparks is recovering nicely. Though he says it still hurts a little if he has to cough or laugh. He told me privately how much he cares for President Sylvestry. And, his severe injury made him realize how fleeting life can be. So, he intends to ask her to marry him. I will grant a recovery leave. He can pop the question, then.

George returned to Rigil aboard his Theatre One Mobile Hospital. We're in contact, daily. He wants to plan the mission to Eta Pegasus as soon as he's cleared for full duty. I keep telling him to think about getting well, instead. Then I assure him, we'll wait for him to go after the Isesinis. He hasn't been confined too long, but I sense he's getting quite anxious. It's hard to keep a good man down.

....

On February 5, as were breaking out of FTL mode at Rigil, the courtroom's half-filled for the Judge to hear a specially scheduled motion from Simmons. He's asking for a lengthy delay because there was an enormous amount of evidence turned over at the discovery hearing. And, he says he needs time to travel to interview witnesses and investigate events for his own team.

Justice Onasta grants his motion and extends the standard pretrial argument date to March 30. There is an outburst as attendees yell boos and catcalls.

"That's enough!" She yells as she slams her gavel. "I will have calm in my courtroom, or this will become a closed trial. Our laws give every defendant the right to a fair trial. And, they favor the accused when it comes to preparation. So, I will hear no more of this. The very next disruption will cause me to ban observers for the duration of these proceedings!" she snapped as she slammed the hammer again, rose, and exited.

It's time for a break. The past two years have been a grind. But the last six weeks have been all-consuming. Almost all my time has gone to my work. There was even a two-week period without my family. So, I notify El and Roh and take a week off.

Bryant, Fred, and I head down to Rigil. It's a little breezy this time of year. There are times when you can go for a swim in the lake but most days require a light jacket. So, we don't plan for water sports. If the opportunity arises, we'll take it. Instead, we concentrate on the new amusement park, Rigil New York's beautiful downtown, and OFSA Headquarters.

That may sound a little strange for a holiday, but Bryant is always asking. And, as a C&C, I have some exceptional privileges. If I want to show him everything, no one will stop me or say a word against it. Of course, that's impossible. The campus is so big you can't take someone through it all in a week. But, it is great to see how fascinated and appreciative he is as I guide him through his exploration.

Chapter 27 Anguish & Recovery

Monday, February 26, 2272

"We really don't grieve for people. We mourn the hole created in our own lives."

V. Adm. Marie Bryant.

February has been brutal. That's why I haven't written anything in so long. In the early part of the month, we were all very actively assisting in recovery operations. At the same time, we were redeploying to resume our responsibility throughout our territory. But, on Tuesday, February 6 the entire Orion Federation stopped. I've read about times that generated widespread grief, but I have never seen so many cases of crying people. And, I haven't ever had to console so many.

George seemed to be enjoying a rapid recovery from his injuries sustained when the Vallhalla's Flag Bridge was breached and depressurized. But, the doctors say an embolism had formed and moved to his brain. That morning, he had such a severe stroke. He died very suddenly.

It was a terrible morning for me personally. He was the man who gave me a chance. George was my teacher and counselor. And, George and Marie are my best friends. I was advised by secure e-mail and informed a public announcement would follow three hours later. I did not want my family or my associates to see my immediate reaction. So, I e-mailed Roh, El, and all Staff I have a routine contact with that I would be locked in my office for a couple of hours and did not want to be disturbed under any circumstances. Then, I went to my en-suite bathroom, shut the door, sat on the toilet seat lid, and wept like a baby for what seemed like an hour. I tried to rise and leave several times, but found myself in convulsive sobs each time. Though I'd nearly forgotten the feeling, it was like what I suffered when Helena died almost ten years ago on March 24, 2262. I felt hollow and in physical pain, and had to rise, lift the lid, and throw-up several times.

I guess about half an hour elapsed before I could steal myself to return to my desk. I took my pad, connected to our mainframe, located the files, and just scanned pictures of us together for another twenty minutes as I shuddered with violent bawls. This is a personal disaster of immense magnitude. It is hard to describe the blackness descending on me. Though my logic tells me there are many other people central to my life, I feel my it's pointless, at this moment.

.

An hour later, I've gotten hold of myself. I know George was significant, but my family is really everything to me. I need to be there for Marie. And, I need help my wife, son, and all my Zeta team through this gloomy time. Logic wins in the end.

I return to the washroom, grab a clean shirt, wash up, and change. I know I need a little more time for my pink eyes to revert to normal. I will have to speak to my people and my family, soon. So, I sit and make some notes. Then, I read them over and over again so I can get through it from memory. That way, I won't break down, myself.

"Fred, can you grab Bryant and come up to my office. I need to see you both." I said to her image on my screen.

"Certainly. We'll be there in ten minutes."

When they arrived, I asked Bryant if he'd like a juice, milk, or soft drink as Fred helped herself. We moved to the conversation pit after acquiring our chosen beverages.

"Byant, I need to explain something to you. And, your mother hasn't heard this either. It's going to be hard to understand. But, I will try to help you."

"Are you all right, dad? You're not sick are you?" There was fear in his voice.

"No, I'm fine. It's not me I want to talk to you about."

"What's wrong, daddy?" He yelled with tears welling in his eyes as he reverted to the name he hadn't called me in over two years.

"Just relax and let me tell you. I'm trying, but you keep interrupting."

"I'm sorry, daddy. You're scaring me."

"I don't mean to scare you. Our family is okay. That's not what this is about. But, I do have bad news about someone else. It's about a person you like a lot."

"Who daddy? Did someone die."

"As a matter of fact, yes. Uncle George died this morning. His body had been badly injured when his ship was attacked. It kept trying to heal itself. But, this morning he died."

"Are you okay, daddy?" Bryant asked. Tears were streaming down his cheeks as he heaved for breaths.

"Yes, Kurt. Will you be okay? We all loved George, but he was your closest friend." Fredricka queries softly.

"Yes. It hurts a lot. But I will be alright. I needed two and a half hours before I could tell you. But, I think we will all deal with it together. We'll help each other." I wrapped my arms around both and pulled them close. We held the hug for several minutes.

"Son, are you going to be okay?"

He nodded through streaming tears as violent paroxysms shook him visibly.

"What about Atina, daddy?"

"This will be very hard for her, son. But, she and Aunt Marie will need a little time alone. Then, we can go see them. It will help to have people nearby who love them. We can go tomorrow.

Mom will stay with you for the rest of the day. I need you two to look after each other. My people don't know, yet. I have to tell them all." They nodded as I returned to my desk and tapped in an order to empty both Hangar Decks and remove the retractable dividing wall as quickly as possible. Then, I directed all off-duty personnel and all in Zeta that were able to attend to report to that area in an hour. After that, I sent a quick message to Marie. I told her I'd be there as soon as possible.

"Will you be okay?" I asked softly as I looked from one to other.

"Maybe soon. We'll help each other." Fredricka replied.

"What about you, Daddy?" Bryant asked.

"This will hurt inside me for a long time. But, each day that pain gets a little less. I will be okay.

I'll try to be there for you as much as I can. But, this will cause a lot of pain throughout our entire Federation. And, it will mean changes in the OFSA. So daddy may not be there all the time. King David, your Aunt Grace and all your uncles will be devastated. And Aunty Marie will need us the most. She loved your uncle very much.' I explained as tears involuntarily welled in my eyes again. "You two head back home. I'll see you there in a few hours." I finished as I walked them to the door.

I was startled to find Roh and El quietly waiting outside. I waved them in as my family left in tears. Both were frozen watching my loved ones withdrawing wracked with remorse.

"What the hell's going on, Kurt? Are you dying, or something."

"No. But, you better grab a drink. I know it's early, but you may even want to make it a stiff one. Then, we'll sit and talk."

My system annunciator cried out several times as they were serving themselves. I checked my mail. I was being summoned to a Commission meeting on Rigil. It was scheduled for eighteen hundred hours. I had suspicions. I knew they'd discuss burial rites. But, I also knew there'd be more. It was inevitable.

"I have bad news.' I explained softly as I headed for a perch on a couch. 'Fleet Admiral George Bryant died a few hours ago. A clot formed from his injuries and caused a massive stroke. He was my mentor and my best friend. And, I know you both loved him, too." I observed quietly.

Tears sprang from both Officers eyes before I'd even finished. El sobbed, and Roh moaned and rocked as she bawled.

"When's the service?" El whispered through violent heaves.

"I don't know, yet. But, other things will happen, too. There will be changes. They will be immediate. The place Admiral Bryant occupied in the OFSA is massive, and everyone will want to fill it quickly, though I don't think anyone can replace, George.

There's a Commission Meeting on Rigil at eighteen hundred. I want you both to accompany me. Roh, can you make sure the Hangar will be ready. We're supposed to meet most of Zeta there in twenty minutes. I will need you both at my side during that event." I stood up.

"We're there for you, sir," El said.

"I know. And, I'll be there for all of you." I whispered.

I spent the next ten minutes preparing the Zeta notification memo. I put it on the system and set it for Command-wide release in half an hour.

....

At eighteen hundred, the remaining C&C are all seated in the Commission's large conference room. I'm not feeling all that well. I didn't take the news well, myself. Then, there was the trauma of informing my family and another when I announced it to twelve thousand people who all broke down, instantly.

I'm at my usual place at the table as is everyone, except George. As I look about, I note I am not the only one with bloodshot eyes and a swollen face. Grace quickly calls the meeting to order.

The next hour was expended discussing funeral arrangements. The King wanted a State Funeral with full honors but had been convinced to hold it on Rigil, for a multitude of reasons. It would be attended by all Federation Heads of State and our allies and most trading partners. It would be broadcast live throughout the Federation since we'd seeded all our remaining space with the new communications relays in the last month.

Then, Grace deftly maneuvered discussion to George's replacement.

"I know everyone's feeling very miserable, right now. But, this is a topic that has to be discussed. Epsilon is the OFSA's premier tactical Command. And, without the proper leadership, it won't be as capable."

"What about Stevens?" I asked trying to deflect the most likely suggestion.

"Tom's expressed on many occasions that he's gone as far as he wants to. He says he's too old to move up that last notch." Steven Nichols explained as Tom nodded in agreement.

"Then, you're the next best choice.' I responded to him. 'Your tactical skills are exceptional, and you were trained by him."

I'd run this scenario in my head many times, over the past few hours. I knew how it would end. But, I hoped I could change the seemingly preordained outcome.

"Maybe that's all true. But, I've been running a regional Command for a long time, now. I haven't had to make wide-ranging strategic decisions in years. There's only one person with the skills necessary whose had his finger in that pie the whole time. And, I think you know who I'm talking about." Steven replied.

"Look. If you're speaking of me, I already have a major Command that's mobile and gets into tactical situations throughout our territory. But, it's a specialized one. It's Commander needs skills specific to its legal, enforcement, and intelligence responsibilities."

"There are others who can replace you, there. But, you're the only person that can come close to taking over for George." Grace said as she turned a letter to me.

The letter was from the King in his official CIC capacity and the Secretary of Defense. They wanted me moved into the Command "whatever it takes to convince him." And, they wanted me to take on the role of Chief of C&C for Tactical Operations.

"This is all very flattering. But, I think there are better people." I tried to explain.

"The entire Commission believes you are the right choice." Savign piped in.

"I need a bit of time."

"We're adjourned for fifteen minutes!" Grace barked and slammed her gavel.

....

"You knew this was going to happen, didn't you? That's why you asked El and me to come along." Rho whispered.

"Yes. But, don't misunderstand. I am honestly reluctant to replace George because I believe no one can. But, I was pretty sure I'd have to take it. And, I think El should replace me." My Deputy jerked upright as I mumbled the response.

"Me. You want to make me a C&C?"

"Why not. You do a great deal of my job now. And, you have expert knowledge and experience in IGB's little intricacies."

"Yes, but there are a lot of Level elevens with a lot more experience and seniority."

"Maybe. But, none have your skill set."

We returned to the meeting.

"Can we clear the room for a few minutes. I'd like to discuss this with my peers alone." I asked as a commotion broke out at the door. It was King David.

We all jumped to attention.

"Relax. This was one meeting I didn't feel I should miss. I need to speak with Kurt before you continue."

We exited and strolled the halls together as we talked.

"I know how hard it must be to consider assuming a role that was held by your best friend who has suddenly passed on." David offered.

"It's not just that, sir. I am feeling pretty guilty. George died to save me!"

"What do you mean?" He asked inquisitively.

"The Examiner was severely damaged and taking heavy fire. George was killed because he ordered the Valhalla to shield us until we could maneuver the ship to a safer orientation."

"George didn't give that order. He didn't see your dilemma because he was busy surveying Epsilon moves. It was Tom who directed the action. And, I can tell you, he's feeling like shit, right now. I spoke to him a couple of hours ago. He's beside himself with remorse. George was his best friend, too. And, you might want to know, he suggested we look at you to fill the role.

And you know those final letters you tactical people always write in case you die. In his, George believed you were the best man to replace him as head of Epsilon."

"I'm stunned. I don't know what to say."

"Say yes to the offer. Take the position. Everyone but you knows you're the right person for that particular job."

"If I agree, I'd like you to consider one request. It's not a demand, sir. But, I think you should promote Elasima to replace me. He's level eleven, already. And, I know there are others with longer careers. But IGB is very specialized, and he knows all its complexities. It would take someone else a year or more to understand. And, he'd actually be running it in the meantime, anyway."

"I hadn't thought that far ahead, yet. But, you're right. I can't argue with the logic. But, the question is you, at this moment."

"You know I am loyal to you and would do whatever you ask of me, Your Majesty. Of course, I'll take it. And, thank you for explaining the Valhalla's move. I will try to help Tom out."

"Let's get back in the room. And, by the way, I'd like you and Tom to present the eulogy."

"That's the toughest job you've ever asked of me," I said as we crossed the sash.

"I don't mean to hijack your meeting, but I need to say something if you'll calm these people down!" David announced to Grace.

"The meeting will come to order. King David wishes to address the Commission." She slammed the mallet then gave him a nod.

"I have convinced Admiral Brubacher to accept the assignment as C&C Epsilon Command and the post of Tactical Chief of the C&C. I would also like your unanimous acceptance to promote Admiral Elasima and assign him as C&C Zeta Command. He's not the most experienced Level Eleven Admiral. But, he's the most qualified for this position."

Grace placed a motion to support both appointments before the board. There was no discussion. There was solidarity in the group that night.

"What about Chiefs?" Nichols asked.

"I'll be happy with Moe. We know each other. And we worked together, before. El knows and likes Roh. I'm sure he won't want a change." I opine.

"When?" Savigne inquired.

"Tomorrow aboard the Valhalla at eleven hundred. Epsilon's still here. The Valhalla and several others are just completing testing after all the repairs. We can do El aboard the Examiner at noon and head to Rigil for the luncheon. The two Commands can host their evening's celebrations." Grace suggested.

"That's fine. But, I will post announcements, immediately. It will allow Moe to prepare for the event and it will answer the questions and doubts Epsilon is feeling." David responded to a room full of nods.

"Let's get El and Roh in here," I said.

Everyone in the corridor was summoned into the room. The announcement was made to them. El was asked about Roh, and she was questioned about him. Both were happy with the arrangement.

"I have one other proposal I'd like to make?" I injected before Grace could gavel the meeting closed.

"What's that Admiral Brubacher?" She inquired.

"I'd like to rechristen the Valhalla the FSS George T. Bryant and put a memorial plaque aboard her. I'd also like to retire one flag office with his name on it and designate the George T. Bryant the flagship of the Federation." I suggested.

"I like most of it,' David observed. 'But, I think you're going too far with the office. It would be hard for others to live with - especially Marie if she stays aboard. And, I'm planning to have the Rigil HQ named the Admiral George T. Bryant campus."

"Yes, you're right. But, I'd like to propose the rest.

"Once we've completed your reassignment, we'll conduct the renaming of the ship," David said after a unanimous vote.

....

As I stood in front of more than twelve thousand in the Hangar of the Bryant after the Assignment ceremony, I couldn't help wishing the circumstances were different. We'd all be a lot happier if George was still with us.

I'd been received with great fanfare an hour earlier. Though I could see the remorse in the thousands of faces, I also felt I was already accepted by the majority of personnel in the Command. The Assignment and Transfer of Command rite were relatively short. As CIC, King David read the order, presented me the Epsilon patches and pennants, and shifted all Epsilon and OFSA Tactical Command Codes to me. Then, I made a brief statement.

"Ladies and Gentlemen and Officers and Crew of Epsilon Command, Mr. Secretary of Defense, fellow C&C Commission Members, visiting Officers and dignitaries, and King David, I am humbled at assuming the job Admiral Bryant handled with such ease and composure. I was part of Mobile Fifth RAC when it was created.

George Bryant was my mentor and my best friend. I loved him like I would an older brother. I only succeeded because of a second chance he gave me when others might have tossed me away. He saw something in me that many may have missed in those days. There has never been a better friend, and there will never be a more capable Commander. I know I cannot replace him or fill his shoes. But, I can try to walk his path.

And, I am honored to have been assigned the foremost tactical Command in the Federation. I know it is manned by the best of the finest. You were all loyal to Admiral Bryant. I will try to earn that respect from you, too.

Like George, I believe it is not the leadership that makes Epsilon a success. It's the more than three million Epsilon people who risk their lives daily to serve our Federation. I also believe I cannot gain your loyalty if you don't feel you have mine. So, I will strive to show you all that I will fight for you - work for you - try to protect you.

I was proud of Mobile Fifth RAC when I was a part of it, years ago. And, from a distance, I've always maintained admiration for you and George. You are brave, honest and forthright. Each and every person under Epsilon's umbrella would give their lives for their King, Command, and each other.

It's my hope to change very little. My command style is a lot like George's because I was trained by him and people he directed and trusted. Epsilon is not broken. And you know what they say. If it ain't broke, don't fix it.' I had to stop as the entire crowd cheered.

'What you're familiar with will remain intact. Admirals Stevens, Moahu, and all the other Epsilon leaders are people I respect. I hope to cause little disruption in their tasks and obligations. That way they can maintain stability in your lives.

I want to thank you all for welcoming me. Our futures will be filled with many trials. But, I believe we'll all enjoy many great times together, too. And, it's my hope we are a family."

Though I presented it in a subdued and solemn manner, it was received as if it was some great oratory. I could not believe the response as the ovation lasted a full five minutes.

I finally brought everyone to order explaining I had to be aboard the Examiner shortly for a similar ceremony for my replacement. Then, I announced the party we would hold that evening.

"I would like to invite you all to tonight's celebration. But, I'd like to add a special note. Many of you do not feel like rejoicing at a time like this. And, that is reasonable and understandable. But, it is customary to hold the event, and George Bryant loved revelry. It was Admiral Bryant who directed Admiral Moahu to create these fantastic Command level events many years ago. And, the other Commands have followed the Epsilon lead, making it an OFSA tradition.

And, it will be an excellent opportunity to recall and applaud George's vivacity. He was a great man who will always be in our hearts and minds, but he enjoyed life. And, if you'd asked when he was alive, he'd have told you a festive wake is a better way to remember than a solemn funeral.

So, while we may acclaim the transfer tonight, let's use the occasion to trade *Admiral Bryant stories* and shout our tributes to the life he lived. There will be plenty of time to show our respect at somber memorials in the coming days. For tonight, let's all remember the joy he brought us. I hope you'll all find your way to the Hangars of our Epsilon Command vessels."

Before leaving, I dropped in on Marie and Atina. After spending ten minutes gently consoling both, I asked her to stay on the FSS Bryant and continue to run her Command from there. She'd been uncertain until I made the suggestion, but decided she'd take up the offer. I explained that my family would always be there for them and we felt they were a part of us.

"I saw your appointment on the viewer. Your speech was magnificent. And, the sentiments it conveyed will never be forgotten by me. Atina and I will make a short appearance at the wake, this evening. It is a delightful idea and the way George would want a memorial."

....

Aboard the Examiner the ritual took more time. It involved a promotion ceremony along with reassignment and elevation. So, it was close to two hours, instead of the twenty minutes, it took aboard the Valhalla.

El made a short speech that reflected on the events around George's passing. It was a masterful presentation that reassured everyone in Zeta. Then, I took the podium and addressed the crowd.

"I'm not sure - but, I don't think I've been on this end of a reassignment.' There was the low din of soft chuckles from throughout the assembly.

'But, I am happy Zeta will be run by Admiral Elasima. Besides his competence, he is one of the most loyal people I know. And, that wasn't just bestowed on me. It's freely given to everyone in IGB.

A great many of you have been with us since the formation of the unit. A lot more came along as we matured and expanded. But, all of you have always given your best and done everything asked of you. You have been unwaveringly devoted to Zeta Command and me. And, you've all worked for El for years - some directly - some indirectly. So, nothing's really changed.

So, it's my hope you will extend the allegiance you've always had for me to your new Commander.

For my part, it's been an honor leading IGB. You have made me proud. We have always completed every task assigned us with vigor. I will miss you all." I stepped down and turned away as I finished. I didn't want them to see the tears in my eyes.

Chapter 28 Seeking Justice

Monday, April 15, 2272

"I'm for justice no matter who it's for or against." **Malcolm X**

We didn't get this mission started until a week ago because I felt Epsilon required recovery time and I wanted to witness and comprehend all its capabilities. And, of course, we needed to conduct a memorial service almost all Epsilon personnel could attend. Below us, things are incredibly intense on the surface of Eta Pegasus, and we've temporarily lost contact with the Marine Corps Commands. Up here, we are still mopping up remaining active Isesinis base stations, cruisers, and satellites. It had taken extensive planning and effort to reach this stage with our combined Mobile Fifth RAC, SOCC, Polemista, and Spiel Forces. Over two thousand warships and three and a half million people had cleared a corridor and surrounded Eta Pegasus the home of the Isesinis. As we exited our jump thresholds, we perceived covering clouds of orbiting debris created by SOCC's preparatory mining of circling enemy assets. But, it all didn't happen by accident.

....

On Wednesday, February 28, 2272, nearly four million filled the OFSA rotunda, its patios, and gardens and all the streets along the processional path. It tested Rigil's facilities to the maximum since only just over a million live there permanently.

My first order of business was to hold a meeting of my senior team. Admiral J. Coquinas, Admiral Palikiko, Admiral Kura Neko my Tier One Commanders, and General Shellots my Marine Army Commandant joined Tom Stevens, Moe and me in my office. I issued orders directing my team to instruct all their ships to park in high stationary orbits. And, they were all to run on reduced power since it only takes thrusters to correct any trajectory decay for the five to six days those procedures were employed. I also directed them to grant leave to all personnel, effective immediately except for the smallest possible skeleton crews. Everyone was to be recalled and aboard their ships by no later than eighteen hundred March 4. That allowed two days to disembark, two to reboard, and the full day of the memorial on the planet.

Since Rigil doesn't have enough capacity for that many visitors, I also authorized the distribution of all the Transferable Field Sheltering (TFS) units our ships carry. That included providing mobile hygiene stations for landed personnel to use. Each ship stores enough TFS equipment to house everyone aboard in case a need suddenly arises to abandon ship in favor of a planet or moon. Each Commander was instructed on the cooking gear, water purification capability, and emergency medical stations they should provide to secure the numbers they were dispatching. The encampment turned into a giant temporary city with millions housed along the shores of the Lake. Flag and Senior Officers, politicians, and dignitaries took up all the motel, hotel, and lodge accommodations. By February 29, I received calls from all the other arriving HQ Commands to discuss deployment of their attendees. I explained how we were handling ours.

The funeral march and rites were conducted on March 2. George was memorialized by the King, the SOD, myself, Tom Stevens, and Marie Bryant. His gilded casket, replete with Federation Insignia and OFSA badge rested atop a six-wheeled open carriage drawn by four white Arabian horses. It led a convoy of a dozen landaus pulled by black Arabians. The Royal Family rode in the first. Marie, Atina, Tom, myself and Admiral Savage were in the next. I was also one of six Admiral pallbearers who laid him in-state on Feb 29 then, transported him from carriage to a mausoleum on the grounds of the OFSA, after the funeral. He was laid to rest there.

Though we'd honored him at the reassignment party, I ordered up an official Epsilon wake. Tom, Pal, Grace Tonaka, Marie and I shared stories from the past. Several wars had made things quite somber in the past several years. But, we all concentrated on the devilish unrestrained humor George displayed more frequently around the time of the forming of Mobile Fifth RAC. There were lots to raise a toast to, and even more that garnered a laugh or two.

On March 5, I ordered Epsilon forces to break orbit and move to Wolf 359. The trip is over a day at our slowest cruising speed. We would do nothing for five days after we entered the quiet system with the tiny red dwarf. We'd use the six days to contemplate our loss.

Tuesday, March 12 found me in another day-long meeting with my senior team. I didn't issue directives but conveyed my need to see all of Epsilon's capabilities. I asked them to run low-pressure drills that tested all their Fleets' proficiencies, so I could watch. I explained they were not being graded - I just wanted to see everything. But, I wanted the troops to know that. I didn't think they should be under pressure, yet.

Then, I scheduled another meeting for the following Tuesday, to discuss an impending mission.

Once they'd all left, I contacted El and asked if I might speak with Sparks to get some intelligence information I needed. He replied that I didn't need his permission but it just shows respect, so I will always seek El's authorization.

I asked General Sparks to release Suvayeek intelligence of the Eta Pegasus system to me along with anything else he had pertaining to it and Isesinis formations in their own space or near ours. Half an hour later, I had nearly a five hundred page book to contend with.

On March 20, I summoned Admirals Coquinas, Palikiko, Laft, Neko, Stevens, Mohahu and General Shellots to my office. I explained the picture I was trying to form and split the document among us by spatial regions. That gave us each a little more than seventy related pages to scan. Each Officer would be able to build an image of their area and together we'd assemble a mosaic. By entering their summaries into my system, we created a current three-dimensional representation of enemy deployments.

I projected the 3-D video image in the air over the conversation pit. It was evident the Isesinis had about seventy percent of remaining forces at or near their homeworld.

"It's like Fort Knox!" Stevens observed referring to the once impregnable gold depository.

"Yes, but I don't believe their intention is fortification," I said.

"What are you thinking?"

"I believe the fastest way to restore services and rebuild plants and technology is to bring home the Fleet and use its Engineering capabilities, parts stores, and manufacturing ability to rebuild everything quickly. There's no doubt they can defend, too. But, I believe their primary purpose is reconstruction."

"That makes a lot of sense." Moe injected as everyone else nodded agreement.

"So everyone take a look at this model and give me your opinions on how many ships and bases are within ten light years of Eta Pegusas. Then, I need you to tell me how many you think are within a ring from that perimeter out another ten kilometers. I'll sort of average your estimates and make some quick decisions from that information. Finally, I need you each to prepare a list of enemy flotillas within your region, by location. I will make some more accurate decisions based on that data. We'll meet again once I have a draft idea for a plan. I'll update all of you Tier 2 Commanders, and you will have to get together with your Field Operations and prepare your part of a battle. From what I see here, we'll need more forces than Epsilon has. I'll seek sizable representation from the

Spiel and Polemista. And we'll need a significant contingent from SOCC. Any thoughts from any of you?"

"Yes, Kurt. What about advanced mining?" Pal suggested.

"Yes. We'll do it again. I don't see any other way to succeed, and as far as we know, the Isesinis still haven't figured out our cloaks. Anyone else?' I asked. There were negative wags all around. "Okay then, let's start with Pal and just go from left to right. Everyone give me your numbers, please."

It took nearly an hour for me to record all the figures as they rhymed them off. Each worked on their particular list when not engaged in their presentation.

"So, generally, we'll need to mine the ships in this corridor.' I outlined a pathway within our 3-D mock-up. 'Then we'll want to booby-trap all the GPHC stations around Eta Pegasus. It seems there are none of those in outlying regions, anymore. And, we'll require intense up-to-the-minute intelligence on each of the Fleets in the outer-donut region. It'll take one to three days for them to receive a distress call and the same time for them to return to defend the planet. So, we can't be more than two or three days accomplishing our goals."

"What will our objectives be?"

"Primary is to capture their Emperor. Secondarily, I want to destroy as many remaining Baseships as possible. Finally, we should demolish any military production assets they've resurrected. Hopefully, we'll get a formal surrender, if we're successful."

"Why do you want that passageway cleared?" Admiral Coquinas inquired.

"That'll be our staging and exit area. We'll use Limpets on everything in there and finish off any remaining vessels when we land. One Epsilon and one Polemista Theatre will hold the pathway while the other five go to Eta Pegasus with three more Polemista and Spiel Tier Three operations. We'll take up high stationary orbits above the enemy facilities on the planet that holds the Empire's leader and government. Once all space-borne Isesinis ships are subdued, we'll land a couple of hundred thousand Marines with heavy armor and artillery. We'll send down more when they've secured the Capital and have a beachhead. They will conduct ground operations outlined in the plan. I want them to pacify the entire planet. We need more surface surveillance to be confident of our facts. But, we definitely have to grab the Emperor. So, let's meet again tomorrow at eleven hundred. We can have lunch, together.' I stood up as I ended my explanation. 'Dismissed!' I barked. Then, I added, 'General stay behind, please.

As is the usual protocol, the last person out shut the door. General Shellots and I stood just inside. My hand rested on the doorknob.

"How are you, Donald? How are you doing in the new assignment?" I quietly asked.

"Fine sir - better than I thought I would. It's a big job though."

"Yes, that's true. But, no one's ever been more ready than you are. You Commanded Svesion's Second Corps for a year. You had eighty thousand before. The next job is an Army.' I paused in thought for a moment. 'No one can train you for that. And this particular Marine Army is the biggest one. Now it's nearly six hundred thousand in three substantial Corps. But, still - you know all the ins and outs from your Zeta Second Corps experience. It's the same but bigger."

"Yes, sir. I tell myself that every day." He responded with a sheepish grin.

"You realize it's fifteen years since we met aboard the Shenzhen?"

"...seems like yesterday."

"I've kept my eye on you. I have confidence in you."

"Thank you, sir."

"Are you up for this ground operation? You're going to have to lead it. It'll take more than two full Corps, in all."

"Yes, sir. Field maneuvers aren't a problem. It's administration that's so much bigger."

"I know what you mean. Anyway, you'll do fine. But, don't hesitate to seek me out if you need to." I opened the door.

He saluted and exited.

....

An hour later in his Office just a few doors down from mine, General Donald Shellots looked over the ground recon reports. A few decisions came quickly.

He'd need a blanket bombardment of all known defensive positions in the Capital City region. After a formidable attack, the tactic would need to be altered to a perimeter assault that would restrict bombing to a toroidal profile surrounding the opening salvos as his landing-crafts made their way through the open central corridor onto the surface. And, those deployment operations would consume considerable time since it would require three round trips of the twenty-four hundred eighty-seven large transport vessels to land the two hundred fifty-eight thousand Marines he deemed necessary to secure the territory in the initial landing. That's one full Corps and a Division. An equal number would organize over

216

the following two-week period as OFSA Marines sweep over the planet. A final Division would be held in reserve in case exit, or fortification assistance was needed. Each of the two large Groups necessitates an additional thirty of the heavy-landers to deploy all their armor and artillery. In the end, Shellots will have dispatched over a half million to this world's surface to deal with land-based battlements.

He wrote me a memo requesting the strike, suggesting it for after all orbital Isesinis assets were destroyed and as a prelude to his invasion. The message told me it would take nearly thirty-six hours to dispatch all divisions included in the first landings. This would have to be considered in my own preparations.

Then, Shellots summoned his Corps Commanders.

It took nearly an hour for Lieutenant General Richard Montpelier to make it from the FSS Sif. Palikiko's FSS Midgard and Coquinas FSS Asgard were nearer, so Lieutenant Generals Yberil and Mashuka were already relaxed with a drink in hand when "Monty" arrived in Donald's doorway. It took him nearly ten minutes to pay his respects and grab a cocktail before getting comfortable.

"I wanted to gather to discuss our impending operation." Shellots began.

"What operation is that, Donald?" Mashuka asked.

"Are you being mischievous?" Shellots smirked.

"No, sir. It's obvious we're about to conduct an operation. I was seeking clarification and details. No disrespect was intended." Mashuka responded as his face flushed.

"And none was taken. You are so easy. It's the way you talk. You leave yourself so open, and I just love to pull your chain." Donald responded with a laugh.

"So what's happening?" Monty cut in impatiently.

"We're on our way to Eta Pegasus, soon. We'll be there by April 10. And, we're expected to capture the Isesinis' Emperor and pacify the planet.

I have already requested a heavy shelling of the capital. It will expand outward, leaving us an expansive disc to land in." General Shellots began but was interrupted.

"Those are risky landings. We never know if our forces will be killed by friendly fire." Monty injected.

"Let's not worry about that here. I can take steps to minimize that possibility.

Anyway, one Corps and an attached Division will execute the initial incursion. But, that'll entail nearly twenty-five hundred LCs and thirty HLs for the heavy stuff. You will have one hundred twenty-eight Carriers to launch from so I suggest waves of two hundred

217

fifty-six. That will put twenty-six thousand on the ground in each surge. The same size force will land every ten minutes over the next two hours. It seems to me that if you overload each vehicle a little and borrow some large shuttles, you could land by Brigades. I suggest you have a Division Commander in that very first Group. The Corps Commander should arrive with the last Major General. Depending on the initial bombings, those first two Brigades may face problems. They must deploy quickly on settling, and they'll only have a little over thirty-one thousand personnel and limited artillery and armor to defend with. But they must hold their ground until the next contingent arrives later.

At the same time, we can send nine HC's at a time from all our SuperCarrier Class Vessels. But, I think that would be too much for a Brigade to have to manage. So, I believe we should deliver just five heavies at a time. The Brigades will be able to use them and won't have to worry about protecting any unassumed hardware.

The Corps Commander should stay mobile until a good portion of the second Brigade is on the ground. Tying up personnel to set up headquarters could leave the force vulnerable, at first. Once you have enough troops landed, the Corps and two Brigade HQs could be raised together.

We'll execute from our staging point thirty-six hours after the first landing. That first wave will quell the Capital. Once that happens, we'll send another group of the same size so all forces can begin fanning out. Those landings will take longer. They can be deployed as our perimeter expands and they're needed.

The remaining Division will be held in reserve. It will be sent in as reinforcements if someone gets in trouble or when we need exit fortification."

"Who's got Job One?" Lieutenant General Mashuka queried.

"Corps One will be the primary assault unit, and they will be supported by one of your Divisions. Corps three will execute the second surge with another of your Divisions. And, your third Division will be the reserve unit.

I need you all to sit with your immediate subordinates. Show them the current intelligence and have them help you build a plan for each of the stages you're involved with. Then, we'll reconvene and modify the whole thing to ensure it meets our objectives and all the schemes are coordinated into a single assault strategy. And Generals Yberil and Mashuka should sit together to discuss how they'll organize the second leg of the battle.

Rules of Engagement are in Force. No mishandling of prisoners, no genocide, and no *accidents*! Everything we do must be *by-the-book*. Do you all get it?" The three nodded as Donald finished.

They chatted for another half-hour before heading off to the Flag Officers' alcove in the Officers' Mess.

....

In their respective offices, Admirals Palikiko, Coquinas, and Nguyen were meeting with their subordinates to plan their specific operations for the coming adventure. All three included the leadership of the Spiel and Polemista Theatre strength units. One of Coquinas' Theatres was being held in reserve. Otherwise, the three had very similar responsibilities. Each would move in to destroy remaining enemy assets after the detonation of the hidden mines.

General Donald Shellots joined each individual meeting. He expressed his need for accurate bombardment targeting to permit the window his forces needed for the landing without endangering them. Each Tier 2 Admiral assured him they would enforce the most stringent standards on their Theatre Operations regarding any surface bombings during the campaign.

....

While the others were conducting their briefings, Laft was already joining Admiral Corgos Basi at the target. Between the two Commands, they'd finish all the booby-traps before the rest of Epsilon arrived. It's slow, perilous, meticulous work. But, it has to be done.

....

By Saturday, March 23, the eight of us were in my office again. Each leader presented a short summary of their distinctive plan as they handed me the documents. Though I need to examine them all in depth and combine them with Epsilon's general strategy, they seemed to account for everything. The proposals ranged in size from four hundred twenty to five hundred seventy-two pages apiece. Tom and I would be busy combining it into one homogenized approach.

"I'll need some time to look these over. In the meantime, I'll buy you all breakfast." I said as I rose to my feet.

....

We resumed discussions at thirteen hundred hours on Tuesday, March 26.

"We've analyzed all your proposals. The only modifications are at the very beginning. And, those are only to combine it into a collective strategy. All of you provided very complete, concise, and thoughtful schemes. So, I am returning them approved but within the overall battle plan. Please note the assigned Mission Number on all documents, from now on.

I've programmed all the variations, I could see based on counter-moves the Isesinis might make. However, there aren't a lot of those if the SOCC and Epsilon SF parts of the operations go as planned. An abort will be triggered automatically if that campaign fails or falls short by any substantial amount. We'd go at a later date once we have a way around that. But, as far as I know, the enemy still does not see our covert vessels or understand why we destroy so many of their warships and Bases so readily. So, I am assuming we will not need to invoke the Mission Termination.

Half of Epsilon SF and half of SOCC are employed in the mining operation. Current reports indicate they have nearly completed their task. The other half of Epsilon SF and a Fleet from SOCC are mining the opposing vessels along the corridor we intend to use for entry and withdrawal.

There are only two systems known to the OFSA on a vector somewhat close to Eta Pegasus. They are HR 8799, and Alpha Pegasus referred to as Markab by us. The first is an inhospitable place and the second offers resources we may need. So, we will stage at Markab. Though it brings us closer to our antagonists, it is still about twenty parsecs from Eta Pegasus. That means a week in a vortex if we do that leg at thirty percent. So, we will land there first and then one and a half light-years from our enemy in open space. And, that could be a dicey move. Though it is easy to hide a single craft in the void, it becomes almost impossible when you're trying to conceal around nearly two thousand warships, bases, mobile hospitals, and supply ships - each bigger than a large town. We are projecting a parking lot that is a sphere with a thousand kilometer radius. And, that many exit thresholds create quite an energy reading on any nearby sensors.

But, we have cloaked SOCC squads patrolling the region, and the Suvayeek are meticulously surveilling the site. Right now, that spot is vacant and there are no patrols or deployments within ten light-years except Eta Pegasus.

So, we'll stop at Markab for a full day then move on to our staging point. We'll launch our attack from there, after another day's rest.

At around eleven hundred on April 13, our reserve Epsilon, Spiel, and Polemista force of three hundred eighty-four warships will head out to their assigned positions. They must plan for re-entry to standard space by four hundred hours April 14. At twenty-one hundred hours, twenty-six minutes, on April 13, the main force will launch for Eta at twenty percent. Our assault time is scheduled for precisely six hundred, April 14. At three hundred hours forty-five minutes on April 14, SOCC and Epsilon SF vessels along the corridor will activate all detonators. They must be satisfied they've allowed a few rival ships to send off messages. At five forty-five in the morning, SOCC and Epsilon ships at the target planet will begin detonation of orbiting assets.

When we break into space at six hundred, we need half a Threatre to fan out and circle the globe along its equator and a similar group to travel a polar orbital path. They should be at different altitudes, both much higher than the main body of OFSA vessels - but not in synchronous trajectories. Their job will be to look for surviving Isesinis HQ Stations, Cruisers, Carriers, Observation Platforms, Shipyards and Communication Satellites and destroy them. The remaining part of the main force will take up their positions in stationary paths over their assigned targets. Tier 1-1 Threatre1 will have six Fleets directly above the Capital City. They are to target all large government buildings, Royal Residences, commercial transportation systems, air transport concerns, spaceports, troop bases, military manufacturing and assembly facilities, and known martial formations within ten kilometers of the municipality. All other groups will program their specified targets into their control systems.At six hundred hours fifteen minutes, all of these vessels will begin bombarding their assigned targets. I have estimated it will take half an hour to raze all listed targets not already destroyed in the previous mission. But, the six Fleets over the Capital will cease firing in the inner five-kilometer radius of their objectives and employ dense creeping fire to widen their outer perimeter to fifteen kilometers.

At six hundred hours thirty minutes, General Shellots will begin dispatching his force to the surface. Around a quarter million will land in that wave. That will take thirty-six hours. But, he requires eight hours to get the first hundred thousand troops on the ground. Until then, we will continue firing into the donut created around the Capital's center. I cannot stress how important it is to impress on your tactical and weapons control personnel how essential accuracy is during this phase. We cannot afford a mistake. We do not need our own killed by friendly fire.

Once the General has his first Division on land, I will be making decisions based on his needs. On the ground, he's the boss. Make sure your Corps Commanders know its a joint mission under his direction. Any of your people you place on the planet for support are just that - no matter their rank. Donald Shellots is in charge.

If anything goes wrong and we are forced to withdraw, one Polemista and one Spiel Theatre will come forward in the Corridor and assist our retreat while the rest of their Fleets and the Epsilon reserve guard the corridor.

When the Marines have secured the Capital, a second contingent will join the first over the period of a week as all ground forces expand our circle of influence until we've acquired and pacified the entire continent. Thank goodness all civilization is on just one. I expect those operations to require up to a month.

Marine priorities are the capture of the Emperor and the submission of the planet. They are also attempting the destruction of anything that can be used to reconstitute their Space Military. However, we'd like to leave them with a limited functioning Army, Navy, and Police Force for enforcement reasons. We are not trying to bomb them into the stone ages with this operation - just remove them from interstellar space warfare.

Any questions?" I finish as I scan everyone around the room.

....

Lieutenant General Montpelier had dispatched Major General John Corkeran to oversee the first wave of surface landings. They'd pinpointed the government center which had been brutally shelled from orbital platforms. Corkeran arrived in the first wave with his First Division's Alpha Brigade. More than thirty thousand Marines were able to land, acquire their heavy armor and artillery, and establish their Regimental and Battalion Headquarters as Corkeran entrenched the Divisional one. Ten Companies were immediately dispatched to probe the area seeking residual enemy forces. They were to deal with smaller contingents and call for help if needed. General Corkeran's operation became the temporary communications' hub. It reported to Montpelier while initiating and relaying orders to outlying Brigade Commands. By midday, his second Brigade had landed permitting the establishment of a ring of eight Regimental Headquarters that surrounded the central operation.

All the while, dust and smoke wafted over the region carried from the continuous flashes and rhythmic thunderous explosions just outside their perimeter. All of Corkeran's troops wore environmental protective gear to deal with all the pollution. Looking up in any direction, John observed the similarity to being in the calm eye of a powerful storm. Ground level was a wasteland full of craters, pits, rubble, scrap, bodies, and various limbs.

Major General Iflan Idanderfor landed among the first LCs carrying Beta Brigade. He established his HQ alongside Corkeran's. Montpellier went ashore with the first wave of troops from Second Division and grounded his base alongside the other two. But Division Two, Three and General Mashuka's First Division would move to outer boundary positions one hundred and twenty degrees apart and distribute their Brigades amongst the ones already on that border. As Division One held the center and the bombardment was expanded outward, they advanced, swelling their limit to the most distant area previously bombed. By twenty-two hundred hours April 15, 2272, a complete Corp with an additional Division was on the ground and prepared to protect the landing area as another similar-sized assemblage landed over the next week. Meanwhile, the aerial assault ceased on the third day. Marine Companies would call in this type of support if needed as they fan out throughout the continent. By April 17, Lieutenant Generals Montpelier, Yberil, and Mashuka were all ensconced in their Centres with flexible webs of subordinate Command Centers that would follow the action.

This massive Eta Pegasus Marine Central Command with its ten Senior Headquarters and all the HQ Staffs was a sight to behold. But, that's what it takes to control the movement of just over half a million troops and all their supportive hardware.

However, it quickly became apparent the Isesinis civilization reflected the Communist Dictatorships of Earth's twentieth century. As OFSA Marines moved on each military production plant, they'd find sizable bases of Isesinis forces placed nearby as protection. So, it was not uncommon for pitched battles to ensue requiring targeted aerial bombardment or Mobile Fifth RAC Raptor support. And, it was also evident that the enemy wasn't going to submit easily. Constant counter attacks on the Central Command proved that.

....

On Thursday, April 18, 2272, Captain Joe Markland, Two Corp's, Second Brigade, Fourth Regiment, Able Company Commander, received orders to secure an aerospace engine factory in Ikuk, a medium-sized city in the Isesinis Northern Province. He sent Platoons One and Two towards an easterly entrance as Four and Five headed to the western one. He led the third platoon himself as they attempted penetration at the front doorway.

The entire manufacturing operation protruded from the sheer granite face of a lofty hill and was shielded by a rocky ledge that jutted over the whole exposed factory roof. Another group of buildings half a mile to its east occupied a similar recess in the solid wall. Its military guard dressed in the customary Isesinis armor led Markland to assume it was an armed garrison.

Captain Markland planned to assault the factory without engaging the barracks. Approaching in silence by stealth would allow them to take the plant without facing the military. And, if the enemy became aware of the action, their troops would need ten minutes to reach the battle site giving Able Company plenty of time to prepare a defense.

But from the moment the three spearheads gained access, he realized he'd dangerously underestimated the situation. The concentrated resistance was conducted by the six-foot-tall armored soldiers, but he couldn't help being amazed at the sight of the swarthy diminutive factory workers scampering to safety. Markland had never seen the Isesinis out of their protective gear. He'd later realize that five hundred enemy troops guarded the establishment from within.

All the action was in corridors leading to the central production area. Close-quarter hand-weapon and physical fighting ensued as Captain Markland observed a large contingent leaving the nearby enemy garrison in answer to a call for help. He ordered his platoons to pull back to rocky outcroppings outside the building - some defending against those coming from within and some facing troops arriving. Meanwhile, he called for help. Fourth Regiment advised they'd directed two Companies to assist, but they were at least an hour away. By that time, Isesinis forces were targeting his five platoons with barrages of mortar and light artillery fire. Arms, legs, heads, dirt, blood, and pieces of flesh rained down as his people were being blown to bits. He called for aerial support and was advised the Carrier FSS Thor was sending down ten fighters that would arrive in ten minutes - a lifetime when you're under withering fire.

"I want A-Platoon to hit those incoming troops with mortar fire. Lay it on, and don't stop until the Raptors get here. You and B-Platoon have to keep up the covering fire. C, D, and E-Platoons return fire on those bastards coming from the factory. We've got enough ammo to sustain a constant stream for an hour. So, we should be okay until our fighters arrive!" Markland yelled into his communicator.

....

Das Kil Stip had analyzed the attackers' formations over the past couple of days and realized there was a possible penetration point he could use for a counter attack. Aerial reconnaissance showed a sizeable Central Command and a dozen or so peripheral ones ringing the main one. The weakness was in their spacing. The OFSA had cleared a five-kilometer disc creating a sixteen-kilometer inner front for them to secure. That meant those Brigade Commands were at least a kilometer apart. Even with deployed guards, there were weaknesses a half kilometer from each Headquarters.

When communications crackled to life on April 18, reporting a noteworthy battle developing at Ikuk, he knew his time had arrived. The Marines would be busy supporting that action and all their other movements throughout the regions they'd expanded into. He'd already developed a plan and was just awaiting the right moment. This was it.

He would send two of his three Divisions to penetrate the OFSA boundary a kilometer apart and head for the hub in two columns, while the third held back in reserve. The objective would be to take out the Central Command decapitating the serpent.

....

At ten hundred on Saturday, April 20, Corporal Joe Camp was just thinking how lucky he'd been that Diamond Company had drawn picket duty on the outer perimeter of the five-kilometer diameter area now occupied by the Mobile Fifth Marine Army. At six feet two inches tall, with an athletic build, natural good looks, and a handsome face trimmed with a mustache and goatee, he refused to don the environmental safety gear that might hide his face. Joe loved to be "cool" and would take risks to maintain that image.

Diamond Company was part of Second Corps, First Division, Third Brigade's contingent. Corporal Camp was just moving from one guard station to another checking on the soldiers in his squad as he mulled over just how calm things were on the boundary.

"Inky Black!" He called as he approached Private Selemina's position expecting her to return the countersign. He stopped short when it wasn't.

"Inky Black!" There was still no reply.

"This is Camp. I need a squad at position DCS1 - ASAP." He whispered into his internal comm as he crouched low peering toward his soldier's location. He was positive the flash of blue he saw was Isesinis body armor.

What seemed like an hour was only five minutes. Camp was joined by another Corporal and ten Marines. Using only hand signals, he indicated the position, a man was down, and the enemy was on site. Then he signaled they should split into two spearheads making contact ninety degrees from each other. His counterpart agreed and silently ordered his people accordingly. Each NCO took a column.

Camp abruptly raised his closed fist stopping his contingent about ten meters short and signaled the presence of fifty moving Isesinis troops. In the lowest possible tones, he advised the Company Commander of the breach and explained he believed it to be the result of the actions by a sizeable force.

"Red Dog. I repeat. Red Dog at DCS1!" The metallic voice would not just be heard by him but every person manning this section of the perimeter.

He signaled his group to turn back. The other Corporal and his men approached their starting point at the same time.

"Let's get to cover." He whispered as his counterpart nodded. All Federation Marines in the area would all be seeking protection after monitoring the call.

225

Corporal Camp was the last man down the sewer opening and was still sliding its lid in place when all hell broke loose. Raptors were reeking havoc on the formation he'd encountered.

....

In his office, Shellots was concerned. The Raptors sent to assist Camp's squad had spotted widespread enemy incursions in that section of the line, from the air. Regular reports were arriving from the five senior Commands on the surface. He sent down orders that Second Corps First Division should handle it until help joined in to fortify the central headquarters. Then, he ordered his reserve Division down to assist those resisting the enemy counterattack. Finally, he asked for continuous Raptor support in that area. When he attempted communications with his ground HQ, only silence was returned.

After a moment of near panic, he called me to ask for continuous live reconnaissance imaging from over the Headquarter's region. It was all still there with no signs of damage or enemy troops when he was finally able to examine the scene. All he could do was wait.

....

By seventeen hundred on April 20, two full Divisions were engaged in the operation to repel the intruders. In numbers, it was a pretty even match. Roughly sixty-five thousand troops from each side met each other. But Federation Marines had three distinct advantages. They were supported by light and medium armor, had control of all airspace, and though well protected did not wear the bulky robotic suits that slowed their opponents. And, of course, they knew head-shots didn't work. You needed to target the Isesinis in the center of the chest to actually hit the suit's operator.

Those small blessings turned the battle by midnight. After losing nearly ten thousand, Das Kil Stip ordered his people to withdraw.

Marine losses from the Isesinis attack were pegged at two hundred eleven dead and four hundred fifty-two injured. And it took until two hundred on the twenty-first to replace the antenna that had been destroyed by an incoming missile. By eight o'clock in the morning, Shellots ordered his reserves to return to their ships. The remaining troops would begin to push outward expanding their control. The goal was to reach a radius of ten kilometers from their Headquarters by sixteen hundred on April 23. Then, they'd begin columnar thrusts to other cities with essential military facilities.

Meanwhile, Corps One's Intelligence Office was sweeping up local government personnel and interrogating them.Some were brought up to the Bryant where I attended the questioning with Admiral Marie Bryant in tow. I still trusted her to have the best instincts regarding interview subjects. On April 22, we learned where the Emperor was holed up. He was in an underground tunnel we'd never have found on our own.

....

Like all the Kils, the Emperor was quite tall and relatively handsome. His family came from the same tribe. We knew we had him when we located an Isesinis in glittering gold armor. This was totally unique attire. We questioned him for a while, but it was like talking to a stone. So, we advised him he'd be charged with war crimes and tried in a legal court of law. He was also told he could face the death penalty.

Each of Fifth Mobile's Supercarriers holds a full contingent of courtrooms and each Fleet's Carriers contain a Circuit Court. So, there'd be no delay in charging him. We learned he was known as Kire Fask. Kire equates to the title of Emperor on Earth and Fask is his family name. He showed his surprise when the indictments contained that information on April 22. We placed him under heavy guard in an Admiral's suite and kept him supplied with meals prepared by captured Isesinis cooks using homegrown foods.

On our first of several visits, I did all the talking. He never uttered a single word. And, Marie sat in silence observing his reactions. But, he began to communicate the fifth time I arrived at his door.

"Are you trying to kill me with kindness?" He inquired as he waved a hand indicating his quarters.

"No. But, you're the leader of a world. No matter how I personally feel about you, I prefer to show you the respect a person holding such an office should receive."

"What do you mean?"

"By what?" I was uncertain what he was inquiring about.

"When you said no matter how you feel."

"I have great contempt for you. I'd like to kill you where you stand. Unprovoked, you invaded our Federation which tries to live in peace. Millions have died - including my best friend."

"I see. You hate me. But, you're a man of honor. So, you wait to hold this sham trial before you kill me."

"It's not a sham. We'll investigate thoroughly. You will have a real defense. Your attorneys will be privy to all aspects of the investigation. It's a civilian trial, so a jury of twelve will determine your guilt under the rules of law enforced by a Judge. You don't have to trust it now. But, you'll see it in action and know it is real justice. It's not the kind your people meted out. In our society, every accused deserves the right to a fair trial."

"It all sounds good. But, I'll believe it when I see it."

"Don't worry. You will."

"When?"

"That's hard to say. We need to seize and analyze a lot of documents on the surface and interview over a hundred people who worked for you. It'll probably take two to three months to determine a course of action."

"Who was this ...best friend?"

"He was the man responsible for defeating Kil Kos. His name was George Bryant. He was an Admiral in charge of the force I now command."

"Did you know him a long time?"

"He took me from the Military Academy nearly twenty years ago and kept an eye on my career, since then. I was at his wedding. He was at mine. Our children play together and are like cousins. His wife is an Admiral, too. She is the one with me when you are interrogated. She has a special knack for knowing the truth."

"So, is your plan to enslave my world?"

"No, just disable its ability to wage an offensive interstellar war. We'll leave when we're sure. And we'll make sure your people can still defend themselves in space and on the planet. We don't take other worlds by force. Our Federation has a hundred and twenty *voluntary* members."

"I know your people like peace. What if I promise to never attack you again?"

"It's too late for you. We have accepted treaties with those who've attacked us before. But, they conducted honorable wars. Your people committed genocide and murder. And, it appears they did those things on your orders. War is bad enough, in the first place. Millions die in these space conflicts. But to kill those who are helpless is criminal. Civilians and prisoners of war should be protected. Kil Kos destroyed an entire planet with all its inhabitants. And, he summarily executed prisoners."

"I see. So, you place a high value on honor?"

"Our entire Federation does. And, our allies do, too."

"What allies?"

"Several non-member neighbors are friendly to us. We have treaties with them. Not all are democracies, but they're all honorable."

"I think you will be surprised if you do an ***honest*** investigation. Genocide and murder are not the policy of the Isesinis. I went to school with Kos. He was always brilliant but sociopathic. It is not my policy to kill prisoners or annihilate helpless worlds. Enslaving them is another matter. It enriches my Empire."

"Who decided to attack the Orion Federation?"

"I did - of course. But, we have a legislated policy for the rules of engagement. It does not include criminal or dishonorable behavior."

"Then why employ those like Kos?"

"You will understand if you get to know our society. Kos is from a very powerful family. His appointment ensured my position. And he had the skills, education, and experience that qualified him for the post."

"Do you mind if Admiral Marie Bryant accompanies me on my next visit?"

"Not at all. I'd like to meet this empath."

I excused myself and left his quarters. But, I stood thinking for a few minutes as I leaned against his corridor doorframe. There'd been a ring of truth hidden within his disdain.

I contacted Elasima asking him to send a large contingent to us. We'd need his investigative team. Then, I spoke with Marie. She'd join me for another visit the day after tomorrow.

Chapter 29 Real Justice

Tuesday, April 30, 2272

"At his best man is the noblest animal. Separated from law and justice, he is the worst." **Aristotle**

Elasima arrived with his Zeta Command at nine hundred this morning. He shuttled over, and we sat with Marie and my team to discuss the situation. By this time, we'd pacified the planet and disabled its offensive capabilities. The planetary military is aware they are expected to maintain order, and we are not there to enslave them or their world. They seem to be cooperating, now.

"El I'm glad you came and brought the works. We have the Emperor aboard. The problem is that I'm not sure he's really a war criminal. For sure Kil Kos was. But, this ruler may have been out of the loop. We need you to really dig in and find out. We'll keep the peace and protect your forces so they can turn over every stone that might be hiding evidence. You're welcome to interview Kire Fask, yourself."

"How do you feel, Marie?" El inquired.

"I attended several discussions with the Kire. As much as I'd like to blame him for George's death, I believe him. I think the war crimes are all on Kil Kos."

"Then there's no point in an IGB interview. I better get a move on." El said as he rose and left the room.

....

A week later, all Isesinis legislation, government documents, and communications were in the IGB's possession. Seven days after that, it was all recorded, translated, and the originals returned to the surface.

As Elisma's people worked at the examination, Mobile Fifth continued to fan out to military-industrial installations all over the planet's single continent. This creates a thinning effect that has to be countered by constant air and armor support. But, it was no longer necessary to fire on anyone. Isesinis forces could see the Raptors overhead and the tanks on the ground. And, the enemy knew that though only a single Battalion may make a visit, they were supported by the rest of their Division - and those by much more. Each tour was accompanied by an Engineering team who were there to determine the type of production handled by any particular plant.

....

On Wednesday, July 3, 2272, Elasima was ready to make a determination. By then, we had successfully disabled most of the ground-based facilities producing materials used in the execution of space battles. But, we left enough intact for the Isesinis to be able to defend against an attack from an outside force. El asked to meet.

"I want you to look this over. We have thousands of documents. They support these. But the ones I'm showing you are the principal directives. In effect, it is patriotic to capture another society. But the Kire is right. They don't condone genocide or needless murder because it reduces the enslaved population. Some people won't be very pleased. I'm going to recommend we don't charge the Kire. He can't oversee someone more than a hundred light years away. He sets the policy and has to hope his people will listen. I don't believe we'd win in court.

After you've examined this material, I'd like you to show it to Marie. Then, I think the three of us should make the recommendation together. The C&C and the King will listen if it's the three of us."

"Leave it with me El. In the meantime, why don't you stay for dinner? And invite all my old friends. I wouldn't mind seeing the gang again. Let's make it Corps level Commanders and above."

"Okay, Kurt. What time?"

"Have everyone show for eighteen hundred with their significant other and any children. I'll bring my team. And, I'll invite Marie and Atina. I'll bring Fred and Bryant along, too. We'll meet in the Admiral's Mess."

Thank goodness the FSS Bryant's Flag dining is so big. Corps-level includes all the Fleet Commanders and above, so there were over two hundred and fifty in attendance including spouses, dates, and children. The galley chef prepared a menu that included a choice of Prime Rib or barbecued Seafood Skewers, braized or mashed potatoes, a vegetable medley and a variety of pastries and squares - all gluten-free though no one ever realized that. They had distinctive entrees of chicken strips, macaroni and cheese, or hot dogs with fries for those children who didn't want the regular fare. Dinner was served with my favorite Gamay and Reisling wines, both bottled by Cave Springs Wineries on Earth. The entire meal was preceded by a garden salad or vegetable soup and accompanied by a variety of coffees and teas. All in all, it was a splendid affair.

....

The next day, El, Marie, and I sat in my office as I placed the call home. We were right on top of recently installed communications relays, so conversation was instant even

231

though we're one hundred sixty light years apart. Grace, Three Tier-One Commanders, the Secretary of Defense and King David were on the other end of the line.

"Kurt, to what do we owe the pleasure of this call?" David asked.

"I'm sure you're up on our reports. The planet is pacified, and we're almost done neutralizing it as a threat. But, we've conducted quite an investigation into the war. I'll let Admiral Elasima elaborate."

"I've sent these documents to you ahead of this meeting. I hope that you had enough time to look them over. I don't want to shock you with my recommendation."

"What recommendation is that, Admiral?" Grace inquired.

"I'm recommending we don't file charges against the Isesinis Emperor. It's apparent from these and a thousand more that he does not condone war crimes."

"How do you feel about this, Kurt?" David queried.

"I concur, sir. That's why I called for El. I felt that way before he arrived. So, I wanted another pair of eyes to examine the whole thing. And, IGB has the resources and skills to ferret out the truth."

"And you Marie; how do you feel about it?"

"I'm the individual here that lost the most personally. So, it's not easy to say this. But I agree. George would not want me to seek revenge for what he'd consider an honest mistake. He'd want justice for war crimes. But, there's no evidence of that here. Kil Kos is the war criminal, not the Emperor."

"How do your investigators feel, El?"

"They don't believe we should file, sir. They think we'd lose in court."

"And the JAG prosecutors?" David asked.

"They say there's not enough to file on here either, sir."

'What about precedence?"

"Sir, we have not filed against our last three attackers because they did not commit what we define as war crimes. Historically, it goes back to when the United States did not charge the Emperor of Japan at the end of World War 2."

"How do you all feel?" The King asked those on his end of the line. Each nodded agreement.

"That's it then. Let the Kire go."

"Thank you all. This seemed like a tough decision because of all that happened. That's why we wanted to include all of you." I observed.

....

"Kire Fask, I'd like to inform you of the results of our examination."

"What have you found?"

"That you were right."

"I don't believe it." The man was startled.

"We found what you said we'd find. We are dropping all charges. We don't believe we'd win a case against you in our courts."

"You *are* very honorable. My people respect that more than anything. My offer of a treaty is still open."

"Will you stay aboard for negotiations? We'd lift house arrest. You could travel about the ship with only minor security restrictions."

"Yes, I'll stay. And, despite the previous constraints, you have been exceptional hosts. I've wanted for nothing but family since I've been here."

"Would you like to bring them up here. They're welcome to see our ship."

"Yes, that would be acceptable."

"Would you come with me? I'd like to show you our Command Center."

"I'd enjoy that."

We navigated the corridors, hallways, and elevators until we arrived on the Flag Bridge.

"This is a massive ship." The Kire observed.

"Nine of these make up the main Command. There are seventy-two Fleets of sixteen vessels and another thirty-six individual autonomous ships not including supply vessels, hospital ships, and security flotillas."

"There are more ships than that here."

"Yes, sir. There is a second Command here. They have thirty-six Fleets and are the law enforcement organization of the Federation. They were here to conduct your investigation. And, there is another group you cannot see." I waved through the observation window as I finished the statement.

Three of my covert Frigates and three of Savign's cloaked Subs turned off their cloaks.

"You have invisible ships?" He was astonished.

"In effect - yes we do. They have cloaking shields that redirect energy making them appear invisible. Nearly a thousand of those were aligned against you. And, our communications are instantaneous anywhere in space. We have learned how to use its natural sub-strata."

233

"So we were destined to lose the war."

"I don't know about that. You almost won it." I offered.

"No, we won the opening round. You were destined to win the war. What about joining your Federation?"

"I'm not sure you'd want to. We require you to adopt a democratic form of government."

"How does that work?

"Your people elect representatives to write laws and maintain the military. There is no Emperor or dictator."

"But, you have a King."

"Yes, but he does not exercise absolute rule. He governs with a Representative Assembly elected by the people. But, we could sign a treaty - agree to peaceful relations - trade with each other if you want - and even protect each other from common enemies."

"Yes, that would be better than membership. I'd lose my job if we join your Federation."

"You don't have to lose it. Make the same arrangement we have with our King. He holds forty-nine percent of the voting power. So, he can often make things happen with very little support. But, he can be overruled. And, such strength keeps the Assembly honest. He has such a big block of votes they don't become politicized. We were an Empire, too. You could be King instead of Emperor."

"This would take time to think over. In the meantime, we should sit down and come to terms on a peace agreement."

"How about a day to spend with your family. Then, we begin meetings the day after tomorrow."

"That sounds good to me."

"In the meantime, I will authorize your reception of our communications channels. There is news of particular interest to you."

"I don't see how Orion Federation News could affect me."

"Kil Kos' trial is just starting. There have been numerous hearings and motions. And, the pretrial arguments were held a while back. The actual hearing begins today."

"We may watch some. But, I am not sure I care about Kos. He handled things very badly."

"Do you mean battle tactics?"

234

"No. I am referring to his personal decisions and actions. Destroying an entire populated planet and killing prisoners is not our way. But, I will probably watch a little."

....

"Have you been following the news, Admiral?" The Kire asked me on our second negotiating session.

"Not really. I haven't had much time. I have nearly a half million soldiers on your planet and another three million people up here to consider. There isn't much time to sit back and watch a trial. How's it going?"

"It was going fine. I am amazed at the fairness built into your system. Federation citizens are prosecuting and defending Kos. But, those handling the defense seem to be doing their utmost to prove him innocent - or at least create considerable doubt about his guilt. But, that's all moot now, I guess."

"What'ya mean?"

"Thirty Isesinis Special Forces broke him out and took him away. He's escaped custody.

"Is this a joke?"

"...No joke, Admiral. And, there's a lot to worry about. A substantial force will still align themselves with him. And, without me on the planet, he will most certainly try to seize power. He is a man of singular focus. So, he will attempt to find a way to resume his attack on the Federation."

"Do you object to suspending our discussions for a short time - maybe a week, or two?"

"No Admiral, I don't mind. In fact, I perfectly understand. But, you know I can be of more use to you on the ground. A significant portion of the population and important families support me. If they see I am still in charge, it may prevent Kos from taking control."

"I agree. But, give me a couple of days to make sure we can suitably secure you. Can you give me details on the support he'd get on the surface?"

It took Kire Fask nearly an hour to complete a picture of all the dominant houses, their military strength, and their political leanings. I excused myself and called for all my senior people, the most senior SOCC Officers and Elasima and his deputies.

....

"El, can you handle Kire Fask for a week or so. I'd like him to be with a C&C?"

"Sure, Kurt but where are you going?"

235

"I'm breaking up my Command, temporarily. Admiral Palakiko's Tier One will remain here to support ground operations and defend the space. She'll have our Polemista and Spiel contingent with her. All the Marines on the surface will stay. Nguyen will take on the space between this position and Earth. Tom Stevens will go all the way to Rigil and work his way back. In case you're not aware, Kil Kos has escaped and is probably headed here. General Shellots, you'll report to Pal, but I will tell you both that I want the surface secured by the end of this week. It's nearly done now, so that's not an impossible goal.

After that, you must get the Kire back on the ground and secure his safety. We need him to run the government. It will help keep Kos from claiming the Empire if he makes it home.

Then, I want you to take this list and have Brigade-strength security forces keep these families in check. They have substantial troops at their disposal and support Kos politically. He is not to have access to or assistance from them. You have my authorization to use lethal force to prevent these people and their troops from backing him - if it's required.

Can, you are to spread your forces along the route and use your intelligence assets to seek out any information that might point to Kos. You are to grab him if you locate him and notify me.

Tom, I will travel with you. We will try to pick up his trail and hunt him down.

Don't forget that Kos is extremely dangerous and an escaped felon. You have my approval to kill if it becomes necessary.

El, I'd also like to ask that you put some of your Intelligence Division under Can's authority, temporarily. He will be spread very thin and will need the help." I asked.

"Certainly, Kurt. I can give him a full Brigade. When is this all being executed."

"I will issue orders for immediate departures. It begins now."

....

In the nine days it took us to return to Rigil, we made several diversions. We sought information in case Kil Kos had previously made it this far. And we examined several uninhabited systems along the direct route to ensure he was not already hiding out in any. But, we struck out at every turn.

I went down to see Grace once we achieved orbit.

"Howdy, Chief," I said as I leaned into her doorway.

"Well, I certainly didn't expect to see you. How come you're here?" She responded.

"I'm back to find Kil Kos. Can you help me?"

236

"What do you need?"

"...All surveillance footage of the holding cell and jail, and all the video we have on orbiting craft, from the day before to the day after the escape."

"I think that can be arranged. You still think like an investigator, I see."

"You can take the boy from IGB, but you can't take it out of the boy." I laughed.

"It'll take about an hour. Want to get a drink."

"I don't know. Fred might not like me carousing with another woman." I snickered.

"Get your ass down to the bar. I'll be right there." Grace injected wryly.

My system annunciator sounded by the time we'd enjoyed our choice of beverage. It was the footage I'd asked Grace for. A quick look told me I wasn't going to figure much out on my own.

"I've got to get back up there," I said as I raised my eyes skyward.

"See you later, Kurt. Come for a visit sometime. You shouldn't ignore old friends."

"I'm not ignoring you, Grace. I'd love a visit. Work hasn't permitted it in a while."

"I know. And, we're all grateful for your success with the Isesinis. See you later, buddy."

"You bet."

....

To this day, I'm thankful for the decision we made to place IGB contingents in all the Commands. But, it was especially helpful, now. I summoned three Lt. Colonels who are IGB Battalion Commanders aboard three of the Supercarriers.

"Colonels, I need your help. I'm sending you each a copy of several videos I have. I need them analyzed carefully. Do whatever is required. I must know how Kil Kos got off the planet." I explained.

"Aye, sir. We'll be glad to help." One responded as they rose from their seats.

"How long?" I asked.

"We should have something in a few hours." The same man answered.

....

I was surprised at the presence of one attendee when we reconvened at nineteen hundred that evening.

"Sir, I hope you will forgive my injection into this situation, but these Marines came to me for advice and support. Their immediate Commanders are all active on the surface of Eta Pegasus. I am the most senior General Staff Officer in Intelligence with intimate knowledge of the Isesinis." Major General Naabaahii observed apologetically.

"...no need to explain, General. I value your input - especially on this subject. But, I have two questions. How come you're on the Bryant? And, why did your people feel they needed your counsel?"

"I'm here because Admiral Elasima included me in the contingent supplied to you. And they sought my advice because they were in disbelief of what they found. They felt it was just too fantastic."

"So, what did they discover?"

"They traced back video surveillance and sensor logs from the breakout. Thirty-one Isesinis executed the mission.' Naaby explained as he plugged his datapad into my projector and displayed the images. 'We follow their party through the corridors and out into an alley behind the jail. They all enter this shuttle.' He stops as he isolates and enhances the small OFSA craft.

'Once we had this view we could follow the vessel into orbit. Then, we saw this." He stopped dramatically as the movie continued. The shuttle became partially invisible as it seemed to hold a stationary position.

"Is it docking with a cloaked vessel?"

"Yes, sir. But, there's more if you keep an eye out."

I peered intently at the image which Naabaahii slowed. There was a brief blip in the cloak as the shuttle bumped the surface of its mother ship. This is common when those inexperienced with these shields attempt to mate with the craft.

"Can you replay that, General."

"Of course, sir." He backed up several hundred frames and replayed at an even slower speed finally stopping in a frame where the cloak temporarily failed.

"Is that one of ours?

"Yes, sir. It's the CSS Elusive. We traced the nomenclature on the shuttle."

"Does Admiral Savign know?" I carefully maintained formalities in the presence of his subordinate officers.

"Yes, sir. She was advised and checked on the Elusive. It has maintained regular check-ins every six hours."

"Do we think the Captain is co-opted, or do we believe that they've been captured."

"Savign knows Captain Johansen personally. She says he'd never defect. She's certain they've been taken."

"We have two problems here. The first is Kos. We want him back dead or alive. The second is our technology. We need to recover the Elusive and seize everyone involved in its theft. None of our enemies exposed to that technology can ever be allowed their freedom.

But, the fact they are maintaining their communication updates leads me to believe they're still in our space and are attempting to prevent any suspicions. I think we can use that to our advantage.

General, I'd like you to assume a post at Admiral Savign's side. Take whoever you need with you. You may have all the personnel and whatever assets are necessary. I want you and your people to monitor those signals and trace back their beams. They can report their position as anywhere in Federation Space, but their transmission origins will tell us the real truth. I will advise Savign. Then, I'll send you her current position."

"Aye, sir. We'll be ready to go." Naabi and his associates stood, saluted, and turned to leave the room. They spoke quietly as they left and marched down the corridor, already planning their strategy in excited whispers.

....

"I know why you're calling, Kurt." Savign displayed her simulated smile as she answered my call.

"Yes, it is about the Elusive. I am sending you a party who will monitor their transmissions to attempt to find the actual origins of their beams. Major General Naabaahii will be accompanied by a sizeable team and their equipment."

"They will be welcomed here. And we will offer them every courtesy.

It sounds like your on a hunt."

"I am. It's personal. George is dead because of that bastard. I'll bring him back to stand trial, or I'll kill him. Either way, I'm not letting him get away."

"I understand Kurt. ...but..."

"What?" I barked.

"Don't let your emotions rule you. You need a clear head, or we could all be mourning your loss next."

"Don't worry about me. Brubacher out." I responded as I abruptly disconnected.

But, I called her back half an hour later after mulling over the conversation.

"I called back to apologize. Sorry I snapped. You're right, of course. Keeping cool is the key to succeeding without unnecessary risk or loss."

"No need to apologize, Kurt. I know how much George meant to you."

....

I have to keep reminding myself that Kil Kos killed my best friend. It's the only rationalization that comes close to explaining being on this hell hole. Polmieria is a small rocky planet with half the mass of Earth that orbits Ross 154 at a distance of only twelve million kilometers. Though it still rotates on its axis, each day/night cycle is just over a week long at its equator. This results in all water on the bright side evaporating into the atmosphere over the three and half days of daylight. Then, it all falls as torrential rain and snow as a region becomes the terminator, resulting in overwhelming floods followed by frozen wastelands that melt three and a half days later when the sun returns. Constant winds of a sixty miles an hour are boosted by gusts one and a half times that velocity. It supports no permanent oceans or lakes. They appear in new places as a region comes into the rainfall area. But, it is pure and clean. You can drink directly from these temporary pools if you dare to remove your environmental suit.

We've been following the terminator line since we arrived on Wednesday, July 31, 2272 - a week ago. Our goal is to locate Kil Kos and his minions if they are in fact on the surface. Regardless of that, we are positive they are in this system. It is also likely that if they're down here, they're moving too. It's the only way to avoid the blistering heat and bitter cold. They could be holed-up in a cave, but that is not likely either since it could end up underwater or frozen in ice. So we keep moving. And as we do we swing from north to south and back again.

Meanwhile, Tom Stevens is in orbit above us, and our Tier 2-1 contingent is searching every square inch of the space both inside and outside the system heliosphere. There are lots of hiding placing. Two Gas Giants offer a couple of dozen moons. But, none of those have water. And those planets are not conducive to humanoid life. And then, there's a massive asteroid belt and another of icy satellites. Good investigative method and logical assumptions led to such intense focus on this small red dwarf.

....

The day after my meeting with Naabaahii and his people, he contacted to my office with additional news. He'd recovered images of the Elusive breaking orbit on a trajectory to Ross 154. He'd also traced the three most recent reports from the craft back to that system. Reviewing relay station logs proved they'd been there for three weeks, by then.

"I don't understand why they'd just sit there," I observed to both the General and Admiral Savign. She'd joined in the hunt because of her missing Sub.

"I do." She responded.

"I hope you're going to share."

"The Subs are not like your Battleships. They use cyclotrons for gravity and are not big enough to support Accelerator technology. They can't produce their own anti-matter. So, each one stores a supply in magnetic traps. Their maximum travel time is about two weeks without replenishment. The Covert Supply Ships offload to each Sub from their Accelerators twice a month. The Elusive was last fed a week before they grabbed Kos. So, they couldn't go very far. And, if they didn't realize that, they're empty and unable to achieve FTL velocities. If they did, they're waiting to capture a ship that can either provide additional fuel for the speeds they need to get all the way home."

"Nichols has Quadrant Four, now. So, I think I'll contact him. We'll take our First there to meet him. Do you want to join in Savign?"

"I can offer two full Fleets without hurting my normal operations."

"Give me a minute," I said as I turned to my screen. I located FSS Indestructible. It's Nichols Command Station and is currently sitting beside a relay unit at Gliese 832, so I'll be able to speak with him face to face.

"Admiral Nichols," I said as his face came on the screen when he answered.

"Admiral Brubacher, how are you? And, how's your mission going? You're still after Kos, aren't you?"

"Yes. That's why I'm calling. We've traced him to Ross 154 - not too far from you. We're heading there now. Do you want in?"

"Of course. I'd do anything to get that son of a bitch. He killed my best friend."

"...my feelings, too. I thought you'd want to come along."

"When will you arrive?"

"We'll be there in two days."

"That's about right."

"What do you mean." I queried.

"By the time I write the orders, and we make the trip, it'll be two days. See you there in forty-eight hours." He disconnected. I flipped back to the other screen.

"So, the hunt's on. That'll put around four hundred warships in the system. And, that doesn't include your subs. How many Marines do we have available, General."

"More than we need for this. I can put a thousand on the planet without hurting our security duties."

"Okay. You two write your orders. I'll send out mine. Let's get that bastard." I said as I rose. "And General, I want you and your people back on the Bryant when we all meet up at Ross."

Now I was part of Alpha team a Company of two hundred and fifty. Three others were spread out along the terminator. We kept running into those closest us as we made our sweeps.

Each contingent landed in nine of the large Shuttles. The vessels provided shelter, food, and sleeping quarters for us while we conducted the hunt. A dozen of us at a time donned environmental suits and searched for three hours - at which time another twelve replaced us. Meanwhile, those remaining aboard launched probes, manned sensor stations, and kept the nine crafts close to us.

Above us, Stevens and Nichols had Lidar, Radar, InfraRed, Ultra Violet, Magnetic, Xray, and visible light sensors scanning both terminator lines intently. If he's here, we'll find Kos. And Tom and Stephen Nichols had Task Force Commands positioned at each nearby relay station looking for any anomaly or spatial disturbance that might indicate a cloaked ship. And, each of those teams was covered by three Covert Vessels supplied by Savign.

"We've found an Orion Federation shuttle. It belongs to Elusive." A voice whispered over our scrambled communications channel.

"This is Admiral Brubacher. Please identify yourself and give your position."

"Captain Mistang of Gamma Company. We're at the southern end of our sweep."

"We're at the northern tip of ours. So, we can't be more than a few klicks apart. We're heading to you." I said as I signaled the Alpha Commander to gather the troops and return to our shuttles.

"Get us in the air and move us true North about eight kilometers. Advise the other shuttles." I ordered.

"Sir, they're farther away than that." The pilot injected.

"We'll have to walk the last mile. I don't want to spoil the surprise.' I replied. 'Everyone suits up." I added.

We flew in silence and landed about ten minutes later. All thirty-five Marines slinked silently from the hatchway as others from nearby shuttles mirrored our actions. We followed the Gamma transponder signal, noiselessly coming upon our quarry twenty minutes later.

"Hound Dog!" I whispered into my microphone.

"Huntsman!" The countersign sounded in my ear.

"We're approaching from your South-south-east," I instructed.

We closed the gap in silence coming upon Gamma Company a few minutes later.

We conversed in sign language. Mistang gave me the direction of the shuttle. He estimated ten soldiers inside since it was one of the small ones. I indicated the area around us, asking him if there were others. He replied that they'd examined over a mile in all directions. No other shuttles were nearby. He also advised that the occupants hadn't left the small craft in quite a while, electing to just move it along as the divider moved westward. He thought they were seeking water or ice to harvest for the Elusive.

I pulled a magnetic charge from my hip pack and indicated we should stealthily place a few along the hatch frame and blow it. He nodded and pointed out five Marines holding up a charge and directing them toward the shuttle. They slinked along silently, placed the bombs and retreated. Mistang counted down the fingers on his right hand. When no fingers remained a Sergeant pressed an icon on a datapad. The muffled explosions fractured the door locks and hinges and the shuttles interior pressure served to blow the hatch twenty feet in the air. Fifty Marines were moving as it launched and were inside the structure in a few seconds. I viewed flashes from behind the fogged windows. Just a few minutes later four Marines were dragging two dead Isesinis while the rest moved six more enemy soldiers at gunpoint. I pointed upward.

....

When I entered the interrogation room, I knew I might not be able to maintain the simple respect we usually paid prisoners. I was also aware that these particular enemy agents would never be released. They knew too much about our cloaking technology. And, I was certain I didn't want Marie with me, this time.

We'd determined the man in the interrogation chamber was the leader of the Isesinis ground team on Polmieria. The Marines had removed his armor leaving him defenseless and vulnerable. And, he was chained to the table.

"Translator on!" I ordered as I crossed the threshold.

"Where's the ship?' I growled. 'Where's Kos?" I added.

My guest only grunted in response.

I swung an open hand slapping him on the side of the head so hard he flew from the chair restrained only when the chain reached its end and snapped him to a violent stop. He fell to the floor whimpering.

"Where's Kos?"

He didn't answer. I restrained myself believing he was still recovering his senses.

"Where's Kos?" I yelled when I saw his eyes refocus on me.

243

He grunted once more. I slapped him again.

"Where's Kos?" I hollered.

"I am a soldier. I don't know space navigation. I can't give you his position."

"Liar! You commanded a mission that landed a shuttle. Where's Kos?" I bellowed again.

"I don't know." He said as he managed to pull himself back into the chair.

I slapped him again. Each time had been in the same place. A large welt was growing into an angry bruise. He slowly raised himself from the floor, returning to the seat.

"I don't really want to hurt you. But, I can keep it up all day - if that's the way you want it. I don't even really want you. I want Kos and your Commander. Kos is a war criminal. And your boss broke him out of our jail. I don't care about the rest of you. But, you're all dead if you don't cooperate." It was a hollow threat. But, I hoped my violent attack convinced him we were capable of it.

He remained silent.

In the momentary hush, I thought about the situation. I didn't actually enjoy physically assaulting a prisoner. But, it did serve to set the stage. Fear could do the rest.

"I'm going to give you a little time to think about this. You can be comfortable. You don't have to suffer anymore. You can eat when you want and visit your friends. Or, we can make this horribly painful. I'll be back in a while." I said as I turned and left abruptly.

Outside the room, I told the Officer in Charge to go in and help the prisoner. He was to offer the man care and food and explain that I'm a loose cannon who is very cruel and unpredictable. I described to the Officer that I wanted the prisoner to trust him but fear my return. He casually sauntered over to a Marine Corporal and discussed the situation in whispered tones. The young man left and returned with a med-kit and two bottles of water.

....

"I'm sorry about that. Our boss is a pretty nasty guy. Let me put something on your face.' The guard said as he fingered the salve he'd opened and gently rubbed it on the man's swelling cheekbone. 'Here, take this bottle of water. I'll be right back with something better. You're starting to swell up." He motioned his own face puffing with his opened right hand as he rose and left the room. A moment later he returned with a cold pack.

"I'm not sure why I'm doing this. It's kind of useless."

"What do you mean?" The prisoner asked sheepishly.

"When he returns, the Admiral will just do it again - and again, until you talk. Whatever benefit you get from this will be wasted. He's pretty tough on all of us, too. But, you really have to worry if he takes out his knife."

"His knife?"

"Yes. When he gets frustrated with prisoners, he'll peel some of the skin right off them. He seems to enjoy it." The Corporal explained as he placed the ice pack on the side of the prisoner's face. The man said nothing. He just looked down at the tabletop in quiet contemplation.

....

When I witnessed the exchange on the monitor, I signaled the Lieutenant who disappeared and returned with a military ka-bar knife. At nearly fourteen inches in overall length, the eighteen-centimeter blade was very imposing and suited to cutting, sawing, stabbing, and skinning.

I turned back to the monitor watching as the two men talked sporadically over the next half hour. It was quiet and unforced. Our Corporal was good at this.

....

"Corporal, excuse us, please. I'll call if I need you." I directed at the young man as I entered the room. It'd been an hour since I last spoke to the prisoner.

"I hope you're ready to chat with me. I don't really want to harm you. It was your fault I hit you before. Please, don't make me do it again. Just tell me where Kos is, and I'll leave you alone."

I waited as the silence dragged into several minutes.

"Remember, I tried to be nice," I said as I reached behind me and pulled the Ka-bar from its sheath. I laid it on the table just out beyond the grasp of his chained arms. There was still silence. I peered into his eyes as I waited. He looked defiant. But then, I spotted just a flick of fear. I reached for the weapon.

"Kos is in the asteroid belt. He is positioned about two hundred kilometers from its inside edge and is in stationary orbit over the planet's trailing terminator line." The man nearly whispered as he intently examined the table top between his hands.

"Guard!"

"Take this man to his cell. Make sure he is comfortable and well fed and get him some real medical attention for his injury.' I instructed. Then, I turned to the prisoner. 'I'm sorry for any discomfort or injury you suffered." I rose, turned, and headed out the door to return to my office.

"We need a tried and tested plan. Finding one of our own Subs is not going to be easy. The technology is designed for avoidance.' I explained to the others attending the meeting I'd called in my office. 'Even knowing its approximate position just means we have to examine a smaller region than we would without that information. I want ideas within a couple of hours," I added.

"I have one right now." Tom Stevens injected.

"Please feel free to expound. Don't hold back."

"Well first, I think we have to use covert vessels in the search. We're searching for Kos. He thinks he's hidden, so he's not looking for us. But using conventional ships means he'll be able to see us. I believe we can use eight crafts to transmit lasers to each other. Though the cloaks are efficient, we should see some distortion or deflection in the beams. We would need three reference points to ensure we hold our positions accurately. That will allow us to align our transmissions precisely enough to determine if they've been altered before reception.

If that fails, we execute a pain-staking search with Marines doing EVA duty. We move our subs inch by inch as our agents feel about for the sub from within our shields."

"Don't you think that's getting a bit carried away!" Savign blurted.

"With all due respect, Admiral, if the first idea fails, I don't see any other choice. If you have a better idea, I'd love to hear it." Stevens countered.

"No, I don't. But, that doesn't mean I have to like yours."

"Savign, I know it sounds a bit ridiculous, but if that's what it takes, that's what we'll do. We can't let this murdering maniac get away. I like Tom's first plan. And, though I don't really like the second, I think it is our only other alternative. I believe we should test out the laser transmission, right away. And while we're actually using it in the field, the Special Forces should be practicing for the substitute method."

"I don't like it, but I agree," Savign added.

"Me too." Steven Nichols piped in. He'd been silent throughout the entire session.

"I'll write the orders to my people. Can you supply a dozen Covert Frigates to support my subs - just in case the bastard detects us and opens fire?"

"Certainly. My CF units are at your disposal." I said as I nodded to Stevens who returned the gesture.

"We'll need twenty-four hours to assemble our force and test the laser theory. Then, another day to get in position." Savign explained.

"So, that's it then. We expect to find and capture Kos the day after tomorrow. Every time I imagine our people aboard the Sub with that sociopath, I wish we could rescue them, immediately." I murmured.

"Me too. That's all I can think about. They might all be dead already." Admiral Nichols added.

....

Nautilus, Poseidon, Neptune, Jupiter, Pluto, Pacifica, Oceana, and CSS Atlantic were chosen to create the web of beams. Testing showed they could circle the suspected area, slowly rotating around a central point to examine a globular region thoroughly. It also showed Stevens was correct. Though a targeted Sub could bend the signals around itself, it could not maintain one hundred percent fidelity. There was just enough variance to make a hidden vessel detectable.

By Friday, August 9, 2272, the eight Subs and one dozen Frigates were in place. They'd circle a section of the asteroid belt that was about one hundred fifty kilometers in radius. Once in position, they turned on their beams, and the entire assemblage began a slow-motion maneuver that turned the disc up on edge, then over on its back as they carefully examined the information on the received lasers. The first orbit revealed nothing. So, they moved inward another hundred miles and repeated the procedure. Then, moved again, and again. On the fourth attempt, they struck gold. Aside from its rocky inhabitants, the field held a reflection where no object seemed to be present.

The Subs and Frigates closed in. The Nautilus and Pacifica dispatched SF Marines to conduct EVA missions to the ghost from within the safety of their subs' cloaks. The Frigates moved in. Each readied an SF team in a shuttle prepped for launch, at a moment's notice. The target was the rear supply hatch on the aft underbelly of the Elusive. It was used for resupply and was not a usual point of access. A relatively long corridor with environmental entrances at either end stretched out from it to the storeroom. No one would be hurt by blowing this opening, though the ship would be rocked violently.

I was notified when all charges had been placed, and the agents were safe aboard their home ships. I ordered the launch of the Marine shuttles. Two minutes later, I ordered the detonation of the charges.

What the enemy saw were a dozen shuttles that appeared suddenly just as their own Sub shook and rumbled violently from the charges that blew away its cargo access. One hundred twenty Marines were in the hallway in less than a minute. Forty-five seconds later, they were in the stowage cubicle. After repressurizing it and removing environmental suits, they began the compartment-by-compartment movement to the Sub's central Bridge.

Nineteen Isesinis soldiers piloting their robotic armor and guarding the crew were subdued with little effort by the overpowering Marine Company. But, Kos was not among them. I ordered them all transported to the Brig of the Valhalla.

....

The questioning went on for days with little result, at first. I even ensured all were able to interact with the prisoner I'd interviewed. Though I did not want to resort to physical pain and psychological manipulation again, I wanted them to know we were capable of these methods.

This time, the technique was more traditional. Each detainee was interrogated for eight hours at a stretch by three Intelligence Officers working in shifts. Each captive was allowed only a single break midway through the examination. Usually, just one Officer at a time conducted the probe, but occasionally two or even all three would create an imposing atmosphere. It's an old technique designed to wear down the subject's resistance.

After three days of silence or belligerence, we stepped it up to four-man teams running twelve-hour sessions with two short breaks and a single small snack midway through the probe. On the fourth day, two prisoners cracked. One overstressed and very strained captive was tricked into blurting out Kil Kos' current location. They had dropped him on the outer planet in the HD-44 1109 system less than nine light-years away. Then, they continued on to lie in wait in an attempt to commandeer Anti-Matter, the FTL fuel they were short of. At standard cruising speed, it would take us less than two days to reach him.

....

HD-44 11909 is a small Red Dwarf with two massive rocky planets and a substantial asteroid field orbiting it. The outer world is nearly four times the mass of Earth, with a surface gravity almost twice that of our home. But, it boasts a lot of flora and fauna, an oxygen atmosphere, and plentiful fresh water. There are small vermin and very large predators over the entire surface. It circles its star at a distance of just fifteen million kilometers but is not yet tidally locked. It rotates on its axis once in every forty-six hours. Its climate is slightly warmer than the Earth enjoys. Though the star is much smaller than Sol, a more significant proportion of its energy is in the infra-red range providing a great deal of radiant heating by conversion to heat over this sphere's vast surface area. This injects significant energy into the environment leading to more dynamic weather patterns.

This satellite's shallow seven-degree tilt, nearly circular orbit, and very slight inclination relative to its star's equator lead to very minor seasonal fluctuations. Temperatures vary by only ten degrees from summer to winter.

The planet has one vast ocean and an elongated narrow one. These separate two nearly identical massive continents. Each starts at about eighty degrees north to seventy-five degrees south latitude and spans about sixty degrees longitude. Extensive forests, plains, and grasslands are parted by long ranges of massive mountain system, enormous fresh-water lakes, and thunderous river drainage systems. Hundreds of habitable islands punctuate its seas. It is rugged, dangerous, and challenging topography.

Locating a humanoid on the planet is quite a chore. Though Kil Kos' sensor readings will be unique, there is close to half a billion square kilometers of land and five times that water area to search. Steven and I have decided to use a pair of complete Tier Two Commands for the operation. I've added the twelve autonomous covert Frigates I have on site, and Savign is supplying thirty-six Subs. We will put three hundred and sixty-eight vessels in stationary orbits. Each will scan an assigned section of the surface. All will be networked to the Valhalla since we are the Lead because this mission is officially our responsibility. I will actually be able to see real-time images and sensor readings of the entire planet twenty-four hours a day.

I have our IT personnel program the sensor system for the Kil and build in a coordinate system providing a prime meridian. Though we will see everything, the system will annunciate readings that indicate his presence. Four days into the search we strike paydirt.

"Your attention, please. Isesinis biological sensor readings have been located at twenty-two point three five seven degrees north latitude by forty-three point six, five, four degrees west longitude, at two hundred eighty-three point five, six meters altitude." The system announced as it flashed a red starburst on the screen at the appropriate location. It repeated the notice until I silenced the audio channel.

It was a small island about two thousand miles off the western coast of the continent east of our designated time terminator. We understood why Kos chose this particular place when analysis indicated the island had abundant fresh water, vegetation, and small mammals, birds, fish, and lizards. None of this world's dangerous predators seem to inhabit the location. It is pristine, provides food, and enjoys a relatively comfortable climate. And, who'd look for him here, in the first place?

I called for a meeting with my fellow C&C.

249

"I asked you to come so we could discuss how we'll approach the capture."

"I don't see the problem. Send two dozen Marines down and grab him." Savign countered.

"It's not that simple. From up here, the island looks small relative to the rest of the planet. But, it's quite large, and Kos is moving continuously. Besides that, his readings have disappeared several times over the past six hours. That means there are probably caves or some other shelter that shield him. And, there are three Isesinis down there. So, I believe he brought some personal guards with him."

"It sounds like we need at least a regiment to land in a perimeter around him and close in." Admiral Nichols observed.

"Yes, that's my thinking, too. But, I was thinking of a Brigade in a five-kilometer radius. That way we can close in with enough coverage to keep him from slipping through our lines. But, we're short. Most of my Epsilon ground forces are back on Eta Pegasus."

"Let me provide the troops. You can still lead the operation. I have no illusions as to who should lead the mission." Nichols replied.

"Sounds good. We'll have Valhalla relay the combined sensor readings to all Company, Battalion, Regimental, and Brigade Commands so everyone can coordinate their movements."

"...seems like a lot of soldiers to catch one man." Savign injected.

"It is. But, I think it'll be necessary. The island's a hundred miles long and sixty wide. That's over fifteen thousand square kilometers. It'll be night down there soon. And, if I were him, I'd find a cave for each evening. We won't be able to locate him. Dawn will come in about twenty-two hours. I think we should start our search then. In the meantime, we can meet with your Brigadier and his subordinate Commanders, if that's okay with you, Steven."

"Absolutely. I'll send for them. I can have them here in an hour."

"That's great.' I said as Nichols began tapping on his pad. 'Let's have lunch together." I added when he'd finished. We rose, left the room, and I led them to our Pub.

"This is General Mitchell." Steven introduced the Brigadier an hour later in the boardroom.

"And these people are Colonels Thad, Shomack, and Shant. And, then we have Lieutenant Colonels Davis, Aktutk, Simnon, Melbourne, Sclotty, Ki, Vingora, Slew, and Danog." General Mitchell said as we moved along the line shaking each Officer's hand.

"And, this is Fleet Admiral Kurt Brubacher C&C, the leader of Epsilon Command and OFSA Tactical Chief of Staff.' Admiral Nichols announced as he held an open hand in my direction. 'He is in command of this mission. You and your operations are temporarily attached to Epsilon and will take your orders from him until the job is done."

"It's my pleasure. I have always had the utmost respect for our Marine Armies. So, I'll tell you now that I'll lay out the general parameters of the mission. But, you will run your Commands without interference. Our goal is to remain coordinated, though. So, everything will run through Brigadier General Mitchell, when we're on the surface.

HD-44 11909b is a planet much larger than our respective home worlds. It has a surface gravity force nearly twice that of Earth. So, you will find it rough going. For sure, you'll need your assist armor. It will take the load off your legs as you march and will aid in lifting. It's warm down there, so you'll be uncomfortable in these suits. Make sure your people pack enough water, and you keep supplies running to them always.

Our mission is to capture Kil Kos. He was the leader of the Isesinis forces that invaded our territory. He arbitrarily destroyed an entire inhabited planet and butchered prisoners of war, so we consider him a war criminal. He escaped just as his trial was starting. Our job is to recapture him. If that becomes impossible, we are authorized to bring him back dead.

The planet has no indigenous humanoid life. It has plenty of vegetation, fresh water, fish, and game. Most of it is dominated by large predators. But, Kos chose this island because it lacks those hunters while still offering lots of wild food and plenty of fresh water.

The island is big. It's over fifteen thousand square kilometers. There are dense forests and plenty of caves to hide in.' I paused to switch on the video projector.

'This is our sensor imaging. Kos and his two bodyguards are the red starbursts in the field. You can see how quickly they're moving. These images are recorded in high resolution. So, you can zoom in and enhance to get topographical information. And, they're in real time. So, you see things change as they do.

The plan is to land on the island in a ten-kilometer circle surrounding their position at that time. Then, we'll close in as quickly as possible and as synchronized as we can. The object is to always maintain the circle and never let any portion of its perimeter open to permit an exit. As we get closer to the target, our lines will become denser restricting his escape even more. We'll position our landing relative to his location at the time. He will not be the center of the circle. It will be based on the direction he's moving away from. We hit the surface with our force anchored opposite the direction he's traveling. In other words, he'll be closest to the troops, he's heading away from and farthest from those he's approaching. That way, by the time we reach him, we should all be together. You'll be able to advance rapidly, at first. But, as you close in, you'll have to slow to ensure he can't slip through your line.

A day on the planet is forty-six hours. So, we'll have twenty-four hours of daylight when we arrive at dawn. I suggest we travel for six hours, rest for two and repeat the process until nightfall. Then, we stop and sleep. But, night's twenty-two hours. So sleep in shifts of four hours, so each man gets at least eight hours over the entire evening. We should reach Kos about midway through the second day.

General, what about your logistical capabilities?" I asked.

"I have two heavy-shuttles at my disposal with crews of ten to fly, load, and deliver. And, they're supported by nearly three hundred aboard our base ship. We can also use transport shuttles to do supply duty while we're on the ground. We'll have fifty-two with us. It'll take three trips to land all our forces. So, I think we should start six hours before the target area's dawn. We'll set up our main headquarters at the portion of the perimeter most distant to our quarry. We'll keep all parked vessels there. Regimental Commands have adequate storage and handling capabilities. So we'll send continuous supply missions to those three operational centers, and they'll distribute locally." The General explained.

"That sounds good. Make sure you have night-vision capabilities. Each Company will need perimeter guards at night, and we may end up traveling during some darkness. I'll be at your headquarters with Admirals Nichols and Savign if they want to come along. We'll bring our Marine Guard Squads down. So, you won't need to concern yourself with additional security. They'll take their lead from your Protective Services people."

"That sounds good, Admiral."

"Send me your detailed mission plans as quickly as possible. Copy Admiral Nichols, too. But, you'll receive final authorizations from me." I said as I rose from my seat at the head of the boardroom table. The ten Officers stood, saluted, and exited the room."

"That went well," Nichols observed when they were gone.

"Your man Mitchell seems good," I commented as we walked towards the docking bay.

....

Saturday, August 17, 2272, I landed in the first wave of shuttles that went to the island. People scurried about as General Mitchell fired off orders to get his Headquarters up and running. Within four hours, we were housed and working out of a mobile all-terrain vehicle with all communications in place and a pot of hot coffee at the ready. It was fully capable of traversing most landscapes and could unblock its own path through even densely forested areas. For those regions with tall hills or squat mountains, it could leap them by employing its limited flight capabilities.

Meanwhile, the three Regimental Commanders were conducting the same exercise as their Battalion Commanders were doing likewise. All the while, Companies were being positioned along the circular line. The fifty-two shuttles repeated the entire process two more times. By sunup, we were set to begin operations as supply vessels continued to drop necessities we'd use during the mission. Mitchell had kept to his approved plan.

The HQ was abuzz with activity. There were constant reports from each of the thirty-seven field Companies, the logistic's Battalion, Intelligence, security, and the Company of Engineers that was continually moved to needed locations. In addition to that and our real-time sensor data, we received hourly weather reports from the Valhalla. In response, Mitchell sent out a constant stream of orders to his Regimental Commanders who would modify and forward them down the chain of command. Each and every Company position was continuously "tweaked" to keep the formation in line and on target.

Though we were traveling in vehicles unlike our footsoldiers, we felt the drain of our additional weight. Every move took extra effort in the heightened gravity field. And, through the early part of the day, we made steady progress as we accompanied the ground troops. Six hours into our journey, we stopped for the first two-hour break. Sitting in the HQ for the trip, I was tired. So, I could only imagine the condition of our people. They were probably exhausted.

The routine continued as planned through the remaining daylight. Then, we broke for sleep and reassessment during the long night.

The next day saw the resumption of the hunt. I watched the screen as the circle began to center itself around the highlighted targets. Ten hours into that daytime period, we were all within two kilometers of our quarry. It was time to stop and plan our assault.

After analysis and consideration, we realized our part of the perimeter was about a half kilometer closer to Kos that the other side was. And, Kil Kos was steadily moving toward us. So we decided to order the forces along three hundred degrees of the circle to advance, while troops in our area held steady. Hopefully, Kos would just walk into our waiting trap.

Mitchell, Nichols, and I donned assist-armor and headed out into the field to join nearby Marines. We watched both sensor imagery and through field glasses.

I was astonished at the vista the scenery of our outside panoramic view provided. The magnificence of the muted malachite colored vegetation and chestnut tree bark contrasted by fluorescent-yellow, electric-purple, and neon-green flora drew an audible gasp from me.

"What's wrong?" Mitchell asked.

"Nothing. The scenery is astonishing."

"I agree," Nichols mumbled almost imperceptibly.

I could feel my anxiety building. But, I wasn't sure if Kos spotted us or just had a gut feeling because just as he came into view about half a kilometer ahead, he stopped and silently signaled his guards who drew weapons and crouched noiselessly in the underbrush. I was aware of the magnification he could gain with the visor of his faceplate, so I indicated that all should stay low. Meanwhile, I was receiving General Mitchell's feed in my headset and knew our troops on the other side of the ring were closing in quickly. He advised them we had the Kil in sight and cautioned them to slow down and allow Kos to come to us.

After a few minutes, the enemy General seemed satisfied and motioned his people to move on. They holstered their weapons. It seemed like forever as they took a circuitous route around dense stands of trees and brush. Finally, General Mitchell felt confident enough to order his men to stand.

"Kil Kos, you are completely surrounded by over five thousand heavily armed Marines. Drop your weapons and stand down!" He ordered.

Though I didn't want to see any of our forces injured, Kos did what I expected and wanted. He paused as if considering the situation, then, drew his gun as he raised his ceremonial dagger. Three soldiers hit him in non-vital areas spewing blood through new openings in his shell and beating him to the ground. The two guards dropped their weapons and raised their hands just as the rearguard action came upon them. Though Mitchell had referred to the number of troops on the ground, they were stunned at the force sent to apprehend them.

....

Monday, August 19, 2272, saw Mitchell, Nichols, Colonels Thad, Shomack, Shant, and I in the Valhalla's JAG Circuit Court as new charges were laid against all but the man I'd slapped around in the interrogation room. It seemed likely a competent defense attorney would get him off because of the abuse, so the prosecutor felt we shouldn't press it. Kos sat in a wheelchair at the defense table. We were all asked to give testimony on his escape and recapture, and I presented a summary video record of it all as part of my statement. The Kil's lawyer objected on the grounds it was condensed and failed to show all the detail. The local prosecutor countered by advising we'd be happy to run it all, but there would be nearly three days of video evidence to present. Then, he introduced a sworn affidavit from the video editor attesting to the fact that he attempted to capture the gist of all the events in the two-hour presentation. The judge ruled that though the entire video may be needed for a trial, the abstract was satisfactory for the pre-trial hearing. Then, he ordered Kos held in isolation in a facility the Judge Advocate General's Office deemed secure enough for a criminal of his notoriety and capacity. In the meantime, I was tasked with ensuring his safe imprisonment aboard the FSS Bryant until we returned him to Earth. Shackled hand-to-foot, the fallen General was handed to my personal guard and me. I took him to my office.

"Have a seat, Kil.' I offered but continued regardless of his choice of action. I knew he might find it impossible to move from the wheelchair to a more comfortable perch. 'I want you to know, I have a certain amount of hostility towards you. In fact, I'd have been happy if we'd have killed you back on that planet. But, I also know you're most likely going to spend the rest of your life imprisoned in isolation. Death would be a relief, but my people do not like executing prisoners - even if they're the kind of scum who'd destroy millions of non-combatants without compassion. So, I wish to show just a little mercy. I will keep you under heavy guard in quarters designed for people of my rank. With certain restrictions, you may use all its facilities. We will need three days to reach Earth, so I suggest you enjoy the interval and the time you spend incarcerated during your trials. Those jails will not be too harsh either because in our system you are innocent until proven guilty in a fair trial and must be treated accordingly until that happens."

"I thank you for the courtesy. But, I believe your *fair trial* is just a farce. And, I don't think for one minute I won't be executed." He spat with contempt in his voice.

"You shouldn't be so sure. Your Emperor already faced a court. The evidence indicated he did not order or approve the actions you executed, aside from the war itself. So, he was found innocent and is back on your home world, right now. He is in charge again.

"I don't believe it!" Kos shot back, though his face gave away his surprise and uncertainty.

"You will be able to speak with some of your people who were there. Ask them. In the meantime, enjoy your stay aboard the Valhalla.

"I sense your disdain is more than just what you call war crimes." The statement was more of a question.

"You're responsible for the death of my best friend during your attempt to resist your first capture. I would personally like to kill you where you stand. But, that is not our way."

"Was he a Kil?" Kos queried.

"Yes. But, in our service, he held the rank of Fleet Admiral and was one of Ten people who control our Force of nearly four thousand vessels. I was and am one too. We were equals. I have assumed his Command since his death. He was my friend and teacher for twenty years. And, for much of that time, I worked for him."

"I'm sorry for that, then. Because good military leaders are hard to find. Especially if, they're proficient at coaching. The fact you are now a General proves he was a great one."

"You are so arrogant. And, you think in only military terms. The man was my friend!"

"I cannot understand that. I am not made that way. I have loyalties to some people. But, I do not have friends. I don't feel anything when those close to me die. It's their duty, after all."

"We'd call you a sociopath in our world. A person that hasn't the capacity to feel what is normal in his society and can kill without remorse. Sociopaths do not have empathy for anyone else and must satisfy their own needs first."

"That doesn't make sense. You are an Admiral and are responsible for thousands or even millions of deaths."

"That's true. But, it doesn't mean I am not bothered by it. It just means I do what I have to - to defend our way of life. I don't commit atrocities or *senseless* murders. I kill to protect my people and don't enjoy it like you do."

256

"I'm sorry. But, I can't understand that perspective."

"I know,' I said and repeated. "I know." as I waved a hand to the guards to remove the man from my office.

....

On Tuesday, December 3, 2272, Kil Kos was found guilty of genocide, the murder of prisoners of war, and escape from lawful custody involving loss of life, as I expected. But, to my surprise, the Judge sentenced him to death by lethal injection. The execution was set for Tuesday, July 1, 2273. Though the presiding Justice said the date was to give adequate time to hear the mandatory appeals, I couldn't help but wonder if she'd intentionally planned it for the Orion Federation Founding Day celebrations. It seemed a little morbid, but Orions all over the Federation sought revenge and wished to celebrate it.

Marie discovered my mistreatment of the enemy soldier but didn't offer the reproach I'd expected. Instead, she thanked me for doing what was needed to bring George's killer to justice.

"I know that kind of behavior is usually repugnant to you. So, if you begin to feel you can't live with the guilt, come and talk with me. I'll try to help you through it. You did what was right." She offered.

"Thank you, Marie. I know you're probably correct. But, for the moment, it's not bothering me. I'm sleeping soundly each night. But, I will seek you out if a problem develops."

On Tuesday, January 7, 2273, I was again in orbit around Eta Pegusus aboard the Valhalla. This time, I was there to wind down all operations and resume negotiations with the Kire. It took nearly ten days to get all aboard their home vessels and send them on their way. Tom Stevens remained with one Tier 2 operation to ensure my safety. And two Fleets of subs and a dozen covert Frigates stayed hidden - just in case.

Kire Fask was very welcoming. He hosted several festive events in my honor in the evenings as our tough negotiations went on throughout the days. But, on January 9, he surprised me with an announcement.

"Admiral, I have been reading your constitution since I was captive on your ship."

"You were our guest Kire. We never treated you like a prisoner."

"That's true. But, you weren't going to let me go, at that time. I think I was still your prisoner." He chuckled.

"Okay. I'll give in on that one. For the first few days that might have been true. But, you became a friend. What did you wish to say about our charter?"

"I like it. It is a most impressive document. And, I especially like the way the Federation handled a Monarchy. It is very unique. I have instituted actions that would enshrine such a system here. I would remain King, and my family would hold the royal reigns into the foreseeable future. But, we would use the same power division formula used by your Federation. The Fasks would no longer be absolute rulers."

"Would you want help? We could provide advisers to guide you through the process. We learned from several attempts. You would not need to make the same mistakes we did."

"Yes, that would be appreciated. But, more than that, we wish to join your Federation - after a reasonable waiting period, of course."

"We'd appreciate that. But, it presents another huge problem."

"What's that?"

"The space between our border and yours. And, possibly more. We already patrol eight million cubic light years. We would be forced to expand to manage a much larger region. We like to occupy spherical zones. It's easier to maintain the borders. So, we'd have to enlist all the other worlds from our current border to the new one at one hundred sixty light years. That would mean patrolling over twice the current volume. We'd have to double the size of our OFSA."

"That's not an insurmountable issue. On this half of your border, you have allies, and we have confederates. It would take some effort, but you only need to convince those on the other side of your globe. And, we are technologically advanced. We'd adopt your designs and build half the required expansion Fleet as our initiation fee. Some investigation revealed that you'd expand from over nine thousand systems to nearly twenty thousand. And, you'd probably rise from over a hundred fifty members to around three hundred. You'd have a much larger population to draw recruits from. And, the increased revenue should cover the inflation of your force and patrol responsibilities. And, the Isesinis would be at your side. We are formidable, you know."

"Yes, I know. And, I like the idea. But, I'd have to check with the council. Treaties are one thing. But, enlisting a new member that starts a chain reaction of expansion is above my authority." I responded with a smile.

"I understand. Let's finish this treaty. Then, I'll give you a formal proposal to hand your people. It can have a five or ten-year period to give time for the expansion. I just know it'd be good for us, a lot of other worlds, and the Federation."

"You give it to me. But, make it ten years, and I'll recommend it. In the meantime, you'd have to move to the democracy."

"We'd do that even if you said no. I like the idea."

It took another two weeks, but we signed our first contract on January 23. The Kire presented his proposal immediately after the agreement was sealed.

On Monday, May 1, 2273, Grace Tonaka retired. It was decided that the Rigil facility would be directly run by an Operations Superintendent who'd report to the Chief of General Staff. There would be no local office for the Chief. One of the six Five-Star Admirals or one Five Star General would serve as COGS. And, that person would serve a four-year term from their mobile Headquarters.

On Tuesday, May 2, 2273, I was appointed Chief of General Staff of the Orion Federation Space Agency Command and Control. But at my urging, Fleet Admiral was designated a Level Thirteen category and a new Level Twelve rank was created and called Fleet Admiral Lower Class. It was still a Five Star grade and senior to Four Star Admirals. I nominated Tom Stevens for the rank as Deputy Mobile Fifth Commander. And, I proposed Stephen Nichols as Deputy Chief of OFSA Command & Control.

On Thursday, May 15, 2273, King David signed a statute into law making George a Hero of the Federation and creating an Admiral George Bryant Holiday to be celebrated on August 1, every year.

On Friday, May 30, I received notice that as apprehending Officer I was expected to attend Kil Kos execution as one of twelve witnesses. I spoke to Steven Nichols and Savign. They'd received the notice, too.

On Tuesday, July 1, 2273, our observer panel gathered at the Orion Penitentiary on Rigil, after all of Kil Kos' appeals were denied. I found it utterly repugnant to watch someone put to death in such a fashion. But, it was like ending a chapter in the Federations history.

Life went on relatively routinely after that. There were the Epsilon missions to here or there to remain at readiness in case of attack and to assist a Quadrant in regular patrols. There were inter Tier One level war games that were held on a periodic basis.

For his part, El was as busy as I'd been when I was Inspector General. He honed their operation further. They could conduct a hundred and twenty assorted OFSA examinations and thirty-five planetary ones annually. I especially enjoyed their investigations of Fifth Mobile RAC. It gave us time to visit while his people were tearing through my operations.

Bryant turned twelve on March 24, 2274. Though I still held loving memories of her, Helena no longer haunted me on his birthday. And, Fedricka and I enjoyed the annual celebration we provided him. He was becoming a superb young man. She was a delightful, loving, and caring wife and mother. She'd found out she couldn't have children. So, Bryant was it for both of us. And, we were happy with it that way.

And, at forty-four, I feel I have the world by the tail. I am doing what I love and making a difference. I have a delightful family and incredible memories. I enjoy power, money, and position. And, my Federation is prosperous and peaceful. On Bryant's birthday, I realize I'm as lucky as anyone can possibly be.

A week after that, the King and Orion Council announced they'd accepted several applications for consideration for membership. They'd be granting those worlds charters on a periodic basis leading up to incorporation of Eta Pegasus and its members in the Federation by the end of March 2273. But, they added they'd annex all regions up to the new border immediately, to respect their promise to the Suvayeek. No Sovereignty would be forced into membership. But, all the space to the new boundary would be patrolled by the OFSA. It made my job a lot harder. As COGS it was my task to build the OFSA expansion plan. I could enlist the help of my partners, but in the end, it was my responsibility.

Back at work on March 25, I received an ominous call. Nichols was telling me there is trouble on the border near the ecliptic line in his Quadrant.

I was shocked when we arrived at his side on Wednesday, April 8, 2274. The spiraling wreckage of nearly a hundred ships and two hundred thirty Raptors he'd already lost was like a slap in the face. As I surveyed the border, I saw the visible portion of the nearly two thousand hostile ships that sensors showed were aligned against us. Nothing ever changes.

End

www.ingramcontent.com/pod-product-compliance
Lightning Source LLC
Chambersburg PA
CBHW070902180626
46817CB00003B/888